THE PATRIOT

'Dear God – and this is Scotland! Like a rudderless ship in a storm! Is there nobody left in the land to grasp the helm? No spirit surviving in this ancient nation? Have we become a race of serfs, cowards and toadies?'

'Not that, Andrew – never that, surely. But . . . we require a lead. It is leadership we lack. Our natural leaders seem to have died out. Many, to be sure, have been executed, or driven into exile. As were you. But you, at least, have come back!'

'Yes, yes – we have a leader, *one* leader again!' Margaret exclaimed, in a rush, eyes shining.

'But do not look on me as one of Scotland's leaders, see you. I have neither the stature nor the station and standing. But I will do what I can. Oh, yes – I will do what I can, God aiding me!'

The Patriot

Nigel Tranter

CORONET BOOKS
Hodder and Stoughton

First published in Great Britain in 1982
by Hodder and Stoughton Limited

Coronet edition 1984

Reissued 1994

10 9 8 7 6 5 4 3 2

British Library C.I.P.
Tranter, Nigel–
The Patriot.
I. Title
823'.912 [F]   PR6070.R34

ISBN 0 340 34915 8

Printed and bound in Great Britain by
Cox & Wyman Ltd, Reading, Berkshire

Hodder and Stoughton Ltd
A Division of Hodder Headline PLC
338 Euston Road
London NW1 3BH

Principal Characters

In Order of Appearance

ANDREW FLETCHER: Laird of Saltoun, East Lothian, a rich property.

JOHN MAITLAND, DUKE OF LAUDERDALE: Secretary of State; Lord High Commissioner to the Scots Parliament.

JOHN HAMILTON OF BEIL: Another young laird, later 2nd Lord Belhaven & Stenton.

JOHN HAMILTON, LORD BELHAVEN AND STENTON: Uncle of above.

WILLIAM DOUGLAS, DUKE OF HAMILTON: Premier Scots peer.

JOHN LESLIE, EARL OF ROTHES: Chancellor of Scotland, later Duke.

ARCHIBALD CAMPBELL, 9th EARL OF ARGYLL: MacCailean Mor, chief of Clan Campbell.

HENRY FLETCHER: Brother of Andrew.

SIR DAVID CARNEGIE OF PITARROW: Brother of the Earl of Southesk, legal luminary.

MARGARET CARNEGIE: Daughter of above.

JOHN GRAHAM OF CLAVERHOUSE: Laird and soldier, later Viscount of Dundee. (Bonnie Dundee of the ballad.)

JAMES STEWART or CROFTS or SCOTT, DUKE OF BUCCLEUCH & MONMOUTH: Son of Charles the Second; Captain-General of the royal forces.

JAMES STEWART, DUKE OF YORK: Brother of Charles; later James the Second and Seventh.

SIR JAMES DALRYMPLE OF STAIR: Lord President of the Court of Session. Later Viscount Stair.

REV. DR. GILBERT BURNET: Scots scholar and divine, former tutor to Andrew and Henry Fletcher. Later Bishop of Salisbury.

Sir Patrick Home of Polwarth: Border laird, later Lord Polwarth and Earl of Marchont.

Alderman Heywood Dare: Taunton jeweller. Purse-bearer to Duke of Monmouth.

Prince William of Orange: Stadtholder of Holland. Later King William the Third.

Princess Mary: Wife of above. Elder daughter of James, Duke of York. Later Queen.

William Paterson: Banker. Founder of the Bank of England. Initiator of the Darien Scheme.

John Hay, Earl of Tweeddale: Great Scots lord. Later Chancellor and Marquis.

Robert Kerr, Earl of Lothian: Great Scots lord. Later Marquis.

John Ker, Earl of Roxburghe: Great Scots lord. Later Duke.

Sir James Montgomery of Skelmorlie: Baronet and lawyer.

Sir John Dalrymple, Master of Stair: Secretary of State, son of Stair. Later first Earl of Stair.

John Campbell of Glenorchy, Earl of Breadalbane: Great Highland lord.

Rob Roy MacGregor of Inversnaid: Captain of Glengyle Highland Watch.

William Douglas, Duke of Queensberry: Lord High Commissioner.

James Ogilvie, Earl of Findlater, later Seafield: Secretary of State and Chancellor.

John Churchill, Duke of Marlborough: Captain-General of royal forces.

Part One

1

The young man frowned as he dismounted in the Sidegate of Haddington. He was, to be sure, a ready frowner; but then, he was a ready smiler too, mobile and expressive of feature, quick to reflect his emotions, temperament and temper both far from placid. His frown now was directed not so much at the clutter of men and horses, children and dogs, all but blocking the street outside Haddington House, which must cause him difficulty in gaining access to the building; for this he was not wholly unprepared, for it was a special occasion. What he had not looked to see was the great coach with its six matching bays and lounging flunkeys and outriders, which all but filled the courtyard of the L-shaped tower-house, dominating all. He did not require to examine the vulgar display of paintwork on the carriage-door, surmounted by the newly-repainted coronet, from earl's to duke's, to recognise whose equipage it was.

He found an urchin to hold his mare, nodded to Willie Bryce, Baron-Baillie of the Nungate, who appeared to be in charge outside, and pushed his way through the crush to the forestair and main doorway, where two burgh officers stood guard, reinforced by two of the Duke's own men wearing steel breastplates painted with coronets, hands arrogantly on sword-hilts. The town-guards knew Andrew Fletcher, however, and passed him inside, with only cold stares from the other pair.

The interior of the house was as crowded as was the Sidegate outside, each of the fine first-floor chambers spilling people out into the hallway and corridors, what they were all finding to do not clear. The place stank, despite its excellent proportions, fine panelling and rich decoration, and not just on account of the throng in the June warmth but because the dark basement cellars below were still serving as overflow for the town-gaol, the Tolbooth in the High Street. In the year of Our Lord, 1678, the gaols of Scotland could be guaranteed to require some extra accommodation.

The young man guessed that what he sought would be found in the finest apartment, the former hall of the house. This, in fact, proved to be the least crowded, folk heedfully keeping their distance. Only half-a-dozen men flanked the great central table with its papers, quills, inkwells, wine-flagons and goblets – and of that number three hovered about the gross, florid, fleshy man who lounged midway on the window-side, wine-glass in hand. Of the other two, one, elderly, short, thick-set but neat, in markedly plainer clothing but wearing a chain-of-office, sat at the head of the table, hands clasped in front of him; the other, a thin, elderly and clerkly individual, bent of shoulder, kept his head well down and his quill scratching over paper.

The young newcomer removed his broad-rimmed hat and bowed – but not too deeply. It was the little man with the chain that he saluted first – for in his own burgh, in theory, the provost ranked supreme. Nevertheless, it was the other, the big, heavy, over-dressed individual further down the table, who spoke.

"Ha – young Fletcher!" he said, thick-voiced. "It's yoursel' – looking liker a whitrick than ever! Eh, Provost? And hoo's Saltoun looking, these days?"

"Well enough, my lord Duke." That was stiff. Andrew Fletcher did not relish being likened to a weasel, even though he was slightly, wirily built, narrow of feature and quick of manner. But the hulking man before him was uncrowned king in Scotland, so he added, carefully, "As is Lethington and yourself, I hope?"

"Ooh, aye – weel eneuch, lad, weel eneuch. Better than some o' my unfriends would hae me – eh, Provost?" John Maitland, second Earl and first Duke of Lauderdale, Secretary of State for Scotland and Lord High Commissioner to Parliament, had adopted a broad Scots accent since he became so largely London-based – as had James the Sixth and First, of sacred memory, three-quarters of a century before, both allegedly finding it to pay, for some reason.

Provost Scott of Haddington moistened his lips, nodded,

10

but said nothing. The three fine gentlemen around the Duke laughed heartily.

Fletcher came forward to the table, but to the Provost's end of it, drew out a paper from a pocket, and laid it down before the little man. "I think that you will find that to be in order, Provost," he said.

No doubt it was the list of scrawled signatures at the bottom half of the paper which caught the ducal eye. Maitland heaved himself up, to lean over and peer at it. Frowning suddenly, he reached out and twisted the sheet so that it faced him.

"God's death – what's this? What's this?" he spluttered, bedewing the letter – for also like the aforementioned King Jamie, Lauderdale's tongue was too large for his mouth and he tended to spray moisture even when he spoke normally – which was excellent excuse for frequent liquid replenishment. "Dammit, man – this is . . . this is a nomination-paper! For Parliament. The election – this election!"

"Yes, my lord Duke."

"You . . . ? Christ God – you! In *your* name!"

"To be sure, mine."

"But . . . !" Prominent eyes all but popping, the Duke glared, breathing stertorously. In his sixty-third year and after the life he had led, full but dissipated and indulgent, he was physically in poor shape – although shape is hardly the word to apply to that man. Corpulent, sprawling, he flopped and shook like a jelly. But there was nothing jelly-like about those pale eyes, however podgy and undistinguished the red and sagging features from which they protruded, choleric but shrewd, menacing.

" . . . for this Haddingtonshire seat?"

"For what other, my lord, would I bring my paper to the Provost of Haddington?"

"Then – how dare you! Devil roast you, man – in my own county! To think to stand *here*! Against my, my . . . against Stanfield!" Maitland had rather forgotten his broad accent in his wrath.

"A choice, my lord Duke. Is that not what an election is for? To give the voters a choice. Of men and policies."

"Insolent!"

11

They stared at each other, elderly man and young. And two greater contrasts in appearance, as in character, would have been hard to find, Andrew Fletcher, at twenty-three, so slight, supple, probably not half the weight of the other, keen-faced, alert, hot-eyed, not handsome but personable, straight and slender as a rapier-blade.

The Duke dropped his gaze, to grab at the offending paper with a slightly trembling hand. It was at the signatures of the sponsors, at the foot, that he looked now. The first, in a large if somewhat shaky hand, was BELHAVEN AND STENTON.

"Belhaven!" he exclaimed, in a positive shower of spray. "Aye – I might have known it! That . . . renegade!"

"My lord Belhaven is a very noble gentleman and my good friend, my lord Duke."

"I say different! And you may tell him so. Let him watch where he treads! And you, sirrah – watch *you*!" He paused, glowering expression changing. "See – you are young yet. Young enough to mend your ways. Put it by, Dand – put it by. Be not used by such as that old fox Belhaven. Gang a mair canny gait!" He was back to the Doric again, poise recovered. He flicked the paper back across the table. "Burn you that, laddie. It's no' too late. And we'll say nae mair about it."

"If you mean, my lord, that I should stand down from this election – then I say no. Not on any score. I regret it if I inconvenience your lordship – but my candidature stands."

"Fool! Knave! Upjumped Hielant scum! God damn you – you will regret this, Fletcher! You'll learn – ooh, aye you'll learn that it doesna pay to tangle wi' John Maitland. You'll no' gain this Haddington seat – but you'll gain paiks and pains aplenty! That I promise you! You'll rue this day . . ."

Deliberately turning his shoulder on the Secretary of State, the young man spoke to the Provost.

"There is nothing else I require to do? For the election? Through you as officer, Provost? If there should be, you know where to find me."

"Aye, Saltoun, sir." They were the first words the Provost had uttered since his entry, and even so the chief magistrate's eyes were on the Duke.

Inclining his head in a still briefer bow than on his arrival, directed somewhere between provost and duke, Andrew Fletcher turned to stalk out.

He was mounted and on his way, before it occurred to him that he had not so much as glanced at the three gentlemen with Lauderdale, one of whom almost certainly would have been Colonel Sir George Stanfield, newly knighted, the Duke's personal nominee, along with John Wedderburn of Gosford, for this double-seat of Haddingtonshire in the Scots Parliament, former sitting commissioner and now his rival candidate for the landward division. One of the others likely would be Wedderburn.

The estate of Saltoun Hall lay some six miles southwestwards of the county town, in the Lammermuir foothills, with Lauderdale's Lethington seat to pass on the way. But Fletcher did not head that way. Instead he rode away castwards, over the humpbacked Nungate bridge and out of the little town, past its former abbey, the once-famed Lamp of Lothian, seat of learning if mistaken piety before the godly Reformation of the previous century. A staunch Presbyterian, Andrew frowned over the errors and follies of men – although in this instance it was women, for the Abbey of Haddington had been the most renowned nunnery in the land. The tragedy was that having so dearly got rid of papacy, now they were having episcopacy thrust down their throats, from the Court at London, by this turncoat and time-server Lauderdale and his like.

But, at twenty-three, that young man could not be wholly preoccupied with the problems and sorrows of his native land, not when riding down the Vale of Tyne, one of the fairest straths of Lowland Scotland, on a sunny June afternoon, on a fine horse and with all the challenge of life before him. Past the fine demesnes of Stevenston and Hailes, Whittinghame and Ruchlaw, he rode, whistling tunefully, these the seats of friends and acquaintances; but today he was bound farther afield, well beyond the whale-back hill of Traprain which rose like a stranded leviathan out of the wide vale, where Lothian was said to have taken its name from the Pictish King Loth. Eight miles from Haddington, where the encroaching foothills

13

narrowed the vale near the great estuary-bay of Tynemouth, at Belhaven, he came to the fortified tower-house of Beil, perched on a shelf above the secret wooded valley of the Beil Water.

His close friend and associate, John Hamilton of Beil, welcomed him warmly, although engaged in his favourite activity of breaking-in a horse – breeding, training and racing horses his consuming passion.

"Andrew!" he gasped, panting from his exertions. "Good . . . to see you. I hoped that . . . you would come. Have you done it?"

The other nodded.

"God be praised! Man, that is splendid! See you – hold this beast. While I get my coat. Watch her – she's skittish . . ."

Leading his visitor up from the paddock in the green valley-floor to the house, he was eager for details. Hamilton's had been the second signature of sponsorship on Fletcher's candidature paper – although he was only just old enough to append it, being a year younger than his friend. Stocky, open-faced, freckled, boyish-seeming, he looked even more youthful than the other.

"Now, let us hope, we shall see a new beginning in this sorry Scotland!" he declared. "You will wipe that Stanfield's nose for him! And go on to greater things."

"Be not so sure, Johnnie. Lauderdale was there . . ."

"Lauderdale? Himself! Here? Back from London?"

"Yes. At Haddington, with the Provost. He was . . . displeased."

"He saw you? Spoke with you?"

"He more than spoke! He threatened me. First he sought to talk me out of standing. Then he told me that I would pay for it. My lord Belhaven too, for sponsoring me. You yourself, perhaps, Johnnie – if he saw your name . . ."

"I care not for that! Damn the man! But – you will wish to see Belhaven. Ah – here is Margaret."

Margaret Hamilton was a smiling if plain-faced creature, little more than a girl really, although at nineteen she had been married to Johnnie for almost three years. It was scarcely a love-match, it all having been carefully arranged in typical

14

Hamilton fashion long before; but they made a happy and wholesome pair nevertheless. She was a great heiress, of course, which helped.

Kissing Andrew, Margaret cheerfully went off to get wine and cakes, to bring them to the wing of the house which the old lord occupied.

John Hamilton, first Lord Belhaven and Stenton, was now in his early seventies, and frail. But the spirit still burned brightly in that stooping frame and glowed intensely in the blue eyes deep-set in the hawklike face – and his had been a vehement spirit indeed. He had been one of the late King Charles's most bold and vigorous cavaliers, fought on many Civil War battlefields, languished in sundry prisons and escaped, and attempted an audacious rescue of his imprisoned monarch at Carisbrooke. After his sovereign's execution, with Cromwell's bloodhounds after him, he had actually feigned death for seven years. With a brother and two servants he had made to cross the great tidal Solway Sands on his way back to Scotland, but had never reached the northern shore, the others bringing only part of his clothing, to sorrowfully announce his lordship's death in the treacherous sinking sands. In fact he had returned to England and gone to work as a simple gardener, at a small manor-house, for those dangerous years of the Commonwealth, until the present monarch's glorious Restoration allowed him to return home in 1660. His only son had died; and he had persuaded the grateful Charles the Second to redestine his peerage to be heired by the young man he had chosen to marry his grand-daughter, Margaret – a kinsman, Johnnie Hamilton, eldest son of Lord Presmennan, of Session, which kept lands and title nicely in the family. His lordship, of the main Hamilton line, was the son of two Hamiltons, the grandson of four Hamiltons, had married a Hamilton and seen his daughter married to another. His wife long dead, now he lived with his grand-daughter at Beil.

"Andrew, lad," he greeted his grandson's-in-law friend. "You get liker your good father each time I set these old eyes on you! A sore loss he was to this land. But his son, now, will make up for his untimely passing, I swear! Eh?" The voice was strong, vibrant, however feeble the body.

15

"That is my hope and prayer, my lord – however lacking I feel in the abilities. Do I find your lordship well?"

"As well as I shall ever be, I think. My time wears to its end. But I too, I hope, have heir to follow on and do the things I ought to be doing! That is, if I can wean him away from breaking horses before he breaks his own fool neck!"

Johnnie grinned. "I have a thick and stiff neck, my lord – as you have frequently told me! And you risked yours sufficiently often – even almost on the block! But – Andrew, here, has in a manner of speaking risked his today. When he handed in his nomination-paper at Haddington. Lauderdale was there. And – displeasured!"

"He was? That overblown toad! Save us – he comes early. Why, I wonder? It is three weeks before the opening of the new parliament. He usually spares us his company until the day before – thank God! Why? He could not possibly have got to hear? Of our plans. In London. To unseat his Stanfield?"

"I think not, my lord," Fletcher said. "At least, he seemed much surprised at my candidature. Angry when he heard of it, yes – but surprised."

"Yet he was there, at Haddington? On the day for the depositing of papers. Not by chance, I swear! He is ever well-informed, is John Maitland – even down in London. He has spies everywhere. He could have learned of talk that Stanfield was to be opposed. But not hear that it was yourself, Andrew. And came to put a stop to it."

"It could be. He *is* well-informed, yes. In more ways than one. He surprised *me* by naming me Hielant scum! Not many would have said that."

"Ah, but he would know your grandsire, old Innerpeffer, know that he came from the North, to Saltoun." Andrew, a Lowland laird with a Lowland name, and with his mother a Bruce, was not in fact so far removed from the heather. His grandfather and namesake, Sir Andrew, a shrewd lawyer, had come south from Perthshire, anglicising his name from Mac-an-Leister, the Son of the Arrow-maker, to the equivalent Fletcher. But when he had in due course mounted to the Bench as a lord of session, he had taken his title not from his new estate of Saltoun in East Lothian – the man he bought it from

16

was already Lord Saltoun – but from his ancestral home at Innerpeffray in Strathearn, where they were a sept of Mac-Gregor. Perhaps that is where his grandson heired his quick temper and high spirit.

"I hope that you answered him suitably?" Johnnie said. "*I* could think of a few things to call John Maitland!"

"No doubt. But I . . ."

"Easy said, here in Beil House, boy," the old lord reproved. "But to his face you might be less bold. Lauderdale may *look* like a horse-couper and worse, but he has all the unlimited power, more's the pity. He has the King's ear, is one of the Cabal, Lord of the Bedchamber, Lord President of the Council as well as First Commissioner of the English Treasury as well as Secretary of State for Scotland. A man dangerous to meddle with."

"That is almost exactly what he himself said to me," Andrew told them. "He said that I would learn that it did not pay to tangle with him. And to tell *you* that, my lord – when he saw your signature as my sponsor. He said that we would pay for it."

"As we may, yes," Belhaven agreed gravely. "Yet we must do what has to be done. Someone must give a lead, make a start. If our land and nation is to be saved. Lauderdale's rule has to be opposed. Scotland must be stirred to action, to be true to itself, to reject the evil policies and corruption which are rending and destroying her. Before it is too late. I am an old done man, by with it. I will do what I can – but that is little now. But you – you are both young, all before you. All depends on you and such as you. Win this election, and you will have your chance, soon. John, here, will take *my* place. Then . . ."

"But, my lord – what chance have I of winning the seat?" Fletcher demanded. "Young as I am, untried, against all Lauderdale's power and influence?"

"A fair chance, lad – a fair chance. Or I would not be bringing down Maitland's wrath on my grey head by sponsoring you! He has many enemies, that man. Even amongst his own kind he is scarcely loved. And though few will defy him to his face, many will be glad to vote secretly against his candidate. And Stanfield, although an able man, is not popular. He is English, one of Cromwell's former colonels. He has

17

made a fair member and has done much for Haddington and the shire. But few there love him either. He is arrogant. Forby, there are still some honest men left in the land, who will vote for the nation's sake, not because they are bribed."

"All my friends are for you, Andrew," Johnnie assured. "They do not all have votes, to be sure. But . . ."

"There's the rub. There are eighty-three voters in all. How many are in Lauderdale's pocket . . .?"

Margaret Hamilton came, with the refreshment carried by a servant, and for a little they observed the courtesies. But quickly they got down to calculations, by no means for the first time. Each of the voters, who qualified only by their land-holdings in the shire, had two votes, it being a double-seat; and nobody had been found to oppose Wedderburn, Lauderdale's other nominee in the seaward section of the county. Indeed, in opposing Stanfield, Fletcher was taking a very great risk, not only to his pocket and reputation but to his very freedom, and all knew it. Try as they would, the three men could not count on more than thirty probable votes – and some of those were doubtful. On the other hand, nor could they identify with any certainty more than a similar number of votes sure for Stanfield, who had been unopposed for the last elections. Wedderburn was in a different category, not a strong man but not unpopular, and a local laird. Not a few would vote for him who would shy at Stanfield; however, he was unopposed, so that did not signify. Which left over a score who might vote either way, depending on their religious scruples, whether they had ambitions for themselves or their adherents in the way of preferment, whether their pockets were empty, and so on. There was one advantage for Fletcher, in that Stanfield, who had done much for Haddington town itself, in establishing industry, mills, dye-houses and the like, could not look to that town for votes; for the burghs of Scotland appointed their own members to the Estates of Parliament, from amongst the burgesses. Nevertheless, shareholders of these enterprises amongst the East Lothian lairds might well vote for Stanfield as, thanks to Lauderdale's patronage, these mills and works were all exempted from taxation.

Long they debated and assessed, considering any and all

18

means by which the odd extra vote might be gained. Belhaven had considerable influence at this Dunbar end of the county and amongst the parish ministers who, by and large, were Covenant-minded and anti-prelacy, which would lead them to vote against the government; on the other hand, Dunbar and district had suffered so much under Cromwell, after his winning the battle there twenty-eight years earlier, that they were pretty staunchly monarchial now and might well choose to support the King's representative's nominee. Not that Fletcher and the Hamiltons were *against* King Charles – only against the policies of his London government, of imposing prelacy and its desire for an incorporating union of the two kingdoms. It was all complicated and difficult.

Andrew took his leave, with a programme of visits and interviews arranged for the period before the election, for the Hamiltons and himself, to seek to persuade and cajole. Belhaven himself would make shift to go and see the Earl of Haddington, across the Tyne estuary at Tyninghame. His support could be crucial. He was a Hamilton too – but was married to the heiress of the Earl of Rothes, the Lord Chancellor, Lauderdale's colleague and crony. With him it would be a near thing.

Riding home the fourteen miles south-westwards through the lovely East Lothian countryside, it did occur to Andrew Fletcher to ask himself why he was doing this, putting himself and his future in grave jeopardy, challenging the powers that had broken finer and wiser and more influential men than himself? Although a good Presbyterian, he was no bigoted Covenantor. He rather admired Charles the Second – even whilst judging him to be sorely lacking in his understanding of the Scottish situation and temper, misguided by those around him. He was instinctively against Charles's brother, the Duke of York, converted to the Romish Church and fanatical about it; but so far these Popish pretensions posed no real threat to Scotland. Misgovernment and tyranny there was – but why did *he* feel compelled to oppose it with all his strength and fortune? His father, Sir Robert, had died young, leaving him laird, in his early teens, of a large and rich estate, an old castle and a tradition of sober well-doing. Neither father nor grand-

19

father, Lord Innerpeffer, would have done what he was doing now, he very well knew; careful, steady men – at least in their public life – disinclined for adventures and dramatics. Not like the Hamiltons, or the Maitlands, for that matter. Yet here he was, seeking to set out on what was little less than a crusade, with the enemy all-powerful. Why? His Highland blood coming out perhaps, vehement, turbulent – like that of his far-distant kinsman, Rob Roy MacGregor? Or his mother's Bruce blood – although the Clackmannan Bruces had been a comparatively tame lot for generations. Bruce? He did not presume to speak of himself, even secretly, in the same breath as the hero-king of three centuries before. Besides, it was Wallace, not Bruce, whom he might wish to emulate – if he dared to let his mind stray that far. Bruce had fought for a throne, power, a dynasty; Wallace only for an idea, love of country, simple patriotism, with nothing to gain personally and everything to lose – as he did. Wallace, indeed yes – and God forgive him for daring to link *his* situation with that of the Patriot.

When he came, with the sunset, to his house, the Abernethy castle extended with its fine 17th-century additions, set between his two villages of East and West Saltoun, such thoughts did not survive the first sight of the place in its secluded foothill valley of the Birns Water. For the wide forecourt area was full of men and horses, reminiscent of the Sidegate of Haddington. But these were uniformed men and their mounts cavalry-horses. Dragoons – and making entirely free with his premises.

Hot temper rising, Andrew spurred in amongst them, demanding what this meant, what they wanted, how dared they off-saddle in front of his house, where was their officer?

A youthful cornet was brought out from the house itself, to announce that his name was Dalrymple, cutting short Andrew's indignant representations with a military gesture, to declare that he and his troop were billeted on Mr. Fletcher of Saltoun until further notice, in the interests of national security. He drew a document from his open tunic to prove it. Although he did not actually read it, Andrew saw that it bore Lauderdale's peculiarly neat signature at the foot.

John Maitland moved fast, it appeared.

Fletcher went in search of his brother Henry.

2

Andrew Fletcher gazed around the crowded Parliament Hall of Edinburgh, at something of a loss. There appeared to be no one to tell new members, or commissioners as they were called, where to go or what to do. The place seethed with people and the noise was deafening. There must be many hundreds thronging the long, narrow hall under the open-beamed roof so lofty. They could not all be commissioners. Supposedly there could only be two hundred and ninety of these – although the numbers varied from parliament to parliament owing to the different proportions of lords temporal and spiritual available. The Scots Parliament, unlike the English, sat together in one chamber, lords, commissioners of the shires and burgh representatives, the Three Estates.

Andrew perceived, then, that quite a number of those present were dressed scarcely in a style to be expected of the occasion; indeed some seemed actually to be selling pamphlets, even snuff and tobacco. He could have brought his brother Henry, after all.

He saw old Lord Belhaven seated alone in stalls near the right-front of the hall, and went to sit beside him.

"I am glad that you were able to make the journey, my lord," he said. "I hope that it has not wearied you over-much?"

"I took it gently, lad – in two stages. Spent the night at Seton with Lord Winton. I would not have missed this parliament – it will be my last. At the next, Johnnie will sit here, in my place. But – I wanted to see you started on your road, Andrew. Your first, my last."

Fletcher had won the Haddingtonshire seat by forty-seven votes to thirty-six, to the great excitement of the county and beyond.

"It need not be so, my lord. You could have many more years yet. When do proceedings commence? The opening was called for noon – now long past."

"We cannot start until the Lord High Commissioner chooses, lad. It is his prerogative – and Lauderdale likes to show who is in command! Although I have known him to start early – and then none could enter because His Grace was seated! But usually he keeps us waiting – and today he will be in particularly ill mood. For which *you* may have some responsibility! Ah – here is Hamilton."

A dark handsome man of middle years, fashionably dressed in London style, came stalking up, waving a scented handkerchief before his prominent nose – admittedly the crowded hall in the summer heat smelled strongly. Men in his path tended to bow as he passed and were loftily ignored; even Belhaven rose shakily to his feet as the newcomer reached him, for this was the head of that great house which cut so wide a swathe in Scotland; although it was odd that Belhaven, himself directly descended from the first Lord Hamilton, should so pay his respects to a man who was in fact no Hamilton at all but a Douglas. William Douglas, Earl of Selkirk, had married Anne, Duchess of Hamilton in her own right, daughter of the second Duke, and had been created Duke of Hamilton for life. Such as he was, he represented the focus of opposition to Lauderdale, whom he hated, the only other duke in Scotland.

"Ha, Belhaven – you are here," Hamilton said. "As well. I shall need every vote this day, I vow!"

"Yes, my lord Duke. The word is that the elections have been managed, pauchled. More than usual. I fear the worst. You are well. After your long journey?" All Edinburgh rang with the story that Duke Hamilton had arrived from London only the day before, after a rushed journey, with twelve coaches and two hundred and fifty men as bodyguard.

"It was devilish hot and tiresome." The Duke's haughty glance, ignoring Andrew Fletcher, was sweeping the crowded hall. "I see damned few friends and over-many unfriends!" he commented grimly. "Maitland is up to no good. He never is – but today he is oily. Ever a bad sign. He tried to oil *me*!"

"You have seen him, then?"

"Aye. I spent the night at Holyroodhouse – of which I am Keeper, you'll mind. He is in residence. So I made my keepership suitably evident to him. Yet he sought to have me

22

come here in his own coach, damn him! Oily, as I say. I told him I preferred my own. But . . . he cooks something. I ken the smell of him."

"He is here, then? But keeps all waiting."

"He is ben there, drinking with Rothes – who is drunk as an owl. Argyll too. A bonny trio!" The Duke turned. "You, young man – what do you stare at? Who are you?"

"This is my young friend, Andrew Fletcher, my lord Duke. Of Saltoun. You will mind his father, Sir Robert? Newly elected for Haddingtonshire. On my recommendation."

"Then I trust that he will vote aright! Nevertheless his place is . . . elsewhere!" And he jerked his head for Andrew to be off.

His quick frown very evident, that young man bowed stiffly, to withdraw, when Belhaven moved round to take his arm.

"Heed it not, lad," he murmured. "It is but his way. Go over yonder." He pointed. "These are the lords' seats."

Pushing his way through the throng to the other side of the hall, Andrew hotly told himself that if this was the man Scotland had to look to for leadership against Lauderdale, then God help Scotland!

Most of the commissioners had not yet taken their seats, but amongst those who had he saw his uncle, his mother's younger brother, Sir Alexander Bruce of Broomhall, commissioner for Sanquhar and a privy councillor.

"May I sit *here*, sir?" he asked, it is to be feared less than cordially. "There appears to be little direction in this place."

"To be sure, lad. Sit by me. Good to see you. My congratulations on winning your East Lothian seat – although I do not know if you have been wise!" Bruce was a large, amiable man, of almost cherubic countenance.

"I am beginning to wonder whether it is a cause for congratulation, sir," his nephew said. "To be elected to . . . this!"

"With our King in London, boy, it is all we have left of government. We must needs make the best of it."

"And make the best of Duke Hamilton too, I take it?" That was tart.

The older man looked at him curiously. "Why, yes. He is none so bad, is Duke William. He has Douglas manners – but

23

what can you expect? He is not afraid to stand up to Lauderdale, as are most. And he has King Charles's left ear, even if Lauderdale had his right! And they do say that the King's right ear is becoming just a little deaf!"

"Indeed? Hamilton scarce chooses the best way to recruit members to his party . . . !"

"Party, Andrew? Hamilton has no party. Hamilton is . . . Hamilton! You will learn. The sorrow that there *is* no party to oppose – only hatred."

He got no further. Two drummer-boys came into the hall beating a continuous rataplan on their side-drums, the signal for members to take their seats and for the unauthorised to leave. Even when these were gone the place was crowded, with no seats for all. Bruce explained that, with all the manipulation behind this election, there was a much greater attendance than usual. Lauderdale had seen that the maximum two hundred and ninety made it – one hundred and forty six lords, fourteen bishops, sixty-five shire commissioners and sixty-five burgh representatives. Most parliaments were fortunate to have half that.

A procession filed in from the left, but only a few inexperienced newcomers rose to their feet, for it could be seen, by the gorgeous robes and copes, that these were only the new Lords Spiritual, at present the most loathed men in the kingdom, the fourteen bishops, and almost all turncoats, led by James Sharpe, Archbishop of St. Andrews and Alexander Burnet, Archbishop of Glasgow, both former Presbyterian parish-ministers. They had been given seats in parliament, by royal decree, only since 1655, after clerical seats had been banned at the Reformation. These went to their places at the end of the lords' stalls, in a heavy silence.

The silence did not last long for, as though to emphasise where the real importance lay, there was still a considerable wait, and chatter was resumed. Then, at last, a full hour late, the drumming resumed and the door at the head of the hall was thrown open to admit, first a file of the royal guard, very fine, who took up positions flanking the throne; then the Lord Lyon King of Arms leading his heralds; then the great officers of state, with the Honours of Scotland, the Earl of Erroll, High

24

Constable, bearing the Sword, the Earl of Crawford bearing the Sceptre and the Earl of Argyll bearing the Crown – odd, when his father had been executed for highest treason. Finally, after a calculated pause, appeared the Chancellor of the Realm, John Leslie, Earl of Rothes, great wig askew and somewhat unsteady on his feet, followed by Lauderdale, the Lord High Commissioner, red of face, rocking of gait, hat crushed firmly down over wig as, deputising for the monarch, he alone could remain covered in that company.

Somebody raised a cheer, tentatively, but it died away unsupported.

Lauderdale went to sit on the throne, keeping his hat on, Rothes collapsed into the chair behind the Chancellor's table, clerks scurried in, with papers, to the two side-tables, the drummers beat a final roll, and all was set for proceedings to commence.

"I declare that His Sacred and Glorious Majesty, Charles by the Grace of God, King of this Realm, has re-appointed me High Commissioner to this Convention of Parliament," Lauderdale intoned in song-song fashion. "Does any here require that such commission be read out in full?"

Since the Duke had been High Commissioner on every occasion since 1670, eight years, none saw any point in further delay.

"Very well. My lord Chancellor – proceed."

Rothes sat forward. The Scots parliament was distinct from its English counterpart in more than the lords and commons sitting together. Here the monarch or his representative actually not only attended but presided in person, although the business was conducted by his Chancellor or chief minister.

"I declare this Convention of the Estates of Parliament, duly called and authorised, to be in valid session." John Leslie, seventh Earl, bull-like, short-necked, stout, may have been drunk as Hamilton had averred, and all but illiterate – he could not spell, certainly – but he gave no impression of not knowing what he was about, even if his words slurred a little. "The business is simple and, God aiding us, should not detain us long . . ."

Thus early, the Duke of Hamilton was on his feet. "My lord

25

Chancellor," he intervened, "you err, I think. Let us have the matter aright. You said this *Convention* of the Estates. I came to attend a parliament, not a convention. Let us begin aright, I say."

"No, my lord Duke – I didna err," Rothes returned, grinning. "I said convention and I mean convention!"

There was immediate uproar in the hall. Undoubtedly almost all present had believed that they were attending a full session of parliament. A convention was altogether a lesser thing, a meeting limited in scope and usually called only for a single purpose; indeed it formerly was the term used for an assembly of the Estates at which the monarch himself was not present.

"A device!" Bruce declared to his nephew. "This is an outrage! But why?"

"Hamilton *said* Lauderdale was cooking something! This is it, then. Not a parliament, at all."

When he could make himself heard, Hamilton, still on his feet, pointed an accusatory finger. "I protest!" he exclaimed. It was at Lauderdale that he pointed. "This is insufferable! I have not travelled all the way from London to attend a convention. The summons was to attend the Estates of Parliament. In the King's royal name. I protest to . . . Your Grace!" That last sounded as though it hurt grievously to enunciate. In Scotland the honorific Grace was offered only to the monarch, not to dukes; but whilst acting as the King's representative and sitting on the throne, Lauderdale was entitled to it.

"I maun put you to rights, I fear, my lord Duke," Lauderdale replied, with relish. "I hae the summons here before me. It is to '. . . attend a Convention o' the Estates o' Parliament'. Just that!"

"But . . . God save us! That is the words always used. For a parliament. A Convention of the Estates of Parliament. Meaning . . ."

"Meaning, Hamilton, a *convention*! In this instance. I should ken, who sent it out. Under His Majesty's signature, wi' His Majesty's agreement."

"Then this is a scandal! We are brought here under false pretences." Hamilton look round over the gathering, assessing

26

support. "My lord Chancellor – I move that this assembly, being a full and lawful gathering of the Three Estates of Parliament, herewith constitutes itself a full parliament and no mere convention."

"Seconded," Belhaven called.

"I must rule you out of order, my lords." It was Lauderdale who answered, not Rothes. "This gathering isna competent so to vote. A convention it has been declared by the Chancellor. Therefore it can only vote as a convention. I has nae authority to turn itself into a parliament."

"The Chancellor can be over-ruled."

"Only by myself. And I dinna choose to do so, my lord Duke."

Hamilton drew a deep breath. "The Privy Council can over-rule the Chancellor," he said.

The tension and stir in the hall was palpable.

"Ooh, aye," the High Commissioner acceded. "Maybe and maybe no'. I could contest that, Hamilton. But I'll no'. Na, na – we'll hae a vote o' the Privy Council, then. Them only, mind. My lord President o' the Council – will ye call a vote?"

Hamilton must have known it to be a despairing gesture from the first. The President of the Scots Privy Council was Archbishop Sharpe of St. Andrews – and there by Lauderdale's influence. So were most of the other privy councillors. When Hamilton's motion was called, it attracted only three votes out of the fifteen councillors present – those of the Earl of Dumfries, Sir Alexander Bruce and the Duke himself. Belhaven was not a councillor.

"Aye, weel – I jalouse we can now proceed to our business," Lauderdale said, sitting back. "Eh, my lord Chancellor?"

The Duke of Hamilton sat down, set-faced.

"So this is how Scotland is governed!" Fletcher said to his uncle.

"Aye, lad, I fear that it is." The older man sighed.

Rothes rapped on his table for quiet. "The duty laid upon this convention is simple but important, fell important," he announced thickly. "It is the matter of granting supply. Just that. Siller! There is uprising, unlawful assembly, riot all over the land. Especially amongst the Westland Whiggamores." He

27

stumbled somewhat over that last. "The local militia, set up eight years ago, cannot maintain the King's peace. Therefore His Grace requires that a new, permanent and established force be set up. Permanent. Paid for by the realm. Not, as now, at the expense of individual lords and lairds. As is right and reasonable . . ."

The acclaim from many of the lords and lairds was heartfelt.

"The cost of recruiting, equipping and paying such force will not be small," Rothes went on. "It will require £6,000 monthly for twenty months. Aye." He wagged a finger. "Sterling that is, mind. They tell me that it comes to £1,800,000 Scots!"

Into the consternation which struck the chamber at this enormous, unheard-of sum, Lord Belhaven's old voice rose strongly.

"My lord Chancellor – would it not be wiser, a deal less costly, and more in accord with Scriptual injunction forby, to pacify our disaffected countrymen rather than assail them with armed soldiery? If we repeal the Act Against Conventicles, all this uprising will die away of itself. That infamous Act alone provokes it . . ."

Rothes rapped on his table. "We cannot discuss here Acts of an earlier parliament. In this convention," he interrupted. "We are here to authorise supply for the provision and upkeep of His Majesty's standing army here in Scotland. Only that."

"I will not be muzzled, Chancellor! I have the right to speak," Belhaven asserted. "None here, I swear, is going to authorise raising, by cess or taxation, the sum of £1,800,000, unquestioning or in haste. When all know that there is no need. That all the unrest in the land is caused by the law against holding conventicles. If our fellow-countrymen wish to worship God in the open air, I say, let them! The ousted ministers do not endanger the peace of the realm, only the sensibilities of certain folk in high places! I say that we should not employ dragoons to regulate each other's consciences."

"I rule you out-of-order, my lord . . ." Rothes began, when Lauderdale intervened.

"I'd remind Lord Belhaven that this United Kingdom is at

28

war with the Dutch. Troops are required to repel possible foreign invasion. You'd no' have us invaded by Hollanders?"

"Does Your Grace anticipate a Dutch descent upon Scotland? If so, I swear that you are the only man in this hall to do so!"

That produced the first laughter of the session.

"I but inform you that the raising of armed forces is for more than the putting down o' conventicles, man. The King's government has the whole peace and security o' the realm to consider."

"Expensive consideration – at £1,800,000! End the Conventicles Act and no new troops will be required in Scotland. Accordingly I so move . . ."

"Not accepted," Rothes ruled. "This convention cannot repeal an Act."

"It can strongly advise the King's Grace to have the Act repealed, at least – you cannot deny that? I so move."

"And I second," Hamilton said. "I am told that troopers of Queensberry's Regiment have been quartered in my palace of Hamilton and in my town and shire of Lanark. This is an outrage! *I* am no Covenanter or conventicler! I demand the removal of these soldiers forthwith."

"I support," Crichton, Earl of Dumfries announced. "The man Grierson of Lag and his troopers has occupied many of my properties and townships. It is not to be borne!"

"If your lordships will sustain Westland Whiggamores, you'll need to abide the consequences!" the Chancellor said. "This is but self-seeking. No valid motion to put to the convention."

Greatly daring, Andrew Fletcher stood up. "May I speak, my lord Chancellor?" he asked, his voice stronger probably than he intended. "*I* am no Westland Whig and there are no conventicles where I come from. Yet dragoons have been quartered in my house at Saltoun, without cause. This as threat and warning. I say that if we are to have military government it must be sanctioned by this house – not otherwise. To sanction more military first is out-of-order. I support the motion."

All turned to stare – and none more pointedly, deliberately and offensively than the Lord Chancellor.

"Who is this young man?" he demanded. "Who presumes to tell *me* what is in order and what is not?"

"I am Fletcher of Saltoun, my lord. A commissioner for the sheriffdom of Haddingtonshire. With as much right to speak as any here!"

"On my acceptance and under my ruling, sirrah – only so! Mind it. You may sit down."

"I have not finished, my lord Chancellor – with respect. I appeal to His Grace – who has already advised me on the matter of standing for this Convention of Parliament!"

There were breaths indrawn all around. Everywhere men sat forward in their seats. This was almost an unheard of challenge from a new commissioner. Even Bruce of Broomhall laid a warning hand on his nephew's arm.

Lauderdale leaned forward, not back, in his throne. "I advised this young man to let a few mair years pass before tangling wi' his elders," he observed, almost genially. "Let him have his say, or we'll suffer the mair, I vow!"

Andrew frowned at this avuncular reaction, which brought a titter from the assembly. For a moment he hesitated. Then he bowed. "I thank Your Grace. My concern is to draw attention, before a vote is taken on this matter, to the dangers of letting loose the military on any countryside and the troubles and uprising this can provoke amongst otherwise law-abiding folk. I am reliably informed that a force, a horde rather, of high-landers, my lord of Argyll's men in the main, I understand, have been brought down to occupy the districts of Carrick, Kyle, Cunninghame and Renfrew. Eight thousand of them, no less, billeted on the folk without payment, despoiling, looting, and encouraged to do so by their leaders – I will not call them officers! As a result there is unrest, violence, near rebellion – which many claim to be the object of the Argyll invasion! Rebellion – so that there should be excuse for this military government we now hear of!"

There was uproar in the hall, with, amongst the din, shouts of "Aye! Aye! The truth!" from West Country members.

Rothes beat with his fist for order. When he could make himself heard, he strongly declared that he could not allow such seditious amd shameless talk. It was no speech of support

30

for a motion but a disgraceful attack upon a noble and distinguished lord who was most generously providing of his manpower and substance to aid in the maintenance of the King's peace. That his lordship's Argyll militia were necessary in this situation was clear proof of the urgent need for the provision of regular forces of the Crown, for which this convention must make supply. He called upon the Earl of Argyll to reply, and refute this young man's unfounded allegation.

MacCailean Mor, Chief of Clan Campbell and 9th Earl of Argyll, was a somewhat nondescript individual, little more prepossessing than had been his executed father, the great Montrose's deadly foe, but lacking his snake-like and dangerous character. Not eloquent, he rose reluctantly, muttered briefly that his people were in the South-West for training in aid of the civil power and were entirely well-behaved. He sat down.

That was scarcely well-received by the West Country members. As clamour rose and Hamilton got to his feet again, Lauderdale waved to catch the Chancellor's eye, and nodded briefly.

"We have a motion, seconded and supported – however ill-advised. We shall vote of Lord Belhaven's motion and waste no more time." Rothes paused. "But I warn all to consider well *how* they vote! The motion is to advise the King's Grace to repeal the Act Against Conventicles. Those in favour, show."

So they came to the test. Andrew, hand raised, looked round the crowded chamber – and his heart sank. Some few were eager, as was he; more were hesitant to declare themselves in favour, but the vast majority were obviously going to sit tight, do nothing, even many of the Westland lairds and burgesses.

"Aye," Bruce sighed at his side. "There's the way of it! Lauderdale has sown his seed – and here's the harvest! Bribes, promises, threats and falsified elections, and we see the result!"

There was no need to count. Less than one-third of the gathering voted for the repeal of one of the worst Acts ever to have stained the fame of this most ancient parliament, an Act of such intolerance, of Lauderdale's devising eight years before, that even King Charles had thought it extravagantly severe, with up to the death penalty for attending the outdoor religious services of the dismissed parish ministers who would not accept episcopacy and the rules of bishops.

"The motion falls," Rothes declared. "We return to the business before this convention – the authorisation of supply for the King's forces."

"No use opposing further," Bruce murmured. "We will be outvoted by the same majority."

Andrew bit his lip in impotence.

"I move that the sum required be authorised," the Archbishop of Glasgow said quickly.

"I second," the Earl of Linlithgow added, as promptly.

"I move against," a new voice spoke up, that of a grizzled, burly man of weather-beaten good looks, Sir William Scott of Harden. "I have call to, I say – for I have been fined £1,500 for my wife attending at a conventicle. £1,500, my lords and friends – which much moneys, I am assured, have been gifted to Sir George Mackenzie of Rosehaugh, yonder, the King's Advocate . . ."

Once more there was uproar.

From a special side-bench a handsome, fine-featured man rose, one of the cleverest individuals in the kingdom. "As one of the Crown's officers, I request the protection of the Crown against such slander, Your Grace."

"And you shall have it, by God!" Lauderdale cried. "Any further such-like attacks – aye, and any further ill meddling in matters no' before this convention – and I shall instruct the King's Advocate to proceed against such as attempt it, whosoever they be! I warn all. I will adjourn the session if this continues."

Into the silence the Duke of Hamilton laughed, and waved his handkerchief. He was one whom even Sir George Mackenzie would not dare arrest.

Rothes spoke. "We have a motion, seconded and supported. That the supply be granted. It has been moved against. So must be voted upon. I call . . ."

Hamilton rose again. "I move a third and relevant motion."

The Chancellor swallowed, looked at Lauderdale and shrugged. The Duke had every right so to move. Curtly he nodded. "So long as it *is* relevant."

"It is. Before this great sum is authorised, this convention is entitled to hear more. How the sum was arrived at? By whom? And why? Might it be for other than the raising of troops? Before I left London I heard talk at Court that the Duke of Lauderdale was going to bring back from Scotland a notable gift for the King's Grace. Which would perhaps restore the King's favour towards him – for the said Duke has been losing place of late, you should know! This great sum of money, I suggest . . ."

"Silence! Silence, I say!" This was a bellow from the throne. Lauderdale was on his feet, features more congested than ever, both fists raised and shaking, a dire sight. "This I will not hear, from any man! I . . . I . . ." He pointed a quivering finger at Rothes. "Enough! I adjourn this session. Adjourn, do you hear?" And leaving his seat he lurched unsteadily over to the nearby doorway, flung wide the closed door, and out, leaving the Chancellor, the officers of state with the Honours Three, the royal guard and the clerks to straggle off after him, as best they could.

Pandemonium reigned in Scotland's Parliament Hall.

* * *

That evening Andrew and Henry Fletcher made their way down Edinburgh's crowded High Street, from their lodgings in the Lawnmarket, past the High Kirk of St. Giles – now being called a cathedral and seat of a bishop – and the Parliament House behind, as far as the Canongate, to the town-house of the Earl of Southesk. The city was packed, of course, and the streets athrong with folk, especially all the hangers-on of the lords and lairds, a noisy, quarrelsome, drunken element.

Henry was a little uncomfortable. He was a sensitive young man, very good-looking in an almost girlish way, two years younger than his brother and very different from him in almost every way. They were very good friends, however, with Andrew distinctly protective; they had been twelve and ten respectively when their father had died. Although Henry had not been invited to Southesk's house, his brother would not hear of him being left alone for the evening in their lodging. It was Sir David Carnegie of Pitarrow, Southesk's brother, who

33

had come up to Andrew as he was leaving the Parliament Hall, and suggested that he might care to dine with them that evening, mentioning that Belhaven would be there. The Carnegies were reputedly an open-handed lot – and presumably anti-Lauderdale.

At the tall tenement within Little's Close, off the Canongate, they were welcomed casually but uncritically, with no one seeming to realise that there was an uninvited guest amongst the many already present. Henry relaxed.

Belhaven, after congratulating Andrew on his intervention earlier, introduced them to Lord Southesk, a big, genial man, son of a difficult father, and brother of the equally difficult wife of the late and famous Marquis of Montrose. Nowadays the Carnegies found it an honour to have been connected with the Great Marquis; it was not always so.

Southesk and his brother made much of Andrew, for whose courage and initiative of the afternoon they expressed admiration. But they warned him as to the consequences of Lauderdale's enmity – as indeed did all.

When they sat down to dinner the brothers were placed in the care of a young woman, who sat between them – which pleased them both, for she was good-looking and friendly and they had had their eyes on her from the start as the only other person present approximately of their own age. She proved to be Margaret Carnegie, daughter of Sir David. They found her easy to get on with, suitably impressed with Andrew but careful to be equally attentive to Henry.

As the meal progressed, his elders from farther up the table sought to bring Andrew more into their conversation. He was flattered, but in the circumstances would rather have talked to the young woman. They were, of course, concerned almost entirely with the political situation, and gloomily so. The general opinion was that Lauderdale would have everything his own way, as usual, and that there was little that anyone could do – not in Scotland, anyway. Only in London might the man's fall be encompassed.

Although much the oldest there, Belhaven was the most optimistic. "I say that Maitland gives too many hostages to fortune. He makes mistakes, for he is not all clever. He has his

34

stupidities and weaknesses. And that woman he has married could much endanger as well as enrich him. One day he will make a large mistake – which we may latch on to. How say you, Andrew?

"He may well make the mistakes, my lord. But how do we latch on? From what I have seen today, we will not latch on to anything! We many of us may hate Lauderdale and all that he stands for. But that is all. We are not united, have no common policy. Each goes his own way. That will never bring Lauderdale down."

"And you see a way, lad? To unite men who have nothing in common save hatred of the man?"

"I say that we need a party. I am no lover of England and *their* parliament. But they can teach us something here. They have parties. Large groupings, who agree on a policy, or various policies. And vote with that party, even though not always agreeing with *all* the policies. So they wield power. We have only individuals – and wield none. Lauderdale and his cronies can pick us off one by one."

Not a few of his seniors began to speak at once. As host, Southesk prevailed.

"We have never gone in for parties, Mr. Fletcher. The Scots Estates are not like that, not made up so. We are free men all – save perhaps some of the burgesses, of whom I know little. We must remain our own men, not ruled by any party."

"You are ruled by the Duke of Lauderdale, my lord! Is that to be preferred to making cause with others who think as you do? When nothing is more sure than that, if his London masters have their way, there will be no Scots Estates at all, only the English Parliament incorporating the Scots."

There was silence at that, and Andrew himself felt a pang of apprehension over having spoken so to an earl, his host, old enough to be his father. But at his side, Margaret Carnegie nodded to him approvingly, murmuring 'Good! Good!' and he was encouraged. Interested also that this young woman should be concerned in such matters.

Her father it was who spoke. "I fear that there is much in what Mr. Fletcher says. Especially this talk of a union, an incorporating union. It is said that the King is strongly for it.

And his English advisers. Myself, I doubt whether Lauderdale would wish to go so far, since it would reduce his own power. But it is something that we will have to beware of, ever more keenly. Or England will have achieved by words what she has failed to achieve over six hundred years of warfare!"

There were cries of 'Never! Never!' from around the table.

Belhaven nodded agreement. "This is the greatest danger facing us – the loss of our birthright, freedom. Beside that, all else pales. The King, no doubt, sees it only as an administrative reform, to facilitate his rule from London. He no doubt means well. But his grandsire, King James, would never have countenanced it, for all his failings. It could be the end of Scotland as an independent nation."

"It has not come to that, yet," Southesk said.

"No. But this of the new standing army could facilitate it. Give added power to London – for nothing is more sure than that such army will be London-controlled. As well as draining Scotland of these vast moneys."

"Could there be any truth in what Duke Hamilton suggested, my lord?" Andrew wondered. "That the raising of the troops might be only an excuse? That the money, or most of it, might really be only for a gift to the King – who is ever short, they say, with his extravagances?"

"God knows, lad! It is certainly a strange and unheard of demand."

"This Highland Host, as they call it, of Argyll's, in the West – it could all be part of a deep-laid ploy to foment trouble, which could be called rebellion, and so for requiring more soldiers, so providing excuse for the levying of the money. Especially if, as Duke Hamilton hinted, Lauderdale's repute with the King is sinking. Could there be truth in this also? My uncle, Sir Alexander Bruce, also said as much."

"Hamilton is straight from London and the Court. He should know."

"No doubt. But this is but speculation," Sir David Carnegie put in. "Interesting but not immediate. Our problem is tomorrow. How to prevent that supply being granted? This enormous sum. Lauderdale can win any vote in this convention, as he has scurvily contrived. How can we thwart him?"

No one was in haste to answer that. Daring again, Andrew spoke up.

"Delay," he suggested. "We cannot win a vote. But we might delay. Few are prepared to stand up to Lauderdale. But many must doubt and fear. Even amongst those whom he has bribed and bought. Such vast moneys must give all pause. So delay might be accepted. Propose commissioners to enquire. Into details. At least prevent a rushed vote. Two matters would allow reason for this. First the great rigging of the elections, making false all voting. A committee to enquire into this. Second, the amount of the moneys demanded. How such great sum was reached should be enquired into. Another committee of the convention. Delay, give time to rouse the land."

"By God – that is a notion!" Scott of Harden, he who had suffered the £1,500 fine, exclaimed. "It might work."

"At least it would give us something to fight for – not to be swept away on a snap vote," somebody else said.

There was general approval, and Andrew's credit rose further. It was decided to recommend this procedure to the Duke of Hamilton next day. Even though there was no party, as such, the Duke was accepted as the obvious leader against Lauderdale, because of his rank and their mutual hatred.

If young Andrew Fletcher had any tendency to swelled-headedness, it was sorely tested that night by the acclaim of his elders. But what went to his head more was the unaffected praise and favour of Margaret Carnegie, who made no bones about expressing her sympathies and encouragement. Indeed, as she said farewell to the brothers at the close-mouth later, she emphasised her concern.

"Would it be possible, Mr. Fletcher, for me to attend at Parliament House tomorrow? To watch and listen? I have heard that it can be allowed. For friends of the commissioners. It would greatly please me."

"*I* wanted to go, today," Henry said. "But Andrew feared that it would not be permitted."

"They drum out all unauthorised folk before Lauderdale comes in," Andrew explained. "But today I saw visitors remaining, at the side of the hall. Two ladies whom I knew not. But I did recognise Willie Talmash, as they call him. And *he* is no commissioner." Lauderdale had married as his second wife the notorious Elizabeth, Countess of Dysart in her own right, an evil influence in two kingdoms. Her first husband had been an Englishman, Sir Lionel Tollemache, and this Willie was their son, Lauderdale's step-son. "If fifteen-year-old Willie can sit through the sessions, then you can, I say!"

"Good! Then allow me to be your escort," Henry put in quickly. "Delighted, sir . . . !"

* * *

Next noonday, consequently, Andrew was in no hurry to take his seat in the Parliament Hall, being more concerned with awaiting his brother and Margaret Carnegie at the outer entrance, behind St. Giles Kirk, and then conducting them to the place where the visitors had sat the day before. They were not long settled there, however, before one of the officers of the guard came up, and peremptorily ordered their departure.

"On whose authority, sir?" Andrew demanded, flushing.

"On His Grace's own," the other asserted.

"Well, I'll be damned! This, this is insufferable! I am a commissioner. And these are my guests . . ." A thought occurred to him. "How does the Duke of Lauderdale know that we are here?"

"He has been informed. And it is not permitted for such as are not commissioners to remain in the hall during sessions."

"But – William Tollemache, a mere boy, was here yesterday. Throughout. The Duke's step-son . . ."

"I know nothing of that. I have my orders. These are to leave, sir."

"No! If the Duke's step-son can remain, my brother and this lady can."

"Please, Mr. Fletcher!" Margaret Carnegie had risen. "I will go. I certainly desire no trouble, embarrassment. Say no more. I will leave . . ."

"No – do not, I beg of you. This is a disgrace! Not to be truckled to."

"I cannot remain. You must see that. Not now." She turned to Henry. "Will you take me out, please. I am sorry, but I must leave."

38

Henry nodded.

"Then *you* come back, Henry," Andrew urged. "We cannot just give in to this. A matter of principle."

"Very well . . ."

The High Commissioner again delayed his appearance well past noon, so there was time for Henry Fletcher to return and resume his seat, however uncomfortably.

At length Lauderdale and Rothes came in, all upstanding. In the ceremonial of the bestowing of the Crown, Sceptre and Sword and the official seating, movement at the side of the hall caught Andrew's eye. Two officers were hustling Henry out, hands gripping his shoulders.

Hot temper rising, Andrew had to restrain himself from hurrying to his brother's aid. He clenched his fists and waited.

Lauderdale heavily announced that the session of the convention was resumed, after adjournment. But he warned sternly that he would adjourn again, if necessarily finally, should there be further improper and disloyal behaviour. To ensure such proper behaviour and to remind all present of their legal duty to the monarch, he had drawn up a short declaration, which all should sign, confirming their entire loyalty to the King's Grace. Lacking this, and hearing of some of the words spoken the previous day, His Majesty might well come to believe that Scotland was being led to rebellion. No doubt the Duke of Hamilton would be the first to sign.

Clerks came down with copies of a paper for signature, as the company murmured. Andrew stood up.

"Your Grace," he called loudly, "while this is done, I have protest to make on a matter of procedure. My brother has just been escorted from this hall by your officers. I am entitled to ask why."

Rothes it was who answered. "The young man taken out had already been warned to leave. He returned. He is not, I understand, a commissioner or authorised officer. So has no right to be present. He will be lodged in the Tolbooth until this session is over. Lest he should again seek to make entry."

"The Tolbooth . . . !" Andrew all but choked. "This . . . this is an outrage! He has committed no offence. I demand that he be released."

"No, sir."

Voice quivering, Andrew sought to control it. "Tell me, my lord – is it an offence for one who is not a commissioner to watch during a convention session?"

"It is, yes."

"Then, sir – order your officers to arrest that youth standing there!" Andrew's pointing finger jabbed towards where, at the side of the doorway by which the official party had entered, young William Tollemache stood watching the proceedings. "Confine *him* in the Tolbooth – beside my brother."

The hall all but rocked with excitement. Even Rothes turned to stare behind him, for the moment at a loss.

Striking whilst the iron was hot, Andrew went on. "He was here, where my brother was sitting, all yesterday's session. As were . . . others. Not commissioners. Will Your Grace order the release of my brother, forthwith, make apology, and allow him to return to this hall?"

Lauderdale cleared his throat. "No, sir – I will not. Mr. Tollemache is here at my request. As my, my servant. For my convenience. I may require . . . that he fetches things, papers, suchlike. From my coach. Or from Holyroodhouse." Nothing could make that sound less than feeble.

"Then should he not wait outside, Your Grace? If my brother must . . ."

Strangely, Lauderdale was rescued from his predicament by the Duke of Hamilton. That haughty individual stood up and rapped on his chair for suitable quiet.

"Your Grace – may I suggest that you and this young man settle this personal disagreement at some more suitable time and place? For myself, I see no reason why I should have to wait while this unseemly bicker goes on. No doubt others feel the same." He raised a copy of the paper being circulated for signature. "This writing affirms all loyalty to King Charles and supports the royal prerogative – which I am glad to sign. But it goes on to condemn the Covenant and all its supporters. I am no Covenanter – as once were *you*! The inference here is that in supporting the King we hereby declare against those who hold to the Covenant. This I am not prepared to sign."

There was considerable murmur of agreement.

"Did not King Charles himself sign the said Covenant?" Belhaven pointed out. His voice was weaker today and he did not rise when he spoke. Yesterday presumably had been overmuch for him.

Andrew fumed, but stooped to listen to his uncle who was tugging at his sleeve.

"Sit, lad. You can do no more. At this stage."

"But . . . it is disgraceful! And Henry . . . ?"

"Let it be. Henry will be let out anon. Nothing to be gained by offending Hamilton. So much depends on him . . ."

Unhappily Andrew sat down.

Hamilton at least gained some small advantage in getting the words treasonable and seditious inserted in the declaration before Covenanters' activities, which enabled him, and all, to sign it – Lauderdale making it very clear that refusal to sign would entail expulsion from the session, as refusing to admit the King's authority.

While this was going on, the Earl of Southesk rose to declare that it had come to his hearing that not a few of the elections for this parliament and convention had been grievously misconducted and rigged. Since this would of course affect votes taken and decisions made, he would move for an enquiry.

This was the signal for Andrew. He seconded and moved further that a committee of enquiry be set up by the convention itself to investigate the entire issue of elections and how they were conducted. Sir David Carnegie and Belhaven signified agreement, as did others.

Rothes huffed and puffed. But as no such enquiry could change the voting strengths of this assembly, he did not rule it out-of-order. Names were put forward for this committee, with Carnegie as chairman, and the thing went through without a vote.

So far so good. Andrew felt a little better.

Before any other tactic could be developed, Argyll briefly moved that the vote on the King's supply be taken, Archbishop Sharpe seconding.

Southesk rose to assert that, since his previous motion was carried, implicit was the understanding that the voting strengths in this convention were, to say the least, at issue and doubtful.

41

Therefore no vote today could accurately reflect the will of the nation – especially on so important a matter as this. He moved no vote and decision until the committee had reported.

Rothes, as expected, ruled that the convention had not been proved *not* to be properly representative. Until it was, it could and must act. The counter-motion was therefore unsound and the Earl of Argyll's motion stood. They would vote.

Again Andrew jumped up. "If a committee of enquiry is acceptable for the lesser matter of election-rigging, how much more necessary for this greater matter," he cried. "Here is the largest sum of moneys ever demanded of Scotland. £1,800,000 Scots! Every man in this hall will have to put his hand deep into his pocket, I say! Think of it, my lords and friends – there are 290 of us here, representing lordships, baronies, shires, burghs, dioceses. How many times goes 290 into 1,800,000? Have you all calculated it? I will tell you – 6,200 times. Heed that – 6,200! Will you all go back to your houses, your coffers, your burghs; those who elected you, and find £6,200 each? Are you prepared to do this? Without enquiry? On the word of . . . some London clerk! I say a committee of enquiry first!"

Bedlam broke out, everywhere men on their feet, shouting. Rothes shouted and beat his table as loud as any, but few paid heed. Lauderdale's florid features were working and he seemed to be shouting also. Belhaven, Southesk, Carnegie, Bruce, Scott and others were all claiming to second the motion. But it was the main body of the members over which Andrew stared – and a grin spread over his face. For it was at these that he had aimed – and, it seemed, aimed truly. They were hit where it hurt, in their pockets. Although, probably, few could take in the real meaning of a million pounds and more, most scarcely having even heard the term before, all there could envisage £6,200 – and quake at the thought that each might have to find such sum, or at least contribute deeply to it. With £300 a fair annual value for many a respectable estate, the thing, put this way, was quite overwhelming.

Lauderdale and Rothes, whatever else, were no fools, realists to recognise the situation. The latter went over to consult the High Commissioner, and only a brief exchange was necessary. Returning to his chair, the Chancellor awaited quiet.

"A committee of enquiry is accepted," he said curtly. "Four. Names?"

Thereafter all was wound up in minutes. Four names were put forward, all as it were neutral in theory – and all of whom, undoubtedly, would be bribed, threatened or otherwise got at by Lauderdale, before they reported. To that extent all there realised that here was no true victory or defeat. But it was the first time in his 'reign' that the uncrowned king of Scotland had been halted in his course, publicly, out-manoeuvred, humiliated. When he stamped out of the hall thereafter, his whole demeanour proclaimed the fact.

The young man who had encompassed this was surrounded by well-wishers, congratulators, hand-shakers – many of whom no doubt would have voted against him had it come to the crunch. He was appreciative but far from ecstatic. Over-modesty was not part of Andrew's nature; but he also had a strong sense of reality and recognised that this was only a superficial triumph, one step on a long journey. And, to be sure, a hazardous step – of that he scarcely required the many warnings he received.

He went off to spring Henry out of the Tolbooth.

3

Being a commissioner elected to the Scots Parliament in the later 17th century was scarcely onerous as regards duties of attendance, for the King seldom called sessions more than once a year and often less frequently. So Andrew Fletcher was not overburdened with parliamentary work. There were, however, other duties to which a parliamentarian was expected to devote himself, one being a member of the Commission of Supply for his own county area. It was distinctly ironic that this should become one of his responsibilities, involving him in quite a lot of work, since amongst other duties it included the raising of cess and levies and the finding of supplies, forage, fodder, quarters and so on, for the King's forces in that area – and when he returned to Saltoun after a few days of private meetings in Edinburgh, it was to find that the troop of dragoons quartered on him were not only still there but had been doubled, and on direct orders of the Secretary of State, Lauderdale. Apart from the inconvenience and mortification of this situation, it did of course inflict a serious financial burden, with one hundred-odd men and their horses to feed and sustain for an indefinite period.

All this was made more galling in that Saltoun became in effect the military headquarters for East Lothian, since the total strength allotted, or imposed, on the county was two hundred and forty regular horse and four hundred militia foot, and these were to cover a large area amounting to some one hundred and fifty square miles; it was obvious therefore that Saltoun, in the Lammermuir foothills, had the lion's share of the mobile troops and was bound to become the important centre. At any rate, here the commandant for the shire took up his abode meantime, no doubt directed to do so.

This officer proved to be a surprise. He was not at all the usual military type, but a brilliantly handsome man in his early thirties, stylish, cultured, personable, by name Captain John Graham and kin to the Marquis of Montrose, laird of the estate of Claverhouse near to Dundee. More interesting still, he proved to be related to Margaret Carnegie, his mother having been a daughter of the first Earl of Northesk, younger brother of the first Earl of Southesk. Recently returned from the foreign wars, with a commendation from the Prince of Orange – whose life he had saved at the Battle of Seneff – he was something of a poet, like his famous relative, and an extraordinary character for a professional soldier. But if Andrew hoped that he would, in consequence, be undemanding in his occupation of Saltoun Hall, he was disillusioned. Graham was charming, excellent company – but he had a steely glint to his darkly-attractive eyes. That he could be ruthless emerged from some of his anecdotes of the foreign wars; and they had proof of it when he had one of his own troopers flogged insensible for stealing one of the Saltoun farmyard chickens – this although the troops were billeted there at Andrew's expense. That young man came to the conclusion that John Graham might well cut his throat if ordered to do so by Lauderdale or to whoever he owed military obedience.

Lauderdale had returned to London almost immediately after the convention, leaving Rothes the Chancellor and Mackenzie of Rosehaugh the King's Advocate, in command in Scotland – but to do his bidding. So far, apart from this extra military presence at Saltoun, there had been no further impositions or punishments, despite the dire warnings. But Andrew was by no means lulled into heedlessness. He knew that Lauderdale had a long arm and an unforgiving nature – the more so possibly as his fortunes declined.

And that was the tenor of the talk which emanated from the South, that autumn. Lauderdale's star was in the descendant. There had been an alleged Popish plot uncovered in London by someone called Titus Oates, seemingly an ex-Puritan and also an ex-Jesuit, who was now being hailed as a national saviour, setting England by the ears, and all leading, oddly, to a change of government. Shaftesbury, the Lord Chancellor, was now Prime Minister, after being in the Tower. He hated Lauderdale and was working for his downfall. The King so far remained his friend, or at least continued to use him, reputedly declaring that, though complained of by the people, he did not appear to have done anything contrary to the interests of his sovereign. The news heartened Scotland.

Andrew had ample to occupy his mind and time besides policies and affairs of state, and their consequences. He had a large and productive estate to run and was much interested in land-improvement, experimenting with the reclamation of wasteland, increased yield of crops, drainage and the like. Full of restless energy, he was not one to find time hanging heavily or to be at a loss for activities. Henry helped him in many of his interests but lacked his brother's driving force.

One matter Henry did greatly help with, and gladly enough, was the letters. Andrew had not forgotten his assertion that the Scots Parliament required some sort of party structure, however loose, if it was going to be able to stand up to Lauderdale or any other High Commissioner. So he set himself the task of writing to a large selection of the lords and fellow-commissioners whom he thought might just possibly be receptive to the idea. The letters, although almost identical, all had to be written carefully in his own or Henry's hand – but he did not sign any, after much consideration. Some of the recipients, no doubt, might guess from whom they came; but there were two reasons against putting his name to them. The present masters of Scotland might well assert that the contents were designed to controvert the regime and so could be classed as seditious if not treasonable, thus giving excuse for the arrest of the signer. With the death-penalty even possible for attending a conventicle, such was far from improbable. Secondly, his name on such proposals would more or less tie him to actually join any party which developed; and since he was too new an arrival on the scene, and too young, to seek the leadership, he wished to retain his independence and freedom of action meantime. Henry disagreed with this attitude, and Andrew admitted that it was in a way contradictory; but he had a strong instinct not to become fully committed to any leadership of which he might possibly disapprove. For an advocate of the party system, Andrew Fletcher was in fact something of a misfit.

The organisation of the delivery of the letters was a major headache and expense.

Keeping Captain Graham in ignorance of the letter project was difficult, for he was apt to be very much present with them that autumn and winter at Saltoun. Excellent company, he frequently dined and spent the evening with the brothers – nor did they seek to freeze him out. He made no secret of the fact that he disliked his present duties; he was a fighting soldier not a billeting-officer or quartermaster. And he was a useful source of information, able to tell them much of current affairs that they were interested to hear. He had friends at Court, in especial his kinsman the present Marquis of Montrose, commander of the royal horse guards, who had indeed obtained for him this present command; and he seemed to hear of much that went on at Whitehall and Westminster. He revealed that Lauderdale was indeed in ever worsening odour, had lost his English position as First Commissioner of the Treasury, with the King under strong pressure from Shaftesbury to set up a

House of Commons enquiry into corruptions and misappro-
priations of Treasury funds – which Lauderdale could hardly
deny, but asserted were perpetrated wholly to carry out the
royal policies in Scotland. But he was still a Lord of the
Bedchamber. Just how much money he had brought back from
Scotland, in July, was a secret between him and his royal
master; but it was known that it was vastly less than had been
expected. The committee of enquiry set up by the convention
had quite quickly tabled its findings; and while undoubtedly its
members were largely in Lauderdale's pocket, they had come
to a compromise, acceding that troop-raising was necessary
but suggesting, as a first payment, only £150,000 not
£1,800,000. Of the 22,000 troops the money was alleged to pay
for, only one quarter, 5,500, were presently authorised.
Whether even these would materialise, who could tell, with
how much of the £150,000 going into King Charles's pocket,
or Lauderdale's own? John Graham personally hoped that
the troops *would* be raised – and himself given a decent
command, commensurate with his status in the Continental
wars. An interesting blow-by-blow of the entire business was
that Shaftesbury was, for his own purposes, now claiming that
the entire 22,000 were in the process of being raised, not to put
down Scots rebels but to be available to invade England. In the
Titus Oates atmosphere and Popish plotting, this went down
well with the House of Commons, however unfair to
Lauderdale.

Henry Fletcher declared that he did not know why Andrew
wanted to get mixed up in politics, from all that he had so far
learned of them.

Captain Graham had some further and more inspiring
information for them. It seemed that the Earl of Southesk and
his household came south each year from his seat of Kinnaird
in Angus, to winter at his town-house in Edinburgh. Almost in
the same breath the Fletchers demanded to know whether Sir
David Carnegie came also – to be assured that usually he did.

Presumably John Graham would pay visits to his kinsfolk in
Edinburgh . . . ?

* * *

"I read your letter with much interest," Sir David said, having to raise his voice above the jigging strains of the fiddles and the skirling and stamp of the dancers. "You made a good case. Whether many will agree or no, I cannot say. But I think that you have convinced me, at least."

"You . . . you realised that the letter was mine, sir?"

"My dear Fletcher, it could not have been from anyone else! It was but an enlargement of what you said when last you were in this house. Besides, I could hear your voice in every line of it."

"M'mm. Will others recognise it so easily, think you?"

"I daresay – unless they are exceeding dull! Although few heard you here that night, to compare. But I warrant that Rothes and the Privy Council have copies before them, and have few doubts as to who wrote it! As well that you did not sign, nevertheless."

"They cannot be *sure* it was me."

"No. But they will be watching you, all the time . . ."

The dance ended, and Henry brought back Margaret. She was flushed and sparkling-eyed, very lovely. John Graham also came up, with his partner, Catherine, Margaret's elder sister. She was strikingly handsome rather than lovely, and they made an eye-catching pair.

When the fiddlers struck up again for the next dance, a schottische, Andrew and Graham each turned to Margaret at the same moment. Smiling, she curtsied to her kinsman but accepted Andrew's arm.

The Highland Schottische is an energetic exercise, for pairs, one in which all the breath is required for the dancing rather than for conversation. But when, midway, there was a welcome pause for recovery, and they found themselves at the far end of the fine room, Margaret found breath enough for speech, still holding Andrew's arm.

"You would appear to get on sufficiently well with that gallant cousin of mine, Mr. Fletcher," she said, nodding her head towards Graham. "Despite being, shall we say, on opposite sides."

"Yes. Yes – he is excellent company. And, and does not thrust his views upon us."

48

"No, he would not. But he will listen, I think?"

"Oh, yes – he is a good listener." Andrew found it rather difficult to concentrate on this polite exchange. Margaret Carnegie had a particularly shapely bosom and the exertions of the schottische ensured that it was now in rhythmic but distracting commotion.

"I would be careful what you tell him, nevertheless, seeing so much of him as you do."

At her tone of voice, as it were deliberately light, he raised his glance to her face. "You mean . . . ?"

"I mean that, in your position, the less that you tell him, probably, the better, Mr. Fletcher."

"You think that he is not to be trusted?"

"Oh, John is to be trusted! Trusted to consider his own best interests always. Trusted to do his duty, however unpleasant for others!"

"You do not like him?"

"In fact, I do. We get on very well. But then, *I* am not in danger of offending the King's government. I have known John all my life, and even admire him – or parts of him. But . . ."

The fiddlers resumed and the dance recommenced. There was no further opportunity for private talk. But Andrew was not prevented from thinking. And his thoughts, on the whole, were gratifying. It was not that he did not take seriously the young woman's warning; after all, it merely confirmed his own impressions of John Graham; and he *had* been careful of what he said in that man's presence. What interested him was Margaret Carnegie's evident concern for him, that she had felt impelled to make an opportunity to speak as she had done. He danced the more lightly for her warning.

* * *

Light-hearted dancing was but seldom indulged in as 1679 advanced and dark clouds gathered over Scotland. Everywhere the repressive measures of government produced the predictable, indeed calculated, reactions in the people. A letter of Lauderdale's which got into other hands was much quoted. 'Would to God they would rebel that so I might bring over an

49

army of Irish Papists and cut all their throats!' Men and women were arrested in ever-growing numbers, imprisoned, tortured and executed – either for attending the outdoor services or conventicles, or for sheltering the ousted ministers, or for protesting against the activities of the military quartered upon them, who stole and beat and ravished without check, indeed encouraged officially to do so. The policy of 'eat them out of house and home' was widely imposed. And the Scots, being Scots, clung the more fiercely to the Covenanting principles that a man's form of worship was no business of the state; supported more doggedly the parish ministers who refused to accept the rule of the new bishops; hated and despised more vehemently the said prelates and the rag-bag of the minions with which they filled the churches – the King's Curates as they were called – many of whom had never put up a prayer or preached a sermon in their lives, some scarcely even able to sign their own names. Especially in the South-West, in Ayrshire, Dumfriesshire and Galloway, where the Whiggamores, as they were called, were strongest, resentment developed with unrest, sporadic violence, soldiers were resisted, church-services boycotted, the few who attended booed, the new incumbents mocked in the streets, even assaulted. Even in Haddingtonshire where the Covenanters had never been particularly strong nor vocal, incidents multiplied; and the Bass Rock, off their coast, turned into a state prison for the arrested ministers, was full. Inevitably Andrew Fletcher had become involved, not as an attender at conventicles but in protesting against the policies and their harsh implementation – which, of course, John Graham had to enforce. That they did not actually come to blows was probably more through Graham's forebearance than his host's.

It was at the beginning of May, almost a year after the convention, that matters came to a head. A party of Covenanters, led by two Fife lairds, Hackston of Rathillet and Balfour of Kinloch, waylaid the coach of Archbishop Sharpe crossing Magus Muir near St. Andrews, dragged out the unpopular prelate and murdered him. He had recently insisted on the execution of another would-be assassin; and of course was looked upon throughout the land as next only to Lauderdale in savagery. Nevertheless even pro-Covenant opinion was shocked by the deed – and there could be little doubt as to the repercussions.

Few, however, foresaw the speed and scale of the results. The murderers fled to the South-West, where they could be sure of support amongst the Whiggamores. Rothes and Mackenzie had the excuse they wanted, for drastic action on a major scale. All available military forces were despatched to the area, including Graham of Claverhouse, who was sent to Dumfries with dragoons and militia. Not only so but, with the notorious Grierson of Lag and Johnstone of Westerhall, he was sworn in as Sheriff-Depute – which meant that not only could these officers impose their will militarily but could try and condemn legally as well. In other words, it was martial law.

At a stroke, however, Andrew Fletcher was relieved of involuntary guest and quartered soldiers.

The sequel developed with similar speed. The South-West rose in real revolt. Since the dragoons were at first concentrated on Dumfries and Galloway, the Covenant leadership, such as it was, chose to muster force further north, in Ayrshire and Lanark. Graham advised striking at once to crush any armed rising before it could gather strength. But he was not in command – indeed it was doubtful who was, at this stage, presumably General Sir Tam Dalziel of the Binns, of Russian fame, but he was not on the spot. At any rate, Graham acted with typical vigour and assurance on his own, force-marched his own small command northwards, met the Covenanting force, in much greater numbers than his own, at Drumclog near to Loudoun Hill in south-west Lanarkshire, attacked forthwith and was soundly beaten.

That proud captain's humiliation must have been intense, at being defeated by a rabble of Whiggamore peasants led by completely untrained leaders such as Hackett, Balfour and Hamilton of Preston, who had nevertheless skilfully used the miry nature of the terrain – as Bruce had done in the same Loudoun Hill vicinity three centuries before – to bog down the cavalry horses, so that there were thirty-six dead dragoons to only three Covenanter casualties. Graham had to flee to

Glasgow, leaving Ayrshire and Lanarkshire wholly in Covenant hands.

Scotland rocked at the news. At Saltoun they did not know whether to cheer or to groan. Whilst it could possibly be the beginning of great things, Andrew felt strongly that this was not the way, murder, violence and religious bigotry. And undoubtedly government reaction would be drastic.

Lauderdale might be hundreds of miles away, and battling to retain his position there. But, whatever his faults, he had never been less than decisive. He was still Secretary of State for Scotland, and in only the time taken for the news to reach London, for an interview with King Charles and for his couriers to race northwards, counter-action was mounted in no fumbling fashion. The Duke of Monmouth, the King's son by Lucy Walters, was in command of the royal forces in the North of England – he was, in fact Captain-General of the army since his twenty-first year – and he was directed to march forthwith, with all his available strength, over the Border, and to put down this insolent rebellion with all speed and no mercy. Of the speed, certainly there was no question. The Drumclog affray had taken place on 11th June; within ten days, young Monmouth was in Lanarkshire in major strength. The Covenant leadership, centred on the town of Hamilton, was still undecided whether or not to march on Glasgow. Graham, with all the men he could muster, rode out of that city, joined the Duke, advised immediate attack before the rebel forces could be joined by others, and pointed out an excellent strategic position at a bridge over Clyde at Bothwell. Battle was joined next day, and the Covenanters, to the number of some four thousand, utterly routed at Bothwell Brig. Five hundred were slain on the spot, twelve hundred taken prisoner and the rest fled.

The rising was over.

* * *

It was a strange and unexpected experience for Andrew Fletcher to be an invited guest at the Palace of Holyroodhouse. Although the invitation had come in the Duke of Monmouth's name, Andrew had no doubt that it was at the instigation of

John Graham, who now appeared to be very close to the Duke. *Why* he should be invited was another matter. He went warily.

He found the palace's forecourt packed with coaches and horses, coachmen, grooms and retainers – so clearly it was to be a large gathering. Indeed, when he reached the handsome reception-chamber on the first floor of the old James the Fifth wing, it was to discover that practically everybody who was anybody in Lowland Scotland was present – save of course those who were in prisons up and down the land. That others hostile to the regime were asked, was quickly apparent, for after perceiving Southesk and his brother at the far end of the apartment, the next person he saw was Johnnie Hamilton, whom he had last seen only a week or so before at old Belhaven's funeral. So Johnnie was now second Lord Belhaven and Stenton and entitled to take his due place in affairs of the realm.

Andrew made his way over to his friend's side. "What are we all here for, think you?" he asked. "This was not Rothes' notion, I swear! Nor Mackenzies'." And he nodded towards where the King's Advocate was chatting with Argyll.

"Do not ask me, Andrew. I am a babe, as yet, in such matters. But I am glad to see you. You can tell me what to do!"

At least they were not long kept waiting here. A silence fell on the company as the Earl of Rothes appeared in the doorway, flanked by two guards, who thumped on the floor with their halberds. Then these drew aside and a darkly slender young man appeared, modestly dressed but wearing the ribbon and star of the Garter, behind him a group, prominent amongst them Graham of Claverhouse.

The company bowed – but in various differing degrees. James Stewart or Crofts or Scott, Duke of Monmouth, represented problems as to how he was to be saluted. He was Captain-General certainly. He was the King's son, but illegitimate; at least that was the official line, although there were enduring rumours in high places that Charles had indeed secretly married his youthful love, Lucy Walters, in Holland – which would, of course, make something odd out of his present gracious Queen Catherine of Braganza. Again, the King had no legitimate offspring; which meant that, if legitimated in law, this eldest bastard could become heir to the throne. He was, after all, a Protestant, while the only other contender, Charles's brother, James, Duke of York, was unfortunately an enthusiastic Romish convert. Moreover, Monmouth was married to their own Countess of Buccleuch, head of the house of Scott – they had in fact been created Duke and Duchess of Buccleuch and Monmouth at their wedding, when he was aged fourteen. It was a less than successful marriage, but there were children – so that the Protestant succession might well be ensured. Small wonder, then, if men were unsure how to greet this latest representative of the ancient royal line of Stewart.

One thing was certain – there could be no doubt about his male parentage. Monmouth was all but a reproduction of the King, although somewhat better-looking, with the same sardonic features, long nose and great lustrous dark eyes, inherited from James the Sixth. He stood now in the doorway, smiling faintly, until the stir subsided. Then he raised hand and voice.

"A good day to you all, my lords and gentlemen," he said pleasantly, with just the slightest impediment of speech, another Stewart inheritance. "I thank you for coming to attend on me here. Refreshment is forthcoming. I shall have a word or two to say later, if you will bear with me." He nodded and came forward.

"A change in dukes from Lauderdale and Hamilton, at least!" Andrew said. Various great ones were brought to be presented to Monmouth by his entourage, in distinctly royal fashion. These were, however, very much government supporters. Servitors brought wine and small meats.

Sir David Carnegie came over and was introduced to Johnnie.

"Are we being honoured, cajoled or threatened and warned, Mr. Fletcher?" he asked. "I find this assembly intriguing. But there will be a purpose behind it, undoubtedly."

"I was saying to Lord Belhaven that this duke is an improvement on Lauderdale and Hamilton, sir. However peculiar his position."

"Be not too hard on Hamilton, my friend. We would be a

54

deal worse without him. But this Monmouth will want something of us – or we would not be here."

"I do not question that, sir. How is your daughter, may I ask?"

"Sufficiently well, I believe. Although to tell truth I see little of her. She spends most of her time, dressed like a fish-wife, carrying baskets of food up to the kirkyard of Greyfriars!"

"She is here? In Edinburgh?"

"Why yes. Has been this past week. I had business in the law-courts. But any small gain I made out of my suit, Margaret is spending on feeding the starving unfortunates at Greyfriars."

"They are starving? The Bothwell Brig prisoners . . . ?"

"They are not being otherwise fed, I understand. Save by sundry soft-hearted folk of Edinburgh. And such as my daughter. Over one thousand of them penned in the kirkyard, without shelter or care."

"But – I had heard that this Monmouth was more kind? Or less harsh?"

"Perhaps he is. Or perhaps merely he does not enjoy hangings and shootings. Prefers something less . . . abrupt!"

"I did not know of this of the prisoners. It is shameful! Perhaps I might accompany Mistress Margaret? See for myself . . .?"

A further thumping of halberds gained silence for the Duke.

"My friends," he said modestly, "I am no orator, as some here. So I ask forbearance. I have come to Scotland at a sorry time, and would have wished it otherwise. But I consider myself no stranger amongst you. After all, my wife and children dwell here. And from here come my illustrious ancestors. It would please me, indeed, to be here more often, even perhaps to reside here myself."

He paused, as though there was some special significance in that.

"It is my hope that the changes which must be made in Scotland hereafter may be as little to the hurt and discomfort of all as is possible. But change there has to be – let none think otherwise. As this uprising has shown, a firmer hand is required. Firmer and less distant. But, also more fair, more

55

understanding, I am assured. Therefore my message to you all is clear, but that of a friend, indeed almost one of yourselves. Trust and support my royal father's policies – his concern for you is great. Aid, not hinder, his new officers. Guide your people to do likewise and to forsake their rebellious ways. For their own and your good. And all will gain notably. This I promise. Fail in it, and I fear for Scotland – indeed I do! In sorrow. That is all, my lords and fellow-subjects. I thank you for listening patiently."

There was some some applause for this peculiar speech from amongst the government supporters, led by Rothes. But the great majority present were silent, eyeing each other doubtfully, wondering what it meant. On the face of it, there was nothing here to have brought them all to hear, platitudes, woolly nothings. Yet there was nothing woolly about the speaker or his manner; the reverse indeed. Moreover it appeared that this was all that he had come to say, for thereafter the Duke began to move slowly towards the door again.

"Did I come all the way from Beil to hear that?" Johnnie demanded, low-voiced. "What is he at?"

"There must be more to this than there sounds," Sir David asserted. "Monmouth is no fool. Here was some message – other than the obvious."

"Certain points he seemed to stress," Andrew said. "That there was this change coming. New officers. A hand firmer but less distant. Could that mean Lauderdale's hand removed? And this of his own fondness for Scotland – of which we were not aware hitherto!"

"Lauderdale, yes – it could be the end of Lauderdale. Perhaps Monmouth is to replace Lauderdale? Preparing his way? Coming to bide here . . . ?"

Further speculation was cut short, as the Duke reached the door, by a touch on Andrew's arm. He found Graham at his side.

"Come and have a word with the Duke, my friend," that man said.

Surprised at this summons, belated as it was, Andrew could scarcely refuse. As they went, to follow Monmouth out, he said to the other, "Do I congratulate you on your military activities, since last we met? Or otherwise?"

Claverhouse shrugged. "Who knows? I did my duty, as I saw it. A soldier takes failure and success as they come. As must you, Fletcher."

Still wondering just what that meant, he found Monmouth and his group waiting in an ante-room off the main stairway. If it was himself for whom they waited, then perhaps the Duke was not anxious to be seen speaking to him?

"This is my friend, Andrew Fletcher of Saltoun, my lord Duke," Graham presented him. "A man of some parts."

"Ah, yes – I have heard of Mr. Fletcher," Monmouth said civilly. "From whom was it? Perhaps it was my lord of Lauderdale?"

"Perhaps, sir," Andrew acceded carefully. "Depending on whether you heard good or ill!"

"So? Now, which would it be? How say you, Colonel Graham?"

"I think that my lord of Lauderdale may have been a little . . . prejudiced."

"Ah – who knows? Perhaps our Mr. Fletcher was also? But . . . both loyal subjects of my father."

"That certainly, my lord Duke," Andrew agreed, still more carefully.

"To be sure. Then may we hope that we can rely upon so loyal and able a subject to aid in the King's cause hereafter? In a new . . . dispensation? To the much advantage of all."

Andrew moistened his lips. "I would hope so, sir. That the King's cause should be mine also is my earnest prayer."

"Well said, Mr. Fletcher – well said! But . . . you fear otherwise?"

"A, a new dispensation, my lord Duke, could put much to rights."

"Exactly. So say we all. So – may we rely on your aid? To help bring about this happier state?"

Pressed thus, as into a corner, the other hesitated. He tried to be in all things honest; and this was difficult. "I hope so," was the best he could do.

"It could be much to your gain, my friend," Monmouth added.

Andrew was usually of a temper to give as he got — and he resented both the cornering and this suggestion of personal advantage. "My own wellbeing is not for consideration, sir," he said. "But that of many others is at stake. Even now. I had heard that your lordship made a more generous victor than did ... some we are used to! Yet your Covenanting prisoners, a thousand of them, are penned like cattle in the churchyard of Greyfriars, here. And unfed. This in the King's name!"

Monmouth looked unhappy and his attendants outraged. "This pains me, Mr. Fletcher, I assure you," he said. "But — the matter is not in my hands. I am but the military commander. At present. The prisoners are in the hands of the civil power."

"They were *your* prisoners, my lord Duke. And you represent the King's Grace, do you not?"

"Sir — do not speak so to my lord Duke!" one of the gentlemen hotly, when Monmouth waved him silent.

"I treated these people fairly, Mr. Fletcher. Although they were rebels. There were no hangings and shootings, no reprisals on their supporters."

"Yet this offence against humanity and decency is perpetrated in the King's name, even as we drink wine in this palace!"

"I will speak with the King's Advocate, sir. But I cannot promise anything. The matter rests with others." The Duke frowned, nodded briefly and turned away, the interview obviously at an end. Then he looked back. "Remember, Mr. Fletcher — your aid will be looked for. And valued."

John Graham looked at Andrew cynically. "You should have been a soldier, Fletcher. A captain of light cavalry, perhaps? But not a general, I think!" And he sauntered after Monmouth.

* * *

"Tell me about the Duke of Monmouth," Margaret requested. "They say that he is handsome and civil both. And like his father."

"I have never seen his father — who does not come to Scotland! But I found the Duke civil enough. As to handsome I know not. I judged him a little strange. A mixture. Perhaps because he was playing a role for which he was not suited."

"And that role was ... ?"

58

"Politician! I think that he is honest. No dissembler. Yesterday he was trying to act the politician . . ."

Her laughter interrupted him. "Mr. Fletcher – do I hear aright? *You* calling politicians dishonest, dissemblers! You who are becoming so notable a politician?"

He frowned despite himself. "I would hope to prove that it is possible to be both. Both honest and in politics!" That was distinctly stiff, not to say pompous. Realising it, and that with a large basket of bread, hard-boiled eggs, milk-pitchers and the like over his arm, pomposity was less than suitable, he changed tune. "He was seeking both to warn us and to lead us, I think. And finding it difficult. Between what he had been told to say and what he wanted to say."

"I think that you must really have liked him?"

They were walking up the Cowgate of Edinburgh westwards and having to pick their way heedfully, both on account of the crowded narrow thoroughfare and to avoid the unpleasantness underfoot for those not automatically conceded the crown of the causeway by their superior dress and manner. Today neither of them were clad at their best, to say the least. Margaret Carnegie might not look very like a fish-wife as her father had suggested; but she wore her oldest available clothes. Andrew had borrowed an old plaid from one of the Southesk servitors, despite the summer warmth. The reason for this was that any persons of rank seen taking comforts for the prisoners would certainly be reported on, and might well suffer, Advocate Mackenzie's spies being everywhere. Andrew would not have cared greatly, but implicating Margaret was a different matter.

Where Cowgatehead merged with the wide Grassmarket, directly below the towering cliff of the Castle-rock, the steep access to the kirkyard rose between high walls – but long before that the stink of the place was reaching them.

"I did not *mislike* him. But I was much exercised. To know what he was at. I have thought much on it, since. I think there was much to learn. It is my guess that Lauderdale is down. That a new Secretary of State will be appointed, to rule Scotland. And that Monmouth hopes to gain the office. Yesterday he was seeking to prepare the way. To make, if not friends, at least to find supporters to aid him when he comes."

59

"My father thought similarly."

"Yes. But there is more to it than that. King Charles is said to be in failing health, although not yet fifty – and lives as loosely as ever. So there is much talk of the succession, since he has no lawful children – however many otherwise! We know that there is a party in England who seek to have Monmouth legitimated and so made heir. A Protestant – and so keep Catholic James of York out. But there is a further whisper, here in Scotland. That the two crowns could be separated again, Scottish and English. They have been united for only seventy-five years. It could be that if Charles dies and Monmouth is not legitimated first, and so York becomes King in England, then Monmouth could be proclaimed King of Scots! All Presbyterians would rather have that than any Catholic, I swear! And he is Duke of Buccleuch, names himself Scott and has a Scots-born son as heir."

"Mercy – you think that is possible?"

"I do. And I think that he does, also. It would account for much of what he said yesterday. If he was ruling Scotland anyway, as Secretary of State, or High Commissioner, in place of Lauderdale, it would all be the more simple. And if he makes himself liked by the Scots people, it would aid, the more merciful victor, the moderate man and a Protestant! And he *is* the King's eldest son . . ."

There was no opportunity for more meantime. They were climbing the ascent to the graveyard which, in the late Queen Mary's reign, had been granted, in the grounds of the Grey Friars' Monastery south of the Grassmarket, to replace the old burial-ground of the High Kirk of St. Giles, which had been not only overfull but its space required for extensions of the Parliament House, the law courts, the Mint and other government buildings. At the heavily-guarded gate in the high perimeter wall, however, Margaret turned right-handed, westwards, along a narrow outer wynd.

"It is wrong of me, weak," she confessed, "but with the wind from the west, the smell is less grievous at the far side. And there is an alehouse there, Mother Pringle's, overlooking the kirkyard, where I have an arrangement."

Andrew certainly voiced no reproach.

Some distance along, near the West Port in the city wall, they
60

came to the tavern, a low-browed rendezvous for drovers and country-folk coming with their produce to the Grassmarket. Margaret led the way indoors, uncaring for the noise, semi-darkness, alternative smells and rough company, to make for and climb the stairs at the rear. These led up to small, grubby bedchambers on the upper floor, into the first of which, on the south side, the young woman turned and shut the door behind them.

"This I have hired, meantime," she confided.

Crossing over to the window, she tugged it open. Immediately the sounds and smells from below were overwhelmed by others from outside, the stench of unwashed, untended, wounded and massed humanity in warm weather, the noise loud, prolonged but various, rising and falling in waves, shouts, groans, cursing, raving, hymn-singing. The house had been built directly against the monastery wall, so that they looked immediately down into the kirkyard. Andrew gazed out, appalled at the sight. He had not visualised it as so utterly shattering. Twelve hundred men packed into an area of about three acres which was already crowded with tombstones and monuments, was in itself something scarcely to be comprehended. When all these had had to live in that space for weeks, without any facilities or shelter save for one well, many of them wounded and sick, the enormity of it all beggared description.

"Dear God, this is beyond belief!" he exclaimed. "This is ... hell on earth." Their appearance at the opened window seemed almost to make things worse. A sea of faces, bearded and filthy, turned in their direction and a forest of imploring hands rose high. It could not be said that there was a rush towards them, the unfortunates being too tight-packed for that. But there developed a sort of surge, in which scuffling and fighting grew, to get near them, below the window, and hoarse yells and pleas and supplications drowned all other noises.

Margaret had a rope attached to her basket, by which it could be lowered the score or so of feet to eager hands. But she waited, calling for Master King, explaining to Andrew that this was one of the outed ministers, much respected, who would be able to ensure some fair distribution – otherwise the strongest and toughest would grab all. Eventually a black-clad elderly man, with a shock of white hair, struggled forward, flanked by stalwart supporters; and into the hands of these they lowered the basket – to be rewarded with a benediction pronounced with quivering fervour and upraised hand amongst the many others.

Embarrassed they drew back. Voice as quivering as the clergyman's, in her emotion, the young woman wailed that it was so little, so hopelessly little for all these people. Only a very few would taste of what she had brought. It was always the same – she left feeling more useless than when she arrived.

When they hauled up the basket again, now containing the empty milk-pitchers from the day before, Andrew emptied his pockets of such coins as he had with him down into those hands so urgently beseeching, in the hope that some of the soldiers of the guard might be persuaded to buy food surreptitiously for the unhappy folk – and felt ashamed as he did it, as though arrogantly bestowing largesse on wayside beggars.

They actually hurried away, somehow guilt-ridden at being free and clean and well-fed.

"I *asked* Monmouth to help them," Andrew muttered, as they emerged into the wynd again. "Pray God that he does! And God's curse on those who can perpetrate this on their fellow-men! And in the name of the King and religion . . .!"

"Yes," she said.

4

It was the Parliament Hall again, awaiting the entry of the High Commissioner – and this time all had been properly done, in traditional fashion, the officers of state, the lords and commissioners and burgh representatives having ridden or marched through the Edinburgh streets in procession, as provided for in the old Riding of Parliament. To that extent it was an improvement. And it was, in fact, to be a parliament and no convention.

But as far as Andrew Fletcher was concerned, there the

betterment ended. He was only there, as it were, by the skin of his teeth. Not because the Haddingtonshire electors had failed to vote for him but because the Chancellor's office had declared that his own and his colleague's, Cockburn of Ormiston's, election was invalid, for unspecified reasons, and that therefore the two opposing and government-sponsored candidates were elected instead. This despite the fact that the actual voting figures were leaked from Haddington, and gave Fletcher and Cockburn a massive majority. The court party could hardly have expected Andrew, at least, to lie down under this – so presumably there was more to the manoeuvre than met the eye. He had promptly appealed to the Committee on Disputed Elections, set up at the former convention, and this had duly pronounced in his favour – but only just in time for Andrew and Cockburn to be able to take their seats. They were wary, in consequence.

There was more than that amiss, to be sure. Conditions were no better, despite the fall of Lauderdale – he had been forced to resign as Secretary of State the previous year, 1680, not by the Scots but by the English government, and was now living in retirement at his London house, allegedly afraid to return to Scotland. Indeed under Rothes – who had succeeded as Secretary of State and been promoted duke – the persecutions were almost worse, though perhaps less efficient. But by an extraordinary coincidence – or else divine intervention, as claimed by the Covenanters – a new situation had suddenly developed. Only the day before, the Reverend Donald Cargill, a zealous ousted minister, had been hanged for publicly cursing and actually excommunicating the King, the Duke of York, the Duke of Monmouth, the Duke of Lauderdale, the Duke of Rothes and General Tam Dalziel; and that same yesterday Rothes, Secretary of State and still Chancellor, had taken a seizure and expired. So Scotland was now freed of both men who had for so long ruled her in the King's name. But, led by Sir George Mackenzie, the King's Advocate, there were plenty of others to carry on their work with equal enthusiasm, Andrew had no shadow of doubt. This session of parliament ought to indicate the way things would now go – although inevitably the Chancellor's sudden death must effect some disarray.

The hall, in consequence, buzzed with anticipation and speculation.

Instead of the drummer-boy, four trumpeters appeared, to blow a right royal fanfare sufficient to rain down dust from the hall's roof-beams, to usher in the official party. The last to appear, before the High Commissioner's entry, proved to be Sir George Gordon, Lord Haddo of Session, only recently promoted to be Lord President of the Court of Session. Now, seemingly, he was to act as Chancellor in place of Rothes. A murmur ran through the assembly. Gordon was an able lawyer and ambitious, but not reputed harsh or dominant in the Lauderdale-Rothes tradition. Whose choice, then, was he?

More trumpeting heralded the King's representative, and all must bow. James, Duke of York strode in, tall, soldierly, alert, better-looking than his brother, with considerable dignity and a quiet assurance, a remarkable change from the High Commissioner they were used to. Few present, despite his reputation, could feel other than that this must be an improvement.

Andrew, for one, reserved judgment.

It was a strange sequence of events which brought James Stewart to that throne-like chair, instead of his nephew Monmouth, as all had anticipated. The King's continuing ill-health had brought the question of the succession ever more to the fore in both kingdoms, in England plots and counter-plots, rumours and scares proliferating. Charles himself was said to be leaning more and more towards Roman Catholicism, although always known as the Protestant monarch – however minimal his religious fervour. As a result, the House of Commons, in a sort of panic, passed a bill specifically excluding the Catholic York from succeeding. The House of Lords threw this out and a crisis developed. A plot was thereupon alleged to kill both the King and his brother and put firmly-Protestant Monmouth on the throne, illegitimate or otherwise. Few actually believed this, but it was thought expedient meantime for both brother and nephew to leave England. Oddly it was the son, Monmouth, whom Charles sent into exile overseas; whereas his brother James was sent northwards to Scotland as High Commissioner, in a totally unexpected reversal of roles. So James Stewart now sat there almost as monarch – and the sudden death of the Secretary of State and Chancellor only added to his authority.

He was a curious man, now aged forty-eight, undoubtedly a better man morally than Charles, courageous, determined, able; but religious where his brother was not, lacking in humour where Charles was the reverse, stiff and uncompromising where the King was seemingly pliant. Now he spoke briefly from the throne, in jerky, military style, formally conveying the King's greetings to his loyal subjects, reading his commission, announcing regret at the untimely death of the Duke of Rothes, announcing that he had chosen the Lord Haddo to take his place as Chancellor meantime – and so passing the business over to that somewhat hesitant individual, a slight, small-featured man, his face almost lost under his great wig.

After a certain amount of wordy preamble, very different in style from York's, he came to the bit. "It is His Majesty's desire that the Estates pass two acts. One, an Act of Succession to the throne. The other an extension of the English Test Act of 1671, applying to Scotland, suitably amended for this kingdom. The King's Advocate will speak to these."

Bloody Mackenzie, as he was now known, had difficulty in making his pleasantly-cultivated Highland voice heard in the din that arose. To have the two most controversial issues of the times as it were thrown at them thus, with the assertion that they were to be passed as King Charles and his brother desired, shook even that sychophantic assembly.

"My lords and commissioners and friends all," Mackenzie said soothingly, "here are two essential matters, essential for the peace and good governance of this realm. Matters which we can nowise shirk, if we do our leal duty to our sovereign-lord and to his people. None can deny it, nor should. First, this of the succession. This indeed calls for no debate. The King's Grace – long may God preserve him – has unhappily no lawful offspring. Since he does not now enjoy good health, it is necessary that his successor be named and accepted. This is incontestible. There is no choice, to be sure. Our High Commissioner, the King's royal brother, is his only lawful kin and undoubted heir to the throne. None here can say otherwise."

To say otherwise, and in the said brother's presence, was certainly not easy, in fact impossible. Objection could only be on other grounds.

The Advocate, chief law officer of the crown, did not wait for others to grasp the nettle. "Some have suggested that our good friend the Duke of Monmouth should be named in the succession. But this, my friends, is impossible. We can only here act within the law. And the law says that none illegitimately born may heir the throne. That is the position of my lord Duke of Monmouth."

"He could be legitimated," someone called.

"He could. But only at the behest of one person – his father. And the King has not chosen to do so. He has chosen his royal brother. This assembly must accept this."

Men looked at each other, silenced. Put thus, the matter seemed unanswerable. Unexpectedly it was MacCailean Mor, Earl of Argyll, of all people, who took the bull by the horns.

"My lord Chancellor," he said, choosing his words carefully as well he might, "the law of Scotland, as enacted, declares that whosoever is King of Scots must adhere to the Protestant religion. Lealest subject as I am, I must ask is my lord Duke of York prepared to abide by this enactment?"

Breaths were held as the crucial answer was awaited. Argyll had been Lauderdale's and the King's man; but it seemed that his hatred of Rome was stronger.

The Duke sat stony-faced, silent.

Again it was Mackenzie who spoke. "My lord, you are right, to be sure, about such act. But may I remind you that we cannot here be concerned with it? For it was passed before the crowns were united and refers only to the King of Scots. We are now part of a United Kingdom. It is a new and double crown, to which earlier legislation cannot apply."

Exclamation resounded.

"I therefore must rule your question out-of-order, my lord," Haddo said.

"My lord Chancellor, I protest!" Andrew exclaimed, jumping up. "Parliament cannot be muzzled in this way. The laws of Scotland cannot be swept aside by, by default! That Act made

66

this a Protestant realm, requiring a Protestant monarch. That cannot be denied. Therefore no mere dynastic arrangements subsequently can change it without parliamentary authority."

"My lord Chancellor – young Mr. Fletcher's enthusiasms are refreshing and well-known! But not being bred to the law, I fear that he must not try to teach me my business. I assure him, and all, that in law this assembly has no authority to require that a possible successor to the throne of the United Kingdom must adhere to any specific religion. As a good Protestant myself, I might feel that this could be advisable – but that is a different matter."

"Then . . . then, sir, if that is so, it may become necessary to *dis*unite or separate the two thrones again!" That came out in a rush. "If only so may the will and authority of the Scottish people and parliament be upheld!"

Now there was uproar, a dozen men on their feet at once, shouting.

The Chancellor's gavel at last gained quiet. "This is disgraceful!" he declared, but unhappily. "I cannot allow such, such sentiments to be expressed. And in front of, of . . ." His voice tailed away.

James Stewart sat expressionless.

"My lord Chancellor – may I advise this headstrong young man?" the Advocate asked. "And for his own good. What he has just impetuously suggested is in fact treasonable. A direct attack on the integrity and powers of the crown, and in the presence of the crown's representative. Men have died for less, many men! Spoken outside the privilege of this parliament it would be my duty to arrest the speaker. Let him ponder that – and choose his words!"

"Does Advocate Mackenzie threaten me, Chancellor?" Andrew demanded. "Within this parliament? Duly discussing the constitution of this realm?"

"I do not threaten. I warn. As is my duty. For, my friends, this Andrew Fletcher has already, all should know, made similar treasonable suggestions, and *outside* the privilege of parliament. Written suggestions. I have been very patient, but . . ."

"Proof, my lord Chancellor?"

Haddo looked at Mackenzie, who picked up a paper.

"Here is a letter. Sent by Mr. Fletcher to a commissioner here present. One of many, I understand – as he has done before. It says that should the subject of the succession be raised here, the Protestant adherence must be forced to the vote. And if it is blocked, then the question of the separation of the crowns should be raised, as warning. Do you deny sending this?"

"Is not the signature relevant?"

"It is unsigned, sir. Anonymous."

"Ah. Why apportion it to me, then?"

"Can you deny that the handwriting is yours?"

Only for a moment Andrew hesitated. It probably was not noticed, for the Advocate was handing the letter to a clerk to bring to him. "I see no reason why I should either confirm or deny – since I am not on trial in one of your courts, sir – as yet!" Then as the clerk came up with the paper, he shrugged – and hoped relief did not show. "But since you are so concerned, Advocate, I will humour you. No, that is not my handwriting." There had always been a fifty-fifty chance that the letter was one of Henry's.

Thrown off his stride, Mackenzie frowned.

Haddo quickly reverted to the main issue. "We are asked to accept the monarch's nomination of his royal brother. I do not see how any can refuse, since there is no other lawful heir. We should be glad to do so. Since I am assured by the King's Advocate that any motion to the contrary could be esteemed treasonable, I shall not permit such motion, but declare herewith that this parliament welcomes the King's gracious decision. No more is required of us. I pass to the next business."

Men eyed each other, many undoubtedly with something of relief, treason being a dire word. Andrew's gazing assured him that there was nothing further that he could attempt. Everywhere eyes were careful to avoid his own. Had the Duke of Hamilton been present he might have been prepared to take it further; presumably he was still in London. Even Johnnie Belhaven was absent, thrown from a horse and concussed. Anyway, with hundreds executed for treason within the last year or so, should any man be led to put his neck into a noose?

They were given scant opportunity anyway. Mackenzie was already spelling out the next issue. It was a peculiar one, in the circumstances, for the Test Act had been passed as far back as 1671 by the *English* Parliament, specifically to exclude Catholics from all offices of state, the test being the requirement to partake of Holy Communion as dispensed by the Church of England. This indeed had then forced the Duke of York into exile overseas. Now he was back, and the Act was to apply to Scotland.

The Advocate explained. "This provision is necessary. We live in a time of fanatical separatists and determined nonconformists, folk who rebel and plot and even excommunicate their King and his close servants. Such clearly can have no place in the King's service. Unhappily there are others less evident, who support these secretly, for their own ill ends. These we must root out, in especial from where they could harm the King's cause. Accordingly some test is required, for the realm's safety. It must be simple, but certain, not to be won around. The King's wishes are clear. I have composed these clauses." He took up another paper. "All persons save the King's brother and sons must take oath on entry into any office in Church or State, binding themselves to profess the true religion as defined and established by the laws of the kingdom; to renounce all things inconsistent with it; to accept the royal supremacy on all things ecclesiastical and civil; to declare it unlawful to enter into covenants or leagues or to rise in arms against the government; to treat, consult or determine in any matter of state, without His Majesty's especial command." He paused. "These are the crown's requirements, simply and fairly put. None, I think, should misunderstand them."

Something like consternation struck the assembly – and not only such small parts of it as tended to be critical of the government. Indeed some of the bishops were amongst the most upset – since it seemed to imply that a new monarch could change the religion of the land at will – and the next monarch, they had just learned, would be a Roman Catholic. The noise and disorder made the earlier clamour a mere passing zephyr. In vain the Chancellor banged his table. At length the Duke of York himself rose and quietly left the chamber, after a brief word with Haddo.

This did have a calming effect. Presently the Chancellor was able to make himself heard, to announce that the High Commissioner would return only if and when order was restored. Points could be raised and questions asked, but only in due and proper fashion, with respect for His Grace and the Chancellor. Otherwise the sitting would be suspended.

The Duke must have been waiting just outside the door, for at the comparative quiet he came back to resume his seat.

Immediately there followed a flood of questions and objections, speakers rising one after the other, the Archbishop of Glasgow, the Earls of Argyll, Roxburgh, Tweeddale, Perth, Crawford and Southesk leading. They wanted elucidation on every clause of Mackenzie's statement but especially to be told what was meant by true religion as defined by the laws of the kingdom. They were answered less than adequately by the usually nimble-witted Sir George Mackenzie, unaided from the throne or the Chancellor's table. None were satisfied and it seemed as though chaos would return.

It was then that Sir James Dalrymple of Stair, up till now Lord President of the Court of Session, made his contribution. A shrewd, indeed brilliant lawyer who had been professor of philosophy, he rose to suggest that since in Scotland the phrase true religion could only refer to the Reformed Protestant faith, they should add a sentence to emphasise this. That faith, as all knew, was set forth in the Confession of Faith of 1560. That should be acceptable to all reasonable men.

There was a distinct pause at this, not all present being by any means conversant with the doctrinal pronouncements of the last century. But Dalrymple was a King's man and friend of Mackenzie's, and clever. No doubt this would be a useful safeguard against Catholicism. Few there, if any, realised that this was not the *Westminster* Confession of Faith, accepted as the corner-stone of the Kirk and drawn up much later.

Presumably the Advocate did not realise this either, for he accepted the additional wording almost thankfully, looking at the Duke and Chancellor and getting nods from both.

Since this amendment went down so well, Andrew saw his

chance. He rose, to put forward a motion that, in accordance with the foregoing, to put the matter entirely beyond doubt, a clause be inserted in this test oath, ensuring the security of the Protestant religion. Baillie of Jerviswood seconded.

After agreeing to Dalrymple's insertion, the Advocate could hardly object to this, which seemed merely to emphasise the same point. The motion was passed without contest. Andrew did not fail to notice, however, the glare of sheer hostility from the normally urbane Mackenzie nor indeed the stern unwinking stare from James Stewart.

Many more queries and points were raised as to meanings and details, most skilfully parried or else ignored. None actually came to motions.

The Duke now showed signs of restiveness. Noting it, Chancellor and Advocate clearly thought to move to an adjournment for the day. Andrew considering that, after an adjournment and the usual behind-the-scenes manoeuvrings, threats and promises, the climate of opinion might be a deal less favourable, hastened to get in another motion.

"I move that this test includes a clause which ensures that no member of the Estates, nor yet elector thereto, need take such oath never to attempt to bring about any change in Church and State as now established. As the Advocate's draft would seem to imply."

"The proposed oath does *not* so imply," Mackenzie said curtly.

"I think that it does. Does not 'all persons . . . on entry to any office in Church or State' refer to commissioners to parliament?"

"No sir. Membership of parliament is not an office."

"Nevertheless it would be safer put in words."

"This is pin-pricking, sir. Not to be tolerated." That was the Chancellor.

"It is a motion before the assembly, my lord." Andrew realised that perhaps he was being obstinate, even foolish in this – for there was no stir of support at all evident now, only some shuffling and murmuring. But he could scarcely withdraw without seeming feeble.

"Unseconded," Haddo pointed out.

"I second."

71

That turned all heads, including Andrew's, who almost wished the two words unspoken. They came, surprisingly, from Sir Ludovick Grant of Grant, something of an eccentric who had hitherto taken no part in the proceedings.

Haddo evidently decided that he had nothing to fear. "Does any other support these, in an unnecessary motion, clearly declared so by the Advocate?"

There was silence.

"Then I declare that the motion falls." Quickly he turned towards the Duke. "Would it be Your Grace's wish that today's session be adjourned?"

"Agreed." James Stewart rose. "My lords and gentlemen, enough for this day. When we reassemble, let it be in a spirit of loyal duty and resolve. Until then, I urge you all to consider, consider well, where failure in such duty will lead." The princely gaze swept round, and seemed to linger momentarily on four faces, Argyll's, the Laird of Grant's, Baillie of Jervis-wood's and Andrew Fletcher's, before turning, he stalked out to a trumpet fanfare.

They were warned.

* * *

At Southesk's house in the Canongate that night Andrew found himself held in less esteem than on the previous occasion. Clearly it was felt that he had overdone it, made himself unnecessarily provocative, offended the King's brother, who appeared to be moderate and reasonable, seemed to be allying himself with the fanatics and extremist Covenanters. There was a new regime now, with Lauderdale and Rothes gone, and no successors of like calibre in evidence. They should be given a chance; headlong opposition was not the policy at this stage. Even Sir David Carnegie was critical. And he reminded him of personal dangers in such attacks.

This aspect it was which seemed to weigh heavily with Margaret Carnegie, and with Henry also to some extent. They were only going on hearsay, of course, and were anxious rather than critical.

Andrew, did, however, have a card to play in his own defence, and which made a distinct impact on the company. He informed that after the adjournment he had gone straight to the Parliament Hall library and looked up the old statutes and Acts of the Estates. And the referred-to 1560 Act embodied *John Knox*'s resounding Confession of Faith at the Reformation, no later and watered-down version. And than John Knox there could be no sterner upholder of the Kirk's and people's rights against the crown's. That Confession declared flatly that Jesus Christ was the only Head of the Kirk, and that all its subscribers were bound to 'represse tyrannie' and to 'defend the oppressed' as well as to uphold to the death the Protestant faith. No one would suggest, he thought, that Sir James Dalrymple, of all men, did not know what he was at when he inserted the 1560 Confession and Act. So they must take it that at least one of the pillars of the government in Scotland, the Lord President of Session, was on the right side of this. For this accepted amendment made a nonsense out of the entire Test.

This, of course, intrigued his hearers and went some way towards restoring Andrew in estimation. It was decided, however, by the group present – which was the nearest thing to a political party such as Andrew had advocated – that it would be folly to draw attention to this discrepancy, in the remaining sessions of the parliament lest the thing should be amended and this enormous loophole blocked. For once, the King's Advocate's lack of religious commitment had let down his cause.

And so, in the days following, nothing was said directly about Dalrymple's amendment, although there were many other questions and points raised, some of which came perilously near this vital issue. Andrew held his tongue, although with difficulty, though voting, needless to say, always against tyrannical powers. He had intended to raise and emphasise the disgrace of the recent Greyfriars kirkyard scandal, which had persisted for five long months before, with many of the prisoners dead, some were executed, some few signed a promise to keep the peace and were released, but hundreds were shipped off the Barbados plantatations as slaves – although the ship sank off Orkney and the prisoners drowned. This should have been a cudgel to beat the government, but he was persuaded to silence.

Actually, however, the remaining sessions were rather dull,

73

humdrum and procedural, all the vital issues, like the fireworks, confined to the first day. No doubt James Stewart was satisfied that his warning had borne fruit. He had got what he wanted, the Succession and Test Acts passed. He prorogued parliament, therefore, in theory the master of Scotland.

But it was quickly made apparent that theory and words were insufficient, that the Scots required more than this to hold them down. Opposition to the Test rose on all sides, led by the anti-government faction, Andrew prominent. Leaflets were issued by the thousand, ridiculing the Act and pointing out its inconsistencies and contradictions, much play being made of the 1560 Confession clause, now that it was too late to amend it until another parliament. Even bishops and episcopalian ministers preached against it. The schoolboys of George Heriot's Hospital smeared a copy of the Act with butter and tried to get their watch-dog to swallow it; when the dog refused they publicly hanged it. Refusals to sign were many, especially when the chief judge, the Lord President of the Court of Session, himself declared that he could not in all honesty put his name to such a document which made no sense, resigned his high office and retired to his Ayrshire estate of Stair.

It was not Dalrymple who was chosen as scapegoat but MacCailean Mor, chief of Clan Campbell himself, something neither Lauderdale nor yet Rothes would have done. Argyll, of course, held many offices under the crown, some hereditary. He did not exactly refuse to sign, but qualified his signature – and this was held to be treasonable. Despite his lofty rank he was promptly arrested, immured in Edinburgh Castle and told that he would be executed, as had his father before him. That he made good his escape from the fortress without delay, disguised as his own daughter's maid, and fled to England, was the talk of Edinburgh for weeks. Few had thought him capable of it.

It was in these conditions that Andrew received a summons to appear before the Privy Council at Holyroodhouse, to answer for his failure, as a Commissioner of Cess and Supply for Haddingtonshire, to levy in full the necessary supply of money, forage and victual for the King's forces quartered in that county. This was the old story of over two years before, renewed, when John Graham had been billeted upon him at Saltoun and he had sought to spare the East Lothian folk the worst effects of the military demands. He was not greatly concerned, for many others had done the same and had been merely warned and admonished.

But the evening before he was to appear at Holyrood, they had a visitor at Saltoun – none other than Margaret Carnegie, who had ridden the fifteen miles from Edinburgh, in the windy winter dusk, with only a groom as escort. Henry brought her to Andrew.

"Margaret has come! Come bringing news, Andrew. Ill news. Ridden from Edinburgh . . ."

"It would have to be ill news indeed to prevent me from rejoicing that it fetched her to us all the way to Saltoun!" he greeted, with somewhat ponderous gallantry. "Come to the fire."

"Would that I had happier tidings for you," she said, shaking her lovely head. "Yet I fear that it must mean, mean saying goodbye, Andrew. You must not go to Holyroodhouse tomorrow!"

"Ha! So you have heard of that?"

"Yes. John Graham told us. Or told my sister. He arrived only today, from Wigtown. Summoned to this Privy Council meeting. Or trial, or whatever it is. As witness against you!"

"Graham? Bloody Clavers can only testify what scores of others can do – that I tried to spare our people the worst demands of his military." Bloody Clavers was the title that John Graham had earned for himself in Galloway, in the King's service.

"I do not know about that. But he sends this message to you – and I think takes some risk in doing so. He says that you must go. Before they lay hands on you. At once. Flee Scotland. As Argyll has done. For at this meeting tomorrow you are to be trapped. Made to sign this Test. And when you refuse, as is expected, you are to be arrested. And tried for treason.

"But this is nonsense! I hold no office under the crown. The Advocate himself declared, before all, that being commissioner of parliament is no office."

"No. But John says that they are going to assert that being a

Commissioner of Cess and Supply for your county is such office. Because you can claim expenses, I think. So you are to be caught . . ."

"But, Lord – every representative of the shires is a Commissioner of Supply! During his term. This is sheerest trickery, deceit . . . !"

"It may be, Andrew – but it is what they have in store for you, John says. And once they have you arrested – dear God, I dare not think on it! You know how they must hate you. I have feared something like this . . ."

He stared at her and then to Henry, at a loss for words.

"Thank Heaven for Graham, at least! That you are warned," Henry said. "What will you do, Andrew? You cannot fight this. Against the Privy Council – with the Duke of York behind them, as must be, since he has taken over Holyroodhouse. It is *his* work! If MacCailean Mor could not defend himself, you cannot."

Andrew turned to pace the floor, fists clenched.

"John says that you can only flee, to where this Privy Council's writ does not run – across the Border," Margaret declared. "At first. And then probably overseas – for no doubt they will be able to take you in England, also, in time. But meantime England. Have you anyone to whom you can go? Secretly?"

"Burnet!" Henry said. "Gilbert Burnet. In London. He would help, Andrew. Master Burnet was parish minister here, our tutor," he told Margaret. "An excellent man. Author of books. He now lives in London . . ."

"I cannot just bolt like a whipped cur!"

"What choice have you? They were going to hang Argyll. Think you they will be any kinder with you? You have *got* to go, Dand – to save your life."

"And at once," the young woman insisted. "Tomorrow may be too late. That is why I rode here tonight. When you do not appear at Holyrood, they will be after you. Do not be foolish, Andrew. Heed us – who are fond of you!"

He looked at her, at that face, searchingly, almost hungrily – and she met his gaze frankly. He nodded. "I . . . thank you. Yes, then – I shall go. Pray God, not for long. But I shall go."

"Tonight?"

"Yes."

"God be praised! And my . . . *our* prayers go with you. Oh, I am sorry, sorry! To be the bearer of such tidings. I, I . . ." She shook her head determinedly. "Enough! I must go. Return, before I am missed."

"You will stay here tonight, surely?"

"No. If it was learned that I was here . . . when you are fled . . . there could be much trouble. My father might suffer. My groom I can trust. But I must be back to Edinburgh tonight."

"Then I will escort you. First, before I . . . bolt."

"Do not be foolish, Andrew . . . !"

"It is *my* privilege," Henry declared. "You have other things to do, Dand. And ride in quite the other direction . . ."

So, presently, they made their farewells, a difficult, trying business, with so much to be said and no way of saying it. The normally eloquent and vehement Andrew Fletcher was for once all but wordless, his brother gabbling rather, Margaret strained, in a conflict of emotions. As Andrew helped her up on to her horse, there in the windy dark, they clung to each other for a moment – that was all. They did not even say goodbye, indeed, neither trusting their voices.

Henry gripped his brother's shoulder, and mounted also.

Later by a couple of hours, Andrew did ride in the opposite direction, alone, with full saddlebags, as much money as he could find about the house, sword by his side – and with a sore heart. He did not look back at his great house, but trotted eastwards through the darkened countryside he knew so well, with a thin rain off the sea in his face. At least, on such a night, he was unlikely to be observed.

He went by Beil, where he knocked up a surprised Johnnie Belhaven and his wife, to say goodbye. Johnnie, now recovered from his concussion, agreed that Andrew had no option but to flee the country. He added that, strangely, only the day before, Baillie of Jerviswood had called, and on the same business, flight, warned that he was to be arrested and executed. He was having hastily to borrow moneys, as he went, for he had been so savagely fined for his non-conformity – £6,000, the entire annual value of his estates – that he was all but

77

penniless. He was a distant connection of the Hamiltons. He had gone on, en route for the Border, intending to call on his friend Sir Patrick Home of Polwarth, who would help him – having himself been incarcerated in Stirling Castle by the Privy Council some time before, for four years; Home had then gone to England but was now returned. Probably Baillie would still be at Polwarth, only a few miles from the Border. Perhaps if Andrew called in there, the two fugitives might go on together? Two men Scotland could ill afford to lose.

They would be back, Andrew assured.

Part Two

5

Gilbert Burnet was a strange man, an extraordinary mixture, extraordinary indeed by any standards. Talented, cultured, handsome, amiable, broad-minded, he was yet strong-willed to a degree, all but obstinate, unafraid of giving offence in the highest places yet the gentlest of men in his personal relationships, utterly careless of his own advantage yet forever attracting offers of lofty position. Cadet of the ancient Deeside house of Burnet of Leys, son of a Lord of Session, he had been a Master of Arts of Aberdeen University before he was fourteen years, studied law, changed to divinity, licensed to preach at eighteen, a member of the Royal Society at twenty-one and Professor of Divinity at Glasgow at twenty-seven. Offered his choice of four Scots bishoprics at twenty-nine, he refused them all but chose to become a mere parish minister of Saltoun at thirty. There he stayed for five years, preaching twice of a Sunday, visiting the sick, tutoring the Fletcher brothers and writing his books, particularly his *History of the Reformation*, of both kingdoms. He was offered the first archbishopric vacant but again refused; and, hating the oppressions in Scotland under Lauderdale, removed to London in 1678. He was promptly offered a large city church, but, followed by Lauderdale's spleen, King Charles himself wrote to the congregation ordering them not to engage so dangerous a character. But the Master of the Rolls, no less, despite the royal displeasure, gave him charge of his private chapel, and gained him the Lectureship of St. Clements, with a house. There at St. Clements he remained, writing – and strangely, became the most sought-after preacher in London. And when his first volume of the *History of the Reformation* was published, received the thanks of both English Houses of Parliament.

This was the man, still aged only thirty-nine, who received with joy Andrew Fletcher and Robert Baillie at his St.

Clements house that March day of 1683, to insist that they stayed there as his guests. Oddly enough, Baillie of Jerviswood was a connection by marriage, Baillie's wife being a niece of Burnet's mother. The fugitives, of course, emphasised that their presence must remain secret, if possible – and by the same token must therefore pose some risk to their host, if discovered. But Burnet would not hear of them going elsewhere. He owed his kinsmen shelter, he asserted; and he had always been particularly fond of his old pupil – on whom, of course, he had had an enormous influence. He approved most strongly of their present attitudes and must in consequence aid them in every way possible.

So they settled in at St. Clement's Lane, amongst the narrow, smelly London Thames-side streets. Andrew was able to write a letter to Henry, informing him that all was well, that there had been no sign of pursuit, that the journey down through England had been prolonged, uncomfortable but uneventful, and would he send him some money as soon as possible, for he was woefully short of clothing suitable for the kind of company Gilbert Burnet frequented. He also wrote three or four versions of a letter to Margaret Carnegie, but tore them all up and ended by merely asking Henry to convey his admiration and thanks and devotion to that young woman.

Burnet had an excellent source of information as to what went on in Scotland through none other than the Duke of Hamilton, who made a point of being kept up-to-date. The author's first book had been the Memoirs of the Duchess Anne; and he was now working on a companion-volume for the Duke. So he saw a lot of the Hamiltons and was able to keep his visitors apprised of much that transpired in that country. It seemed that the oppressions of the government grew ever more dire. The Duke of York, who had started out, not exactly by seeking popularity but by acting with seeming moderation and largely leaving political action and persecutions to the officers of state, even becoming a golf enthusiast on Leith Links like his grandfather, was now showing his true colours. There were more and more arrests and executions; edicts and orders flowed from Holyroodhouse, Catholics were promoted to high places, fervent Protestants brought low and the Test

82

rigorously applied. No fewer than eighty Episcopalian ministers, mainly of Lauderdale's appointment, refused the Test and were ousted. The subsequent uprisings of the people were put down with a savagery hitherto unequalled – with Colonel Graham of Claverhouse the name which was apt to crop up most frequently as the greatest scourge, and in high favour with James Stewart. Indeed he was said to have been promised a seat on the Privy Council. Mackenzie, the Advocate, for his part, had been rewarded with the royal barony of Bute. And so on.

Scotland seemed a good place to be out of – but the exiles' anxieties for their kin and friends grew the more.

Not that conditions in England were so greatly better. With ever poorer health, the King's hidden Catholicism became ever more evident, and the English House of Commons, staunchly Protestant, grew ever the more restive. The House of Lords, with many more Catholics, was less so; but the Protestant lords were the more concerned in consequence; and in fact took the lead in agitation and protest. Plots and scares and secret groupings proliferated and talk was all of unconstitutional action, revolt and worse. The house of Stewart, which had survived for over three centuries, appeared to be lurching towards a fall.

Burnet, who had always been a King's man, however frequently he found himself in disagreement with the monarch, was pulled two ways in all this. He was a firm Protestant, but loth to turn against Charles Stewart. He was an upholder of freedom and hater of tyranny, but disapproved of violence and unconstitutional behaviour. When Charles had found it expedient to offer him the bishopric of Chichester, he had refused, but sent the King a specially-composed poem, expounding in notable verse the duties of kingship in a Protestant realm. He sought to remain friendly with men of all views and to avoid implication in politics – or so he declared. Nevertheless those close to him had no doubts as to where his heart lay. And Andrew Fletcher, whose own views had been so greatly moulded by the older man, who had had the rearing of him for five most formative years, knew better than most.

For all that, Andrew was surprised when, a week or so after

their arrival, and with time already beginning to hang heavily, Gilbert Burnet asked his guests if they would like to accompany him to a meeting that evening? They need not worry, it would not be a public meeting; indeed a very private one. Those attending would be exceedingly discreet and trustworthy, and no risk to the fugitives be involved; but they might well find the occasion instructive and might in turn have the opportunity of instructing the others on conditions in Scotland, which might have some relevance to the proceedings.

Intrigued, they were glad to accede. Lying low was a dull business.

They had not far to walk, only two streets further west along Lombard Street, to Abchurch Lane, something of a backwater, where at a wine-merchant's establishment, by the name of Shepherd, they were led through a back-yard, amongst casks and barrels, and up a stair to the merchant's house. Climbing, Burnet asked them if they had heard of the Council of Six. It would have been strange if they had not. All England had heard of the Council of Six, reputedly the most lofty, influential and secret of the political groups and leagues which the present unhappy dynastic and governmental situation had thrown up. Just who the six were was a mystery – but they were highly-placed Protestants, inevitably. Scarcely able to believe their ears, that the allegedly inoffensive, non-political Dr. Burnet should be in a position to introduce them to such company, his charges marvelled.

Mr. Shepherd, a rubicund, bustling and very unplotterlike little man, ushered them into a large chamber, apparently part-office, part wine-tasting room, by the aroma and the many pails and flagons, where, beside a well-doing coal-fire, four men sat at ease, glasses in hand. They were all of middle years, richly-dressed and assured of manner. They rose to greet the newcomers.

"Ah, Gilbert," one said, "here is a pleasure. We are always delighted when you will take wine with us."

"The privilege is all mine, my lords. May I present to you my friends from Scotland, of whom I informed you? Both lairds of substance and some renown, forced into exile."

"But not for long, I hope. Of both Mr. Baillie and Mr.

84

Fletcher we have heard, of course. And quite recently – from my lord of Argyll, no less."

"I fear that you will have heard but little to my credit from the Campbell, sir!" Baillie said grimly. "I am Jerviswood. Argyll helped to fine me £6,000 none so long ago – for non-conformity!"

"You say so? A grievous imposition. But Argyll it seems has seen the light, if belatedly, and changed his tune. We have sent him on to Holland." The spokesman held out his hand. "I am Essex. And these are my lords Howard, Russell and Grey."

Impressed indeed, the visitors bowed. The Earl of Essex was one of the foremost noblemen of England, until recently indeed Viceroy of Ireland, and now Lauderdale's successor as First Lord of the Treasury. Lord William Russell, son of the Earl of Bedford, was one of the most famous parliamentarians of the day, leader of a large faction in the House of Commons. And Lords Howard and Grey were well-known peers, influential in the Upper House. If these were four of the Council, then its illustrious nature had not been exaggerated.

They were sat down, offered a choice of wines, and courteously but authoritatively questioned in detail about the Scottish situation, and especially the Duke of York's behaviour and activities. These men, it seemed, were particularly interested in any possible re-separation of the crowns, such as Fletcher had once suggested.

Andrew explained that this was not in any way a live issue, at present, in Scotland, although it was not infrequently spoken of. He had raised it in the convention more as a threat than anything else.

At this stage another gentleman arrived, proving to be none other than John Hampden M.P., another leader of the Commons, grandson of the famous Parliament general. He was a harsher man, less urbane and seemingly less pleased to see the visitors. He explained that he had been kept late at the House and would have to go back shortly, being down to speak in a debate which might go on into the small hours. With a doubtful glance at the Scots he asked if there was any word of The Sparrowhawk?

"He will be here," Russell said.

They were discussing the probable line-up and voting strengths in the Lords for and against the Exclusion Bill against the Duke of York, when the wine-merchant opened the door again to usher in the sixth member of the Council. And the others all rose to their feet with rather more alacrity than hitherto. Nor were Andrew and Baillie any more sluggish, when they perceived the identity of the newcomer. It was James of Monmouth.

If the Scots were astonished, having thought that the Duke was still in exile overseas, Monmouth seemed little less so on finding there Andrew Fletcher whom he had last spoken to in such very different circumstances in the Palace of Holyroodhouse. They greeted each other stiffly in consequence.

Burnet explained his friends' present state, although Monmouth did not feel called upon to explain his. But it transpired in the conversation thereafter that he was back in England secretly – although his father knew of it. Charles, however ailing, however frequent his blood-lettings and cuppings, appeared still to be playing a two-handed game.

Despite the doubtful glances of the two latest-come members, the other four were quite prepared to discuss their policies in front of the Scots exiles. It seemed that their principal preoccupation this evening was the possible setting-up of a regency. The King's state was precarious, his physicians' remedies growing ever more extreme, and these were weakening the monarch. He was still only fifty-three, but now scarcely in a fit state to reign – although he continued to pursue his pleasures with a sort of desperation. Since the Exclusion Bill had so far failed to pass the Lords, James Duke of York was still the legitimate heir to the throne. But if a regency could be established, and the King persuaded to yield the power to it, then the disaster of a Catholic monarch mounting a Protestant throne might be averted. The Regent, of course, should be Monmouth who was popular with the people, and Protestants – there was no other contender. Charles had innumerable other bastards but they were little more than children and he was not fond of them as he was of his firstborn. Could the King be persuaded to agree to this, even if he still refused to legitimate his son?

That young man, eyed by them all, hesitated. He started to say something and then seemed to change his mind. He just did not know, he said. His father was a strange man, all contradictions; and now in his sickness more unpredictable than ever. He knew that he was fond of himself, in his own erratic way – otherwise he would not have been allowed to return to England, even secretly. But there was clearly a grievous impediment about this matter of legitimation. The King would not consider it. No doubt it was something to do with the late Queen, Henrietta Maria, the King's mother. Also perhaps his own Queen, Catherine of Braganza. He held back, reluctant. And this attitude might equally affect his reception of the regency notion.

"There is some mystery here," Essex said. "We must seek to find out what it is."

"Could it not be the less mysterious?" Hampden put in bluntly. "That His Majesty has all along been a secret Catholic? And holds back mainly because you, sir, are a Protestant? Now that he nears his end, deeming himself in danger of hell-fire if he does not play Rome's game?"

Monmouth frowned. "I do not know. He is not a religious man. And he has withheld this of legitimation for many years. Before he was ailing."

"What is important is not so much the reason as the fact," Russell said. "Is there no way by which we could persuade His Majesty to a regency? It would solve many problems."

"The King has always recognised his brother to be obstinate, injudicious, difficult," Gilbert Burnet put in. "I have heard him reprove His Royal Highness many times. Could you not play on that? Make much of what he is doing, or misdoing, in Scotland? The cruelties and persecutions. These took place under Lauderdale also, of course – but now it is the King's own brother doing it. Heir to the throne. Dividing the nation."

"Charles always supported Lauderdale," Hampden pointed out.

"But he is not a cruel or harsh man, in himself."

"May I speak?" Andrew said, eagerly. "If I may be so bold. Thank you. This of dividing the nation, the Scots nation. That may or may not grievously affect the King. But to divide the

87

crowns — now, that would be a different matter! I think His Grace would do much to avoid that."

"But you said before, Mr. Fletcher, that this of the separation of the crowns again was not seriously considered, not a live issue?" Essex objected.

"It is not, my lord. But it might be made so. More important, could it not be used with the King? To help convince him that the Duke of York could in fact bring it about? He has, indeed, got his Succession Act through the Scots parliament. So if England did refuse him as monarch and Scotland does not, then the kingdoms *are* divided again."

"It could work the other way," Russell pointed out. "Make His Majesty more determined than ever that York be established in England, that the thrones be *not* divided."

"I think not, my lord." Andrew glanced at Monmouth to see how that man was taking this. "The King has sent his brother to Scotland, knowing his unpopularity here. He knows himself to be gravely ill. To make the Duke widely accepted in England would take long — and His Grace is unlikely to have that time. Moreover, I think that the Duke of York is not the sort to take kindly to seeking popularity."

"I agree," Howard said. "I think that it is worth a trial."

"Do you concur, my lord Duke?" Essex asked.

"I see no harm in it," Monmouth said slowly. "But do not ask *me* to put the issue before my royal father. He will only think that I invented it all, for my own purposes — whereas I would shed my blood to keep the kingdoms united!"

Baillie opened his mouth to speak, but shut it again. He for one was no great believer in the United Kingdom.

Soon thereafter Burnet took his leave, with his charges. On the walk back to St. Clements he however expressed himself as well satisfied with the evening — odd, in one so deliberately non-political.

In the weeks that followed, the exiles, although they saw no more of the Council of Six, heard a great deal about sundry other groups and plots and alleged conspiracies; indeed London seemed to resound with such, almost farcically so. No doubt it was all a symptom of the general unrest and apprehension. But the stories circulating verged on the ridiculous. The various cabals gave themselves curious titles, which were duly whispered abroad, uttered dire threats about the Lopping Time and Striking at the Heart, referred to lofty personages as the Blackbird, the Goldfinch, the Churchwarden of Whitehall and so on. New drinking-toasts circulated and grew popular, such as 'Confusion to the Two Brothers, Popery and Slavery!' and 'To the Man who First Draws Sword in Defence of the Protestant Religion!'

Few could take all this seriously; but Gilbert Burnet for one feared serious repercussions from authority. That the Duke of York suddenly returned from Scotland, even if only temporarily, may not have been a result, but it certainly had the effect of further stimulating the unrest and the fears. The general assumption was that there would be major and unacceptable developments. Burnet said that his two lodgers must be prepared to take a hasty departure, probably across the Channel.

Then, at the beginning of June, all erupted. A city tradesman named Joseph Keeling, no doubt well paid to do so and an agent provocateur, announced, with names, a detailed plot to assassinate both the King and the Duke and to place Monmouth on the throne. This was the old story, but refurbished with dramatic and circumstantial particulars. Charles, despite his illnesses, was not to be denied his pleasures, or some of them, and had gone with his brother, by coach, to the racecourse at Newmarket. And, according to this Keeling, the royal coach was to be held up on the way back to London, at the farm of Rye House, owned by a veteran Cromwellian officer named Rumbold, with fifty armed men, and its occupants slain. But, as it happened, an accidental fire at the racecourse premises caused the King to return earlier than intended, and the alleged plot miscarried.

Whether there was any truth in what became known as the Rye House Plot is doubtful. Certainly Rumbold and some others named by Keeling were members of one of the rather wild groupings, and were promptly arrested and put to the question. But much bigger game than this was the objective. It was the members of the Council of Six, and some of their associates, at which the thing was aimed – although all knew

89

well enough that these were not the kind of people to be involved in assassination and the like, nor to associate with such as Rumbold's company of extremists. Despite their lofty rank, however, all save Monmouth were arrested and thrown into the Tower, with some of their close friends.

The worst followed swiftly. Lord Grey contrived to escape, by plying his gaoler with drink, and managed to get away to Holland. Lord Howard proved to be weak, a broken reed, and under pressure signed his name to what their enemies wanted him to say, condemning his friends. The Earl of Essex was found dead in his cell; and Hampden and Lord William Russell were condemned to death for high treason.

With Algernon Sidney, Trenchard and one or two other M.P.s arrested as accomplices, and also condemned to execution, Gilbert Burnet was in no doubt as to his own vulnerability, and that of any guests of his. Indeed the presence of the two Scots exiles in his house was a further menace to him. They must flee, therefore, and at once. Burnet himself refused to do so – indeed he insisted that he must attend Lord Russell, his especial friend, on the scaffold, as minister; but his lodgers must go. He could arrange for them to sail for the Low Countries in one of the many wool-ships, as was being contrived for Monmouth.

Andrew accepted the inevitable. But Robert Baillie said no. He would go back to Scotland, secretly. He had a wife and family there and no brother to mind his estates and send money. He would return to Home of Polwarth, from where he could slip back and forth across the Border at need. There too he could keep contact with his estates. He had intended this, anyway.

Andrew tried to dissuade him, emphasising the dangers, as did Burnet, but to no effect. Andrew, of course, was tempted to do likewise; but he recognised this could only involve others in danger. He would go to Holland where so many Scots exiles received protection from the young Protestant Prince of Orange, William, married to the Duke of York's eldest daughter Mary, herself strongly Protestant. Monmouth, it seemed, was bound there also, not for the first time.

So, in tense circumstances, they parted, all wondering whether any would see each other again.

6

Strangely enough Andrew did not feel so much of an exile in Holland as he had done in London. That small country seemed to be full of Scots; and here he did not have to go furtively but could behave like an ordinary citizen. The people, too, were friendly, a simple, undemonstrative, down-to-earth lot not unlike the Lowland Scots – and of course Protestant.

Andrew arrived at Rotterdam in the spring of 1664, having come by easy stages, via Paris and Brussels. Like so many another of his class and background, he had made the tour of Europe as part of his later education, and so knew the Continent reasonably well. Henry was supplying him with adequate funds, these reaching him mainly at the hands of merchants from Scottish ports, for these kept up a great trade with their various French, Flemish, Dutch and Germanic counterparts, with much coming and going. Some of the delay, therefore, was occasioned by awaiting the arrival of such messengers, at arranged points. Besides, there was no least hurry. Indeed, after the stresses and contentions of Scotland and the confinement, secrecy and dangers of London, this Continental interlude seemed almost like a prolonged holiday, even though Andrew did tend to fret, with guilty feelings of inaction and uselessness.

Henry sent him letters as well as money, which kept him informed of conditions in Scotland and the fortunes of their friends, as well as on estate matters and problems. Henry himself so far seemed to have suffered no real hardship as a result of his brother's activities, save for the further billeting of militia on Saltoun; he was, to be sure, an inoffensive character, who was apt to look well before he leapt, in marked contrast to his vehement and hot-tempered elder brother.

91

The news from Scotland, otherwise, was far from reassuring, with the military now more or less in entire command, an ominous foretaste of what conditions might be like when James Duke of York became King. The dragoons ruled the land, with sword, pistol and spur; and since the dragoons' officers were given sheriffs' powers also, there was no redress in law. Always Lauderdale and Rothes had relied on the soldiers to do their bidding; but now, lacking strong men above them and taking orders directly from the Duke of York, the soldiers had it all their own way. Dalziel of the Binns, Grierson of Lag, Johnstone of Westerhall and Graham of Claverhouse were the names at which even strong men came to blench and women wailed. Graham was indeed now on the Privy Council, that grim instrument of royal power, a meteoric rise. In nominal rule were only titled mediocrities. Gordon of Haddo had been created Earl of Aberdeen; but that did not make a strong man of him. Sir George Mackenzie of Rosehaugh, the Advocate, was the brain of the administration; but he was not the man to keep the soldiers in order.

Enclosed with one of Henry's letters was one from Margaret Carnegie. She wrote kindly, even affectionately, but somehow carefully – as she no doubt felt that she must; but he wished that he could have read rather more into it. She did sign herself 'your devoted friend', however, which might take on a fairly fervent interpretation. He kept her letter on his person, at any rate. When he came to answer it, he found that he too had to be rather more careful than was his usual – which comforted him.

At Rotterdam Andrew found a veritable Scots colony, with its own Presbyterian church, clubs and social hierarchy. Here, of all people, MacCailean Mor was supreme, supported by another Campbell, the Earl of Loudoun, by the Earl of Melville from Fife and many other notables of lesser rank if greater accomplishments or notoriety, including the Reverend Ferguson, known as the Plotter – which, in an age of plotters, was distinction indeed. Andrew was much surprised to discover in this company none other than the recent Lord President of Session, Sir James Dalrymple of Stair who had found it expedient to remove himself rather further away than

Ayrshire from the ire of the Duke of York and the military, once the Confession of Faith business became known.

The United Provinces of Holland, at this period, represented a small enclave of freedom, peace and culture in a Europe otherwise scarcely noteworthy for such conditions – extraordinary, considering how close-pressed by the Spanish Netherlands, the France of Louis Fourteenth and the warring Germanic states which had succeeded the old Empire. William of Orange, son of a Stewart princess and wed to another, although young, was, as well as a noted soldier, a shrewd, solid and reliable character, fairly typical of his people, and had had the good sense to build up the finest fleet in Christendom – which was part of the secret of Holland's independence and security – his admirals' names striking fear in every court in Europe. William and his wife did not appear to object to their country becoming a haven for refugees from many lands – there were even Catholic refugees in Holland. And the great universities of Utrecht and Leyden were beacons of religious thought, philosophy and the arts, unsurpassed in that age.

There were almost as many English exiles as Scots; but whereas the latter tended to roost at Rotterdam the former made Amsterdam their centre. The seat of government was at The Hague; but since they were all within a day's ride of each other, there was a certain amount of mingling – and some friction also, inevitably. The Duke of Monmouth stayed with his cousin, the Princess Mary, at The Hague, but was seen frequently at the other towns likewise.

In all the expatriate groupings the plotting went on incessantly, of course, normal amongst exiles with too little to do. At Rotterdam, when Andrew arrived, the schemes centred round Argyll, naturally, with his great manpower potential in his clan-lands. There seemed to be some doubt as to the ultimate objectives of such Campbell-led endeavours, however fervent the Protestant spirit. Scotland was still ostensibly a Protestant realm and Argyll was a King's man and no republican. It was the Duke of York and his minions who had ousted him; but Argyll was loth to take any real steps which might seem to be aimed against King Charles. Others were less nice, especially the sanctimonious Plotter Ferguson, and MacCailean

Mor was being edged along almost unwillingly. Other Scots were frankly republican in outlook; and there was a religious grouping which stridently urged a theocratic kind of government to usher in God's kingdom on earth – and to hell with the Pope of Rome. On the English front the plotters were much more united, the sole objective being somehow to get Monmouth on to the throne.

Andrew deliberately avoided entanglement in any of these contentious groups. He was not a plotter by nature, preferring open politics, the exchange of views, reform by reason and consensus, not violence and recourse to arms. But his was very much a minority opinion.

In his concern not to get involved in the scheming and factioneering, he sought semi-permanent lodgings somewhere well out of the city and its hothouse atmosphere. He was fortunate to chance on a substantial farmer named Pieter van Heel, outside a dockside alehouse, somewhat the worse for schnapps, whom he rescued from attacking ruffians with the aid of a hastily-drawn if unprimed pistol. Thereafter he escorted the man home to his farm in the Bergschenhoel area two miles north of the city – to the gratitude of the large and motherly Mivrouw van Heel and her amiable daughter. After the ladies had put the farmer to bed, nothing would do but that his protector be fed, and nobly; then, hearing that he was going back merely to a Rotterdam inn, it was insisted that he stay the night. In the morning it did not take long to persuade the visitor that the Van Heel farm was a better place for a young Scottish gentleman to lodge than any city hostelry, and the matter was arranged there and then.

That proved to be a very fortunate incident for Andrew, for not only was he exceedingly comfortable and well looked-after at Bergschenhoel, but Van Heel, despite his weakness for schnapps, turned out to be a notable agriculturalist, practising an advanced land-husbandry which greatly interested Andrew as an improving laird. He had never seen barley such as Van Heel grew and on land, on the face of it, not so good as his own at Saltoun. Also the Dutchman had his own mills, two of them, with machinery much in advance of anything his guest knew. Andrew wrote at some length about all this to Henry, with

94

recommendations. But he did not add that the daughter, Alida, was friendly, generous and very understanding as to a young man's needs far from home and his own sort of womenfolk. Margaret Carnegie seemed a long way away, and love unexpressed. Not that the word love or its Dutch equivalent came into Andrew's head in connection with Alida van Heel; but he found her very much to his taste, nevertheless, of a long wintry night in Holland.

In the reverse direction news from Scotland grew ever more dire. It was not a letter, but the arrival at Rotterdam of Sir Patrick Home of Polwarth, which informed him. Baillie of Jerviswood was dead, hanged. He had been hiding at Polwarth and making secret sallies through the Borderlands from there, involved in an attempt to set up a scheme of emigration to form a Scots colony in the Carolinas, where men could be free to worship God as they thought right. But he had been apprehended, most grievously maltreated, tried for treason, offered his life if he would betray others, and when he refused, although by then a very sick man, hanged in his nightshirt and his limbs hacked off to be exhibited in different towns.

Andrew grieved sorely, and cursed the men who could so use one of the best of their countrymen.

Sir Patrick's links with Baillie and the emigration scheme had become known, and the dragoons came to Polwarth in the Merse. He had fled – but only so far as the family burial-crypt under the floor of his parish church, where he hid in the cold and dark for many weeks, amongst the coffins. There his twelve-year-old daughter, Grizel, brought him small quantities of food, hidden in her clothing and saved from her own plate, slipping out from the castle each night, once the soldiers were asleep, for her errand amongst the tombs. His refuge eventually flooded by melting snows, he had been forced to evacuate it, had managed to reach Tweed and thereafter walked his way down through England, acting as a travelling surgeon, in which he had some skills, to reach the Thames and a ship for Bruges.

Sir Patrick was a useful acquisition for the exile colony, at least for those who sought action, for there was a great clan of Homes in the East Borders, with over a score of lairdships, able to raise a large number of men and mounted Borderers at that, and the Homes tended to stick together. Many who would not follow a Highland Campbell might follow a Border Home.

With February, the time of decision came abruptly. Charles Stewart died suddenly, and his brother lost no time in having himself proclaimed king in both realms, James the Seventh and Second. If there were to be any deeds, in place of the floods of words, now was the occasion.

* * *

Andrew Fletcher gazed round the great assembly in the marble hall of the Stadthuis of Amsterdam, and shook his head.

"This is a folly!" he declared. "A levée, a carnival! Who could take seriously such a gathering? I understood that it was to be a council, a debate, to come to decisions. Not, not a junketing!"

Sir Patrick Home, who had persuaded Andrew to attend, shrugged. "I had not expected so many," he admitted. "Nor this . . . revelry. But the desired end may be gained, even so. The right decisions taken. Group with group."

"I am no soldier, but never did I hear of a campaign being decided upon thus."

There must have been fully three hundred present, Scots, English, Irish, Dutch, Huguenot French, all talking, laughing, drinking, circulating in that great hall with its white marble walls, black-and-white tiled floor, statuary on plinths and mirrors which seemed to double the numbers. Their hosts were none other than the Lord Grey of Werk, the escaped member of the Council of Six, and Anthony Ashley-Cooper, 2nd Earl of Shaftesbury, son of the man who had brought down Lauderdale, now himself an exile. The object of the meeting was to link, if possible, the English and Scots action in the present situation and to create some sort of united Protestant front.

After observing for a while, from their small gallery, the two Scots perceived that there was a certain amount of method in the business. Grey, Shaftesbury and Argyll, with a few of their close associates, formed a tight knot, which moved about the hall and to which aides brought up individuals to say their say, make their contributions or be given their instructions, and then be dismissed. It was a court rather than a conference, and any decisions would be arrived at by the consultants not those consulted.

"I cannot see this resulting in any unified venture," Andrew insisted. "The bedfellows are too odd. And the methods look autocratic without being assured!"

"We shall see," Home said. "Come, and give them the benefit of your views, my friend."

"I am not eager . . ." Andrew reminded. But having come he could hardly refuse further contact.

Sir Patrick was sufficiently important to do his own introducing, and he made much of Andrew to the Englishmen. Surprisingly, Argyll added to the praise – which had the effect of putting the younger man very much on his guard, for hitherto MacCailean Mor had been less than friendly. Grey nodded distantly, not mentioning that they had met previously.

"I have heard of Mr. Fletcher," Shaftesbury said graciously. Under his enormous wig, he seemed to be a handsome man of about forty, in a flashy way and over-dressed. "Heard of his influence in the Scottish Parliament. And of his, h'm, substance. We welcome his adherence to our great endeavours."

"I thank you. But, although I would be sorry to disappoint your lordship, I fear that I can scarcely be said to adhere to an endeavour of which I know not. First I would require to hear what it is?"

"Why, man – the Protestant cause! What else?" Argyll said.

"The cause is scarcely the endeavour, my lord. To what am I expected to adhere?" Perhaps that sounded distinctly stiff from a young man to his elders and betters. Lord Grey frowned.

"What but our joint effort to put a Protestant monarch on England's throne, Mr. Fletcher? Surely that is sufficient? And Scotland's also, of course," Shaftesbury added, as afterthought. "All must know that much."

"Mr. Fletcher keeps himself mighty retired," Argyll observed, geniality wearing thin. "He did not always, I mind!"

"This joint effort, my lords? In what does it consist?"

"In projected landings in England and Scotland, at the same

time, sir," Grey said. "With Protestant risings in both countries, to coincide." That held a hint of impatience. "All this has been talked of for long. Now is the time to act. We must decide on dates, numbers, landing-places, shipping and the like. And, to be sure, moneys. We shall need much money, Mr. Fletcher."

"Ah!" Andrew said.

"It will be, shall we say, an excellent investment, sir," the Earl of Loudoun put in, from the background. "You have, I understand, a rich estate in Lothian. Some small subvention now, some arrangement, and that estate shortly could become much the larger, Mr. Fletcher. When our true King is on his throne. With, h'mm, other marks of royal gratitude."

"I see." But it was at Patrick Home that Andrew glanced, flushing.

That honest man looked unhappy. "I . . . I did not know. I was not aware. Of this . . ." He turned. "My lords, I brought Mr. Fletcher here . . ."

But the lordly ones had moved on, and they were confronted instead by a red-faced, blunt-featured, stocky individual, in rich clothing but lacking something of the manner which should accompany it.

"I am Heywood Dare, Alderman of Taunton," this man announced. "I act purse-bearer and close councillor to His Royal Highness of Monmouth. You may have heard of me. Can I put you down, sir, for some suitable sum? For the invasion fund."

"I think not," That was terse.

"Sir – you are not refusing to contribute? To this most necessary cause. It should be considered a privilege."

"No doubt. But I have other privileges to consider at the moment."

"What could be more urgent, sir? I understand that you are a man of property. In Scotland. If you have not sufficient moneys to hand at this time, I would accept a written warrant . . ."

"Mr. Dare," Home intervened, aware of his companion's famed temper, "I think that you should leave the matter meantime. Mr. Fletcher is otherwise concerned at this moment. Another time, perhaps . . ."

"Sirs, another time may be too late. This most essential invasion must be mounted without delay. It is already almost a month since the Papist usurper grasped England's throne. He must be unseated before he can further secure himself. Every week will count against us. Here is no time for faint-heartedness and penny-pinching. Moreover," Dare leaned closer, dropping his rather strident West Country voice. "Due and heartfelt aid *now* will most certainly merit the most tangible royal appreciation. Office preferment, a knighthood perhaps. Even a baronetcy might be considered – although that would be more expensive . . ."

"My God!" Andrew's clenched fist rose quivering before the other's florid face. "You . . . you . . . !" That temper all but choked him. "How dare you! How dare you, sir! Think to *buy* me, like some huckster! I could horsewhip you for that, do you hear? Horsewhip . . . !"

Home grasped his arm. "Andrew – come. Not now, not here – of a mercy! Let us leave . . ."

"Aye, leave indeed! This place, these people, are beyond all bearing. If I had known that this was not to be a meeting, a council, but a market, a saleroom . . . !"

"Yes, yes – I am sorry. I had no notion of it, Andrew. Let us be off . . ."

But escape just then was contra-indicated. There was a commotion at the principal doorway, a trumpet blew, and with all the flourish of a royal entry the Duke of Monmouth was ushered into the hall. Everywhere men turned to bow.

"Lord – we can scarcely leave now," Home said. "It would be considered an insult."

"He is not King yet!" But Andrew accepted that they must wait, meantime. However hot-tempered, he was not a discourteous man.

Argyll, Grey and the others formed themselves into a tight group round the Duke, to escort him through the assembly. He moved with dignity, slowly, with a suitably regal carriage, acknowledging the salutes and genuflections of the company. As he came level with Andrew and Home, Lord Grey touched the ducal arm and nodded. Monmouth raised his brows, inclined his head and passed on.

99

"At least *he* is not begging for money!" Andrew observed. "Nor, it seems, eager to consult us!"

"No. But now that he knows that we are here, we can scarcely leave. Without due permission. *I* cannot, anyway . . ."

"This is not Holyroodhouse and he the Lord High Commissioner, man! He is but another exile – and the King's bastard!"

"Perhaps. But all here are united in accepting him as the man who should be King. And treating him accordingly. Besides, since I am in Argyll's confidence as regards his plans, I feel that I must stay now that the Duke has come . . ."

"You are? Argyll *has* plans, then? Not just vague hopes?"

"Oh, yes. Plans well advanced. The hopes are that he may convince Monmouth and his people to strike at the same time. Argyll has been planning a return to Scotland long before Monmouth came to Holland, a return in strength and arms. He has Clan Campbell all prepared to rise. He says that when he lands in his own Argyll, nine or ten thousand of his own name will draw sword for him. If a second stroke is aimed at the Lowlands, with Loudoun, Cochrane and such as myself leading, then Scotland, it is hoped, will rise, all Protestant Scotland, North and South."

"Patrick – these are not plans! They are still only vague hopes. Has it escaped your memory that though the Campbells are a Protestant clan, in name, most of the Highland clans are not? And they are united in one respect – they all hate the Campbells! A Campbell-led rising in the Highlands will ensure that the rest of the North will not join in!"

"But . . ."

"And the Campbells are scarcely loved in the Lowlands, as you know well. Have you forgot the Highland Host of a few years back? Eight thousand Campbells let loose in Renfrew, Cunninghame and Carrick, to do their worst, on Lauderdale's business! That will be remembered for long. I say that you could scarcely have a worse name to lead a Scottish rising than MacCailean Mor!"

"Yet he has the men . . ."

The Duke and his party had disappeared into an ante-room at the head of the hall; and from this the man Dare emerged, to push his way purposefully through the throng. It was to themselves that he headed, disapprovingly.

"Sir Patrick and Mr. Fletcher," he jerked. "His Royal Highness grants you audience. Come."

The pair exchanged glances.

"I do not seek such audience . . ." Andrew began, but the Alderman had already turned back, to lead them. Home touched his friend's arm and followed.

They were ushered into the ante-room where about a dozen, mainly Englishmen, drank with Monmouth. An argument seemed to be in progress between two of the company, evidently on the subject of cavalry tactics, the rest listening with varying degrees of interest, the Duke most obviously so. Andrew knew the younger man to be Sir John Cochrane of Ochiltree, son of the Earl of Dundonald and quite a noted soldier. The other was a stocky, grizzled elderly man, plainly-dressed and assertive of manner.

They waited.

At length Monmouth acknowledged their presence and waved the disputants to silence. "Ah, Sir Patrick. And Mr. Fletcher," he said pleasantly, "you find us exercised with matters military. About which, more and more, we must concern ourselves, I fear. I greet you kindly, gentlemen. When last we met, Mr. Fletcher, it was under very different circumstances."

"Indeed, my lord Duke – since when many good men have died."

"Sadly, yes. I grieve for them. In especial, to be sure, my royal father."

As all murmured suitably, Andrew merely inclined his head slightly.

The Duke went on more briskly. "We are here, however, concerned with practical and very essential affairs. And would welcome the counsel of you gentlemen. You, Mr. Fletcher, are prominent in the Scottish parliament – or were. In the event of my lord of Argyll's landing and rising being successful – for which we pray God – how would the Scots parliament greet a proclamation of myself as King, think you? Protestant King of Scots?"

Andrew hesitated, as well he might. "That, sir, would depend on many factors," he said, at length. "On who proclaimed it. When. Where. And whether the rising was successful in the *Lowlands*. In our parliament not one commissioner in ten comes from the Highlands."

"M'mm. We would hope, to be sure, that the Lowlands would indeed rise strongly to our Protestant banner. But my lord's intention is, of course, to land first in his own Argyll, raise the clans and then march south. Would proclamation of myself as King not greatly aid his reception in the Lowlands? In especial, if I landed meantime in England, to raise that kingdom also?"

Andrew drew a deep breath. "With all respect, sir – and to my lord of Argyll – I much doubt it. The Highlands and Lowlands seldom see eye to eye. And my lord is very much of the Highlands – at least in most Lowlanders' eyes. And even in the Highlands there are . . . clan animosities! Since you ask me, my lord Duke, I must answer in truth that such proclamation by the Earl of Argyll would be unlikely to serve your cause."

There was a murmur, fairly consistently hostile, from the company. Argyll looked outraged.

Monmouth did not, however. "Are you against any such proclamation, Mr. Fletcher? Or only if made by my lord of Argyll? Or other from the North?"

Again Andrew hesitated. "It is difficult to say, sir. You are but little known in Scotland. You have a Scottish name and wife and title. But . . ." He could hardly say that he left his Scottish wife, the Duchess of Buccleuch and Monmouth, whilst he lived elsewhere with the Countess of Wentworth.

"Does His Highness's royal descent and ancient Stewart blood mean nothing to Scotchmen?" Grey demanded, frowning. "Or *Lowland* Scotchmen!"

"Indeed it does. But then, the Duke's royal uncle is equally . . . blest!"

"But he is a Catholic, man!"

"I have not forgotten, my lord. But this of a proclamation could work both ways. Parliament – the Scots Estates – might well prefer to make anything such, themselves. In more constitutional fashion. If at all."

102

"So you are against it, Mr. Fletcher?" the Duke put to him, flatly.

"As a means of aiding an invasion and rising, I think that I am, sir. Unless you were present in person."

"That I fear would not be possible. In Scotland. I shall be sufficiently occupied in England! It is not my endeavour, Mr. Fletcher, to *separate* my father's crowns. I hold the United Kingdom indivisible. It was only that if, by having me proclaimed King in Scotland first, it might aid in my English campaign, that I might contemplate it. Clearly you consider it inadvisable. Do you agree with him, Sir Patrick?"

"In this of a proclamation, yes, my lord Duke, I do. In the matter of Highland and Lowland differences and lack of co-operation, I am less sure."

"Ah. One other matter, then, gentlemen – and it arises from your last point, sir. How much Lowland armed support is likely? When my lord of Argyll lands and raises my standard? Sir John Cochrane, here, fears no great deal. But my lord of Loudoun is more hopeful."

"I also am hopeful," Home declared. "I believe that Scotland is just waiting and longing to throw off its shackles!"

"Excellent! And you, Mr. Fletcher?"

"I have no wish to disappoint, my lords – but I am less sanguine. Remember that the nation is in some degree cowed. The military are in complete control. There has been twenty years of repression and persecution. It *may* have bred a spirit of rebellion and resentment – but that may not work wholly in favour of the royal house!" That was as gently as he could put it. "Again, the people's natural leaders have been driven out, imprisoned or executed, as a matter of policy – so that those on whom effective rising would depend, in the first place, are not there. The Kirk, the Church, would be strong for a Protestant revolt – but the Kirk has been stamped upon and decimated deliberately, by order from London, throughout all King Charles's reign! I say that . . . ." Belatedly he recognised that he had probably said enough, by the expressions of his hearers.

"Thank you, Mr. Fletcher," Monmouth said stiffly – and then, surprisingly, was actually interrupted.

"This young man speaks sense." It was the stocky, elderly man who had been arguing with Cochrane.

"Indeed? You think, so, Colonel Rumbold?"

Andrew was more surprised than ever. Rumbold was the name of the Rye House Plot ringleader, at whose establishment the alleged assassinations were to have taken place; and he had been one of Cromwell's Ironsides colonels. So this was presumably the same man escaped from the Tower – which was sufficiently significant. Although most of the others growled their offence, the Duke eyed the older man thoughtfully.

"I had not thought that any Scot, any *Protestant* Scot, would so disapprove of what I seek to do!" Argyll declared. "To cry down our attempts."

"My lord, I do not disapprove. Of all efforts to right Scotland's wrongs. My concern is that your attempts, and mine, should be successful. For a failed attempt would be worse than none. And we should not shut our eyes to facts. Your clan is one of the most powerful in the land – but one of the best-hated! Perhaps wrongly. But that is not the point. I say that any invasion and rising in Scotland should, in the first place, be led and headed up by other than Campbells. Let them join in, by all means – but not seek to take the lead."

"But nobody else is doing so, man!"

"Are the Scots so altogether wretched? Cowed, you said, I think, that they will not rise?" Alderman Dare grated. "So broken a nation?"

In answer, Andrew did not trust himself to look at the man. Instead, he spoke as to Colonel Rumbold. "Scotland groans under the most harsh and rigorous military occupation, with men, women even children hanged, shot, drowned, tortured. For as little as having even a kinsman attend a coventicle, a religious service. My lord of Argyll himself was condemned to death for refusing the Test. You, sir, are a soldier, I understand. You know, if any does, what the military, in total command, can do to a people. Your Oliver Cromwell held down all England so for sixteen years, did he not? How many successful risings did the English make, against you?"

There was silence.

It was Monmouth who spoke, then. "So, Mr. Fletcher, you advise against all military ventures?"

"No, my lord Duke, I do not. Such invasion and rising, aimed at England firstly, might be successful. For there the military are not all-powerful. But you have made it that way – or your father did – in Scotland. A successful landing in England might well spark one off in Scotland. But not the other way."

"I see. Then, sir, I thank you for your counsel – however unpalatable! We shall consider well what you have said. I bid you a good night. Sir Patrick – perhaps you will stay with us a little longer?"

Bowing, Andrew took his leave. He certainly had had enough for one night, as evidently had the others.

* * *

Later, thinking it over, Andrew came to the conclusion that he had had enough for considerably more than one night. He was filling in his time in exile by writing a book, a sort of discourse on the affairs of Scotland incorporating his views on government. He had reached a stage where he wished to use the hopeless misgovernment of Spain under an imbecile king, as an example, and recognised that a sojourn in Brussels, the capital of the Spanish Netherlands, would greatly assist his knowledge. So to Brussels he decided to repair forthwith – before any more unpleasantness developed, any more requests for money or involvement in plots and schemes, of which, to say the least, he was in no wholehearted support. Two days later, then, he was on his way to Brabant, Brussels, lying some eighty miles south of Rotterdam. Patrick Home at least was sorry to see him go – as was Alida van Heel.

It was three weeks later, in his temporary lodgings near the Cathedral of St. Gudule, that he was surprised to be visited by a messenger with a letter from the Duke of Monmouth, no less, urging him in most pressing terms to call upon him at the Hague palace at his earliest convenience. It was a friendly letter, modestly worded, with neither flourish nor command about it, and was signed, not Monmouth, nor yet James Scott nor even Crofts, but James Stewart. And as a postscript was a note to add that a particular friend of his had arrived at The Hague.

Andrew was in a quandary, of course. He did not want to get further involved; but nor did he wish to seem discourteous. And, to be sure, the writer might well become his liege lord before too long. But it was, of course, the reference to a friend's arrival that intrigued him. When, questioning the messenger, he elicited the fact that it was Dr. Gilbert Burnet, he hesitated no longer. He would leave for the Hague in a day or two; he had all but finished all he could do in Brussels anyway.

He had not visited the Dutch capital since his youthful tour, and even then had not aspired so high as the Stadtholder's palace of the Bosch. Here he found Monmouth to be occupying a rear wing of the great establishment, with quite a little court of his own – at which he was less than pleased to see the man Dare, the Plotter Robert Ferguson, as well as Colonel Rumbold, Grey and others. Although he asked for Gilbert Burnet, none appeared to know of him, so presumably he was not staying at the palace.

However, when after some delay, the Duke received him privately in a gilded saloon large enough to house ten score, Burnet was therein, the only other occupant.

Monmouth was thoughtful in allowing Andrew to greet his old tutor, with some emotion, whilst he himself strolled over to gaze out of a window. It seemed that London had become quite too hot, under James the Second and Seventh, to hold such as Burnet, and he had betaken himself first to Paris then to Italy, and now here he was at the personal invitation of the Prince of Orange himself.

"It was good of you to come, Mr. Fletcher," the Duke said, presently. "Sir Patrick Home informed me that you were in Brussels. I hope that this has not too greatly inconvenienced you?"

"I was practically finished at Brussels, my lord Duke."

"Let us dispense with lordings and highnesses since we three are alone, my friends. I asked you to come, because I seek your advice. Again. And at Dr. Burnet's urging. He believes that you will give me good counsel, personal, close counsel. Each time that we have met I have conceived that you are not only an honest man but shrewd and well-informed – if outspoken! And such are, I fear, distinctly rare. A man in my situation is surrounded by men with ... shall we say, other qualities! Schemers, self-seekers, trimmers and fanatics, not to say toadies. Not all, of course. But too many. So much of the counsel given me is what these wish me to hear, or what they believe I myself would wish to hear. Not what I *require* to hear. You, I think, will be otherwise – as Dr. Burnet assures me. He has a high regard for your abilities. Will you so help me, Mr. Fletcher?"

"Why, sir, to be sure. I much appreciate your trust. Whether my poor advice will be of any service is another matter. I fear that Dr. Burnet's esteem may not be altogether warranted! Our friendship cozening him! In what way can I help you?"

"It is in what my great-grandfather James called statecraft that I seek counsel. I am short on statesmen to advise me, I fear – however many politicians! From what I have heard, and what Dr. Burnet tells me, that is *your* great interest." He paused. "I want to know how best to reach the people. Not only the lords and gentry but the people. When I land on English soil again. What do I do? Apart from fight! Proclaim myself King – or not? At once? Issue an appeal to arms – or not? Wave the Protestant banner? Promise reforms of government, lower taxation, repeal of the harshest laws? Or is all this too lofty for the common folk? How say you?"

"You are set on this invasion, then?"

"Yes. Argyll sails in four days' time. I have promised to move within days thereafter. So that the Scots will hear of it and be heartened."

Andrew frowned. "I regret it, sir. I know that it is argued that such a move should be soon. Before King James, your uncle, has time to entrench himself. But I would say to wait. He is a man of harsh, stern methods. Every month that he is on the throne will see the people of England, Protestant people, more afflicted, more hardly used. And so growing more ready to welcome an invasion ..."

"It is too late. I have given my word. Moreover, matters here push me to it, Mr. Fletcher. My uncle has sent an envoy to the Prince of Orange here, requesting that he no longer permits me to remain in Holland, and hints that he might have to consider making an edict removing the heirship to the throne from his elder daughter, Mary, William's wife, to the younger, Anne. So William wishes to be rid of me. I had thought to go to Sweden – but am committed to make the great venture in England instead. Preparations are in train. We sail in a matter of days."

"What then am I to say to you? Only that I do not advise that you proclaim yourself King, in England as in Scotland. Announce rather that you have come to defend the Protestant faith. Issue a call to arms, in that defence. But leave the parliaments to proclaim you monarch. If you have the parliamentarians on your side, it is half the battle. And you have more hope of that in England than in Scotland, meantime."

"You think so? How else may I woo the parliamentarians?"

"You might ask them, sir, to bring in a Bill of Legitimation. Ask it in friendly, even respectful fashion. The English parliament is sovereign. In Scotland it is the *King* in parliament that is sovereign. So this could not serve there. If an Act was passed legitimating your birth, it would much help. And involve the members in your cause. Even if it failed to pass the Lords, that could serve you. Provide an issue – the Lords against the people! All to stir up feeling, rouse the nation."

The Duke rose to pace the floor, glancing over at Burnet. "Dr. Burnet is right – you have shrewd wits, sir. But . . . there is a matter here which, shall we say, holds me back. The fact is, my friends, I *require* no legitimation!"

They both stared.

"Few know of this, gentlemen. And I tell you in greatest confidence – for I feel that I can trust you. My royal father, you see, for his own reasons, made me promise not to publish the matter. As price of his continued goodwill. I possess my father's marriage-lines to my mother!"

"Good Lord . . .!"

"My lord Duke . . ."

"Aye – my father, as Prince of Wales, secretly married Lucy Walters, here at The Hague, in 1648, when he found that she was with child by him. It was kept very close. For his father, King Charles the First, was prisoner in England. And his mother, Queen Henrietta Maria, in Paris, had forbidden anything such, and threatened to cut his allowance from the King of France. Later, when both my grandfather and grandmother were dead, the politicians persuaded my father that to let it be known that he was wed to a commoner was no way to regain his throne. Then, it was considered expedient that he wed a princess, Catherine of Braganza. And so the thing must remain hidden – or it made that royal marriage a fraud. So it has remained." The Duke spoke it all tensely, through tight lips.

His hearers exchanged glances. "I do not know what to say . . . Your Royal Highness!" Andrew said.

"Say nothing, my friend – as I have done all these years. But you will understand why I am loth to seek legitimation by any parliament!"

"No, no – that would be an equal fraud!" Burnet exclaimed.

"Perhaps. But . . . it could be worth doing, nevertheless," Andrew said. "Even though in truth unnecessary. It might well please the people. And help to bring parliament to your side. An acknowledgement of its power. Promise of your good relations with it, hereafter. Unlike your uncle's!"

"M'mm. I will think on this. Have you any other counsel for me?"

"The Church, sir." Andrew looked over at Burnet. "Perhaps Dr. Gilbert has so advised? I mean the *English* Church. For the Scottish Kirk is in hopeless disarray. No so in England. It is a Protestant Church, alarmed, with a Catholic monarch nominally at its head. Address yourself to the churchmen."

"I agree," Burnet nodded. "It could do much. The Church can provide a voice in every parish. To stir up the people. More than any other can do."

"If you, sir, as a Protestant monarch, could be preached in every pulpit!"

"Yes – yes, I see. That is good, wise. Anything else, my friends?"

"Only that I would hope, Highness, that you could yet delay this venture. Until the time was more ripe, England more eager to be rid of your uncle."

"Impossible, I fear. It is too late to halt Argyll's sailing. And I have agreed to sail within days of his." The Duke held out an open hand. "Mr. Fletcher – despite your most evident lack of eagerness, it is my hope, indeed my urgent desire, that I can persuade you to accompany me. Dammit, man, if I was but your King already, it would be my royal command!" And he smiled.

Andrew shook his head, wordless.

"Consider it, my friend. Dr. Burnet, I seek your kind offices on my behalf. He will, perhaps, listen to you. He could serve me passing well . . ."

They took their leave.

Burnet, there as guest of the Stadtholder, was himself lodging in another wing of the vast palace; and nothing would do but that Andrew should stay with him meantime, permission already sought and granted.

So much for non-involvement.

7

Andrew paced the deck of the frigate *Helderenberg*, on which he now knew every plank and nail and mark. It was the 31st May and he had been on this wretched ship for eight endless days, waiting, waiting, there off Texel Island at one of the mouths of the Zuider Zee. They had been due to sail on the 24th, and even that was a grievous delay; for Argyll had eventually left for Scotland on the 2nd and Monmouth had agreed to follow within six days. But delay had succeeded delay, part of it due to sheer inefficiency on the part of the Duke's lieutenants, for there did not seem to be a practical or reliable man, in Andrew's estimation, amongst them. But, to be sure, most of the trouble had been caused by lack of funds for purchasing the necessary arms and ammunition and other warlike supplies, for chartering this frigate and the three tenders which were to accompany it; likewise for paying the accumulated debts of the various exile-adventurers owed here in Holland – which proved to be an unexpectedly major item. Although money had been promised from England, none had materialised. Argyll's part of the joint venture seemed to have run off with a large proportion of the funds, with it starting first – these largely supplied by a rich widow named Smith. The Duke had been forced to pawn his valuables; also Lady Wentworth's jewels. Andrew himself, in the end, had had to put his hand deep into his pocket, despite his dislike of Dare, the paymaster, and his grave doubts anent the entire project, which he found himself somehow supporting. It was to be hoped that things would improve once they reached England.

So far there were only about fifty men on board, apart from the Dutch crew, and few of these such as to inspire boundless confidence. None was a man of any notable substance nor repute. Not that this in itself was of great importance, assuming that their fighting qualities were right; but well-known names could much help recruitment once they landed. When it had come to the bit, most of the aristocratic English exiles, for one reason or another, had found it inexpedient to accompany the expedition at this stage, although they promised to come along later – and the Scots, of course, save for Andrew and the man Ferguson, had gone with Argyll. Strangely, also, for reasons which Andrew had not fathomed, the only two real soldiers of Monmouth's entourage, Colonels Rumbold and Ayloffe, had both been sent with the Scottish expedition.

It was late of a blustery afternoon before those on board saw what they looked for – or two-thirds of it – coming northwards up the wind-tossed inland sea from the direction of Amsterdam. These were the two tenders, little more than square-sailed Dutch barges, which were to accompany the frigate, loaded with supplies. There should have been three.

When the tenders came alongside to unload their passengers, Andrew saw that there were only some thirty of these, although many more had been expected; and apart from Monmouth himself and the Lord Grey, there were only Alderman Dare and the Reverend Robert Ferguson, of the leadership group. It transpired that Sheldon, the English envoy at The Hague, on King James's orders, had been endeavouring to have all sailing halted, as an act of hostility; and his son-in-law, William, had reluctantly made a gesture of appeasement by ordering an arrestment of the tenders at Amsterdam – but only after they had been due to leave. Unfortunately they had suffered the usual delays, and they had had to make a last-minute dash for it. And making a dash in heavy Dutch scows was something of a contradiction in terms. One of the tenders had been caught and held – which of course was a major loss. Nevertheless, the survivors seemed to be in fairly high spirits at what they saw as their first victory.

Andrew Fletcher saw it otherwise, and said so. "This is serious. Apart from the loss of men and vital supplies, it means that London knows all about this enterprise. Not only that we are sailing, but *who* sails and our small numbers."

"So long as they do not know where we intend to land, that is of no great moment," Lord Grey asserted.

"I think that it is. Eighty men, wheresoever they land, can represent little more than a fly to be crushed, against the might of England. Our only hope, as I see it, is that this may in fact so lull the authorities there that they do not trouble to take any very urgent steps against us, at first, and so give us time to assemble support on landing."

"Henry the Seventh, sir, landed with fewer men and yet won his kingdom."

"Yes, my lord. But Henry Tudor had previously made certain that the nobility were waiting and ready to welcome him. We have not."

"In this venture, Fletcher, we can do without such faint-hearted talk!" Heywood Dare growled. "That, certes, is not how thrones are won! If you cannot do better than make moan, by God, you should keep silent!"

"Damn you, Dare!" Andrew's voice quivered and his hand dropped to his sword-hilt. "You, *you* call me faint-heart? You will take back those words or, or . . ."

"Gentlemen, gentlemen!" the Duke intervened. "Enough – enough, I say. In my presence. Save your ire for our enemies, of a mercy! Let us have no talk of faint-hearts in this company. Now – let us be on our way. Set sail, at last. The Dutch ships may yet seek to detain us. Where is our shipmaster . . . ?"

Andrew and Dare glared at each other, but inclined their heads towards the Duke.

So, with Andrew almost wishing that the Dutch *would* appear, to prevent this unhappy enterprise from sailing, the anchor was raised and the sails unfurled. They had been lying in the lee of Texel, one of the string of low, sandy islands which rim the Zuider Zee. They skirted this, now, west-about, in order to proceed into the North Sea opposite the fortified port of Den Helder. No notice seemed to be taken of them there. Emerging into the open sea, with a half-gale sweeping up the Channel from the south-west, they realised that what they had thought was rough water in the comparatively sheltered reaches of the Zuider Zee was a mill-pond contrasted with conditions outside. All that Dutch seaboard is shallow and shelving, conducive to short, steep seas. The vessels bucked and heaved and rolled, as they turned to head downwards towards the mouth of the Channel, having at once to tack directly into wind and seas. Hot tempers, like dispute and argument, quickly sank away, as practically all the passengers went down with sea-sickness.

Andrew was only slightly affected. But even so he did not enjoy that voyage. The unseasonable weather maintained, squally with rain-showers and cold enough for February. The old frigate was far from comfortable, accommodation primitive, food of the poorest. What it would be like in the two tenders was only to be imagined. Day after day the wind blew in their faces, so that continuous tacking, left and right, was the only way of making progress, and a slow progress indeed, made still slower by the necessity of not outsailing the lumbering, barge-like tenders, which much of the time appeared to be lost, save for their sails, under a smother of spray. Three full days out and they were still only off the mouth of the Schelde, not much south of the Hague. Andrew had little difficulty in keeping himself very much to himself, for sickness kept most of the company in their bunks, amidst a dire stench. Indeed, in the main, he saw most of James Stewart himself, who also seemed to be more or less immune to the nausea and to whom Andrew grew ever more attached. He was not a strong character, perhaps, with much of his pleasure-loving father and flighty mother in him; but he was genial, intelligent and unassuming, considering his position. Andrew only wished that he was a better judge of men. They held long talks, and the younger man came to the conclusion that he would

113

make a better king than any of his last three predecessors, at least.

Their destination, he learned, was the English West Country, with a landing at Lyme, in Dorset. The argument was that the people of those parts were at once more Protestant and more sturdily-independent of London than any others south of Wales and Yorkshire. Also, Heywood Dare, from Taunton, had allegedly much influence thereabouts and strongly advised such landfall. If these seemed to Andrew inadequate reasons for such an important decision, he recognised that he might be prejudiced where the goldsmith was concerned; and also that he was insufficiently knowledgeable about England to be able to pontificate.

Beyond all calculations, even with the weather slightly improving, it took them eleven days to reach the Dorset coast. At least the adverse conditions seemed to have prevented English shipping from searching for them. They made their landfall at Portland Bill and then turned away westwards across the wide mouth of Lyme Bay. It seemed that they were going to drop Heywood Dare, by small boat, off Seaton, at the far end of the thirty-mile wide bay, after dark, from whence he would make his secret way to his own Taunton, to publish the news there and raise recruits. The vessels would then turn back across the bay for Lyme itself, there apparently being no landing-place for larger ships, and the unloading of supplies, at Seaton. There they would disembark and raise standard.

This they did, and Andrew for one was not at all distressed to see Alderman Dare disappear in his small boat, into the gloom of the June night, on his twenty-mile road to Taunton. But it all took longer than allowed for and it was broad daylight before they won back to Lyme harbour, within the shelter of The Cobb breakwater, at the east end of the bay. Andrew advised that they stand out to sea again until nightfall, to land in darkness, so that their small numbers might not be apparent to all; but everyone was impatient now to be ashore and on with the great venture, and Monmouth gave orders to draw in to the quay, there appearing to be no opposition. There were only two other coasting craft presently in harbour.

What followed was at least suitably dramatic and emotional.

The Duke led the way down the gangplank, to drop on his knees on English soil and kiss the ground, others following joyfully. He uttered a short and rather embarrassed thanksgiving to God for a safe landing and sought divine aid and guidance in their undertaking. Then he drew his sword and held it high, shouting forward, to the cheers of his supporters, watched open-mouthed by sundry seamen and a few fishermen and locals.

They marched for a couple of hundred yards or so behind the unfurled blue standard which Lady Wentworth had stitched for them, erected this silken banner at the roadside, cheered loudly, and finding nothing else to do, turned and wandered back to the ship again, to proceed with the unloading.

That evening, in the George Inn at Lyme, the invaders ate their first good meal for some time, thankful to have a steady floor beneath them, and toasted the success of their champion. The Duke then made known his decisions and dispositions. He himself would exercise overall command in the field. Lord Grey and Mr. Fletcher meantime would be joint Masters of the Horse. Heywood Dare, when he returned, would be Commissary and would lead the foot, until further arrangements were made. The Reverend Ferguson – who had been secretary and chaplain to the former Earl of Shaftesbury – would compose and publish the manifesto which was to draw all men of goodwill to their side. And so on. There was, to be sure, precious little alternative to these appointments. Meanwhile their task was to assemble and train men.

So next morning the Protestant rising was proclaimed at Lyme and in the surrounding small towns and villages of the rich Dorset-Somerset-Devon countryside, the squires and parish ministers were being approached personally. There was a moderately successful reaction amongst the latter, but the former hung back notably. Which was doubly unfortunate, not only for the failure to give a lead to the common folk but because it was from these that the essential horseflesh was looked for to mount their hoped-for cavalry. Lacking funds, they could not *buy* mounts. Andrew, with the others, tried his hand, or rather tongue, at this recruiting, but with only modest success, his Scots voice an obvious handicap.

No evident opposition developed. And, hearteningly, from the small towns such as Axminster and Bridport, and the villages of the Char and Axe valleys, rather than the estates, volunteers began to come in, in fair numbers. Some few brought rusty swords and old pistols, but most arrived armed only with cudgels, billhooks and sickles.

This continued for a second day. With a couple of young curates to be his mouthpieces, Andrew did better, and was gratified to return to Lyme in the evening with a tail of no fewer than ninety-two men, mainly small tradesmen and apprentices from the towns, with a few countrymen, farmers' sons, cattle-men, thatchers and one or two waggoners with the very necessary vehicles and draught-horses for transport.

But straggling through the little town of Colyton on the way back, they heard the local clergymen declaiming from the town-cross a proclamation. Listening, Andrew realised, appalled, that it was Ferguson's manifesto. It was, indeed, no suitable and dignified statement of aims and claims but a tirade, rabble-rousing perhaps in parts, but in the main tedious and off-putting to any intelligent man. And ill-advised and mistaken in much that it declared, if not actually dangerous. It referred to the Duke as King James the Third and Eighth, it proclaimed his uncle as not only an usurper but as responsible for the Popish Plot of 1678, even the Great London fire of 1666, the murder of Essex and Russell and many others, and much else. It even suggested that he had poisoned his brother, Charles to obtain the throne. It declared the present parliament illegal and brought in the Catholic interest – which might have had some truth in it but was not calculated to woo the parliamentarians to Monmouth's side. Altogether the thing was a disaster, appealing only to the extremists and the wildly irresponsible. Andrew hurried on, to urge the Duke to withdraw it at once.

But at Lyme, alternative excitements prevailed, with Lord Grey at the centre. Apparently around mid-day a report had come in that a small band of militia had arrived in the Shave Cross area to the north-east. Grey, with the thirty or so horsemen that had managed so far to mount, and about one

116

hundred oddly-armed foot, had been sent to investigate, and if possible effect their first victory. His lordship had returned alone some three hours later, on the best horse, in a dire state. They had been quite overwhelmed, he declared, all but trapped. He had only just managed to escape. A large body of the enemy were advancing. They ought to get back to the frigate and cast off, before it was too late.

Monmouth, it seemed, had been less precipitate, had prepared for swift evacuation but had sent out scouts to report on the situation. And presently these had come back not only with reassuring news but with Grey's little force, which they had come across returning cheerfully to base, intact and actually with a number of new and well-armed recruits, prisoners from the militia company which had fled before them, and these having decided to throw in their lot with the insurgents.

So the rising had had its first little victory, after all, however modest. But at the sad cost of all faith lost in the Duke's chief lieutenant and joint Master of Horse.

The new adherents were, of course, only local levies of no great quality, but welcome, especially for their arms and the boost they gave to morale. Andrew gained a useful and modern cavalry pistol and some shot. One of the militiamen, a sergeant and better informed than the rest, was able to tell them that the Duke of Albemarle, dull son of a great father, was put in charge of the Devon and Somerset militia, to hold the rising in check until the Earl of Feversham, a Frenchman, came down from London with the main royal army. This news was on the whole good, since it seemed to mean that they had only the part-time local forces to face meantime – and by today's showing these were scarcely crack troops. Also that perhaps King James in London did not trust his English nobility, in that he was entrusting the anti-rising leadership to a Catholic foreigner.

At the council-of-war in the George that evening – at which Lord Grey sat noticeably silent – Andrew did raise the matter of the manifesto, urging its immediate retraction, to Ferguson's voluble offence. But the general reaction was that while his objections might be valid, the matter paled into insignificance before the military situation and should be left meantime – although no further copies would be issued. The real debate was on what to do next – action. A messenger had arrived from Taunton informing that Dare had managed to muster some three hundred foot and about forty horse, and, marching through the night with these, should reach Lyme in mid-forenoon. More would follow. So although they had no great army, they would add up to almost eight hundred men.

There were two schools of thought. One, to strike whilst the iron was hot, break out from this Lyme area and take the initiative, hoping, believing, that more and more would flock to their standard. The other, that this breathing-space, before the royal army reached the West Country, should be utilised to drill and train their distinctly motley force into some sort of fighting units able to face the militia with confidence. The Duke himself favoured the latter course.

Andrew urged otherwise. "It is clear that the gentry are not going to rise until they see evidence of our strength – and we need their support for leadership and, more important perhaps, for their horses," he contended. "They will not see that in eight hundred men drilling and counter-marching at Lyme, little more than a village. A demonstration of strength and confidence is necessary. And the occupation of a large town equally so, to quarter and feed our men and to enhance our repute. Also we have proved that it is from the towns that we are going to draw our numbers, in the first place. The town corporations and craft guilds are our strongest allies meantime. So I urge that we march on Exeter, or, better still, on Bristol. Right away. And it will be further for the London army to come to us, giving us more time. And showing the flag in a new area."

There was some support for this, but Monmouth was doubtful.

"I feel that it is too risky, with untrained men and less than one hundred horse," he said. "We should have a few more days here at Lyme, building up, drilling, weapon-training and trying to collect more horses. Then we might head for Bristol and try to bring in the Welsh. My mother was Welsh . . ."

That had to be accepted.

In the morning, however, the Duke came to where Andrew was holding a weapon-training exercise on the pebbly beach –

and learning to master his own new pistol in the process – to say that he was sorry if he had seemed to ignore his counsel the previous evening; but he felt strongly that this training was essential for such raw recruits. But he did agree that some gesture, some flag-showing move, was advisable at this juncture. After yesterday's fiasco with Grey, he thought that Andrew should take a party of horse and make a tour through the countryside, looking for militia in the Vale of Honiton area, where such had been reported. A surprise raid there might prove profitable and salutary.

Andrew was nothing loth.

It was at this stage that Dare and his Taunton company entered Lyme after their all-night march of almost thirty miles, weary but in good spirits. Andrew, despite his dislike of Dare, did not fail to cheer. He was, to be sure, almost as interested in the quality of the horses as of the men, in his present capacity of Master of Horse. Most of the beasts, being townsmen's mounts and even dray-horses, were fairly dull stuff, but two or three were good stock, in especial a fine bay mare taking his eye. He decided to ride that on this day's ploy; for thirty miles, at walking pace, was not likely to have overtaxed such an animal.

Leaving the newcomers to rest and refresh themselves, he selected some fifty horsemen of a sort and, mounting, rode off westwards.

They made quite a good day of it, although they saw no militia. At Colyton they were told that the local company of the soldiers had gone to join the Duke of Albemarle at Bath. But after proclaiming Monmouth and the Protestant rising at the cross and receiving quite an ovation, Andrew asked to be taken to the militia-barracks in the old castle-prison; into which they broke without compunction and helped themselves to all the remaining arms and ammunition stored therein, quite a considerable haul. Thus, cheered, they rode on to Honiton and back by Wilmington, the country entirely open to them. Andrew wished, however, that they had been riding north to Bristol.

They returned to Lyme in the evening, without major incident but with some satisfaction in their assessment of the general state of the country, as to strong and swift moves by

Monmouth. But in the stable-yard of the George Inn, such thoughts were banished from Andrew's mind. He had just dismounted when Heywood Dare emerged from the rear door of the hostelry, redder of face than usual and pointing at him with, of all things, a horse-whip, features working.

"You, Fletcher, you Scotch rat!" he shouted. "You stole my horse!"

Scarcely believing his ears or eyes, Andrew stared. "What . . . ?"

"You stole my horse, I say, damn you! Mine! I have been waiting for you. I *bought* it. And you took it, curse you! Thieving Scotch scum!"

"Lord, man, are you out of your wits? Have you been drinking? I only borrowed the beast. For duty. This is an armed force, not a private riding stable! The horses are for the cause, not for . . ."

"Liar! Rogue! Wretch – I'll teach you your lesson, Fletcher!" And the man raised his whip.

"Put that down, fool! Down, I say! Have you forgot – I am Master of Horse?"

But the whip flicked back and then struck down. And although Andrew threw up an arm to protect his face, he was too late. The lash cut across ear and cheek and throat.

"You once . . . threatened me . . . with horse-whipping!" Dare panted. "My God – we'll see about that!" And he raised the whip again.

A red mist before his eyes, shame and fury and lacerated pride rather than the pain which he scarcely felt at that moment, Andrew's hand dropped to where his sword should have hung. But it was still in its saddle-scabbard, cavalry-fashion. Instead his fingers gripped the pistol-butt projecting from his belt. Staggering back, he whipped the weapon out.

Lunging at him again, a pace forward, Dare brought the whip down. The pistol, still primed from the day's sortie, was thrown up. But not in time to prevent the second lash. Andrew pressed the serpentine trigger and the flint-lock and cap was released. The charge exploded.

Shot at point-blank range, Heywood Dare crumpled and fell, while the other gazed aghast, gulping, trembling.

Dare was dead before they got him back into the inn.

* * *

The Duke of Monmouth paced up and down his upper chamber, brows drawn, features tight. ". . . I repeat – you will have to go," he said.

"Yes, Highness. I am sorry."

"Sorry, man! Why keep saying that you are sorry? God knows, we are all sorry! More than sorry – desolated. You have, at one blow, removed two of my most needful supporters and friends. Dare and yourself. For I can no longer keep you with me. You must see that? When Dare's people learn of this – if some have not already heard – they will be hot for *your* blood! You cannot hope to lead my troops now. You must flee. And at once."

"Surely there is some way that I can serve Your Highness still?"

"Not here, not now. One day, perhaps. See you – you have committed what could be named murder. On English soil. You are condemned for treason in Scotland – now you could be condemned for murder in England! You cannot stay here, in this country."

"I could go secretly. To Bristol or otherwise. On your behalf. Seek to prepare your way . . ."

"No. It is impossible. I cannot be seen to employ you. Dare had much influence in this West Country. His death will not be forgotten or forgiven. Whatever the circumstances of it. No – you must go. Go at once aboard the *Helderenberg*. Tonight, secretly. She was to sail in two days' time. I will have the shipmaster to sail tomorrow, early. She is bound for Bilbao in Spain. Where the rest of her cargo is destined. You will be safe there."

"Safety, sir, is not what I seek!" That was anguished.

"I daresay not, Mr. Fletcher." Monmouth's features softened. "So I must seek it for you. Somebody must."

"What can I say? I blame myself, more than Your Highness can ever do. I have an evil temper, I know. Gilbert Burnet often warned me of it. And my brother. But . . . I was much provoked. Whip-lashed . . ."

121

"Yes, yes. God knows, I might have done the same myself! If I blame you, it is because of the hurt to my cause. But it is done now and cannot be undone. I am going to miss you greatly, my friend. For, temper or none, I have valued your counsel and your company. Even if I have not always acted on your advice. Dare's *company* I can do without! But he was loyal and useful, however ill his manners. I needed you both."

They eyed each other in silence. Then the Duke held out his hand.

"I am for my bed now. I advise that you get yourself down to the ship. I do not want you here in the morning. But – God speed, my friend! I hope your road is not too grievous. Perhaps we shall meet again in happier circumstances. If I gain my throne, I shall not forget your aid and goodwill."

Andrew shook his head, wordless, as the other ushered him out.

An hour or so later he slipped out of that back door of the inn, with his valise and without other farewells, and made his way down through the June night to the quayside, a man lost.

8

At the port of Bilbao, where the Pyrenees join the Bay of Biscay, in Northern Spain, Andrew Fletcher waited. He was getting used to a life of waiting now – but this time he did so differently, lethargically not impatiently as was his nature, almost uncaring of the passing days and weeks of that hot summer, idle, depressed, drinking too much. He was forced to wait there. Bilbao was a busy wine-exporting seaport, with much coming and going of shipping. On arrival in the *Helderenberg*, he had sent a letter to Henry, by a vessel bound for Dysart in Fife, giving some news of his situation and requesting money from Saltoun. So he must stay until there was a reply. Besides, where was he to go? No alternative destination drew him – save to Scotland itself, for which he was

122

direly homesick. But that was impossible; he would be arrested as a traitor and hanged.

Those were the most grievously unhappy months of Andrew's life. Having a man's death on his conscience was like a leaden weight all his waking hours. He belaboured himself for letting his temper take control of him and for having failed Monmouth, set his hand to a task, however reluctantly, and then had to throw it up and flee ignominiously, leaving others to the test. All savour was gone from living, the future not only uncertain and dark but pointless.

His outlook was by no means lightened when, about a month after his arrival, a ship from Bristol brought news from England, desperate news. Monmouth's attempt was over, finished, ended in complete disaster. There had been a battle at Sedgemoor, a mere score of miles north of Lyme – so the Duke had remained in that area, after all – which had developed into something of a massacre of the innocents. Feversham's regulars had cut down the insurgents like ripe corn – and thereafter slaughtered vastly more, as prisoners. The royal troops had then instituted a reign of terror in the West Country; and a judge, Jeffreys by name, was sent down from London to give a gloss of legality to the savagery but in fact, by his heartless and indiscriminate mockery of justice, multiplied the horror many-fold. Monmouth himself had escaped the slaughter but, with his uncle putting a price of £5,000 on his head, he had soon been captured and was now in the Tower of London awaiting trial for high treason.

Andrew grieved. He had, in truth, hardly expected success; but this bitter calamity and appalling aftermath desolated his already stricken spirit. He even found occasion further to blame himself. If he had been there, he might just have made some difference. At least he would have pressed his utmost to have a move made to take Bristol, before Feversham could come up. And who could tell how much Dare's death had contributed to the result, through the offence of his Taunton recruits? The entire ill-conceived enterprise might have been fated from the first, as he had felt in Holland; but his own failures could have made it all worse.

He belaboured himself unmercifully. The thought that his fit

123

of temper had in fact probably saved his own life, by bringing him here before the debacle, only added to his distress.

He had to wait almost another month at Bilbao, well into August, for a reply to his letter to Henry – by which time his funds were running low indeed, despite having moved into a cheap dockside bodega and restricting his feeding and drinking. When at length a shipmaster from the port of Leith sought him out, with a package of money, the enclosed letter was from Margaret Carnegie, not Henry. Even so it did not yield him joy, for it was no love-letter. It was announced that Henry had been arrested and was immured in Haddington Tolbooth. Men known not to be in sympathy with King James's government, or awkward for other reasons, were being arrested on all hands, since the failure of Argyll's rising. MacCailean Mor himself was dead, executed. He had landed, it seemed, in his own Kintyre, but only some two thousand of his Campbells rallied to his banner. After delay, and argument with Cochrane and Home, he had agreed to march on the south-west Lowlands, Ayrshire and Lanark, where they hoped for support. But the Marquis of Atholl, at the head of enemy clans, caught up with them in the Dumbarton area, the rebel army broke up without any major battle and Argyll himself was captured. So all collapsed ingloriously, with predictable and terrible consequences. Margaret did not say what had happened to Sir Patrick Home and Sir John Cochrane. Her letter was stiff, stilted, clearly written under stress. There was no mention of the money enclosed, but it was considerably less than Henry had been sending; Andrew got the impression that it had, in fact, come not from Saltoun at all but from Margaret herself or her father – and was the more unhappy. She wished him well and signed herself 'your loving friend'. But that was insufficient to cheer the recipient.

Nevertheless all this did have the effect of spurring Andrew, in some measure, out of his deepest depression. It made him angry, for one thing, that his brother should be being made to suffer for his fault. His first reaction, of course, was to seek to take ship back to Scotland forthwith and exchange himself for Henry. But common sense quickly assured him that this could be profitless for them both. The authorities would not free

Henry just because they had caught himself. He might well be able to help his brother more effectively by remaining a free man and seeking to exert some influence. Also there was some comfort in the fact that Henry had been confined in Haddington, not in the grim fortress of Edinburgh Castle – which, like the Tower of London, was so often the first step towards the scaffold. He himself would have been immured therein, he had no doubt. But the Tolbooth of Haddington was a much less ominous prison, for merely local malefactors. The probability was that no very dire fate was planned for Henry, his incarceration but a precautionary move.

So, when he wrote to thank Margaret, he also sent a note to her uncle, the Earl of Southesk. That nobleman, although far from pro-government, was influential, High Sheriff of Forfarshire and married to the Duke of Hamilton's sister, his aunt married to the Earl of Traquair, the Lord High Treasurer; also he was careful never to actually involve himself in what might be labelled seditious. Andrew urged him to do all that he could to get Henry freed, perhaps in conjunction with their uncle Sir Alexander Bruce of Broomhall, of the Privy Council. He added that he should use unstintingly any revenues from Saltoun which might be useful in this respect. The sort of persons who were presently ruling Scotland were, he surmised, the sort who might well be susceptible to discreet bribery.

Although Andrew knew no especial desire to go anywhere else, there was no need now to remain longer at Bilbao, of which place he had had more than enough. He would have gone back to Holland, where Gilbert Burnet presumably still remained, with the other Scots exiles who had not joined the ill-fated Monmouth expedition. But he recognised that his presence there might well bring down trouble on the innocent heads of those befriending him. With the Monmouth disaster, William of Orange, the Stadtholder, would be all the more apt to yield to pressure from his father-in-law, King James, now stronger than ever before; and someone who had committed legal murder in England as well as taking part in a rising, might well be unwelcome. Paris and Brussels, likewise, were too close to England for security. He probably would be wise to keep to southern Europe meantime. He had visited Rome as a

125

youth, but never Greece. He might wend his way in that direction – and send word for more money to come to him at Rome.

It was at this stage that further word reached Bilbao from England. Monmouth was dead, executed by his uncle, despite many pleas for mercy. It was apparently Ferguson's manifesto which had sealed his fate, the proclamation of him as King, therein, together with the ridiculous allegations that James, as Duke of York, had poisoned King Charles. So now there was no rival to Catholic James for the thrones of the United Kingdom. And that strange, humourless man was demonstrating his power. Everywhere Catholics were being promoted and Protestants displaced, with many time-servers hastily changing faiths. Parliament was prorogued when it protested, and its members appeared to be impotent. Laws previously passed were arbitrarily suspended. The Archbishop of Canterbury and six other Protestant bishops were arrested and put on trial. Catholic troops from Ireland were brought over and quartered at Hounslow, to keep the London population quelled. In the West Country the insufferable Judge Jeffreys had been reinforced by three others, and further encouraged in his ghastly work by being given a barony. Clearly this was to be an example to the rest of England on what could be expected in the event of further Protestant unrest. The Killing Times had come to England; and the Earl of Feversham, and his lieutenants Kirke and Churchill, rivalled Jeffreys in their orgies of blood and unbridled savagery, the military counterparts of Dalziel, Grierson and Graham of Claverhouse.

Much shaken by these tidings, Andrew learned something else – that news could travel in more directions than one. Only two mornings later, with his plans made to leave Bilbao, he was knocked up early at his bodega by town officers, arrested on the orders of the Alcalde and escorted to the town gaol. He was surprised to find there the shipmaster of the *Helderenberg* and the pilot who had navigated Monmouth's expedition, and whom he had not seen since landing. He was, however, allowed no speech with them. He was not ill-treated, and allowed to have his few belongings brought from his lodgings. In answer to his protests, he was assured that his

126

arrest was on orders from Madrid. It seemed that the English envoy there had received information from England that Fletcher was in Bilbao, and was to be extradited and sent to London for execution – not trial, for apparently he had already been tried in his absence and found guilty both of murder and of treason. The English resident would, no doubt, be coming for him in due course; although whether or not Madrid had agreed to extradition was not clear.

If something was required to jerk Andrew Fletcher out of his apathy, this served that purpose. A healthy wrath and indignation boiled up in him, his temper and wits both proving to be not dead but only dormant. He decided that he had to get out of that gaol, and quickly.

He tried bribery first, although this might leave him woefully short of money for his journeying thereafter. But his gaolers proved impervious. He sought means of effecting a break-out, but had to accept the fact that his cell was proof against any such attempt. He wrote a strongly-worded protest to the Alcalde of Bilbao, pointing out that he was a *Scottish* citizen and that no representations of the English ambassador had any validity in his case, requesting immediate release and offering to appear before any judicial tribunal. Unfortunately his Spanish was only rudimentary so that this had to be penned in English. He also engaged in some doubtful prayer – doubtful because he considered that his Maker might well think this an insolent liberty on the part of one who had taken a fellow-Christian's life, obnoxious as the creature was.

Oddly enough, it almost looked as though it was this last endeavour which bore the fruit. For the next morning there was an almost incredible development. Andrew had just awakened after a restless night and gone over to gaze out of the barred window of his cell, cudgelling his brains afresh to think of further steps he might take to gain his release, or at least to improve his situation vis-à-vis the Spanish authorities, when he perceived an old bearded man of venerable appearance standing alone in the forecourt below and gazing up at his window. To see such a one in such a place at such a time, was improbable in the extreme. When this antique-looking, stooping gentleman saw him at the window, and raised his handsome silver-mounted staff to gesture, he was the more surprised. The gesturing was equally unlooked-for but perfectly clear as to intention. The staff pointed vigorously behind Andrew and to the left, where was in fact the door of his cell, then traversed along in an easterly direction for some distance, then spiralled downwards and pointed out into the said forecourt. This done, the visitor went through the performance again, exactly as before. Finally, he jab-jab-jabbed with his stick at the door-position behind Andrew in the most urgent manner, touched frail hand to his wide-brimmed black hat, and turning, limped over to the heavy iron outer gate, opened it, and passed through, closed it quietly behind him and disappeared down the street.

Utterly astonished and at a loss, Andrew stared after him. But there was no further development. He could only assume that the old man was mad. Yet how had he got in, and at this hour? Apart altogether from why? And how was it that the outer gate was open, or at least unlocked? This was a prison, after all.

Almost against his own judgment Andrew left the window and went over to the cell-door. There was no handle on the inside, but he pushed against it – and with a faint creak the door swung open. Thoroughly amazed now, he peered out into the long corridor beyond. There was nobody in sight. He paused, wonderingly.

Thinking back, then, he recollected having been aware of some sound outside, some time before he had roused himself to rise from his straw palliasse. That must have been this door being unlocked. Which meant . . . ?

With a sudden unreasoning hope he almost went hurrying down that corridor there and then. But his wits reasserting themselves, he went back, closing the door again quietly. He threw such belongings as he had unpacked back into his valise, put on his coat, and, taking up the bag, re-opened the door and went out.

He tiptoed along that corridor, heart in mouth, thankful for the snores from inmates of the other cells to help cover his footsteps. At the end there was a turnpike stairway – the spiral described by the old man's staff. Down this Andrew stepped, one tread at a time, scarcely daring to breathe. At the foot it

128

opened into a guardroom, devoid of door or barrier. From the stair he could see three men therein, his warders; but they were all slumped on benches and over a table, apparently asleep.

Hesitant indeed, the prisoner paused. Then, deciding that there could be no turning back now, he crept on down, to inch across the guardroom, past the sleepers. He had a crazy notion that they were not asleep at all, but only pretending, and were watching him throughout.

If they were, they did not react to his presence. In a state of disbelief he reached the massive iron-bound door beyond, with its grille. This did have a handle, and when he pulled it the door opened on oiled hinges. He slipped out and gently drew it shut behind him.

He was now in the cobbled forecourt, empty save for strutting pigeons. It was no more than a dozen yards to the outer gate through which the venerable guide had disappeared. That gate Andrew knew to be unlocked. Having to restrain himself from taking to his heels, he walked quietly over to it, tugged it slightly open, and slipped through, into the street.

The gaol was situated in a long, climbing alley between the main square and the old bridge. At this hour there were only two people to be seen: a woman carrying a pitcher to the well and an old man leading a laden burro – but certainly not the same old man. Look as he would, Andrew could see no sign of his extraordinary visitant. Without actually thinking it through he had somehow assumed that he would be waiting for him out here, to give further guidance or at least to explain.

The need to get far from that gaol, however, was the strongest urge he knew just then. Delaying no more than moments, he set off down the street towards the bridge over the Nervion to the dock area, trying not to seem to hurry noticeably. He kept glancing over his shoulder; but he did not appear to be followed.

His mind began to work more coherently. Deliberately he put from him any groping for explanations for this extraordinary situation. That must wait. His first impulse was to make for the quays and stow himself away on a ship. But was that not just what he might be expected to do? He could not be sure which vessels would be sailing with least delay, without making dangerous enquiries. Bilbao was very much sea-related, although some miles up-river from the coast. Because its hinterland was almost wholly mountainous, the Pyrenees to the east and the Cantabrian chain to the west, with landward communications steep and difficult, almost all coming and going was by ship, save for the local peasant and market traffic. So surely he should seek to do the unexpected, and get away by land. And since the Pyrenean terrain was clearly much more rugged, lofty and therefore less populous, that would be where, probably, he would be least looked for. Also it was at least in the direction he would wish to go.

He was fortunate in that it was a market-day and folk from the hilly countryside were already beginning to stream into the town, over the bridge, with their produce and goods for sale at the stalls, loaded on burros and mules. Andrew was glad to mingle with these – but recognised that his garb and bearing would make him conspicuous. This was scarcely the time or place to try to purchase local clothing. But he did see a youth leading two donkeys, one laden with pots and wine-jars, the other with tall stacks of wide-brimmed hats of plaited straw, one of which he contrived to buy, no doubt paying many times its market price. Under this he felt a little less exposed, although perhaps this was an illusion.

The tide of peasants was going in one direction, at first, into town; however, presently, some men and boys began to straggle back, with the unladen donkeys, to do their day's work in the fields, leaving their womenfolk to sell the produce. When Andrew perceived amongst these the youth from whom he had bought the hat, he attached himself to him, and went off over the bridge in his company, however oddly that young man eyed him. At least no one challenged him.

The youth was returning to an upland village called Sante-stella, a few miles on the difficult road to Durango, south-eastwards. Andrew sought to gain his goodwill by indicating, in his halting Spanish, that he was escaping from one of the tax-gatherers of the Spanish government, so universally hated throughout the Basque country, who appeared to think that he was a smuggler from one of the foreign ships – this said with a wink, to suggest that he might be just that. Whether he was

130

believed he did not know, but at least the young man made no objection to his company, even shared some bread and cheese with him, and by the time they reached his village, was prepared to do even better. He made the most of his opportunity, sold Andrew some old clothing and a tattered cape; and though he could scarcely sell one of his mother's two burros, acted broker for another one, with a neighbour, together with halter and pack-saddle, at a price probably unsurpassed in Santestella in living memory. Thus equipped, and with an adequate supply of very basic foodstuff, the traveller took his leave and the road over the passes to Durango.

A mile or two on, where a track branched off due eastwards, just for safety's sake, Andrew branched off likewise. Such commercially-minded peasants might just possibly be persuaded to sell information about him, hereafter.

So, with his droop-eared, less-than-lively but evidently amiable donkey, he trudged eastwards through the comparatively empty Pyrenean foothills, scarcely able to believe his good fortune.

He had plenty of time now to ponder over his curious attainment of freedom. He could only assume that his presence in Bilbao had become known to more people than he had realised; the fact that the *Helderenberg* master and pilot were in custody was possibly significant. He had heard that there was a small English colony in the town, wine-traders in the main, and one or two Scots amongst them; but he had carefully avoided contact. Presumably amongst these was one, or some, who learned of and sympathised with his position, either as a fellow-Scot or as an English Protestant. And whoever this person might be, he must be influential in some way. Perhaps the Alcade himself had helped, at least so far as turning a blind eye to the rescue arrangements; he had been civil enough at Andrew's arrest. It was an open secret that many of the Basque notables were far from in-accord with the central authorities in Madrid and glad enough to avoid co-operation when it could be done without repercussions. No doubt the warders had been bribed to leave the doors unlocked and to feign sleep, knowing that they would not be punished.

131

Whatever was behind it all, the thing was heartening as it was welcome. And Andrew Fletcher needed enheartening, at this juncture, almost as much as he needed his freedom.

For the first time for months, he faced the future, however unknown, with some cheer and anticipation.

9

So commenced a most strange interlude in that man's life, scarcely fanciful, for it had reality and incident enough, but as it were unrelated to anything that he had known previously, and free in a way that his exile in the Low Countries, even his long-ago Grand Tour, had never been. He saw none of his own kind or class, nor wished to do so; he went at his own – or the burro's – pace, wheresoever the spirit led him, so long as it was in the general direction of far-away Rome, time utterly unimportant; he derived a simple but real pleasure from seeing new places and new things, perceived much in essential daily living which hitherto he had not recognised or had taken for granted. As a stranger in a strange land he went warily but awarely. All his experiences and contacts were not joyful ones; but he found instruction as well as challenge, of a modest and practical sort, in all. He became, perforce, something of an expert on Spanish character, customs, food and drink, and the Spanish outlook on life, so utterly different from, for instance, the Scots. And he learned to know himself, in consequence, better than he had ever done – which is always good for any man. Born to riches, prominence, privilege, and with the gifts of intellect and leadership, he had nevertheless been largely shielded from much of the elementary frictions and stresses of ordinary life, save for those which his choice of politics as a career had brought upon him. Now, drifting through high Pyrenean Spain with a donkey, he began to catch up on what he had missed – and on the whole enjoyed the experience, even if sometimes only in retrospect. And his guilt over what had happened at Lyme, although it did not disappear, faded somewhat.

Although on the whole it made an undemanding progress, save in small everyday matters of travel and communication, there were occasional dramatics. There was the night, for instance, in the Jaca area of the upper Aragon valley, when he was set upon by two armed ruffians in the tiny inn where he was the only guest. Afterwards he was not entirely dissatisfied over the way he had comported himself by flooring one of his assailants with a kick in the groin and knocking almost unconscious the other with a half-full wine-beaker – thereby winning himself a distinctly rusty old sword and dagger, whilst leaving one man moaning on the floor as his colleague bolted. Also, since he was certain that the shifty-eyed innkeeper was hand-in-glove with the attackers, he had the satisfaction of not only leaving without payment but of helping himself to a smoked ham for good measure, when he made it clear that he knew better how to handle the sword than had its previous owner.

Thereafter he made his way to the small town of Jaca where he managed to buy a small old-fashioned pistol and some ball and powder, much as he now hated the weapon and what it represented in his life. At least he would travel the more securely.

This purchase left him the more short of money and he began seriously to consider means of spinning out his remaining small funds and even, if possible, of earning more – something he had never before had to think of doing – for it was a long way to Rome. There seemed to be little that he could do amongst these mountain people which they could not do better for themselves. He was beginning to give up hope in this respect when, one night, lodging with an old village priest, he learned that the man, becoming crippled with rheumatic trouble, could no longer write, nor could anyone else in the village. As a result the little church's missals, breviary and lectionary, hand-written, were becoming tattered and unreadable because he could no longer hold pen to transcribe them. Since these were in Latin and Andrew was well versed in the humanities, he spent a couple of days there doing what was

133

necessary, and earned the first wage of his life, modest though it had to be. More important, the priest, much gratified, assured him that he would be welcome at the many small monasteries scattered through those remote valleys, where it seemed – oddly, to Andrew – that monks able to write were in short supply and monastic documents frequently in need of transcription.

So the traveller began to call at the monasteries, and to his considerable advantage. Not only was he indeed able to earn his keep and more, by transcriptions and other writing tasks, but because of what he was able to see and study in the libraries, scriptoriums, repertoriums and museums of these establishments. Always interested in history and mankind's long struggle towards enlightenment, scientific advance as well as better government and justice, he found much to fascinate him in these places, quite apart from purely religious matters, amongst books and manuscripts usually unconsulted for many years. For he was surprised at the intellectual degeneracy of most of these mountain monasteries and conventual houses. Perhaps those in Lowland Spain were in better shape – although he had gathered in Bilbao that the Holy Church, in His Most Catholic Majesty's domains, was presently in a sorry state of backwardness, ignorance and superstition. He found the monastic clergy in the main friendly enough, even amiable and hospitable; but unlettered, not notably pious and seemingly lazy. Their fairly general lack of appreciation of the worth of much that previous generations of their orders had accumulated in their archive-rooms at least held some advantage for Andrew Fletcher; for his own very evident appreciation of these things quite often resulted in him being offered books, illustrated manuscripts and other items in return for his scribing labours, not all of which he felt bound to refuse in very shame. So that, as time went by, his burro became loaded more richly probably than any other donkey in Spain, to its owner's wonder, considering that he was now practically penniless and living from day to day, hand-to-mouth.

To the problem of money, however, in late November, he unexpectedly was presented with a partial solution. He had crossed out of Spain into the independent little mountain

134

principality of Andorra, where at its capital town he discovered, of all things, that the chief treasurer of the little state, indeed the banker to the ruling Prince-Bishop, was a Scotsman from Edinburgh, married to an Andorran wife. This individual, John Kerr by name, was in effect almost the real ruler of the place and its five thousand inhabitants, for the Prince-Bishop, being Spanish and holding also the Spanish bishopric of Urgel, only occasionally visited the principality and the Council consisted almost entirely of unlettered peasants. Kerr was responsible for developing tobacco-growing in a big way on the lower mountain-slopes which seemed to be most suitable for the crop, and this was proving a highly profitable industry, for the smoking of the weed was now being accepted as providing immunity from the plague. So he had become very rich himself, as well as enriching his patron and indeed the peasantry. Kerr was delighted to meet Andrew, for no other Scot had ever come visiting Andorra in his time; and like all his compatriots in voluntary exile, he loved Scotland the more for being far from it – though without any real intention of returning there. And he knew Haddingtonshire and Saltoun Hall, his father having been a goldsmith and clockmaker in Edinburgh, and in fact having made a special chiming-clock for Sir Robert Fletcher on one occasion, Kerr recollected. A good Protestant at heart, although nominally a Catholic here serving a Catholic bishop, he was agog to hear all that Andrew could tell him about the state of affairs both in Scotland and England – despite being comparatively well-informed already it was clear, as, a banker in a small independent state on the verges of Spain and France, he had to be.

The great advantage to Andrew was, of course, that John Kerr was well aware of the richness of the Saltoun estate and therefore of his visitor's credit. And, being in the money business anyway, he was able to advance cash upon a bill of credit on the bank in Amsterdam which the Scots exiles made use of for their sustenance and where Andrew's substance was known and respected. So meantime the traveller's financial difficulties were over.

Andrew stayed with Kerr and his handsome and hospitable wife until well after the Christmas season, at their urgent invitation, whilst the Amsterdam arrangements were being finalised, these taking a considerable time naturally; so that the two exiles were able to bring in the New Year of 1687 in suitable Scots style.

When all the credit facilities were at length completed, Andrew was almost loth to move on. But his presence here would become known in time. Also there would, he expected, be moneys awaiting him at Rome, which must be seen to. And his readings in the monasteries had further whetted his desire to visit Greece, the very cradle of democracy and responsible government. Now, at least, he would be able to head for there in more normal style.

He left his burro at Andorra la Vieja, bought two horses, hired a young Andorran as groom and attendant, and said farewell to the Kerrs – this in February 1687.

He had heard of no hint of any hue-and-cry on his account.

10

Almost exactly a year later, Andrew found himself back in the Stadtholder's palace of The Bosch at The Hague, with Gilbert Burnet, something he could scarcely have foreseen, especially as he had arrived from Hungary of all places. Not that his arrival here was really remarkable; English, Scots and Irish exiles were indeed flocking to Holland again from all points of the compass, drawn as by a magnet, many of them directly from England itself. The reason was simple in the extreme. King James was making life unbearable for all save Roman Catholics, and even for the more democratically-minded and freedom-loving of these. Protestant England was on the verge of revolt and everywhere eyes were turning hopefully towards Holland and its Stadtholder, Prince William of Orange, the Protestant's champion, and his wife, James's elder daughter, who was heir to the throne and herself strongly Protestant. William was a warrior-prince who had even managed to hold up the victorious march of Louis the Fourteenth of France. Surely he must now come to the rescue of Protestant England, not to mention Scotland.

James Stewart, that obstinate, humorless, pious man, had the bit between his teeth with a vengeance, as lacking in judgment as was his ill-fated father Charles the First but lacking that noble-seeming monarch's personal charisma. He had no least notion of compromise nor seeking to gain his ends gradually, but was determined to put back the clock and make his kingdoms wholly Romish without delay. He had, in fact, applied to the Pope for England – Scotland was not mentioned – to be re-admitted officially to the Vatican hegemony, after a century and a half of Protestantism. He attended Mass in all the official trappings of kingship. He put Catholics in power everywhere – and when the Church of England bishops protested, he arrested seven of them, including the Archbishop of Canterbury himself, and clapped them into the Tower to await trial for treason. Not only this, but he was now ruling as an absolute monarch, ignoring his parliaments and levying taxes, and customs and excise, without the authority of the legislatures – and when the House of Commons refused to advance him personal revenues, accepting a pension from Louis of France. His toadies and boot-lickers controlled and mismanaged all, the unutterable Judge Jeffreys now Lord High Chancellor of England and hanging all who stood in the King's way.

So appeals went out from all quarters, high and low, to William and Mary at The Hague – come and save us! And, from The Hague itself, appeals went out all over Christendom – come to Holland, all Protestants and lovers of freedom and justice, to aid in the great task of liberation.

This message had reached Andrew Fletcher, from Gilbert Burnet and Sir Patrick Home – whom it seemed was safely back in Holland – by means of the credit-forwarding arrangements through the Amsterdam bank. That Andrew should have been fighting the Turks in Hungary, under the Catholic Duke Charles of Lorraine, was, for that matter, a strange development in itself. He had never got to Greece. At Rome, collecting his money sent direct from Scotland, he had found something of a crusading atmosphere prevailing, with young

137

men of spirit enrolling on all hands to go help drive the Infidel Turkish invaders out of Hungary. Although this was basically an Imperial and Catholic endeavour, Andrew, like many other young Protestants, saw nothing incongruous in answering the Emperor's urgent call, backed by the Pope in Rome. It caught him at a time when he was tiring, just a little, of drifting through Europe as a sort of interested but uninvolved spectator. His was a vehement and enthusiastic nature which was apt to demand action. Moreover, he still had a sense of guilt over the death of Heywood Dare, and taking part in this joint Christian endeavour might help a little as penance, against the common enemy of Christendom. So he had postponed Greece meantime – where, of course, the Turks were in force also – and gone to lend his sword, along with many others, to Duke Charles of Lorraine, the Imperial commander-in-chief, in this latter-day crusade. And in Hungary he had in fact distinguished himself, fighting in two set battles, including the great victory of Mohacs, in August, and in many skirmishes. He had actually enjoyed the experience, single-minded, having no doubts as to the rightness of his cause for once, and finding soldiering to his taste. Indeed, after Mohacs, he had been singled out for promotion, by Duke Charles, to a colonelcy of horse, when Gilbert Burnet's letter reached him, urging this alternative crusade to restore the Reformed Faith and democratic government to his own land and to England. Patrick Home's rider, to the effect that it was time that Andrew did something positive to protect his own interests, also made its impact – for he informed that when he had escaped from Scotland, although Henry Fletcher had been released from Haddington Tolbooth, the government had held another trial of Andrew himself, *in absentia*. This time not only had he been found guilty of further treason over the Monmouth business but had his name declared infamous, to be blotted out of all records as though he had never existed, a price put on his head, and his estates forfeited and given to the Earl of Dumbarton, one of King James's Scots minions – and, oddly enough, brother to the Duke of Hamilton. This last, of course, meant a drying-up of Andrew's source of revenue, and Amsterdam could no longer honour his bills of credit.

So, what with one thing and another, the new colonel took his leave of the Imperial army and made his way back to Holland whilst funds lasted.

He found the quite small area between The Hague, Utrecht, Amsterdam and Rotterdam, no larger than many a Scots county, a hive of excitement, intrigue, rumour and plotting again. Thousands of refugees, exiles and adventurers of many nationalities had flocked thither from near and far, by no means all of them reputable or even nominally Protestant. All talk was of an imminent invasion of England, although details and planning were notably absent. Fire-eaters and soldiers of fortune were in the ascendant, even Plotter Ferguson was back and active as ever, having somehow escaped in the Monmouth debacle. Andrew, distinctly disenchanted, tended to see it all as something of a rerun of former follies.

There was a difference, however. William of Orange was not the Duke of Monmouth. He was substantial, ruler of a rich country with a standing army and the most powerful navy in Christendom. Moreover his wife was undoubted next-in-line to the United Kingdom throne. And he was a cautious man, not be to be rushed, despite the clamour of the exiles. As important, the appeals for action from England were now a flood, and coming from high quarters as well as low, with promises of armed support and money. This invasion, when it came, would surely have little similarity to the last.

With such great influx of strangers, accommodation was hard to find and expensive – and now, after an interview with the Amsterdam bankers, Andrew found himself all but penni-less again, and was forced to sell some of his precious acquisitions from the Spanish monasteries to rich Hollanders. But Dr. Burnet, now acting as chaplain and adviser to William and Mary, had actually become a naturalised Hollander to avoid the demands of King James that he should be sent home to stand trial, still had his quarters in a rear wing of the royal palace and insisted that Andrew lodge with him, declaring that the Stadtholder approved. Indeed, it seemed, William desired speech with the visitor, information as to the Hungarian situation and other matters. Andrew's fame seemed to have burgeoned in extraordinary fashion, to his own discomfort, his general reputation having become a notably muddled combination of wily politician, brilliant soldier, escaper, dashing adventurer and dangerous man to controvert, especially when armed with a pistol.

He had his interview with the Prince one evening in mid-March, a private audience, with the Princess Mary also present and only Gilbert Burnet in attendance. William, now thirty-eight, was a short stocky man, not handsome but with strong features, heavy brows and a notably hooked nose, features which could seem formidable but which also could on occasion light up with sudden bursts of humour, even gaiety. Although generally solemn, as became one bred a strict Calvinist, he had a sort of slow affability and was not proud in manner unless provoked. Andrew was very much aware of a pair of hooded and particularly shrewd eyes. This was the man whose life John Graham was reputed to have saved.

"So – the celebrated Mr. Fletcher!" he was greeted, in fluent but heavily-accented English. "We have heard much of you. But Dr. Burnet assures us that you are less fearsome than you are painted!"

Andrew bowed. He did not know whether to bow first to the Princess, as heiress to his own country's throne, or to the speaker as reigning prince here, so he aimed his genuflexion approximately between the two.

"I am honoured that Your Royal Highnesses receive me," he said. "And grieve over my reputation. But I hope to learn by my mistakes."

"Well said, sir – well said!" William approved. "We all should do that."

"You have suffered much, Mr. Fletcher, for your ... convictions," Mary said. She was a plump, dark woman with no pretensions to beauty but with the large lustrous Stewart eyes to relieve a rather sad expression. Married for eleven years and still childless, and permanently at grievous odds with her father, she no doubt had reason for sadness.

"Less than many, Highness – who have paid with their lives."

140

"True. Let us hope that not many more need do so. That the time of freedom and betterment is near."

Burnet had said that the Princess was more keen on the invasion venture than was her husband.

"How goes the warfare against the Turk, Mr. Fletcher?" William asked. "Is he being pushed back. We hear little."

"Yes, sir. On the whole it goes well, since Mohacs. I believe that the Infidels will be thrown back to their own land during the coming campaigning season. The Duke of Lorraine now marches on Slavonia and hopes to win Belgrade before winter slows his advance. This summer should be the vital one."

"Then let us pray that it is equally so for ourselves!" Mary exclaimed. "For England. And Scotland also, to be sure."

"H'mm." Her husband paced to and fro before the great log fire of the private library. "We must be sure, my dear, that the time is ripe and that we are fully prepared, before we make any moves," he reminded. "With your nephew's rash attempt before us as warning."

"Yes, yes, William. But all is now changed from then. Is it not, Mr. Fletcher? Could the time be more ripe, indeed? With England straining to revolt. Seven bishops in the Tower – even Canterbury himself. I hope that you are going to aid us in our great endeavour, sir? As you aided poor Monmouth. And the Hungarians."

Andrew glanced at the Prince. "*My* aid, Highness, would be of but little value, I fear. His Highness has military leaders by the score to call upon, so much more able and experienced than am I. And I am but a poor man now, my estates confiscated. Forby, my first concern must be with Scotland . . ."

"Ah, yes, my friend," the Prince cut in. "And it is about Scotland that I wish to consult you. And not as a soldier. I know that you have not seen Scotland these last years, but Dr. Burnet assures me that you know your countrymen better than most, and the temper of the people. Tell me – how would the Scots people look upon a Hollander replacing their king?"

"A Hollander with a Stewart wife!" the Princess added.

Andrew hesitated, as well he might. Of all peoples the Scots were perhaps the most clan-conscious, concerned with genealogy, blood-lines, descent. Their ancient monarchy was

141

the oldest in Christendom, and although the Stewarts were a far cry from the original Celtic/Pictish kings, they *had* the blood, through Bruce and his non-Norman ancestors. But – a Dutchman!

"I cannot declare, Highness, that such would be their choice – had they a choice," he said carefully. "But . . . your royal lady, here, would be welcomed, to be sure."

"Are you saying, sir, that my wife only should claim the crown? The Scottish crown. To become Queen of Scots? And myself only a consort, a, a dependency! That I would never consider."

When Andrew made no comment, Gilbert Burnet spoke. "Your Royal Highnesses, if I may be so bold? The Scots may not *seek* a monarch not himself of the ancient line. But since there is no other lawful Stewart heir save King James's two daughters – as yet – they would, I believe, wish to have the elder lady and her husband as monarchs, joint monarchs. Especially when that husband is the most noted Protestant prince. Also a renowned warrior – always important with my countrymen. I believe that they would welcome such solution. And, h'mm, hope for offspring."

There was a silence at that last rider.

"Is that possible in the Scots monarchy?" William asked. "A joint wearing of the crown?"

"My great-great-grandsire did so," Mary said. "Henry, Lord Darnley, married Mary the Queen and became King. To be sure, he himself was a Stewart."

"That was the Crown Matrimonial, Highness," Andrew ventured. "Slightly different, if I may say so. In the gift of the Queen Regnant. Henry Stewart was not full monarch. Could not reign of himself. Had he been alive when Queen Mary abdicated, he could not have been King in her place. That was their son, James the Sixth."

"I would not be prepared to be such a puppet!" the Prince said. "It must be better than that."

"There is another possibility," Andrew went on, slowly. "Take the precedent of your own nephew, Highness – the Duke of Monmouth. He was created that, in England. But in Scotland he married the Countess of Buccleuch, in her own

142

right, and they were created Duke and Duchess of Buccleuch and Monmouth. And that was accepted as lawful, in Scots custom. A joint dukedom. He was not Duke-Consort of Buccleuch, or in his wife's right. If it was lawful for a dukedom it could be lawful for a kingdom." Even as he spoke, it flashed across the speaker's mind that in fact, if Monmouth's claim to possession of Lucy Walter's marriage-lines was truth, then there *was* an alternative Stewart heir-to-the-throne, a Protestant and male heir, the young Earl of Dalkeith, son of the Buccleuchs. Andrew forbore to voice this thought however.

"Ha!" William said. "This sounds more hopeful. I had forgotten the Buccleuch dukedom."

"Is all this so important?" Mary wondered. "Since the throne is now a united one. My great-grandsire, James the Sixth, became first King of the United Kingdom of Great Britain, in which both thrones are included. If the *English* ask you to be king, William – as they are doing even now – is that not sufficient?"

"Sufficient in law perhaps, my dear. But I am concerned over the wishes and feelings of the Scots. I need the support of Scotland in this endeavour – or at least not its enmity. The Highlands are largely Catholic still, we know. I do not want a Highland army marching to support your father. We know what happened to Argyll."

"Argyll was a Campbell!" Mary Stewart said shortly.

"You see – the Scottish concern with blood and clans!"

Burnet intervened again. "Your Highnesses – Scot as I am, I believe that you should leave the Scottish situation meantime. Concentrate on England. Once you are King in England, sir, the Scottish problem will be less difficult. From all that I have heard, the Scots are in no position to mount an invasion of England in support of King James. He is scarcely beloved, even in the Highlands. I say invade England with your Protestant army, under cover of your great fleet. And when you sit on the throne at Westminster, I think that you need not fear Scottish opposition."

"So say I," Mary nodded.

"Would that it were so simple! There is so much to be considered first. My States-General are suspicious, even hostile. They see me, as King of England, forgetting my own

143

Netherlands. Of leaving the Low Countries open to Louis of France's ambitions. I have to carry my people with me – if for no other reason than to ensure the aid of my army and fleet. I tell them that if, with England, I lead a great confederation of Protestant states, then the Netherlands are the more secure. And I will never desert my Dutch people. But . . ."

"Promise them gold, English gold, and they will come round!" his wife advised. "Also trading rights in the English colonies. Your Dutch will listen to that talk!"

"Then there is Louis. He cannot but know of this projected invasion. His spies are everywhere. James is his cousin, his pensioner and fellow-Catholic. He will seek not only to warn him but possibly also to support him in arms. This is partly what concerns my States-General. The fear that the French will descend upon the Netherlands whilst I am engaged in England."

"The victory over the Turks, Highness, may help in this," Andrew suggested. "The Emperor, as I see it, is Louis's chief rival and preoccupation. Now, with this Hungarian war all but over, the Imperial armies will be freed from that entanglement. Which means that King Louis will be watching the East again, rather than the North. The Brandenburgers talked much of turning on France. Until he sees how the Emperor will move, with Turkish defeat, Louis will I think hold his hand . . ."

"So, as I say, the sooner you move to England the better," Mary asserted.

"I will not move before all is in readiness – both here and in England. That could be fatal. As Monmouth found out. We cannot do anything before June, anyway. That could be all-important."

Andrew looked from one to the other. At an audience one did not cross-question royalty. But his raised brows were eloquent.

"June, Mr. Fletcher," William repeated. "We have sure word that James's Queen, his second wife, Mary of Modena, is with child. Due in June. If the child should be a son, and lives, then all is changed. My wife ceases to be heir to the throne. A male heir would alter all."

There was silence again.

144

"It is suggested, Highness, that this pregnancy is ... suppositious," Burnet said.

"Suggested by those who would wish it so, my friend. Or those who would have me to act precipitately. *My* information is otherwise."

The Princess looked sour.

"So we must wait," her husband went on. "But waiting, we need not be inactive. God knows, there is much to do. And you, Mr. Fletcher, will, I hope, be prepared to aid us. You have had recent and active experience of warfare. Distinguished yourself, all say. Although I will have some thousands of my own troops, I trust, to support me if and when I move, for good reason much of the army must be English and Scottish volunteers, few of them with knowledge of soldiering. So such as yourself will be invaluable." He raised his hand, smiling, as though to forestall any objection. "Even if you refuse to accompany any expedition, for your own reasons, I think that you cannot refuse to help train these good folk who presently all but swamp my small country? I shall need every able officer I can find."

Andrew could only bow.

"Keep us informed, my friend, of anything you hear as to the Scots situation. And your thoughts thereon. We shall be grateful."

"Thank you for your attendance, Mr. Fletcher," the Princess said.

The audience was at an end.

11

If the feeling of having been through all this before had been strong eight months before, when Andrew had first returned to Holland, it was still more so now. For once again he paced the deck of a ship anchored off Texel, impatiently waiting after long delay. Again he was in two minds about being involved at all. And again he had very little in common with most of his companions.

But there were differences, admittedly. For one thing, this was a powerful ship-of-war on which he stood. And the nearby reaches of the Zuider Zee contained, not a couple of lighters in addition, but a great fleet of vessels, warships and transports, marshalled in long rows. Moreover, this was late October not June, so that the wild weather which had held them up for ten days was at least not so unseasonable, however frustrating.

William of Orange's ambitious project, over which that prince was little more enthusiastic than was Andrew Fletcher, had been postponed well beyond the provisional June date, despite continuing and ever more urgent appeals from England. The information about the Queen's pregnancy had proved correct, but the term of delivery was wrong. Mary of Modena had indeed produced a child, a son, but not until the beginning of October. So now there was a Prince of Wales and the dynastic situation had become considerably more tense. But despite William's first notion that the arrival of a male heir to the throne would much retard his own chances, it seemed that the reverse actually applied. At least, the pleas for swift action had become ever more pressing, from England, with the contention that the longer the child, named James again, lived the more difficult it would become to unseat the father. Also, the birth had more or less coincided with the trial and surprising acquittal of the seven bishops and this had touched off such an upsurge of popular rejoicing, and resentment against the monarch, that King James had to seek security in the midst of the army of Catholic Irish troops brought over and assembled at Hounslow. There, in a panic, he issued a unilateral declaration of indulgence for Catholics and Protestants both, without parliamentary authority and contrary to law. But this was too late and rejected on all hands. Prominent Protestants were united in their advice to William that now was the time to strike; conditions would never be more favourable – and failure to act might well mean a spontaneous civil war breaking out in England. Seven of the most influential, the Earls of Devonshire, Shrewsbury and Danby, the Lords

146

Delamere and Lumley, the suspended Bishop of London and Admiral Russell, had sent imploring messages to The Hague. And the Prince had been persuaded.

So Dutch and foreign troops were hastily mustered at Nimeguen and a fleet assembled in the Zuider Zee, under the command of Marshal Schomberg and Generals Bentinck, Dykevelt, Keppel, Van Hulst and Herbert, with a number of exiled leaders – of which Andrew Fletcher found himself almost inevitably one. The amassing of the force had gone well, better than might have been expected at short notice, for the Dutch were efficient enough. But there had been a hitch, when Lord Sunderland, one of James's intimates – who presumably considered that he ought to butter both sides of his bread – sent secret word to William that the King had an undertaking from Louis of France, in that should William move, a French army would be sent to invade Holland and take the city of Maestricht, to deter the Dutch from sailing. So the Prince had detached half of his Netherlands force to go to save Maestricht, which left him with some 14,000 men for the venture, 8,500 of them Hollanders.

Ten days of squalls and unfavourable winds had followed and William had delayed his own embarkation, at his States-General's request. But now, after a change in the wind at last from south-west to due east, orders had come to sail. The fleet would reassemble at Hellevoetsluis on one of the arms of the Maas estuary, some ninety miles southwards, where the Prince would join it and from which a dash across the mouth of the Channel might be made with some hope of avoiding the English navy.

Moving such an armada into sailing formation, the warships encircling the transports like sheep-dogs, took time. The hope was that James's fleet would be loth to tangle with the renowned Dutch shipping, or too disaffected for its commanders to risk anything such. Admiral Russell had indicated that this might well be so. At any rate no sign of opposition had shown itself by the time that the windy October dusk enshrouded the great concourse of vessels as it moved, breeze half-astern, down towards the Channel.

Andrew appeared to be the only Scot aboard the flagship

so far, and kept pretty much to himself, turning in early.

Sailing at the speed of the slowest, daylight found them only off the old Rhine-mouth, some fifty miles down the flat, featureless coast. There was still no report of English naval presence which cheered all save the few fire-eaters. The wind swinging slightly into the north, they were able to make better time, but the shipmasters shook their heads gravely, fearing that this change of direction would go too far.

By mid-day the wide mouth of the Haringvliet arm of the Maas estuary was opening to port and they turned in, almost due eastwards now, the wind unfavourable again. Hellevoetsluis port was some way up and reasonably near to Rotterdam. Here William and his close entourage came aboard, and Andrew was glad to be joined by his friends Gilbert Burnet and Sir Patrick Home, along with other Scots.

A curious atmosphere prevailed on the flagship, with none of the false confidence of the Monmouth venture, little feeling indeed of high endeavour, but no desperation either, rather a sort of inevitable commitment and a dogged determination, suitably Dutch. William himself was no enthusiast, but he was very much in command, a strong, stern man who knew what he was doing and would do it without fail, for he had a streak of ruthlessness.

Nevertheless the doing of it was again delayed. The wind and weather altered again, south-westerly gales and driving rain, and so continued. Indeed on the 26th October there was a really violent storm, where even in the comparatively sheltered Maas estuary the ships were in grave danger of being driven aground and wrecked, and the state of the men crowded aboard became dire, with morale plummeting and assertions, even amongst the leadership, that fate was against them and that every day lost sank their chances further. Andrew for one did not see it that way. He argued that the weather would equally keep the English fleet storm-bound; that James and his advisers would not look for invasion in such conditions; that Louis would be unlikely to move his armies either, and that seasick men would quickly recover once their feet touched dry land. In his opinion, if they set off the moment sailing conditions were at all possible, however uncomfortable, even

148

dangerous, they would be presented with a wonderful chance to avoid a sea-battle and the possible massacre of transports and gain an almost unopposed landing, with the French behind them immobilised. William was inclined to agree with this assessment, although many of his lieutenants were now urging that the entire project be put off until the spring – this group led by one Wildman, an English expatriate politician, eloquent but consistently overestimating English strengths and Dutch weaknesses. But the Dutchmen were uneasy too, fearing that the estuary would freeze over and trap the shipping, as so often it did in early winter.

On 1st November the wind abated somewhat, although even in the Haringvliet the seas remained daunting. William gave the command to reassemble – for the fleet was now scattered over a wide area. It took until the evening tide before all could be marshalled in some sort of order, and at last they set sail for England – many declaring that they were heading for certain death, not by land but at sea.

Andrew felt strangely detached, as though it all had very little to do with him. *His* thoughts, hopes, ambitions, like his heart, lay five hundred miles to the north.

It certainly made an appalling passage. The gale and seas prevented them from tacking northwards as intended. The fleet could not be kept together. Visibility was very poor and signals could not be transmitted. Even the great ships-of-war suffered direly; what it must have been like on the overladen transports and horse-ships beggared the imagination. Then, next morning, the wind strengthening rather than sinking, it swung into due east, and under almost bare masts they blew rather than sailed before it, spread over endless miles of tossing, grey-white sea. Some vessels had to tow others, their rudders smashed. How many might be lost nowise could be ascertained.

It was on the third day out before the leading ships passed into the Channel proper, between Dover and Calais and into very slightly more protected waters. There was no sign of the English fleet – no doubt this easterly storm would keep it bottled up in the Thames. By dark they were as far west as the Isle of Wight. That night a council was held in the large low-decked poop-cabin of the flagship, all the leadership crowding in. Andrew did not feel himself to be in that category, but William sent for Burnet, Home and himself.

Decision now had to be taken. Where to land, and when. Whether couriers should be put ashore, if possible, to send warning to certain powerful supporters, the Earl of Bath in especial, who was now governing the West Country and a hidden adherent. And so on. There was much debate. It was agreed that the landings should be in the West, not only in that the hatred of James was strongest there, the more so since Judge Jeffreys' savageries, but because it would take longer for the King's mainly Irish army to reach them from Hounslow and so give time for Protestant supporters to rally and, very important, for a sufficiency of horses to be commandeered adequately to mount the invasion force. In this discussion Andrew's first-hand experience in Monmouth's problems and mistakes were invaluable. William declared that he would like the actual landing to be the next day, 4th November. As it happened, this was both that Prince's birthday and his wedding anniversary. A strict Calvinist, he did not believe that it might bring him luck; but he did think that the fact might encourage his troops. The exiles there, however, pointed out that the following day, 5th November, meant a great deal to the English people, whom it was even more important to encourage to rise in action. This was the anniversary of that other Protestant deliverance, of James the First and Sixth from the Catholic Gunpowder Plot of Guido Fawkes of eighty-three years ago, and it was still celebrated throughout the land. What date could be more apt?

That was accepted, and Torbay was decided upon as the best place for the main landing. It had to be as sheltered as possible from the east wind and yet large and open enough to accommodate the whole fleet and, at the same time, not guarded by forts and, especially, with a beach available where the horses could be disembarked. Torbay, tucked in behind Hope's Nose, had all these attributes. Some advised Plymouth, some thirty miles further west, where Lord Bath was based. But that of course was a fortified port with a garrison, and Bath's predilections might not be shared by his whole command.

Better the main landing at Torbay, with perhaps secondary assaults at Dartmouth and Brixham, round Berry Head.

Such planning was all very well, but carrying it out in present conditions was less easy. All next day they tacked about in the Channel, fretting, those who were not sea-sick impatient, cursing the delay, conditions and the weather, even the competence of the high command. Shipmasters were at their wits' end to hold a fleet of almost five hundred assorted craft approximately together. At night this proved to be quite impossible and dawn of the 5th November found most of the ships far to the west, indeed almost off Plymouth. There was despair in many quarters, even Gilbert Burnet declaring that it seemed predestined that they should never set foot on English soil – but praying heartily nevertheless.

Whether as a consequence or not, however, the wind changed into south-by-west in mid-morning, to shouts of thanksgiving. And in some four hours, with this behind them, the bulk of the fleet was again approaching Torbay.

The new wind, to be sure, blew straight into that wide bay, with Hope's Nose now offering no protection; but Berry Head at the southern end served as an alternative breakwater and the landing was fixed for Brixham on its north side.

So at last the anchor-chains rattled down all round that horn of the bay between Brixham and Goodrington, William and his entourage stepping on to English ground at Brixham harbour itself.

"So, Dr. Burnet?" he asked, almost jovial for that grave man. "What do you think of the doctrine of predestination now?"

"I think only of the providence of God, sir – and thank Him, as ought we all."

"Well said, my friend. Let all heed it. But now – to work."

* * *

It was only twenty miles to Exeter, where William planned to base himself meantime, but it took them three days to get there. Not because they had to fight their way; no opposition showed itself. But the landing of so many men, and especially of horses and artillery, in stormy weather, even on comparatively sheltered beaches, was a protracted business indeed. And in fact the weather deteriorated once again, the wind swinging back into the west and strengthening, which did not help – although they learned afterwards that it had almost certainly aided them greatly, for the English fleet had won out of the Thames and into the Channel, in strength, and could have disrupted the landings. Instead, this new gale from the south-west drove it to take cover, and it got no nearer Torbay than the sheltered waters of Portsmouth.

During this waiting period William looked for the Earl of Bath to declare openly for him and to give a useful lead to all the South-West. But although other locally-based notables, such as the Earl of Abington and the Lords Colchester and Wharton came forward, there was no word from the Governor at Plymouth. They were thankful, therefore, that they had not relied on the man and made their landing at Plymouth as some had advocated.

This reticence had its effect elsewhere in official quarters, not unnaturally. Although common folk hailed the Prince of Orange as a Protestant saviour, their betters held back. When the invaders reached Exeter at length, it was to find the Bishop and Dean fled, the magistrates nowhere to be seen and even the lesser clergy and merchants wary. Saviours they might be, but their co-religionists had had all too vivid experience of King James's and his Lord Chancellor's behaviour towards rebels, so perhaps they were not to be blamed too hardly.

The period of waiting was not wasted. This time it was not a case of roughly training unarmed countrymen but of marshalling and disposing to best advantage an already trained army, some half of it veteran troops. Volunteers who did come in were welcomed and formed into units of a sort, to be sure; but these were used mostly to send, in parties, around the countryside to spread confidence in the venture and encourage others. Andrew Fletcher, like many another of the Prince's staff, took a group of these each day to collect the so necessary extra horses, of which literally thousands were required. William did not have the time for ordinary dealing and buying. The animals had to be commandeered, but he insisted that all should be paid for, even though at modest price. It was not a pleasant duty, but this was war, and it was better than bloodshed.

After a week of this they had sure word that James had arrived at Salisbury with his army. The trial of strength appeared to be at hand.

Two days later informants reported a large cavalry force under Lord Cornbury only some twenty miles away, in the Crewkerne area. Preparations were in hand to counter this move when another report, from what was considered to be a reliable source, brought the astonishing information that this Cornbury and a Colonel Langston were actually intending to change sides, and to bring over this entire cavalry command to the Prince.

This was the sort of stirring news the invaders required and longed for. William at once detached two regiments of horse, mainly English, to go forward to investigate and welcome the new adherents if the thing proved to be true. Andrew went along.

If he, for one, required any further demonstration of the follies, mistakes and sheer nonsense of much of war, he obtained it now. They got as far as the open valley of the Otter when, across the undulating country they perceived the ostensible enemy appearing out of woodland a couple of miles away. Spurring on to meet them, but prepared to change into battle formation at short notice, they observed first that Cornbury's force had halted in a long straggling line, presumably at sight of themselves; then, after an interval, that the force appeared to be breaking up in confusion. While they were still a mile apart, the bulk of the King's cavalry began to wheel around and dash off, back into the woods. Only its left wing, about a regiment strong, remained in position, waiting. Four times that number had bolted.

Mystified, the Prince's horse rode on, although very much on the look-out for trickery. But as they neared the stationary royal troops, an officer came out to meet them. Saluting, he shouted that he represented Colonel Langston, who craved permission to bring over his regiment into His Royal Highness Prince William's command.

So, amidst relief on both sides, cheers and back-slapping, they came together, in the process perhaps another hundred or so coming back out of the woodland from the bolted regiments. It seemed that someone had started a rumour that they were being betrayed, that once they had yielded to the Prince of Orange, they would all be massacred by the heathen Dutchmen; and Lord Cornbury had fallen into a panic and ordered a hasty retiral. Langston had kept his head, fortunately.

If all this bemused such as Andrew Fletcher, at least it gave them the impression of poor quality troops and leadership on James's side.

In the days that followed, of a miserable wet and windy November, that impression was powerfully reinforced as more and more of the royal forces transferred themselves from Salisbury and Portsmouth to Exeter and the forward base William established at Axminster, in groups and companies and whole regiments, until it appeared as though James was left only with the hard core of his Irish Catholic troops. Ships, too, arrived in Torbay – although the royal fleet as such stayed where it was. It was an extraordinary situation that developed, in fact, a curious war of marking time, as with an hour-glass in which the sand dribbled steadily from one end to the other, which meant the winning and the losing, without a blow struck. No further forays were risked by the King; and the Prince was wisely content to wait.

Crisis-point was reached after two weeks of this. News kept coming in of notables and whole cities all over the country declaring for William, York and Newcastle amongst the first. London was said to be seething. The Earls of Devonshire and Danby had each mustered a sizeable force for the Prince and were marching south. Then the Duke of Grafton and the Lord Churchill arrived at Axminster from the royal camp, to kiss William's hand; Grafton was an illegitimate son of Charles the Second and Churchill was James's chief military adviser. And then the final blow – the Princess Anne, the King's second daughter, with Lady Churchill, fled from Whitehall north to Northampton, where she declared herself Protestant and denounced her father.

That was enough for James Stewart. He promptly sent an envoy to William proposing a conference to discuss terms, suggesting possibly that his son-in-law might act Regent,

154

himself retaining only the title of King. He also sent to London for his wife and the infant prince to join him.

William agreed to meet him, making suggested terms which, as was later reported, James declared were better than he would have expected. Nevertheless, that strange man, having sent off his Queen and baby son in a frigate to France, seemed entirely to lose his head. For, instead of setting out to meet his son-in-law, he secretly deserted the rump of his army and fleet, hurrying off at three in the morning with one Sir Edward Hales, in disguise as his servant. Apparently not trusting any of his ships' captains, he boarded a small fishing-boat which Hales had hired, to make the hazardous crossing of the Channel, throwing the Great Seal of the United Kingdom into the river en route. However, they had not got far from the shore when local fishermen, who, imagining them to be escaping Catholic priests such as were now in flight all over England, apprehended them and, despite all protests, carried him back to their own part of the town. Here the King was recognised. Better that he should not have been perhaps, for crowds gathered to abuse and threaten him. Had not Sir Basil Dixwell been brought to his rescue, that might have been the end of James Stewart. Dixwell, however, continued to hold him secret captive.

Meanwhile the word spread that the King had abandoned his supporters and left the country. Now the flocking to William became a flood. Church-bells rang throughout the land as they had not done since Charles the Second's restoration. The Prince decided to move towards London.

But advisedly he and his entourage took their time. Not only was the country in a state of turmoil, but in these southern parts chaos developed. This was because James's last command to his general, the Earl of Feversham, was to disband the army forthwith. And it transpired that there was no money to pay the troops. So a horde of angry and resentful Irish were let loose, leaderless, and went rampaging, looting and raping far and wide. This produced inevitable reaction, with mobs gathering to protect and retaliate – and to attack all foreigners as precaution. Any soldiers were suspect and Dutchmen tended to be taken for Irishmen. Such fighting and casualties as this strange campaign produced occurred now.

William reached the town and castle of Windsor, on the Thames, before the news reached him as to his father-in-law's true position, that he was not fled to France after all but was held prisoner in the house of one Dixwell outside Portsmouth. Astonished, and against the advice of certain of his counsellors, the Prince thereupon sent one of his aides, Zuylestein, back south-westwards, to order the King's immediate release, with permission to go where he pleased, so long as it was not to London.

The slow advance towards the capital was resumed.

Surprise and indignation was general, therefore when, a few days later, the Prince and his party learned, at Sion House only a few miles from the city, that James was in fact back in Whitehall and indeed had just held a Privy Council. Not only that, but the news came via a royal courier who actually brought a summons for Prince William to appear before the unpredictable monarch and Council at St. James's Palace in two days' time.

For the first time Andrew Fletcher saw William of Orange really angry – and it was quite a fearsome sight. His wrath was as much against the Privy Council as against his father-in-law, for reported attending were men who had sent messages to The Hague imploring him to come and take the throne. He forthwith sent a high-powered group, led by the Marquis of Halifax, the Earl of Shrewsbury and the Lord Delamere, to Whitehall, to announce that he would indeed be at St. James's Palace in a couple of days but not for any meeting with King James – only with the Privy Council. And he would come to it with his full armed strength. James had forfeited all right to the crown and must retire out of London before then, to await his, William's decision as to his disposal. That was all.

And so they waited at Sion, not without tension. The Council would come to heel, no doubt; but how would the notoriously volatile London mob behave, in its hatred of foreigners – and undoubtedly William of Orange, although half a Stewart, would be esteemed a foreigner. The Londoners had brought havoc to great causes before this. There might have to be fighting yet.

Next noonday however, a joint deputation arrived from the Privy Council and the Lord Mayor and sheriffs. They declared that they awaited Prince William's command; that King James had retired to Rochester with only a small party and his chaplains; and that the citizens of London were everywhere proclaiming His Royal Highness as saviour. They were lighting bonfires and had dragged Lord Chancellor Jeffreys from his house and all but pulled him limb from limb.

It looked as though the thing was done, at last.

* * *

William paced the floor of the Whitehall Palace chamber, watched with varying degrees of concern, apprehension and wariness by about a dozen men, most more splendidly-dressed than the Prince himself, who was more plain soldier than lover of show and ostentation. These were all great ones, Dutch and English, save for two – Gilbert Burnet and Andrew Fletcher. Why the latter should have been summoned to this meeting he could not imagine. Burnet was different, for he was William's constant adviser as well as chaplain, and had already been offered the bishopric of Durham, the greatest in England after the archiepiscopal sees of Canterbury and York; he could well now rank amongst the great. But Andrew, since coming to London, was seldom in any close association with the Prince and had already applied for permission to leave and return to Scotland.

"The position is intolerable!" William declared, not for the first time. "And I will *not* tolerate it for much more long." Sometimes when he was upset, his normally excellent English suffered a little. "Unless you wish for me to return to the Netherlands. Where I am *required*. Not, as here, kept waiting like some, some lackey!"

Cries of protest and dismay rose from the English lords, against grunts of approval from the Dutchmen.

"Your Royal Highness – bear with us, of your clemency. And do not, in God's name, desert us!" the Duke of Ormond exclaimed. "The position is most difficult. Decisions cannot be taken lacking the proper authority. This is a kingdom not a, not an electorate. The King is the fount of all lawful authority and lawful appointments. King James has not abdicated and is still on English soil. However inconvenient this is. He only can order the recall of Parliament, for Parliament to take the decisions that are required."

"Your Oliver Cromwell got over that problem without great difficulty forty years ago, my lord!"

Throats were cleared at mention of that ominous name.

"For your own sake, Highness, all must be done in due order," the Earl of Nottingham said, almost reproachfully.

"But *nothing* is being done, sir – nothing!"

"Your Highness will not allow us to approach the King for his permission."

"I will not, Great God! To do that is to admit that he still reigns. And he does not. What of this Privy Council? If King James had died, been killed by that mob, what then?"

"Then, sir, the Lord Chamberlain would have had to call the Council together to appoint a Council of Regency until the heir to the throne was declared monarch." That was Shrewsbury.

"Why not now, then?"

"Highness, the Lord Chancellor is in the Tower awaiting trial for his grievous crimes. You would not seek *Jeffreys'* authority?"

"The heavens forbid! But you, my lords, are almost all members of the Privy Council, I think? Can you do nothing without that oaf Jeffreys? Can you not appoint a new Chancellor?"

"Only the King can do that, sir."

"Christ God grant me patience! We do things better in my country, I promise you!"

"Highness," Gilbert Burnet put in. "King James, at Portsmouth, sent you a courier with a letter proposing a meeting. He suggested that you should be Regent. That letter bears his royal signature, royal authority. If Your Highness would agree to be Regent, even if only for a short time, that signature and suggestion would suffice, I think. The problem would be solved."

"I shall not be Regent, Dr. Burnet. I have told you. A regent rules only for another; that other *reigns*. So the Regent is

158

servant to the monarch. I will not play servant for any man."

There was silence save for William's pacing steps.

The Bishop of London spoke; he was an adviser of the Princess Anne's. "Your Royal Highness – if you sent for your wife to join you here, perhaps the King could be persuaded to abdicate in her favour. She, his eldest daughter. She would then become Queen with your royal self consort."

"No, my lord Bishop. No man can esteem a woman more than I do the Princess. But I am so made that I cannot think of holding anything by apron-strings. Nor can I think it reasonable to have any share in the government unless it be put in my own person, and that for the term of my life." That was slowly, heavily, said. "Moreover, to send for my wife from The Hague would take time. Am I, and my army and supporters, to wait here, on the whim of an ageing man who had thrown away his kingdom but clings to its crown?"

"You are saying, Highness, that you will be neither Regent nor Prince Consort?" Halifax put to him. "Does that mean that you wish to be King?"

"Yes."

"Yet, sir, it is your wife who is – or was – heir to the throne. Before this infant prince was born. Would you override her right?"

"I would not. My wife must be Queen. But I will not be a mere consort. We must be full King and Queen together. And the government mine."

"But . . . but is that possible, Highness?"

"If it is in Scotland – as I am assured." William glanced over at Andrew. "Then it can be here, my lords. King Charles created his son and his wife, the Countess of Buccleuch, Duke and Duchess of Buccleuch and Monmouth. Together, each and both, full duke and full duchess, neither consort. He did that here, from Whitehall. Do you question his right?"

The Englishmen eyed each other doubtfully. There were some murmurs about damned Scots and bastards.

The Prince waved a hand for silence. "You must see to it, my lords. And quickly. Send to James at Rochester and persuade him to abdicate. And to recall your Parliament as his last act as King. The Parliament and Council proclaim my wife and

159

myself King and Queen. It is understood? Else I return to my own country and meddle no more in your affairs."

The finality of that had its effect on all. It also allowed an aide to come forward to deliver some message to William, who nodded.

"General the Lord Dundee honours us with his presence, gentlemen," he declared. "He is, I am assured, a friend of Mr. Fletcher's. So perhaps he is not so black as he is painted!"

Andrew looked nonplussed. He knew of no Lord Dundee. Presumably he came from the Scots army, which had marched south over the Border at James's command on the first news of William's landing, to support the English forces which never fought. Unopposed, it had got as far south as Watford and there halted when it learned that no one else was going to draw sword for King James. Since when, in idleness, it had been making a considerable nuisance of itself to all concerned, nobody knowing quite what to do about it.

The aide came back. "Major-General the Lord Viscount of Dundee, Your Royal Highness," he announced. Behind him the handsome, debonair figure of John Graham of Claverhouse strode in, to bow and smile and wave a lace-edged handkerchief, very much at ease.

If Andrew was astonished, he was more so in a moment when Graham paced right up to William and was shaken warmly by the hand and even clasped to the princely bosom. Then he recollected the story that Graham had once fought in the Orange Guards and had saved the Prince's life at some battle.

The English notables looked highly disapproving.

"My lords," William told them, "when I said that this new viscount was a friend of Mr. Fletcher's, I could have added that he was a friend of my own also. In that, fourteen years ago, I owed my life to his braveness on the field of Seneff. He now commands the Scots force at Watford, and I have asked him to come here, under my safe-conduct, in order that the problem of the Scottish troops may be dealt with in friendship. But first may I congratulate the General on his new dignity? King James made many errors, I fear. But not, I say, when he made our friend viscount! Recently, I believe, my lord?"

"Less than a month ago, Highness," Graham agreed with his brilliant smile. "I swear that I am the newest-fledged nobleman of two realms!"

"Was that the price of you bringing your rabble over the Border?" the Duke of Grafton demanded, a rough diamond to be half-brother to the late mannerly Monmouth.

"My rabble, sir, was in duty bound to support the King of Scots. And still is. As to price, what did your mother pay for *your* dukedom?"

"Hrr'mm. Enough!" William exclaimed. "In my presence there will be civil speaking." He paused. "My lord of Dundee – what did you mean about supporting the King of Scots? Still?"

"I mean, Highness, that whatever may be the position here in England, James Stewart is still lawful King of Scots. And while he remains so, I and all other of his leal subjects must support him to our utmost. However great our admiration for your own royal person."

"M'mm. I see. Do you agree with that, Mr. Fletcher?"

Andrew cleared his throat. "Yes – and no, Your Highness. Yes, in that the King of Scots is entitled to the support of all Scots, irrespective of what the English may decide. But not if he has broken his coronation-oath to defend the Reformed Faith – since our duty to God ranks before even our duty to the monarch."

"Well, said, my friend. My lord – is that not true with you also?"

"I fear, Highness, that I have never been quite so religious of mind as my friend Mr. Fletcher, alas – whom I rejoice to see, after so long."

"And your duty towards King James – to what does that constrain you in this present tangle?" the Prince demanded. "Your army at Watford?"

"Why, continued support for His Grace, sir. Until he tells me otherwise. The King ordered my force to march south to his aid. So I, and it, remain until the King gives me different orders."

"But this is folly, sir – folly! James is not making a fight of it. So he has no need of your troops."

"He has not told me so, Highness."

161

"He tells nobody anything! He but sits at Rochester saying nothing, doing nothing. You cannot keep your Scots at Watford, idle, plaguing the good folk there. It is beyond all reason."

Graham shrugged.

The Prince pointed a finger which shook a little with his suppressed ire. "You are not so sure of your position as you have us to believe, my lord. I know your state. I am well-informed. Many of your people have deserted you and gone back to Scotland. Some go every day. You have now little more than three thousand left. You cannot hold even these for much longer. I have five times so many standing to arms. I could destroy your force in but hours, sir!"

"You could try, sir. But you *have* not tried. And will not, I think. Since you will not wish to offend Scotland, in this pass."

"Damn you . . . !" With an obvious effort William controlled himself. "See you, my lord – we are old friends and need have no quarrel between us. Why dispute? There is nothing for you here, save in my goodwill. James cannot use your men and your support now. Take your troops back to Scotland and we shall forget all this. And when I am King you will be the gainer, I promise you – and hope that you will serve me as loyally."

"That I can only do, Highness, when King James gives me his permission. Have I *your's*, to go speak with him?"

"Great God Almighty – go, then! Yes, go to James at Rochester. Tell him to face facts and truth. Tell him what harm he is doing to his kingdoms by his stubborn pride. Tell him to abdicate soon. And face facts yourself, my lord of Dundee! Go – and, Fletcher, go with him. If he is truly your friend, try to make him see sense! Off with you both . . . !"

The two Scots bowed themselves out.

"It is good to know that we are such good friends!" John Graham said, smiling, but dryly, as they walked down the corridor.

"It was news to me, also!" Andrew answered, stiffly. "Although I suppose that it could be said that I owe my life to you. For the warning you sent me at Saltoun those years ago. For which I have never had opportunity to thank you." That took some getting out.

162

"It was the least that I could do. In return for all your . . . hospitality!" Graham changed his tone. "So now you are in William's camp. We seem fated to be on opposite sides."

"I would not put it so. I am scarcely in William's camp—I am in *Scotland*'s camp. James was not good for Scotland, so I am against him. It is as simple as that. I desire the weal and freedom of my nation and people, only that. If William will give us it, I am for William. Not otherwise."

"Still the simple high-minded patriot! William Wallace's latter-day successor! I would have thought that your experiences, persecution, forfeiture, exile and the rest, would have taught you better. You have paid dearly for your lily-white hands, man!"

"Whereas you, whose hands are stained with the blood of your own countrymen – aye, and women and children too – are General the Lord Viscount of Dundee! I would not change places with you, John Graham."

The other quickened his pace but said no word.

In the palace courtyard, where sentries stood stamping their feet against the cold and Graham sought his horse, he turned.

"You are something of a fool, Fletcher," he said. "For a man with the wits to be otherwise. You could do great things, I think, reach the heights. In especial, placed as you are now. If you stopped your looking at the stars and instead considered the solid ground at your feet, for once! Are you going to stay here in England, with William? Or come back to Scotland?"

"I return to Scotland just as soon as I may."

"I thought so. See you, Scotland is not going to accept your Dutch William as King of Scots, even though he is half-Stewart. Not easily. James may not be popular or the wisest of monarchs. But he *is* of the line of our ancient kings, in direct descent. And he has a son, which William and Mary have not. Moreover, James has been taught his lesson. He will never be the same man again. Especially if he is guided aright. Come back to Scotland, Andrew, and help to guide James. I think that I can promise you a fair reception. Help James to be the sort of ruler you conceive Scotland to require. If he is cast out by the English, as seems likely, but remains King of Scots, then he will be a chastened and different man. You would have much more chance of influencing him than you would the triumphant Dutchman."

Andrew shook his head. "*I* think not. William is an honest man, James is not. William has been reared to rule through a States-General, a parliament of the people. James considers kings to rule by divine right. And James's hands drip with blood – as *you* should know! No – I shall never support James Stewart."

"The more fool you, then. You may rue that decision, one day. Well – tomorrow I go to Rochester – and we shall see what we shall see. Who knows, you may be in Scotland before me. If so, I wish you no ill. But remember that you are still forfeit there, an outlaw with a price on your obstinate head! It will not be easy for you – and *could* be if you would but heed me. James's men still rule. So do not act your usual rash self!"

"I acknowledge your kind thoughtfulness, my lord."

"Oh, be less damned prickly, man! You are devilish hard to serve! God knows why I seem to like you!" Graham grimaced ruefully. "I think of you as Honest Andrew – and you think of me as Bloody Clavers! Ah, well – so be it. If you see my good-looking cousin, your good-sister, before me, convey my admiration, will you?"

"What? What did you say? What good-sister?"

"Why Margaret Carnegie, to be sure. Did you not know? She wed your brother Henry in the spring – a notable match."

"Margaret! Married! To Henry! Dear God – it is not true?"

"But, yes. Were you sent no letter . . . ?"

He received no answer. Andrew Fletcher turned on his heel and went striding off over the courtyard cobblestones without another word.

Part Three

12

Andrew Fletcher's return to Scotland at the turn of the year, after his long exile, was very different from anything he had in the past sustained himself by imagining. Instead of coming home in joy and relief at a long ordeal and deprivation over, and a reuniting with those he held dear, he found himself to be still something of a furtive fugitive, still an outlaw in his own land, still a man without a home and, worst of all, having to face the brother he loved married to the woman he loved.

He had intended to travel north with Sir Patrick Home but in the end Home decided to remain with William's entourage meantime until it became clear how things were going to work out in the dynastic and political situation – for of course he also was an outlaw and a wanted man in Scotland. But he could not persuade Andrew to stay. Neither Burnet nor even William himself. Indeed Andrew's last interview with the Prince had been an unfortunate one, with William first talking almost of desertion and then, when that proved unavailing, seeking to make Andrew a sort of secret agent and envoy to test out opinion in Scotland and try to turn influential figures towards an acceptance of himself as King of Scots on James's hoped-for abdication. Andrew had said, cautiously, that he would do what he could; but that, of course, he would have to have the Prince's assurance that if he gained the Scots throne his reign would be as the Scots constitutional tradition required, King of Scots not King of Scotland on the English model, ruling through and with the Estates of Parliament, as it were the clan chief of the community of the Scots, the voice and upholder of that supreme community of the people, not as had been the last three monarchs since James Sixth and First died, who sought to rule by divine right, arbitrary and absentee. And, to his surprise – although perhaps it should not have been – William turned on him coldly, sternly, to declare that he would give no such undertaking, to him or to any man, that the powers, prerogatives and conduct of princes were not for discussion, much less for bargaining, with subjects.

Their parting, therefore, had been coolly formal.

Instead of Home, Andrew in fact made the journey northwards with a very different type of companion, by name William Paterson. This man, son of a Dumfriesshire farmer, although almost exactly Andrew's own age, had already had a most extraordinary career. Bred for the Church, he had fled Scotland with his parents during Charles's persecutions of the Covenanters, gone to Bristol, then England's chief port for trade with the New World, and there in due course become imbued with the desire for trading adventure, and sailed for the Americas. Across the Atlantic he appeared to have managed to combine the activities of colonial trader, money-lender, missionary and buccaneer, unlikely as this combination might seem. Presumably it was the last which at length made it advisable to leave the Carolinas in something of a hurry and return to Europe – but not to any part where King James's writ ran. So, like so many others, he had arrived in Holland; and it was in Amsterdam that Andrew had first met him, where he was acting as a sort of broker between the aristocratic Scots exiles and the banking-house which dealt with the Fletcher finances. He had come to England with William's train in some paymasterly role; and although he and Andrew had so little in common, they had got on reasonably well. He now desired to visit his family again, after the lapse of years, a comparatively rich man, and suggested that Andrew should travel with him. The latter was, in fact, hardly in a position to refuse, for he was now in an impoverished state. Whilst he had been a member of William's close party he had had little need of money; but now he was on his own again and feeling the pinch. Paterson indeed had lent him money in a professional capacity, on the security of his estates in Scotland. In his company Andrew was able to travel more comfortably and swiftly, even in winter conditions, than would otherwise have been possible. On the way he discovered that his strange compatriot, belonging to a breed of which he hitherto had had little or no experience, was a fascinating companion, all but bursting with ideas in the realms

168

of trade, commerce, banking and colonisation, ideas completely new to the contemplation of a Scots laird but in which Andrew perceived that there could possibly be great benefits for Scotland.

They parted company at Tweed, Paterson to head westwards for Dumfries, but agreed to meet soon again in Edinburgh. The exchange of ideas had not been all one way and Andrew in his turn had planted some seeds in the other's fertile mind.

Riding alone up through the Merse, with his own Lammermuir Hills beginning to loom ahead, Andrew Fletcher was all but overcome with emotion. It was nearly six years since he had last trodden his native soil, and he had pined for it like most other exiles. But there was more than that to it. He had a love for Scotland and its people beyond all telling; and to be once again in his own land worked so powerfully upon him as to bring tears to his eyes, at this well-remembered vista or that, all so often conjured up before his mind's eye in far and alien places. Especially as, after the rather featureless moors and undramatic scenery of North Northumberland, the change to verdant Tweeddale, the rolling green loveliness of the Merse and all the Border hills which rose everywhere like leviathans from the far flung sylvan expanse, was so sudden, so breathtaking.

Nevertheless, despite emotion and a sort of heart-breaking delight, he went warily, Home's and Graham's warnings in mind. His political enemies still ruled here, however doubtful now their stance, and he was a condemned man in law. So he avoided most of the haunts of men and the castles and great houses of former friends, to ride by little-used byways and to thread the sheep-strewn Lammermuirs by tracks he had not followed since boyhood. He emerged eventually, as the early dusk was falling, in the throat of a little pass under Watch Law on Lothian Edge and looked down and out over the fair land of East Lothian to the distant waters of the Forth estuary, a lump in his throat. His eyes turned first, of course, westwards, towards the shadows some ten miles away that represented the woodlands, fields and pastures of his own Saltoun. Sighing, he did not head in that direction but turned his horse's head

169

downhill directly northwards into the mist-filled foothill area of Spott and Stenton. It was quite dark when he rode into the courtyard of the House of Beil.

His welcome by Lord and Lady Belhaven and Stenton could scarcely have been more wholehearted. It was as though he had been gone only a week or two – although Johnnie, and Margaret too, had changed in appearance somewhat, as no doubt had he. Johnnie was heavier, broader, more stocky but just as cheerfully good-humoured; and his plain-faced, gentle lady more matronly, more self-possessed, as became the mother of a four-year-old son – and obviously to be a mother again shortly – but just as unassumingly kind. Andrew was just in time for the evening meal, held early in country fashion.

It is to be feared that, however excellent the provision, he scarcely knew what he was eating, in trying to answer the flood of questions with which his hosts inundated him as they sought to learn of the adventures and experiences of six years of active exile, Johnnie agog, Margaret in wondering concern. But at length Andrew called a halt, flapping his hand.

"Enough! Enough!" he exclaimed. "Surely it is my turn now? There is so much I want and need to hear, have to know. First of all – Saltoun? Henry? And, and . . . his wife!"

His friends eyed each other.

"Henry and Margaret are well," Johnnie said, carefully for him. "They have been wed since the spring. They suit each other very well – eh, my dear? As for Saltoun, they do their best."

"Aye. To be sure. They are . . . happy together?"

"Oh, yes. Or, so it would seem, Andrew. Did you think . . . otherwise?"

"No, no. But – it was a surprise. To me. I only learned of the marriage two weeks ago. In London. From Claverhouse, of all men."

"You had not heard? They would send a letter . . . ?"

"No doubt. But placed as I was, letters could miss me. In April, May, I was in Hungary, fighting Turks. I am glad that they seem happy. Henry deserves his happiness." That was strongly, almost harshly averred. "Now, Saltoun? You say that they did their best. What does that mean?"

170

"It means that it is difficult for them, Andrew. In difficult times. Henry is a marked man also, you'll mind. He was imprisoned. Not that he had done anything but be your brother and send you moneys. But that was enough. I tried to get him released; but I am a watched man myself, with little influence. It was only the Carnegies who got him out. When he returned to Saltoun, it was to find Dumbarton's steward lording it in the Hall, his people managing the estate and farms. Henry was shown the door."

Tight-lipped Andrew nodded.

"He came here for a while. Then went to stay with the Carnegies at Pitarrow in the Mearns. Sir David and Southesk know the Douglases – Dumbarton is second son to the old Marquis of Douglas. They worked on him, Dumbarton, to at least let Henry return to Saltoun. Said that he knew the property better than any hireling. And could get most out of it – for Dumbarton! So that he could at least keep the place in fair order for the day that you won it back. Dumbarton is a soldier – he is, or was, commander-in-chief in Scotland – with no knowledge nor care of farming and lands. He was not satisfied that he was being well-served by his steward and the others. He did allow Henry to return, but not with any authority. Only to advise and keep an eye on the steward. Not to stay in the Hall. He let him have your small dower-house at West Saltoun. So there they roost, he and his Margaret. Doing what they can to keep the estate together – although the revenues all go to Dumbarton."

"I see – yes, I see it all. The Carnegies have been . . . very good."

"Oh, yes. Sir David is one of the shrewdest lawyers in the land. He and Southesk have friends and influence in the highest quarters. Although not of the King's party."

"And Margaret has been so good, so patient and helpful. To Henry, and in your interests, Andrew," the other Margaret put in. "She is a dear."

Their guest cleared his throat. "I shall not fail to thank her," he said. "This man, the Earl of Dumbarton? I know nothing of him, save that he was awarded my forfeited estates. Why? Why him? What sort of man is he? You say he commands the army

171

here. So Claverhouse – the Lord Viscount Dundee – serves under him?"

"Yes. As I say, he is a soldier only. And an able one, I am told. He learned his trade in the foreign wars. As did Graham. A younger son, as the Lord George Douglas, he inherited no lands or fortune, so made his own way. King Charles thought much of him. Created him Earl of Dumbarton, for his services in the Dutch war – when Graham was fighting on the other side! King James brought him back to Scotland and appointed him commanding General. He it was who brought Argyll to ruin. But he had no lands, only the title. Saltoun was confiscated and given to him. That is all I know. I have never met the man. Otherwise I have heard no particular ill of him – unlike his lieutenant, Graham."

"He will not hold Saltoun much longer, will he, Andrew?" his hostess asked. "Now that King James seems to have fallen?"

"That I do not know. Indeed I know little or nothing of the situation here in Scotland now. In England, all hangs in the balance. I think that William will win the day. There. For James is hated. But here? How is William esteemed? How strong is James's grip? Or, at least, that of his supporters?"

"It is hard to tell," Johnnie admitted. "On the face of it, all is as it was. James is still King of Scots and his minions hold all power and positions. But they are uneasy, no doubt of that. They draw in their horns somewhat. They are mainly Catholics, of course – or pretended Catholics! Whilst the people are staunchly Protestant. The people are for William, I think. He is half-Stewart, after all, and married to a Stewart."

"Yes, the people. But unhappily, it is not the people who make the decisions, but their betters! Men like yourself and myself, Johnnie – God forgive us! The nobility and gentry, man – what say they?"

"Damned little, Andrew. In this pass. Keeping their eyes and ears open and their mouths shut, for the most part. Waiting to see how the cat jumps!"

"Aye – the leaders of the nation! Must it always be so? But – if the English accept William as King, will *they*? A Dutchman?"

172

"I do not know. Would you? You, who have suggested before now that the crowns might be separated again?"

"That was a threat. When the King was behaving tyrannically from London. I still say that it may be necessary, and right. But not to keep James Stewart on our throne. If so be it that the new monarch will rule as the King of Scots should, in and through Parliament, preserving our ancient liberties, then there is little harm in him being King in England, too."

"And your William will do so?"

"William must be shown that only so can he be King of Scots."

"You will tell him so?"

"I have already told him so. And it will be my endeavour to see that the Scots Parliament tells him so also, in no uncertain voice."

"Aye – so Scotland has its old Andrew Fletcher back again! And not before time. For there is much amiss, much to be done. Not only in Parliament House. But you will have to take your time, Andrew. To watch your step. Go cautiously at first. You could still be arrested and executed without trial. For you are tried already, in absence, and found guilty of treason. Whether they would dare to do it, I do not know. But they might, man, they might, for you could be a thorn in their flesh."

"I will watch, never fear. I have learned how to survive, in these last years. Is the country quiet, or is there much unrest?"

"Quiet! Lord, Dand – you ask that? The land is in a constant commotion. It is all but mob-rule in many parts. This shire of Haddington is not so bad. We are douce folk here. But elsewhere, in the West, in especial, it is bad, bad."

"You mean persecution still?"

"No, no. Rabbling. That is what they are calling it. The mobs hounding out the bishops' men, the King's Curates as they are called now, the ministers who took up episcopacy, on King Charles's orders. They are a sorry lot, on the whole, as you know – but they scarcely deserve this."

"You mean that the churchmen are being attacked again? The clergy. In their persons?"

"Just that. Worse than ever before. Up and down the land

173

they are being turned out of their manses, dragged through the streets, assaulted, some even slain. I heard that as many as two hundred had been violently driven from their livings, their wives and bairns made game of, by the mobs. Even the bishops themselves have gone into hiding."

"But surely this is not tolerated? I have no love for the bishops and their minions, who have cost Scotland dear. But this is no way to deal with them. Is the law not protecting them? The sheriffs and officers? Their own kind . . . ?"

"I told you, our present masters are lying very low. Besides, being in the main Catholics, they are not greatly concerned. They do not love Episcopalians either. To them, it is but one Protestant party savaging another, I suppose. And remember, your friend Claverhouse, who *is* an Episcopalian, is out of the country with his army – the troops who could have protected these curates."

"And what of his chief, this Dumbarton?"

"A Catholic, they say. He would be, for his mother was a daughter of old Huntly."

"Dear God – and this is Scotland! Like a rudderless ship in a storm! Is there nobody left in the land to grasp the helm? No spirit surviving in this ancient nation? Have we become a race of serfs, cowards and toadies?"

"Not that, Andrew – never that, surely. But . . . we require a lead. It is leadership we lack. Our natural leaders seem to have died out. Many, to be sure have been executed, or driven into exile. As were you. But you, at least, have come back!"

"Yes, yes – we have a leader, *one* leader again!" Margaret exclaimed, in a rush, eyes shining. "Grandfather always said that *you* were the hope for the future. Johnnie too, of course – but you in especial. I mind him saying it in this very room, before your first election. But – oh, Andrew, you will be careful? Promise that you will be careful!"

"Sakes, lass, it sounds as though there were sufficient of careful men in Scotland, as it is! But do not look on me as one of Scotland's leaders, see you. I have neither the stature nor the station and standing. But I will do what I can. Oh, yes – I will do what I can, God aiding me!"

"In my small way, I will aid you too, Dand!" Lord Belhaven said.

*　*　*

Andrew delayed his arrival at Saltoun, next day, until evening, as he had done at Beil, and for the same reason – so that here, where he was known by all, he might slip in unnoticed.

There were two Saltoun villages, East and West, about a mile apart, with the Hall in its demesne-land another mile north of both. The East or Kirkton of Saltoun, climbed a gentle slope of one of the foothill ridges, its parish church a landmark; but West or Milton of Saltoun lay hidden in a valley, sheltered amongst old trees, with the Birns Water splashing though the midst. Here were the two mills, the tannery, brewery and other necessary estate utilities. The dower-house stood in its own triangle of land near the western of the two bridges which spanned the river. It was a modest-enough house, compared with the great castellated pile of the Hall, grown out of an earlier miller's house – indeed the original mill-buildings and wheel were still incorporated in the stableyard – improved and extended for the use of the lairdly family's dowagers, unmarried daughters and suchlike dependents. Andrew rode into the dark yard, tethered his horse to a post and, schooling himself and his emotions, went to rasp the tirling-pin at the back door.

Leezie Duncan, Margaret's former personal maid, opened almost immediately. "Losh, you're early, Maister!" she exclaimed, in her strong Mearns accent. "I heard you ride in. It's right dirty night to ride frae Embro in this . . ." Suddenly she stopped, to peer into the outer darkness. "Guidsakes! It's, it's . . . it's no' himsel'? It's – losh, it's the laird!"

"None other, Leezie. Back from my travels. It is good to see you. Is your mistress here? I gather that my brother is not?"

"Aye, sir – or no, sir. Och, sir – here's a right joy! She's ben the hoose. Sakes, but she'll be fair whummled to see you! Here – gie's your wet cloakie and come awa' ben. Eh, but you're looking fine, Laird, for a' that!"

He followed the exclamatory abigail through to the front of the house, to be all but propelled into a pleasant firelit and lamplit room.

175

"See wha we've gotten here, Mistress Meg!" Leezie cried, with a sort of triumph, and stood in the doorway, arms folded over ample bosom.

Margaret was sitting in a wing-chair by the fire, a book in her hand. Eyes widening at what she saw she rose slowly to her feet. She was lovelier even than he had remembered her, now in her twenty-ninth year, still slender but with a superb figure, all woman now, girlhood past.

The man, staring, swallowed, shook his head and found no single word to say.

Behind him there was a kind of whinnied laugh which ended in a choke, and then the door clicked shut.

"Andrew! Oh, Andrew, my dear it is *you*! Andrew – at last! At last!" Book falling unheeded to the floor, she came running to him, to throw herself into his outstretched arms.

Hungrily he embraced and kissed her, her hair, brow, eyes, lips – and it was their first kissing. She did not repel him; indeed she kissed him back, twice, then buried her head against his chest, clutching at him, with something between strangled sobs and laughter.

So they stood holding each other, for long moments – and the stir of her emotion within his arms was no help to a hot-blooded man who, whatever the appearances, was seeking to restrain himself. They did not actually speak, whatever sounds they made.

At length, abruptly, she drew back – but not so far back that she could not still grip both his hands and so held him there, searching his face and features in the mellow light as though for confirmation of something, something vitally important. Presumably she found it, for she nodded, two or three times, even though she sighed as she did so.

"Margaret!" he said, and again, "Margaret!" lingering over the syllables. He did not require to say more, just then.

Again she nodded, as though he had enunciated the whole truth of the matter and no more need be said. But for good measure she added, "Andrew!" again, and led him over to the fireside, hands still in his.

"So long," he got out hoarsely. "So very long. To wait. So hard. The waiting. And now . . . and now . . . !"

"Yes," she said. "I know."

"You are beautiful. And true. And kind. Always you were that. A joy and a warmth, at the very heart of me. An anchor, in all the storms. That kept me secure. But now . . . !"

"But now I am your brother's wife!" she said, levelly, since one of them had to say it.

Pursing his lips he inclined his head and their hands parted.

"It . . . had to be, Andrew," she declared, low-voiced. "And Henry is good, fine. We are . . . very happy."

"I am glad of that, at least!" That was stiff.

"It was for the best," she said, looking into a flickering, aromatic birch-log fire.

"Good! For the best is always . . . admirable!"

"Andrew." She laid a hand on his arm. "You must understand. Or all is . . . a ruin."

He took a deep breath. "Yes. Oh, yes – you are right. Understanding. That is what is required."

"It will come, my dear." She straightened up. "Now – you will be hungry, tired. You will wish to wash, whilst I see to a meal." With relief to both she became the busy, effective housewife, little as he had thought of her as such. "A glass of wine, first? Have you ridden far today?"

"No. Only from Beil . . ."

Later, as they sat at table, with Leezie departed again, although both carefully sought to avoid the subject of the marriage for a while, inevitably they came round to it. They had got to the matter of Henry's release from Haddington Tolbooth when Margaret, in her account of it, hesitated.

"They . . . they required tokens, proofs. That he would no longer work against them, against the government," she said. "It was necessary to give these, give something to convince them."

"But Henry was *not* working against them, was he? He was never the one for that."

"He was sending *you* moneys."

"My own moneys."

"Yes. But you were an active enemy of the government, condemned. An outlaw. So Henry was – how did Father put it? – compounding your offence. So they imprisoned him and forfeited your estate."

177

"Yet moneys continued to come. Less, but still some. From whom?"

"Shall we say from your friends, Andrew?"

"From *you*, Margaret?"

"Only a little. I have not much money. Only what my mother left me."

"Your father, then?"

"And others. Well-wishers."

"All, all compounding my offence! You and your father and others all putting themselves at risk, for me. Oh, Margaret, Margaret!"

"It was the least that we could do. It had to be."

"Had to be? That is what you said before. About your marriage. It had to be. Why?"

"Do you not see? I told you, tokens were required, to win Henry's release. Here was one. If he was to wed Sir David Carnegie's daughter, we, the Carnegies, would stand as, as sureties. I think that is the word. Sureties for his good behaviour . . ."

"Lord! So you sold yourself to get him out! Because of *my* offence. Of a mercy – not that!"

"No, no – that is nonsense, Andrew. Foolish talk. I did not sell myself. I have always been fond of Henry and he of me. It might have . . . come to that, anyway. He had asked me, more than once. To be his wife. So now, it was . . . convenient."

"Convenient! Convenient for *Henry*, yes! But you! And me . . . and me . . . !"

"Yes, for you, too, Andrew. Moneys could still be sent to you. Henry could watch over your estate, for this Lord Dumbarton in name but really for you. I think, not married to a Carnegie, that would not have been possible."

"Damn the estate and the moneys! What of *me*?"

"Yes, what of you, Andrew?"

He blinked at the way she said that, and at her direct gaze across the table. He swallowed.

"I loved you. Love you, now. Always shall do. And hoped. Hoped and prayed . . ."

She moistened her lips. "I am sorry, sorry! But – hoping and
178

praying were not enough, my dear. Did you ever say so? Ever write it in words? Ever act the lover?"

"I could not. How could I? A rebel, a hunted man with a price on my head. How could I offer myself to any woman? But I loved you. And thought that you knew it. And, and might, in your heart . . ." He left the rest unsaid.

She said no word either, for a little, but a single tear trickled down her cheek.

He shook his head, then reached out and touched her arm. "Forgive me, lass. It is done and cannot be undone. You are my brother's wife. It will be difficult for me. But difficulties are made to be overcome, they say!"

"Henry and I are . . . happy, Andrew," she said – and that was almost a plea.

"Yes. So you said. I shall not forget, never fear! Now – tell me of your cousin, John Graham, now so great. I saw him in London. But Johnnie Belhaven tells me that he has married . . . ?"

"Yes. To Jean Cochrane, granddaughter of the Earl of Dundonald . . ."

When, presently, it was time to retire, Andrew took her gently in his arms and kissed her brow.

"My dear," he said. "We have new burdens to bear, I fear. I do not wish to add to yours. But . . . I am going to require your good help. You will know that, and understand? I do, and say, unwise things, at times. We will, we must, inevitably see much of each other. It will not be easy. But with your aid and forbearance, I will contrive it. Not to hurt Henry. Nor yourself."

"I shall need help, too, Andrew – do not think otherwise. Go now, my dear – and good night."

* * *

Henry Fletcher arrived back from Edinburgh the next afternoon; and however mixed were Andrew's feelings over this reunion, those of his brother were of sheer, uncomplicated joy and affection. Which in turn, of course, helped the other to keep his own in order. Henry had changed, in appearance and manner, remarkably little over the intervening years, still the slight, sensitive, vulnerable-seeming young man, attractive in a

179

boyish way, so essentially prepossessing. Whatever his previous doubts and fears as to their relationship in these new circumstances, it was not long before Andrew was feeling as protective as ever towards his younger brother – with, inevitably, a consequent strengthening of his resolve to keep those relations on a right and proper footing vis-à-vis Margaret. He fairly quickly perceived, also, that the protective fondness was not confined to himself, that Margaret's undisguised affection for her husband had quite a degree of motherliness about it – which, somehow, was no little comfort to himself.

Henry, naturally, was eager to learn all that had befallen his admired brother during their long separation and Andrew had to satisfy this to some extent before he could do his own questioning. Since Margaret had heard much of it, he suggested that Henry and he should go for a walk, whilst the light lasted, for he longed for some sight of his own place and old haunts. But Henry strongly advised against this, pointing out that there were now many of Lord Dumbarton's people about the Saltoun district, managing the estate, farms, mills and so on, and these must not learn of the Laird's return lest they inform the authorities. Their own folk, no doubt, were to be trusted; but even these would be bound to talk amongst themselves and the word could soon reach other ears. Little as Andrew might relish hiding furtively on his own property, he could not blink the realities of the situation. There was still a price of £1,000 for his head, dead or alive.

So the brothers had to talk walking round and round the comparatively small walled-garden and orchard of the dowery-house, on that crisp afternoon of early January. On the subject of Andrew's danger, Henry admitted that he was in two minds. His political enemies were still in power and undoubtedly would wish to apprehend him; but whether they would actually execute him now would depend on the dynastic situation and how much protection Andrew could expect from William of Orange.

"I have served William reasonably well. We may not see eye to eye on all matters, but I do not think he would smile on any who maltreated me, Henry."

"So I would have calculated. If he were King. But how likely is he to become King?"

"In England, I think, very likely. But here, is another matter."

"You believe James could remain King of Scots, with William King of England?"

"Could, yes. In law and theory. They are still two kingdoms with two parliaments. But in practice, who knows? All will depend on opinion in Scotland. Which not only I but William wishes me to ascertain."

"So? You have come home still in his service?"

"Not so. I am entirely my own man. But he asked me to discover, and inform him."

"So he *will* protect you?"

"He would probably wish to."

"You do not sound too sure of him, Dand."

"I am not. I admire him as a man and a soldier. He is, I think, honest and no tyrant. And a good Protestant. But whether he would make a good king for Scotland, I am not convinced."

"He could not be worse than James?"

"That at least is certain! But we need better than that."

"Yes. So, do I take it that you are still set on fighting the crown? After all the price you have paid!"

"Not the crown, Henry. I have no quarrel with the crown, as such. Scotland's ancient crown. It is misgovernment from London that I have fought. And will go on fighting. Misgovernment in Scotland by Scots is bad enough. But that at least we should have the power to put right. But misgovernment, even *good* government, from another kingdom – that is intolerable for free men."

They paced in silence for a little.

"What of James?" Henry asked. "We hear only rumours. Wild rumours. Contradictory. Some say that he has abdicated, others that he never will. Some that he has fled to France, others that he is still near London. Some even say that he intends to come to Scotland. Although this I doubt. Now."

"Why now? I think John Graham would bring him back, if he would come. And there is still a Scots army at Watford."

"I doubt it because of what I found at Edinburgh. I went

181

there yesterday, as I do each month, to render a report on the property, Saltoun, to Lord Dumbarton at Edinburgh Castle, or to his lawyer. Yesterday I found Dumbarton gone and the lawyer, Archie Primrose, much upset. He believes him to have fled the country."

"Fled? The Commander-in-Chief!"

"He says that Dumbarton secretly took ship from Leith. A ship bound for Le Havre. Went hurriedly, leaving all behind, save his wife and some personal papers. Primrose does not know what to think, what to do, who to turn to. He says that his father, Archie's own father, Lord Carrington, the Lord Clerk Register, has had word that King James sailed for France on the last day of the year. But whether this is true or not, he does not know. So Dumbarton may have decided to go and join his master."

"Aye, indeed – who knows? There have been so many stories. And James is utterly unpredictable. But it may be so – for he could not remain at Rochester indefinitely. And William's patience must be running out. And if so, Henry, lad – it looks as though we might be getting Saltoun back!"

"I would not be too sure of that, Dand. For it is still a forfeited estate. If not Dumbarton's, then the government's. Which could be worse."

"Nevertheless, as matters are now, I think that James's men here would be doubtful about handing over Saltoun to another. And any such about accepting it. We shall see."

"What are you going to do meantime, Andrew? Till we do see?"

"I cannot remain hidden in your house here, like some skulking fugitive, frightened at being recognised – that is certain. No, I think that I shall go travelling again. But about Scotland, this time. Using another name. Seeking to test opinion, to discover how matters stand, to seek out friends and men I could work with. I have been out of my own country for six long years. I need to learn much, see much, clear my mind. So that when I send word to William, I may do so from knowledge, not hearsay."

"But ... not too soon, Andrew? Not for some time? You must stay awhile, here. Even though you have to lie low.

You will not hurry away from us now, when you are just home . . . ?"

"Scarcely home, lad. This is *your* house – and Margaret's – not mine. And it is a small house to be cooped up in. I am not going to get amongst your feet."

"What nonsense! Our home is yours. Indeed this house is your property, in truth, like all the rest of the estate. But that aside, we *want* you with us."

"Not all the time, Henry. Or *you* may. But I think that your wife would not."

"I swear that she does! Margaret loves you, Andrew. Always has done. I used to be almost jealous of you sometimes. She talked of you so much, feared for you, even called out your name in her sleep! Margaret would never wish you away."

Andrew swallowed. "You are good. Margaret too. But . . . I value your love and affection too much to endanger any of it, Henry. As I might well do by being overmuch amongst you, between you. A husband and wife need their . . . privacy. Besides, I cannot remain penned in the house like a stalled ox! Oh, I shall stay a day or two, never fear. But . . ." He looked sidelong at his brother. "Your marriage? It is . . . good? Happy? You, you suit each other?"

"Yes, oh yes. So very well. She is of all women the most wonderful! Adorable. And kind, kind."

"Kind?"

"Yes, kind. Beyond belief. I do not know what I would do without her. I am not like you, Andrew, a man who can work and fight and live alone. I require . . . support."

"Do not we all . . .?" his brother said.

13

Events rather overtook Andrew Fletcher's proposed programme. By the time that he arrived in Edinburgh, as Mr. Robertson from Strathearn, to put up at a modest hostelry in the Cowgate, at least some of the rumours had been confirmed. King James had indeed departed for France, but without abdicating first. However, as price for being allowed to do so unhindered, he had authorised Parliament to be recalled, the English Parliament. Many of his highly-placed supporters, if they had not already gone, were following him – which was leaving the field fairly clear for William. And Viscount Dundee and the rump of his Scots army was marching homewards.

All this was in England, to be sure. In Scotland the hiatus continued. Leadership, that winter, was indeed all but non-existent. There were no doubt strong men in the country somewhere; but they were biding their time; and time-serving was a matter for judicious assessment, none could deny. When Dundee and his soldiers came back, it might be different.

There was not total inaction. Andrew learned that a group of Scots nobles and one bishop had in fact left for London to urge William to accept the Scottish crown, on certain conditions – although, of course, they had no real authority to do so. The Prelate, Rose, Bishop of Edinburgh, was indeed under attack from his fellow-bishops for this move, for it seemed that the Episcopal Church – which was the official Scottish Church by royal edict – was more in favour of James than of William, who, being a strong Calvinist, could be expected to support and advance the Presbyterian faith. And since most of the nobility and gentry had found it expedient, during the last two decades, to be Catholic or Episcopalian, William's acceptance was by no means certain, even though the vast mass of the people, strongly Presbyterian since the Reformation, were for him.

All this, and more, Andrew learned as he moved about in the Scots capital, in the ale-houses, hostelries, markets and the like, in his guise as a grain, fodder and cattle-dealer from Strathearn. He knew a good deal about these commodities from his running of the Saltoun farms in the past, and so could sustain the image convincingly enough. He did, also, make his presence known secretly, to one or two friends whom he felt that he could trust – Sir David Carnegie, at Little's Close, Scott of Harden, Cockburn of Ormiston; but these he visited only after dark and after ascertaining that they had no other callers. Being mid-winter, most of the aristocracy were staying at their

Edinburgh town-houses rather than on their country estates.

Carnegie, of course, was the best-informed as to the political situation and seemed glad to see Andrew back, however urgent as to his warnings about taking care and doing nothing to draw attention to himself. According to him, although the government figures were indeed lying pretty low meantime, and with good reason, their minions, in their nervous state and left largely to their own devices, might do foolish, unpredictable things. Indeed, at the moment, Scotland was being governed, if that was the word, largely by these underlings, their betters and principals keeping well out of sight. In theory the Drummond brothers were ruling Scotland for King James, at the moment, James, Earl of Perth as Chancellor and John, Earl of Melfort as Secretary of State, both Catholics with a Gordon mother. Their cousin, now Duke of Gordon, formerly Marquis of Huntly, had been appointed Commander-in-Chief in the missing Dumbarton's place but he was not considered to be any formidable soldier. The Earl of Moray, another Catholic, was assistant Secretary of State. Sir George Mackenzie, the Lord Advocate, had fallen out with these gentry and resigned, to be succeeded, oddly enough, by none other than Sir James Dalrymple of Stair, he of the John Knox Confession of Faith, back from exile, and presumably having made himself acceptable again to the powers-that-were. So it was possible that William had at least one friend in the Scots government. But the real strong men of James's party were the two soldiers, John Graham and Colin Lindsay, Earl of Balcarres, second-in-command, both Privy Councillors and both out of the country but on their way home. When they arrived, with their troops, then would be the moment of decision. And it would not be long now, since they were reported to have reached Durham.

Andrew postponed his projected tour of the country for the time being, deciding that for the immediate future Edinburgh was the place to be. Meantime he sent a fairly lengthy report to Gilbert Burnet for onward transmission to the Prince of Orange.

In those two weeks of waiting he returned on two evenings to Saltoun and on one to Beil.

Strangely, it was at West Saltoun that he received the

important news that he, and all Scotland, awaited, on his third visit there, and not from Carnegie or other highly-placed source. Soon after his arrival, another visitor rode into the darkened dower-house yard – William Paterson, from Dumfries. And he was full of news; like money-men everywhere he appeared to have swift and accurate sources of information.

"Both Houses of Parliament in London have declared James abdicant, having broken the essential contract between monarch and people and abandoned the country," he announced. "They have offered the crown to Mary and William, with the effective rule in William's hands. And William has accepted and agreed to a Bill of Rights to limit the powers of the monarchy. He will be declared King and his wife Queen, when she reaches London, in some two weeks' time. Mid-February. So – the die is cast!"

"At last!" Henry cried. "Now we shall see some movement, some advance."

"But James himself? He has not abdicated? From either throne?" Andrew asked.

"No. Or if he has, there is no word of it from France."

"Then how lawful, how effective, is this pronouncement by the English Parliament. *Can* they force an abdication? If the monarch does not agree?"

"They must believe that they can. And they must have the best legal advice, surely?"

"Or choose to ignore it! I would doubt if they can do this. Abdications can be forced, yes – but I would judge that the instrument which makes it lawful, binding, would have to be signed by the monarch himself."

Paterson shrugged. "As to that I know not. But William must accept it as valid, since he is already calling himself King."

"William *desires* to accept it. But that does not make it lawful."

"You sound almost like one of *James*'s men!" Henry exclaimed. "One of these Jacobites, as they are calling themselves. You *fought* for William!"

"Worked for, scarcely fought. Though I was prepared to. I am not against William's accession. In England. Far from it. But if it is not lawful, there could be endless trouble.

186

And of course, it does not apply to Scotland, in any case."

"If William and Mary are King and Queen of England, both grand-children of Charles the First, then the chances are strong that they will become King and Queen of Scots also. Who else is there?"

"There are three choices, I suppose – even four. James could remain King, here. His infant son, the apparent heir, could be King in his place, with a Regent. Anne, his second daughter could be Queen of Scots, with her husband, Prince George of Denmark, Consort. And lastly, as a far cry perhaps, but possible – indeed it might appeal to many – there is Monmouth's son, the young Earl of Dalkeith. Monmouth assured me that he held his father's marriage-lines to Lucy Walters, his mother – a secret marriage, in Holland, but genuine enough, despite Charles's later denials. So young Dalkeith could be the true heir."

"Save us – I never heard of this!" Paterson exclaimed. "What a tale!"

"Nor I," Henry said. "Do you credit it, Andrew? This of a marriage?"

"Yes. Leastwise, I believe that *Monmouth* believed it. He told me in confidence. He did not seek to make anything of it, then – although he might have done had his invasion been successful. He did not show me the paper but said that he possessed it."

"But . . . Lord, this could change all! If it was known and accepted," Henry declared. "It turns all tapsalteerie! Where *is* this paper? These marriage-lines?"

"That I do not know. Monmouth may have carried it about with him. In which case it could have fallen into James's hands, when the Duke was executed – perhaps *why* he was executed! And would be destroyed, you may be sure. Or he may have left it with his wife, the Duchess of Buccleuch. Or it may still be in Holland."

"That document, if it exists, would be worth a fortune indeed!" the money-conscious Paterson asserted.

"Andrew," Margaret put in, "is it your intention to use this information? It could be dangerous, I think."

"I do not know. I have thought much on it, but cannot make

187

up my mind. Without the document itself, there is not a lot that could be done. Only an assertion and no proof. The *threat* of it might be useful – that is all. In the right quarters."

"I think you should be very careful about using it. Or any such threat," she said, earnestly. "You have sufficient enemies as it is. To offend James *and* William, and their supporters – as this would – could be the end of you!"

"Never fear, lass – I shall be discreet on this."

"What is the next move, then, if William has become King of England?" Henry wondered. "He may well consider that he is King of the United Kingdom also, may he not? And therefore of Scotland too."

"I left him in no doubts about that! Gilbert Burnet also will not let him believe so. Nor the Reverend Carstairs, who is another of his chaplains and whom he made minister of the English Presbyterian congregation at Leyden. He is a true Scot and as close to William as Gilbert is. No, I think William will not make that mistake, whatever others he may. Mr. Paterson – you mentioned a Bill of Rights which the English Parliament was insisting on, limiting the powers of the crown? Have you heard of the details?"

"No. Only that William had accepted it."

"This is hopeful, at least. He, of course, has been reared, not as an autocratic monarch, but as almost an Elector, as Stadtholder. So he is no believer in the divine right of kings. We, in Scotland, will have to make up our own Bill of Rights to present to him – a wonderful opportunity to improve the rule and governance of this nation. At last!"

"Do not be too sanguine, Andrew," Margaret warned. "Once William finds himself on the throne in London, he may take a different attitude than he did as Prince of Orange."

"But the Scots Estates of Parliament have the power to *make* him adhere. We must see that they do so."

"And you intend to see that they do!" Henry said.

"I do – if it is in my power."

"Then, whilst you are at it, Mr. Fletcher, see that the discrimination against Scots traders, in England and the colonies, is ended," Paterson added. "There are sore barriers, I have found, unfair and prejudicial. We have been a great
188

trading nation in the past. With France, the Low Countries, the Empire, even Muscovy. Much of that we have lost, because of English jealousy and wars. We can get it back. And better, trade more widely still. With the Americas. When I was there, in the Carolinas, in the lands of the Caribs, in Darien and Yucatan, I learned how vast are the riches waiting to be picked up by men with courage and foresight. I tell you, there is a whole new world waiting . . ."

"Ah, yes, Mr. Paterson – tell us of your exploits and experiences in the Americas," Margaret urged, clearly anxious to get away from the dangerous subject of politics. "Andrew says that you had most exciting adventures."

Nothing loth, William Paterson launched forth.

* * *

It was a month later that they had another significant visitor at West Saltoun, even more unexpected than William Paterson – and again Andrew was there, for Edinburgh, indeed all South Scotland, was in a turmoil and the city was a good place for such as Andrew Fletcher to avoid meantime. The Scots army was home, and James's supporters had taken new heart and crept out of their holes, to resume overtly the reins of power. The name of the Lord Viscount of Dundee was, of a sudden, on everyone's lips; for it seemed that, before fleeing to France, King James had appointed Graham to be his right hand in Scotland, not exactly Lord High Commissioner, since he had called no parliament, more like a viceroy, with command over both military and civil power. So Bloody Clavers was, for the moment, uncrowned king; and he was not the man to falter or to hide his light under any bushel. It was the turn of William's supporters to go to ground, especially in the capital, with the returned army encamped in the park of Holyroodhouse, below Arthur's Seat, and more or less at liberty to hold the city to ransom.

Which made it all the more surprising that the visitor to West Saltoun that evening of early March was none other than John Graham himself, alone save for a single trooper as groom. And, like Andrew, he did his visiting under cover of darkness, even though it was ostensibly to see his Cousin Margaret.

After a somewhat restrained welcome and a purely formal congratulation on his viscountcy, he lost no time in asking for speech with Andrew, declaring that he knew very well that he was at Saltoun and that what he had to say to him was important and could be much to that man's advantage.

So Andrew was brought from the back-quarters, to eye the newcomer warily however affably he was greeted.

"The returned prodigal himself!" Graham exclaimed, smiling. "Only, in reverse, as it were, no? The loser, with all the powers and opportunities to be the winner!"

"From yourself, my lord, I take that as a compliment!"

"Take it as you like, man – so long as you also take my offer and advice. Which I have come here to give you."

"I cannot think that that is likely. We choose different paths, you and I."

"Aye – but you it is who has always chosen the wrong paths. As witness your present state. Why be always the loser? The betrayed, the man cast off?"

"Better than being the betrayer, at least! And who has cast me off now?"

"You ask that? Surely even you . . . !" Graham paused. "But perhaps a little privacy might be advisable?"

"There is nothing that you could say to me that I would not wish my brother and my good-sister to hear."

"Very well. Perhaps, indeed, they will be a good influence! Help me to instil some sense and judgment into that stiff-necked, unyielding head of yours! May I sit, Cousin . . . ?"

Wine set before them, Graham returned to his theme, addressing Margaret this time. "I have come here, at some inconvenience and risk to my name and repute, to try to help this stubborn good-brother of yours, Meg. God knows why – save that I have always had some sort of liking for him, a recognition that, whatever else he is, he is honest! And able, of course – if he would but employ his wits in the right directions! One of the most able men in Scotland – or could be . . ."

"The point of this homily, my lord?" Andrew interrupted.

"Oh, do not be so confoundedly awkward, man! You have been proved wrong and have been let down. I come to offer

190

you a way out, a saving of your position. I can save you – and *only* I can, I think."

"I was not aware that I required the saving. At least, not at your hands."

"Oh, hear him at least, Andrew!" Margaret exclaimed.

'You require saving, yes," the other nodded grimly. "You have fallen between two horses. Both are liable to kick you! I can lift you into the saddle again."

"Stop talking in riddles, of a mercy! You say that I am let down and betrayed. By whom?"

"Lord save us – do you really not know? By William, of course. William has cast you off. Why, I do not know – save that you no doubt have been as awkward and difficult with him as with everyone else!"

"In what way has William cast me off? It is the first I have heard of it."

"He is displeased with you. He is well-served with spies – as, it happens, so am I! You seem to have offended. No doubt in seeking to limit his powers as monarch. So – you are to suffer for it. He will not lift the forfeiture on this Saltoun estate. He has declared it. Mind, he has no right to do so, anyway, since he is not King here. But that is scarce the point."

"What! Not . . . not . . .?"

"No. Not. William has said so. He is not King of Scots but assumes that he is. And he has lifted the forfeiture of the others who have supported him – Polwarth, Jerviswood, Ochiltree, Melville, all young Argyll's lands. But not Saltoun. Only Saltoun is excepted. You are still outlaw, Andrew – forfeited by both James and William! The price of speaking your too honest mind to princes!"

Affronted the other three eyed each other.

"Andrew! After all that you have done for him, for William!" Henry cried. "I cannot believe this . . ."

"It is true," Graham assured. "Have you not seen Home? He is back at Polwarth. And Cochrane, my odd good-brother, back at Ochiltree. In possession again – or thinking that they are. We shall see about that! But not you, my friend – not you!"

"How do you know this?"

"I make a point of having my informants, close to William. Recollect, I once saved his life!"

"Gilbert Burnet would have sent me word."

"Burnet is no longer in William's close company. There has been disagreement there also. Burnet has left Whitehall to become Bishop of Salisbury. That beauty, the cardinal, the Reverend Carstairs, is now William's closest adviser on Scottish affairs. He does not love you, I think?"

There was silence for a little as his hearers digested all that.

"So we come to my offer," Graham resumed. "James is still King of Scots, whatever the situation in England. You, Andrew, in the past have advocated that the kingdoms might be separated again. Now it seems they will become so. *I* am James's representative here meantime. Some time ago he issued an Edict of Indulgence towards Scotland. Admittedly it was intended to permit *Roman Catholics* to be freed from all restraints and forfeitures and to hold office again in the realm. But it nowhere states *only* Catholics. Indeed even some of those damnable Covenanters have made use of this Indulgence to have their penalties lifted, on promise of better behaviour. In the King's name, my friend, I can extend the Indulgence edict to yourself, lift the forfeiture and make you Lord of Saltoun again!"

As the others drew quick breaths, Andrew spoke levelly. "At a price?"

"No costly price. Indeed no more than your simple duty. Be a loyal subject of your undoubted liege-lord the King of Scots, and no longer a thorn in James's flesh. That is all."

"All! You ask me to forswear my dearest principles, all that I have stood for – and call it no costly price? James Stewart is a tyrant, a fanatic Papist and unfit to rule this kingdom, his hands stained with blood – much of which *you* have shed for him! Not for a score of Saltouns would I give him my support."

The other controlled himself only by an obvious effort. "Watch your fool tongue, Fletcher!" he grated. "It could lose you your head! Do not presume on my patience and good will."

"It was neither patience nor goodwill which brought you here tonight, I think, my lord. But need. Political need. You

192

find few Scots – Lowland Scots, at least – prepared to support Catholic James against Protestant William. So you turn to such as myself, whom you think to buy! Had you found Edinburgh in Jacobite mood, I swear that you would not be here now. And *I* might well be in the cells of Edinburgh Castle! No – I am not for sale, for my own estate or other."

They stared at each other, two determined men fated to opposition.

"Think well," the elder said, slowly. "This could be your last chance. You have not William behind you now. Your are alone, man – with many enemies. And I am *not* seeking to buy you. This Indulgence could apply to you lawfully."

"Not in my eyes. It was an arbitrary edict of King James. Issued for his own purposes, without the consent or even knowledge of parliament. Only parliament can lawfully change the law. I could not take advantage of such edict."

"What if *William* had remitted your forfeiture, then? As he has done these others?"

"It would still not have been lawful until it was confirmed by the Scots Estates of Parliament."

"Damnation, man – is there no reasoning with you! No reaching the wits you have buried inside that obdurate head of yours?"

"A while ago you told Margaret that I was honest. I fear that you will just have to accept the fact – even if *you* esteem it stupidity!"

The Viscount of Dundee pushed back his chair. "Then I have wasted my time, coming here. And I meant well by you, Andrew Fletcher . . ."

14

The very next day, judging that the sooner he was away from Saltoun the better, in the circumstances, Andrew rode southwards through the Lammermuir Hills and into the Merse, to

Polwarth-on-the-Green, to consult with Sir Patrick Home. At Redbraes Castle there, the Home seat, he found not only his friend back in residence but the son and heir of another former friend, George Baillie of Jerviswood who, whilst all were exiles in Holland, had married Grizel Home – the same who had brought her father sustenance by night to the underground crypt below Polwarth Kirk, six years ago.

Patrick Home confirmed much that John Graham had said – although his interpretations and reactions tended to be different. He was much troubled that Andrew had been singled out so notably for William's disfavour, and had assumed that he must most grievously have offended. The victim's assertions that he had only emphasised to the Prince the traditional limitations of Scottish kingship and the need for co-operation with parliament and people, set Home's head ashaking. Apparently William had become increasingly touchy on this subject of limitations of power, since the Bill of Rights had been forced on him by the English parliamentarians as price of his accession to that throne. Indeed this was the reason for Gilbert Burnet's fall from favour also, in that he had argued for the Claim of Rights and assured William that conquest, however successful, was no substitute for parliamentary authority in either kingdom. So now he was removed from Court to Salisbury, as Bishop thereof. William, in the end, had had to agree to the English Bill of Rights, if with ill grace, his Queen most strongly against it. So it was probable that he was determined that the same sort of trouble should not develop in Scotland, and looked upon Andrew as a likely leader in such demands. The delaying of remission of forfeiture was no doubt just some sort of warning in the matter, a hint not to muddy the water.

Andrew felt that it was something heavy-handed for a hint – the more so when, a little later, Home asked him if he had received his letter regarding the forthcoming Convention. On enquiry what this might be, the younger man was informed that, in response to the party which had gone down to offer William the Scots crown, the new English monarch had desired to call a Scots Parliament to ratify the proposal. It was pointed out, however, that only the appointed King of Scots could call an actual Parliament; and since William was not that until the

194

said Parliament itself confirmed the matter, the only procedure available was for him to call something less, namely a Convention of the Estates, which would then officially make the offer. To this, perforce, William had had to agree. But since he was in a hurry, and said that he could by no means spare the time to call the usual elections, which required forty days' notice, he had sent out a circular letter to all former members of the Estates, lords, bishops, commissioners of the shires and burgh representatives, summoning them to a Convention in Edinburgh at the end of the month. He, Home, had had his letter for ten days. As, he knew, had Cockburn of Ormiston.

"Damnation – no letter has come for me! To Saltoun," Andrew exclaimed. "Can it be . . . could he be so devilish mean as to do this? To debar me from taking, or at least standing for, my seat? Surely not?"

The other looked unhappy. "I suppose . . . if you are still forfeited, a condemned man, then, then you are still outlaw, in name. And so, and so ineligible to sit in Convention or Parliament."

"Lord God!" Andrew swore, hotly. "Preserve us from princes! This is beyond all!"

"Perhaps the letter has gone amissing? The courier could not find you . . . ?"

"He would come to Saltoun, would he not? No, the only one who has come to Saltoun is Claverhouse. *He* did not speak of this Convention."

"Perhaps he did not know."

"He is well-informed, that one. He would know. He assured me that William had cast me off, and tried to win me over to James. He believes that James's cause, in Scotland, is by no means lost."

"Does he know that there is an English and Dutch army marching north to ensure that it *is* lost?"

"There is? He said nothing of that. Yet – surely it is something that he would know, if it is true?"

"It is true enough. George Baillie passed them on his way home. Under General Hugh Mackay of Scourie. You remember him, in Holland?"

"Yes – a stern, grey man. Is he a good enough general to fight Graham who, whatever else, is a notable soldier?"

"That I do not know. But the word from Edinburgh is that Graham's troops – I suppose that we must call him Dundee now? – that his army is deserting fast. They are largely Hielantmen, apart from his dragoons, and have been away from their homes for too long. They marched south in October. Now, idle in Edinburgh and cursed by the townsfolk, they are heading back for their glens by the hundred. James, you see – and therefore Dundee – has no money to pay them now . . ."

"I see. So – Graham is less strongly-placed that he would have had me to think. Which makes his coming to Saltoun yesterday the more interesting! When is this Convention to be?"

"The letter said at the earliest possible. By the end of the month. But that is scarcely practicable. Duke Hamilton is coming up to preside over it. He cannot be High Commissioner, since such can be appointed only by the King of Scots. He may be in Scotland now – I do not know. But William wants no time wasted, so it could be any time now. I am ready to go at a day's notice."

"Aye – then it is time that I returned to Edinburgh, I think. Even if I am not to be a commissioner for Haddingtonshire, there may be something that I can do . . ."

So Andrew rode north again next day, by the coast-road this time, by Dunbar, to Beil. There Johnnie Belhaven confirmed most of what Home had said, and could add more. His chief, the Duke of Hamilton, *had* arrived in Edinburgh and had summoned the chief Williamite supporters to meet him there the very next day, himself included, at Holyroodhouse, to plan their strategy for the Convention, and to fix a date. That affair was going to be a trial of strength indeed, for James – or at least Dundee, who was acting in his name – had also called for a Convention and would no doubt seek to dominate and constrain it in James's favour. The tale was that he had first intended it to be a full Parliament – since James could lawfully still call one – but had decided against this in case the decisions went against him, and so could claim that they did not carry all weight and authority. No doubt, if he found matters going his way, or James's, he would have the final sessions declared a Parliament indeed.

Johnnie was highly indignant to hear that Andrew had been excepted from the lifting of forfeitures and so would be ineligible for calling as a commissioner. He declared that it made him doubtful as to whether William was worth supporting – save in that he could not be so bad as James. He confirmed that he had his own circular letter, from William, to attend, as a Lord of Parliament; and that Cockburn of Ormiston had been summoned as a shire commissioner. So Andrew's exclusion was the more painfully deliberate.

At least Johnnie had a suggestion to make. Andrew should accompany him to Edinburgh next day. He could ride in the guise of a servant, if need be. And he would insinuate him into Hamilton's meeting at Holyroodhouse, where they would see what could be done.

Andrew was somewhat doubtful as to this last, for his very brief relationship with the Duke of Hamilton all those years ago had hardly been of the happiest. But they would see . . .

*　*　*

It seemed strange, after all his furtive lurking and hiding, to be entering the royal palace of Edinburgh openly, even though Andrew did so as groom and bodyguard to the Lord Belhaven and Stenton. After Johnnie dismounted at the impressive front entrance, Andrew led the horses round to the stableyard-court at the back, to enter the august premises by a rear door, where he discarded his steel-bonnet, heavy sword and liveried cloak and, respectably-dressed beneath, went through to join his friend in the Duke's quarters. Even so there were a lot of suspicious glances cast, both at front and rear, and not confined to Andrew Fletcher. For, at this juncture, Holyroodhouse was also the residence of the Lord Viscount Dundee, the King of Scots' representative, who was occupying the royal apartments, with his lieutenants and staff; and all visitors had had, as it were, to run the gauntlet of inspection by Graham's officers before gaining access – indeed they had had to ride through the rump of the army encamped in the park around. The Duke of Hamilton was Hereditary Keeper of the palace and so had his private wing of the great rambling establishment as his Edinburgh town-house; and Graham could scarcely keep him out, since Hamilton had never actually come to blows with James, and his high rank had always ensured him some sort of links with the royal Court at London. And he was, after all, almost a member of the royal family, the Hamiltons having intermarried with the Stewarts on more than one occasion.

Andrew had realised that his arrival at the Duke's meeting might not altogether please that haughty individual; but he was unprepared for the stir created by his appearance amongst the company at large. To only one or two of those present had he revealed his return to Scotland hitherto, secretly; some others undoubtedly would know of it. But to most there – and some thirty men were in the handsome panelled chamber – his entry came as a major surprise. The majority knew him, to be sure, many in a friendly enough way, others less so; but all, certainly, had heard of him. The fact was, of course, that he did not realise just how celebrated a figure he had become since he left his native land, his adventures, exploits, troubles and links with both Monmouth and William of Orange, all apt for note, discussion and undoubted exaggeration. That he was a condemned murderer and renowned slayer of Turks, allegedly, may have contributed to the interest. There was, accordingly, a nudging and exclamation. Then a loud and authoritative throat-clearing from the fireside vicinity produced an anticipatory hush.

"Belhaven, is that yourself?" Hamilton called, without any noticeable warmth. "And in unlooked-for company, I see!"

"Yes, my lord Duke – and most valuable company!" Johnnie gave back, boldly. "I consider myself highly privileged to be able to bring Mr. Fletcher here. To our much advantage, I am sure." He stumbled a little over that assertion, well rehearsed as it had been.

Andrew bowed, briefly, but said nothing.

Hamilton frowned and tapped a toe on the carpet, seemingly undecided as to what line to take – which was unusual in that man, at least in public. He appeared to have aged considerably since Andrew had last seen him, now in his fifty-fifth year, grown thick, florid and heavy-jowled; but his former assumption of superiority gave no impression of having faded. All awaited his reaction.

"Mr. Fletcher hazards himself in coming here," he said, at length. "No doubt he has his reasons for so doing? Likewise yourself, my lord!" Having delivered himself of this suspended judgment, the Duke turned to resume his converse with those standing near.

If this scarcely amounted to the warmest of welcomes, at least it was not total rejection and dismissal. Even so, Andrew's temper boiled up; but Johnnie's grip on his friend's arm was firm, almost urgent. Whether this would have been sufficient to overcome the latter's conviction that he would be infinitely better elsewhere is doubtful; but reinforcement was at hand. A handsomely saturnine-featured individual from the hearthside group came forward, hand outstretched.

"Ha – Saltoun! How very good to see you again!" he said smoothly. It was Sir James Dalrymple of Stair, Lord President of the Court of Session, chief justiciar of Scotland, now in his seventieth year, although he by no means looked it.

If this development caused surprise, it was not least in Andrew himself. In the first place he had not expected to see Dalrymple in this company. That wily lawyer had played an equivocal part indeed on the political scene. He had been strongly anti-Covenanter and pro-Charles, a trusted colleague of Lauderdale's. Then he had astonished all by his famous volte-face against James Stewart, at the 1681 Parliament, when he upset the government's plans by his trick of getting the Test Act as good as nullified by having incorporated in its wording the wrong Confession of Faith. This had resulted in his having to leave the country for a while and his turning up at William's Court at The Hague – where Andrew had last seen him. But since then he had returned to Scotland, and evidently James's favour, for he was received back into government, first as Lord Advocate and then promoted to Lord President. Now here he was at this gathering of William's supporters, and making himself conspicuous by being first to greet the outlaw whom it was surely the chief law-lord's duty to have apprehended and executed for treason. Moreover, he had called Andrew Saltoun, the lairdly title which was, of course, forfeited with the estate.

199

Andrew shook hands warily. He did not trust Stair a yard, but recognised his astuteness and nose keen to sniff the winds of change; therefore the possible advantages for himself of this greeting.

"I heard that you were back and amongst us," Stair said, pleasantly. "Scotland is the better off, I am sure. Where have you been hiding yourself, friend?"

"Here and there, my Lord President – here and there. You, now, have not *required* to hide yourself, I perceive!"

"That is so. But I am no plotter, sir. A simple man – and the soul of discretion, to be sure! I serve my country as best I may."

"As do we all," a new voice added. It was John Hay, eighth Lord Hay of Yester and second Earl of Tweeddale, a near neighbour of Andrew's, at Gifford. "How good to see you, after so long, Andrew. We have missed you."

How greatly Tweeddale had missed him was a matter for question. He was another who had kept his position and estates by carefully trimming his sails to the winds that blew – which perhaps was indeed the sensible course in such difficult times, for clearly the great majority of the nobility of Scotland had so elected. Related to the Duchess of Buccleuch and Monmouth, yet a supporter of Episcopalian Charles, he had still managed to be a Lord Commissioner of the Treasury under Catholic James as well as an Extraordinary Lord of Session. That he was here at Hamilton's pro-William meeting, like Dalrymple, would seem to indicate which way the tide was flowing in Scotland.

Thus led, others came to greet the returned wanderer, headed by Robert Kerr, Earl of Lothian, Tweeddale's cousin. And perceiving it, Hamilton found it expedient to modify his attitude somewhat and at the same time reassert his authority.

"Fletcher," he summoned, "we are discussing the Convention. Its form and procedures. I understand that we are not to have the benefit of your attendance!"

"So I am informed, my lord Duke." Andrew moved nearer to the fire, to avoid having to shout. "But – perhaps there is time to rectify that matter? A fast courier to King William in London urging reconsideration?"

"Insufficient time, sir. His Majesty requires the Convention to start at the soonest. I am calling it for five days hence. Besides, King William is unlikely to change his mind on this matter, I think." That was pointedly said.

"I wonder who advised him to it?" If that was less coldly enunciated, it was equally pointed.

The Duke shrugged. "His Majesty knows his own mind. And no doubt has his good reasons."

"Then I say that it is a shame and a scandal!" Johnnie Belhaven burst out. "Andrew Fletcher has served him well. Better and more closely, I swear, than any other in this room! Yet he only is singled out for exclusion. You, my lords and friends – have any of you ever lifted a hand for William's cause, much less drawn sword? As have not I. Andrew ventured his life for William. Was a colonel of horse in his army. Yet *we* are all called to this vital Convention and he is excluded. His estate still forfeit. Why?"

There was an uncomfortable silence.

"His Majesty knows his own business best," Hamilton said at length.

"Is it his own business? I say that it is Scotland's business!"

"My lord of Belhaven should watch his words!" the Duke said sternly. "The King's business *is* Scotland's business. And Scotland's the King's. There are sufficient enemies of His Majesty hereabouts, some in this very building, without aiding them by foolish and unconsidered talk!"

"Are you not prejudging the issue, my lord Duke?" Andrew asked quietly. "Scotland's business is not *yet* King William's business. The Estates of Parliament may make it so, but have not yet done so. You refer to William as His Majesty, and rightly. But he is not yet His *Grace*, the King of Scots, I would remind all present."

Again the uneasy hush as men eyed each other.

"That is what we are here to ensure – that he does become King of Scots," Hamilton declared, frowning. "As is his right."

"Tell King William, then, from me, that he has not as good right to this crown as I have to my estate of Saltoun!"

201

Andrew averred. "Can any deny it?" And when none answered him, he went on, "*This* is why William has acted against me. Because I told him the truth. That only the Estates of Parliament could make him King of Scots. And that the Estates would require his promised adherence to the rights and freedoms of the Scottish people, so vilely trampled on by the last two monarchs, before they offered him the throne. William did not like that – and I say that we should be warned that he did not! He is a sound man, strong, a fine soldier and a good Protestant. He *could* make an excellent king, I think – so long as he understands the limits of his kingship. That he has acted as he has done, shows that there is a danger that he does not, a danger for Scotland."

There was considerable stir and exclamation at that, some in agreement, some not. Hamilton could be heard declaring that it was entirely obvious why King William had decided to teach this insolent young man a lesson. The Convention undoubtedly would go a deal more smoothly without him.

It was Lord President Dalrymple who countered that. "This Convention will not go smoothly whether Mr. Fletcher is there or no. Claverhouse will see to that! Do not underestimate him. Nor the strength of his support. William will require every vote that can be mustered. There may well be many who think as Saltoun does. We shall require their votes."

That, from so able and experienced a politician, had a sobering effect. Even the Duke looked a little concerned.

"You believe that Graham can look for much support for James, at this stage?" he demanded. "Is he not totally discredited? Your own presence here, my lord President, would so imply!" That was barbed.

"My presence here, my lord Duke, represents much consideration and judgment – as befits my office! I have come to the conclusion that William would be less harmful a monarch for Scotland than James. Also, I hold it important that the Union of the Crowns be preserved – wherein I may differ from Mr. Fletcher?"

"All men of any judgment support the Union, sir. Therefore few, surely, can support James now, since with William King in England, James as King of Scots *must* break the Union."

"Obviously. So I am here. But not all are enamoured with the said Union, I fear. And others are afraid of William. Many who favour episcopacy would prefer James. Even in England the Archbishop of Canterbury himself, and other bishops – five of them even of the seven whom James committed to the Tower – have refused to take the oath of allegiance to William. Many lords also. They fear that, as a strong Calvinist, he could bring down their faith. And the Catholics, to be sure, will support James – and the Highlands are largely Catholic. So the Jacobites may muster more votes than you think."

"I say that you are excessively fearful, sir."

"Perhaps. But why, then, are James and Dundee so confident, as to themselves call this Convention also? If they feared that it would go against them, would they not rather have shunned it, declared it null since not called by the present King of Scots? Instead, they boast that they will carry the day. I advise your lordships against over-confidence. I think that we may better them – but it may be a close thing."

"We might ensure that certain of James's supporters are not *there*, to cast their votes!" the Earl of Lothian suggested, to a murmur of agreement.

"You are not proposing to use force, my lord?" Stair asked.

"Shall we say . . . persuasion, sir?"

"It would not be for the first time!" Tweeddale observed, grinning.

Hamilton looked thoughtful but did not speak.

Andrew raised his voice. "I would remind all that if it came to using force, violence, the new Lord Viscount of Dundee would be apt to be more successful at it than anyone here! John Graham is a master in such matters. And he has the means and the men, to hand. We need only look out of these windows! I would strongly counsel against any recourse to force."

"That from the slayer of Monmouth's paymaster and sundry others!" somebody commented.

A hot retort sprang to Andrew's lips but he swallowed it. "We are, at this Convention, concerned with the better government of this kingdom, with the rule of law as against tyranny," he asserted. "We must have a great opportunity, such as never before, to ensure that our kings hereafter do not misrule and tyrannise over us. All should be devoted to that end. To ourselves resort to force and lawlessness would ruin all. Would play into Dundee's hands."

"Dundee's hands will be full enough when Mackay's army arrives," Hamilton said.

"And when may that be?" Dalrymple asked. "They march but slowly, I am told. The last news I had, they had not reached York. At such pace they cannot be here for two weeks, even if unopposed."

None could gainsay that. Discussion broke out all over the room.

Sir David Carnegie had arrived. He learned that Andrew proposed to leave right away, seeing no advantage to be gained by staying, since Hamilton clearly would not do anything to improve his state. Johnnie explained the situation. Carnegie urged the younger men to wait at least a little while, until he had had a word with the Duke. Even though that man would not advise William to change his attitude – and there was no time for that to be arranged anyway – he might be persuaded to allow Andrew to sit in on the Convention proceedings as a spectator; which would surely be better than nothing?

"Tell him that if he does not agree, I might apply to John Graham for permission!"

When Carnegie came back it was to announce that the Duke had reluctantly acceded. Evidently Sir David had some influence with that stiff-necked individual. But acceded only on the clearest understanding that Fletcher would on no account utter a word or seek in any way to influence the assembly. At the least hint of any such misbehaviour he would be ejected. Margaret's father added that he had personally given his assurance that there would be nothing of that sort.

With this Andrew had to be, if not content, at least acquiescent. He and Johnnie took their leave.

* * *

Parliament Hall, behind St. Giles, had seen dramatic occasions innumerable, witnessed clash and challenge again and again. But seldom, surely, could the atmosphere have been more tense, charged with a partisanship so vehement and clear-cut, as on this blustery day of March 1689. The assembly, of course, was only reflecting the feelings and excitement of the city outside, of the country at large – or the southern half of it at least, for the Highlands were a law unto themselves. Scotland found itself faced with a momentous choice, which all recognised could greatly affect the lives of every citizen, great and small, for possibly ages to come – William or James, a united crown with England or separate again, Presbyterian – Calvinist even – Episcopalian or Romish, the rule of parliaments or autocracy, the ancient dynasty or a new one. All these and much else fell to be decided – with the vivid recognition that civil war might well result whichever side won, the city already in a state bordering on sword-rule.

In an inconspicuous corner, not where Henry and Margaret had sat on a previous occasion, Andrew Fletcher watched and waited, as keyed-up as anyone there but with the added frustration of having no least part to play in the drama about which he felt so deeply. It was strange to be back in that hall, in any case, after all these years, and so much more experienced a man – wiser, also, he hoped – without being muzzled into the bargain. The strangeness, admittedly, would be shared in some measure by all; for this was the first Convention or Parliament for almost four years, James having insisted on ruling without the aid of the Estates. So to some extent all was abnormal, unprecedented, the numbers attending much reduced from the usual, with many gaps caused by death in the interim and no new elections having been held. The Lords of Parliament, therefore, who sat by hereditary right, much outnumbered the representative commissioners, although the burghs, which appointed their own members from the merchant and craft guilds, were well enough represented – this Andrew being glad to see, for the ordinary folk were more likely to support Calvinist William than were the landed gentry.

The procedure was different, too, most of the pomp and parade dispensed with, since there was no authority accepted by all, therefore no procession through the streets, no fanfares. But at least neither was there any undue delay about getting started. The bells of St. Giles had just finished booming out the hour of noon when the doors were thrown open left and right at the head of the hall, and two men strode in from each side, Hamilton and Dalrymple from the left, Sir George Mackenzie, the Lord Advocate and the tall, slightly-stooping figure of the Marquis of Atholl, on the right.

This produced the first murmur of surprise. John Murray of Atholl was not the man most would have expected to see in such position, from the verge of the Highlands, hitherto not prominent in politics and governmental affairs and indeed thought to be somewhat uncertain in his loyalties. Presumably, then, he had plumped for James. But in what station?

Whilst the hum of conjecture was still strong and these four came forward to the Chancellor's table, to stare at each other from either end, another couple issued from the right-side doorway – Dundee and the Bishop of Edinburgh. These paced in, to place themselves *behind* the said table, facing the assembly and between the other pairs. Dundee was very fine, in the scarlet of a general, with feathered cavalier hat, the Bishop in full canonicals. It all looked impressive and as though well-rehearsed and accepted, compared with the obvious tension in the hall at large.

Dundee raised his hand for silence – and achieved it quickly. "In the name of James, by God's grace undoubted King of Scots, I call upon my lord Bishop of Edinburgh to beseech God's blessing upon our deliberations and His guidance upon our decisions," he announced crisply.

There was another stir at that so early throwing down of the gauntlet.

Bishop Rose raised his sonorous voice in fervent prayer. Sadly, the fervour was not reflected by a major proportion of his fellow-worshippers – not so much because he was only one of the despised Episcopalians but because very little of his prayer was concerned with the forthcoming deliberations, almost all with James Stewart, whose health, welfare and support he sought from the Almighty, whose royal grace and dignity he praised and whose restoration to fullest power and prerogative in both his kingdoms he urgently implored. What other petitions he might have intended to present were lost in uproar.

When it was clear that worship was no longer the main

preoccupation, Dundee raised hand again. But this time he did not gain the desired silence. The noisy protesting grew louder if anything, especially from the ranks of the burgh representatives.

When actual scuffling broke out in the hall between protesters and Jacobites, the platform-party, however opposed their views, quite quickly became as one in their recognition of the need for order and acceptable behaviour, Hamilton in especial very evidently deploring unseemly noise, particularly on the part of the lower orders. He too held up his hand, and when that produced no results, thumped on the Chancellor's table and turned to Dalrymple.

Oddly enough, that elderly lawyer succeeded where his betters had failed. Perhaps it was that he was robed in the full majesty of the law, in great white wig and scarlet, fur-trimmed gown, as chief justiciar of the realm, overawed the burgh members – most of whom, of course, were provosts, bailies and magistrates in a small way. At any rate, quiet returned.

Dalrymple did not yield place to Dundee now. He spoke up. "My lords and commissioners, I greet you. And remind all of the dignity and honourable fame of this ancient Convention of the Estates of our realm and the duty upon us all to conduct our affairs in suitable order." A significant pause. "In the absence of a Lord High Commissioner and of the Lord Chancellor, even of the Secretary of State, I conceive it to be my own duty, as Lord President of Session, duly to convene this assembly as a Convention of Parliament."

The Catholic Chancellor, the Earl of Perth, after being chased by an Edinburgh mob, had fled to Stirling, thinking that the Keeper of that royal castle, the Earl of Mar, would afford him refuge. Mar's refuge proved to be a dungeon in the said castle, where the chief minister of the crown had languished. As for the Secretary of State, Perth's brother, the new Earl of Melfort, he had been more successful in his flight and was now safely in France. Hence the gap in the authority.

A mixture of cheers and groans greeted Dalrymple's assertion. His companions on the platform were trying hard to assess the relative strengths of the one side as against the other, not so much in noise as in numbers.

Stair went on. "Lacking the Chancellor, it will be necessary for a suitable and respected personage to preside over our deliberations. Who could be more suitable than the premier nobleman of this realm, my lord Duke of Hamilton? I so propose, for the agreement of this assembly."

More noise, into which Dundee had to shout.

"Lord President Dalrymple's proposals are interesting but beside the point! *I* represent King James of Scotland here; and the King, when not present, appoints the Chancellor or his deputy. I am a soldier and no presider at debates. In King James's name I appoint the Marquis of Atholl as Chancellor Depute."

Uproar and shouts of Vote! Vote!

The leadership of each side was not yet quite ready to put the matter to the test of a vote, none having been able quite to calculate how such a vital vote would go. It was Sir George Mackenzie, the Lord Advocate, almost as astute a lawyer as Dalrymple, even if the other had bested him that time over the Test Act oath, who intervened to gain time.

"His Grace the King has sent a message to this Convention," he announced. "Surely this ought to be heard before we go any further? Do you wish to read it, or shall I, my lord of Dundee?"

"King William has also sent a letter. By myself," Hamilton declared, his first remark thus far. "I insist that it be read before James Stewart's."

"That would be quite improper, my lord Duke," Mackenzie asserted. "Dutch William may be King of England but he is not yet King of Scots. James is."

"Let him read it first, if so he desires – the result will be the same!" Dundee said, shrugging – to the surprise of many, not least Andrew Fletcher.

Hamilton took it as his right, produced the letter, and holding it this way and that, as though the writing was not of the best, began to read. He was not a very good reader and sounded bored from the start, so that the thing scarcely gripped the company. Yet it was a fair enough message, reasonable and moderate. William greeted all Scots subjects warmly, asserted that his dearest aspiration was to make them a just, fair and merciful monarch, promised to secure the Protestant religion and the ancient laws and liberties of the kingdom and emphasised that a union of the two realms of Scotland and England was the best means for procuring the happiness and welfare of both. He commended all who heard to God's good keeping and prayed that His wisdom might inform their proceedings. If it all rather seemed to lack the fire and challenge which the occasion warranted, perhaps that was the fault of the reader.

The Williamites now could not object to James's communication being heard likewise. Dundee indicated that Mackenzie should read it. The Lord Advocate, of course, was eloquent and a skilled reader and pleader, with a musically sibilant Highland voice. He did his best. But nothing would make that royal message anything other than it was, the dogmatic, unyielding pronouncement of a man utterly convinced that he was God's deputy, undoubted ruler by divine right, and that no question arose or could arise as to his authority as King of Scots. He announced that he expected all loyal and faithful subjects to condemn the base example of disloyal men, and emphasised the dangers which they must needs undergo if they failed to do so; and the infamy and disgrace that they would thereby bring upon themselves in this world, and the condemnation due to the rebellious in the next. He commended all loyal subjects, assured them that his help was at hand, and promised indemnity to the mistaken and disloyal who had the good sense to declare for him by the end of this month at the latest. For all others, the direst of penalties.

Andrew, listening and watching, was as astonished as most others at the blind, arrogant assurance of this man who had failed so utterly and yet continued to act the victor, who appeared to have learned nothing by his misfortunes. Eyeing John Graham, as Mackenzie read, he was sure that he detected an unease in that normally confident-seeming character. *He*, almost certainly, would have preferred to have left that letter unread.

The company sat silent, thereafter, for moments on end. Then an almost animal-like growling began and grew, containing its own threat and menace. As that growling became more like a sustained snarl, Dundee beat on the table with his fist.

"For your further information," he cried, "hear this. I have just had word that King James has landed in Ireland, at Kinsale, with 15,000 French troops lent by King Louis. With more to follow. Everywhere the Irish are rising in his support and are throwing out Dutch William's friends. Soon all Ireland will be his. He has called on the old Irish Parliament to meet. Then – he will come to Scotland! Give him a month or six weeks, he says . . . !"

After that bombshell and the tone of James's message, William's moderate letter, however fair in comparison, seemed the less impressive or inspiring. And there seemed to be nobody prominent on William's side, just then, capable of producing the required fire and inspiration. The one man who might have done it, possibly, was sitting quietly in an obscure corner, having had to promise not to open his mouth.

"I invite the Marquis of Atholl now to assume the Chancellor's chair," Dundee went on, after a pause, grimly.

"No!" That was Hamilton, the reverse of fiery, cold, stiff but sufficiently determined. "I refuse to accept your authority so to do, sir. You have no authority here, save as one Lord of Parliament. And even that is doubtful, since James Stewart had forfeited the Scots throne by misgovernment, and the breaking of his coronation-oath, *before* he made you viscount! *I* shall preside, on King William's instructions."

The platform-party glared at each other.

"A vote, then. A vote," two of them said, almost in the same breath – the two lawyers.

The cry was taken up from various quarters of the hall and, significantly, from protagonists of both factions.

Dundee shrugged.

Dalrymple raised hand, "A vote, then. Those who would wish the Duke of Hamilton to preside, show."

Amidst much excitement, now that the test was come, not only hands shot up but men jumped to their feet, making the counting the more difficult. Eventually it was decided that eighty-six were voting for Hamilton.

Andrew, trying to count the abstainers, could not be sure that eighty-six would be sufficient.

But when the Atholl votes were taken, they proved to add up to only seventy-one. Shouts for a recount produced the same total. The Williamites had a majority of fifteen.

In a din of ringing cheers and angry shouts the Duke moved to the Chancellor's chair and sat down.

Dalrymple bowed to the chair, and turning, moved off down to his place in the body of the hall. After a moment or two of hesitation, Atholl and Mackenzie did likewise. That left only Dundee standing beside Hamilton, who turned to stare at him coolly.

"Will you take your seat, my lord," he directed.

"I will not," Graham answered, quietly but firmly. "As the King's representative, I cannot accept this vote, *your* authority or the validity of any proceedings under such direct denial of the royal prerogative. I shall leave this hall, and thereby remove any further competency from this assembly. It is no longer a Convention of the Estates, merely a gathering of individuals – too many of whom are in manifest and open disobedience to their monarch and so guilty of the crime of treason. I shall, however, seek to ensure that the royal authority is otherwise and vigorously enforced." And turning on his spurred heel, he marched to the door by which he had entered, and out.

For an appreciable interval there was a hushed pause. Then some few of the Jacobite members rose to follow the example of Dundee. But Atholl, perceiving it, turned, rose and gestured, finding his voice at last.

"Do not leave," he urged. "Or the King's cause could go by default. We need to speak for him. Even if we cannot here win a vote."

"The voting is altogether unsound," another voice cried – that of the Archbishop of Glasgow. "Many are not present who should be – because of wrongful and wicked constraint! My lords of Crawford and Cardross are imprisoned in their town-lodgings by the mob. Most of my brothers-in-Christ, the bishops, dare not venture into the streets, or leave their own sees, for fear of rabbling. Other supporters of King James likewise. The Chancellor himself is unlawfully immured. The Earl of Balcarres, new-returned from England, likewise. It is all a shameful travesty of justice, I say. Had all who should be here been able to come this day, the vote would have gone quite the other way, I vow!"

"Sit down, Curate-master!" somebody shouted. "How many better men, who should have been here now, lie beneath the sod because of you and your like!"

"Aye – and what of Graham's dragoons?" another challenged. "He rode here with sixty of them in his tail. No doubt they are out there still, waiting for us! I had to push my way through them to get in, as did others. They spat on me!"

"The Papist Duke of Gordon is not here to vote," a third pointed out. "Why? Because he holds Edinburgh Castle against us, his cannon trained on this hall . . . !"

Hamilton banged on the table with the Chancellor's gavel. "Silence! Enough, I say! This is a Convention of the Estates, not a packmen's fair! All will be done in due order, all speech addressed to and through myself. I warn all, and shall not warn again, but will call officers to eject offenders." He stared around him, almost with distaste at all he saw. "Now – to business. In effect, this Convention has but the one task and duty – to decide on the destination of the Scottish crown. Sufficiently important, none will deny. But important and fateful as it is, it should not take us long, I think. James Stewart has forfeited all right to that crown by his actions. A successor must be offered it, in his place. There is but one successor evident and apparent – William, already King of England. He is not yet King of Scots, for reasons of our ancient laws and customs. We have it in our power to make him so. But – since this is a matter of law and legalities and I am no lawyer, it had better be put to you by one who is. I call upon the Lord President Dalrymple." That was a long speech for one usually curtly sparing in words.

To cheers and groans Dalrymple rose. "My lords and friends," he began, "for those not conversant with constitutional law, it may be proper to explain the differences in this matter between ourselves and our English neighbours. Our Estates of Parliament have a different history, background and function from their two Houses of Lords and Commons. Ours is only one, and stems from the ancient Celtic polity, from the

212

Council of Mormaors or the Seven Earls, later enlarged and made more representative of the realm at large. But losing nothing of its original powers and authority. In it, the King should preside in person, as does a chief in his clan-council – to which it is indeed related, a supreme clan-council. The English Parliament is of Norman-French origin and quite different. The King does *not* attend it. There are many other differences, most of which need not concern us here . . ."

Hamilton cleared his throat loudly, indicating eloquently that that was enough of that.

Shrugging, Dalrymple took the hint. "To the point, then. The English Parliament cannot lawfully forfeit the occupant of the throne. They can seek to force him to abdicate. If he will not do so, then they can unlawfully cut off his head, as they did with King James's father, although against Scots wishes! Or they can, with almost equally doubtful legality, *declare* him abdicate by having voluntarily deserted his kingdom. As they have done with James . . ."

"Unlawful! Shameful! The act of renegades!" sundry Jacobites cried.

"Perhaps. But that is not our concern today. Our position is quite otherwise. We *can* forfeit the monarch. The Council of Mormaors and Earls had always to appoint the King. From one of the ruling-house, yes – but they *appointed*. And whom they appointed they could, in theory, forfeit. The great Bruce himself admitted as much, in the famous Declaration of Independence at Arbroath in 1320. That declares directly that if the King, even one so heroic, should fail to defend the people's safety and liberties, he should be removed and the people make another King. This is the law of this land, and this Council of the Estates can so declare, forfeit and replace. No need to call for an abdication. We have but to declare the crown forfeit by James, for due and sufficient reason – in especial the breaking of his coronation-oath to maintain the Protestant religion. And to offer it to a successor chosen by us, of the royal blood. William's mother was a Stewart princess, as is his wife."

Into the noise Hamilton banged on the table. "Sufficiently

clear," he asserted. "Our right is plain. We have a decision to make. In due form. Does anyone so propose?"

A score of lords were on their feet at once, clamouring for the privilege. From amongst them the Duke chose Archibald, tenth Earl of Argyll, son and grandson of executed earls. A better-looking man than either of those, MacCailean Mor put forward the formal motion that King James of Scots had forfeited the crown and should be replaced by William of Orange, presently King of England. All the other would-be proposers remained on their feet, to second it.

Flatly, Hamilton asked if there was any counter-motion.

Atholl rose, and with every Jacobite in the hall shouting support, his words were lost in the clamour.

"Vote," the Duke said, to the clerks. "The counter-motion first."

A new voice spoke up strongly, that of a heavily-built man of middle years, Sir James Montgomery of Skelmorlie, a cadet of the house of Eglinton.

"My lord Duke – before we agree this motion and offer the crown to William, let us pause for a moment. I am wholly in favour of William. But let us consider. Scotland has suffered much since her monarchs removed themselves to London – misgovernment, ignoring our liberties, rule by favourites, outright tyranny, and the like. King William in his letter promises to observe our rights and laws, as King James did not. But ought we not to make these clear? The English drew up a Bill of Rights before they gave William *their* crown. We should do no less. It is a notable opportunity. We are in a position of strength, the like of which we may never have again. Let us not throw it away by too easy an offer. Let us at least set out our own conditions for good government and the maintenance of our ancient freedoms, in our message to William."

A murmur of agreement arose from various quarters, muted at first, then growing, swelling.

Andrew sat back in his seat, thankfully. For the last few minutes he had been clenching his fists tensely in a fever of agitation lest this great chance was neglected. It had been only with the most stern self-control that he had prevented himself from calling out, promises or none.

From the lords' benches Johnnie Belhaven rose. "If that is accepted as another counter-motion, I second," he said.

"I, too, urge all here to support such prudent provision," Surprisingly, that was James's Archbishop of Glasgow.

There was a pause whilst men considered the implications, especially in view of that last contribution, Hamilton drumming his finger-tips on the table. Clearly there was considerable backing for Montgomery amongst the Williamites; and if the Jacobites chose to follow the Archbishop's lead, even if only for purposes of delay, the counter-motion could be carried.

"To decide upon and draw up such conditions would take time," he observed, at length.

"What matters a day or two?" Johnnie demanded.

"King William wishes no delay," the Earl of Lothian asserted. "Such matters can be negotiated later. I say vote."

The Lord Melville, home from his Dutch exile, seconded.

The Duke frowned. With William's supporters divided, James's, throwing in their numbers, could seem to win. He made up his autocratic mind.

"Very well – I shall allow time for this matter to be considered by all and proposals listed. I therefore adjourn this Convention until two days hence, at noon." He rose, without further remark, and stalked to the door.

Thus, unexpectedly, the session came to an abrupt end, men staring at each other uncertainly.

As movement began, Andrew made his way through the throng to speak with Sir James Montgomery.

* * *

That evening, in Penston's Tavern in the High Street, the upper room was crowded – and with a very different clientele from its normal bibulous citizenry. The wine flowed, yes; but its drinkers were without exception men of standing, lords, lairds and lawyers, most of them commissioners of the Convention – although not all, for Andrew Fletcher and a few others were amongst the company. Indeed it was Andrew and Montgomery who had organised the gathering, carefully inviting only men of wide and progressive views; mainly Whigs inevitably but some with no political affiliations save a known love of their country, although there were no actual Jacobites amongst them. What they had in common was a dissatisfaction with the way that the Convention was being managed and a determination that matters must be improved.

Andrew in fact took the lead, once all were assembled and their glasses and tankards filled. "We have asked you all to come to this tavern, rather than to any private lodging, for good and sufficient reason and purpose," he announced. "In the state in which we find the city and country, to meet in any man's house might well cost that man and his womenfolk dear, either from Dundee's dragoons, other Jacobite supporters or the town mob – which is quite out-of-hand and knows not friend from foe. So much for a leaderless nation!"

Cries of heartfelt agreement greeted that, for none could be unaware of the dangers of the streets, with wild rumours rife, no authority acceptable by all, the worst elements coming to the surface inevitably, a broken and unpaid army loose in the town and Dundee breathing threatenings and slaughters whilst the castle's canon were loaded day and night and aimed down upon the city streets in the name of King James. Prudent folk stayed at home, behind barred doors, and even great lords who seldom moved about without a tail of a dozen or two armed retainers, went warily. In consequence, there was a poorer attendance tonight than hoped for, only about a score present.

"We meet behind closed doors, then, necessarily," he went on. "And by the same token, what we may say must remain secret meantime, lest any or all suffer. So care was taken as to who was invited. We are in each other's hands, gentlemen – and this city is full of informers. If I seem too fearful, to overstate matters, recollect my own position – and therefore your own. I am still a forfeited outlaw and condemned felon. Most of you are magistrates, and know that everyone associating with me therefore commits an offence which could be punishable by death! This under King James's laws – and James is still lawful King of Scots. So I bid you to think well – and if you prefer to leave, do so now."

There was some talk but no leaving.

Montgomery took over, a baronet of ancient lineage but a

216

shrewd lawyer. "So we must be agreed, my friends, that what we have to discuss and decide here, and possibly at other such meetings, is sufficiently important to warrant taking these risks. I say that it is. All know that we have reached a crossroads in the affairs of our nation and are about to make a notable change of direction. But it is clear that too many do not perceive the wise path to take in that direction – or care not – and so may well lead us along the wrong route. And we have been on wrong routes for too long! It is our task, our duty I say, to try to ensure that the right road is taken. Most of us here sit in the Convention. Yet we see that the Convention is likely to fail the nation. So we must plan how we may influence it for the right."

There was loud agreement on that, at least – but thereafter a dozen voices were raised in suggestion and counter-suggestion, accusation, denunciation and the like. Argument developed on all hands.

Montgomery appealed for quiet. "My lords and friends – lower your voices, a God's name! Or all Edinburgh will learn what we are at! We must have order in this or we shall get nowhere. We are only a gathering of like-minded men, a club as it were, with none greater than another. But it seems evident that we require some leadership and direction. A chairman, at least – else we shall get nowhere along that road. I propose to you he whom I would rate senior here, in rank as in age, my goodsire, Lord Annandale."

William, Earl of Annandale, chief of the great West Borders clan of Johnstone, whose daughter was Montgomery's wife, shook his grey, leonine head. "Not I," he declared. "I am no chairman. Give me a saddle, rather, and a sword, and I am still your man! But not this. I suggest to you Mr. Fletcher, who has both the wits and the words for it."

"My lord – no. I thank you – but no," Andrew said. "I am not the man you need. As I said, I could be a danger to you all. As your chairman, the more so. And I am not now a commissioner, and so cannot speak in the Convention on your behalf or otherwise. No – it seems to me that Sir James himself is the man for the chair – he who spoke out so well and boldly this afternoon."

"Agreed," Johnnie Belhaven said.

That was accepted, and in some order they got down to a worthwhile discussion. General agreement was reached fairly quickly on what was required – a Claim of Right to be drawn up, at least in skeleton form, to be presented by the Convention to William, the Scots crown dependent upon its acceptance, and embodying safeguards for the essential liberties and rights of the Scottish people in religion, government and law. That of course was easily said, but less easily defined and detailed, especially with individuals all emphasising their personal priorities, such as the immediate repeal of the Test Act, an end to illegal taxation, no more arbitrary appointment of magistrates, the restoration of the rights of the royal burghs and the need for the regular calling of parliaments. Andrew had his own strong contribution to make to the list – the disbanding of the standing army, which as well as being a most convenient instrument for tyranny, was an intolerable burden upon the nation's resources and a menace to the ordinary citizenry; to be replaced by locally-raised militia companies, such as already existed in some areas, but these to be authorised only by parliament and mustered and paid only when so ordered.

Twenty men cannot draw up any satisfactory and workable document of proposals, and in the end it was left to a trio, Montgomery, Pringle of Torwoodlee and Andrew Fletcher, to do the embodying the next day and to have at least the bare bones of a possible Claim of Right and a list of supporting requirements to put before the resumed Convention the day following, with sufficient voices and votes then to be raised to ensure their due consideration, the others present discreetly to canvass their friends and possible sympathisers meantime.

And so, two days later, when the Duke of Hamilton reconvened the session, he was faced with an entirely new situation, something like the embryo of a party such as Andrew had envisaged and advocated all those years before. It did not, to be sure, command anything like a majority of the Williamite persuasion; but it was able to present a fairly united front and speak with single and decided voice – which tended to be the Ayrshire voice of Sir James Montgomery – but which knew just what it wanted and was prepared to back it all with

218

relevant motions and calls for votes. This, in turn, gave confidence to others hitherto diffident, undecided, but willing to follow a strong lead. Hamilton and the other senior William supporters were not long in getting the message.

That was not the only message of the day. Presumably there had also been a meeting, or decision-making, on the part of the Jacobite faction, which had resulted in a slightly larger attendance, the Lords Crawford and Cardross rescued from their besieged lodgings and two or three other aged or sick noblemen and bishops persuaded to appear. Surprisingly, Dundee himself was present, in the body of the hall, sitting amongst the lords.

It was clearly a most delicate situation for all concerned. Any split in the Williamite voting strength and the Jacobites could carry the day. Which in one aspect strengthened the position of the tavern-party and in another weakened it; for though it meant that Hamilton would have to defer to their wishes more heedfully, they dared not go too far lest they lost more than they gained. And with Dundee there to lead the James supporters, they could be sure that any weakness would be exploited.

When the Duke, therefore, typically abruptly, commenced proceedings by declaring that Sir James Dalrymple would read out the headings of the recommended Claim of Rights which might accompany the offer of the crown to William, there were immediate protests from many quarters. But there was nothing to vote upon yet, and Dalrymple went ahead. As Andrew and the others had feared, it was all too generalised, vague, such as William would have no difficulty in accepting and then more or less ignoring. Lothian proposed it as a motion, and Dundee and Montgomery were on their feet simultaneously condemning it, one as treasonable and the other as inadequate. With 177 present today to vote, 91 were for the rejection against 86 for acceptance.

Much perturbed and offended, Hamilton went into a brief conference with his close colleagues, however unprecedented for the presiding functionary, amidst Jacobite cheers. Montgomery nodded towards the watching Andrew. They had demonstrated their power – but shown also how two-edged a weapon they could wield.

Dalrymple at least took warning and evidently persuaded Hamilton, for when that man brought the meeting to order again it was for Dalrymple to propose a fairly innocuous motion that the Convention forthwith send a message to King William, whose affairs they were reminded brooked no delay, thanking him for calling the Convention and informing him that they were considering resolutions to put before His Majesty along with an offer of the Scottish crown. This was seconded by the Lord President's own son, Sir John Dalrymple, another lawyer, who showed promise of being as able as his father if less pliable and more unscrupulous.

Dundee moved the direct negative and Montgomery jumped up to support the motion.

The vote went 102 for and 75 against.

So now the position was clear, however awkward. The Williamites could win handsomely, but only with the tavern-group's support.

So Montgomery rose again to read out *their* poposals, to an ever-increasing clamour of opposition from the Jacobites. When Montgomery had finished and promptly moved that they be accepted, his father-in-law Annandale seconding, Dundee as promptly moved rejection.

This time there was considerable disarray amongst William's faction, but Sir John Dalrymple shouted that this was shameful, as good as pointing a pistol at William's head, and all true men should vote against.

The vote went 136 against and 41 for the motion.

It was something like stalemate. Neither main faction could win without Montgomery; but his group could not get their own way without detaching quite a large proportion of the main Williamite vote.

Andrew, who had brought paper and pen with him, scribbled a note to pass along to Montgomery, advocating the putting forward of single items of their demands, starting with the repeal of the Test Act.

Lord Melville proposed that they set up a committee of, say, six, to draw up an agreed list of conditions for the Claim of Right, of which the Earl of Annandale and Sir James Montgomery be two members. Obviously the James supporters would not wish to be represented – which left the other four places for the main Williamite faction. This did not suit Montgomery, since they would be out-voted two to one. He said so, and the motion clearly would not be carried. Instead, he proposed the abolition of the Test Act – which would make for fairer representation in the Estates hereafter, as well as having numerous other benefits for free men everywhere.

The Test Act was, of course, universally unpopular, save to ardent Episcopalians. So this motion appealed to most men there, and it was carried by a majority of over one hundred.

Amidst cheers, Montgomery rose to propose the abolition of standing armies, these to be replaced by local militia companies, Belhaven seconding.

This was a different kettle-of-fish, and Hamilton and his friends would have none of it. They perceived, also, what Montgomery was at, seeking to get the items on his list passed one by one. This, as well as being obnoxious, would be a lengthy procedure. The Duke, therefore, banged on his table, declared the motion invalid, as an attack on the *crown*'s prerogative, the armed forces being raised in the King's name and therefore not to be abolished without the King's authority. He then rose, without further warning, announcing that the Convention stood adjourned for three days, and left the hall.

Scotland's Parliament Hall thereafter bore some resemblance to a bear-pit.

* * *

Hamilton's three-days interval proved to be an eventful one for Edinburgh, all on account of a ship putting into Leith haven two days later, one amongst many, for this was the port of Edinburgh. But this ship bore Hugh Mackay of Scourie, William's general, and some of his staff. Frustrated by the necessarily slow progress of marching infantry and ox-drawn cannon, when he had reached Tees he had requisitioned all the shipping available in that estuary, embarked almost all his cavalry, fifteen troops of horse, selected the fastest craft for himself and set sail, leaving his foot to trudge northwards as best they might. So now he was at Leith, less than two miles

221

from the capital, awaiting his cavalry – which inevitably had to use larger, slower ships – but which was expected to arrive in a couple of days. The cavalry totalled, it was reported, some eleven hundred men.

The news of this reached Edinburgh as fast as a man could ride – and of course, set off as swift reaction, cheering amongst William's supporters, consternation amongst the Jacobites, and doubts and fears amongst the ordinary citizens, who advisedly were suspicious of all solidery.

Dundee reacted fast. His own army had continued to melt away, unpaid and demoralised, and such as remained in the park of Holyroodhouse were in no state to fight a battle against fresh cavalry. Able to trust only two or three troops of his dragoons, he sought to cut his way up to the castle with them, to join forces with the Duke of Gordon and his garrison. But the narrow and difficult approach to the fortress, climbing up from the Lawnmarket, had been barricaded off, with timbers, broken masonry and miscellaneous rubble, trenches even dug amongst the cobblestones, to assist in keeping the garrison more or less penned in, besieged. For his dragoons to clear a way through would have taken hours and moreover made the dismounted cavalry extremely vulnerable. So instead, Graham led his squadron outside the city-walls northwards, to the Nor' Loch which lay at the foot of the castle-rock, and riding round the rim of this reached a section of the thrusting cliff which it was just possible for an agile man with a head for heights to climb up. And there his dragoons and such of the townsfolk as were in the vicinity, saw the King of Scots' handsome general, Bloody Clavers as he was known to the crowd, or Bonnie Dundee as the Jacobites preferred to call him, thigh-boots, scarlet-and-gold coat, feathered bonnet and all, go clambering up, hands and knees, scaling the huge perpendicular rock like a monkey, zigzagging, hoisting, traversing, up and up until he reached a ledge immediately below the castle-walling itself, up which no man could climb. But there, above him, heads looked down from an open window, watching astonished. And those below could hear Dundee calling for the Duke of Gordon. Presumably the Cock o' the North was there waiting, or nearby, for a shouted conversation took place, not all of

222

which could be heard from the lochside but in which, fairly clearly, Dundee called upon the Duke to fire some shots from his cannon, one or two into the city itself, as intimation of the King's continuing authority, and two or three in the general direction of Leith, as warning to Mackay. Evidently Gordon expressed reluctance to do this, for Graham urged it again, the louder, and added that the castle must hold out for King James at all costs. He himself was for Stirling, where he was calling a new Convention and Parliament in the royal name, for 18th April; and thereafter he would raise the Highland clans, whose chiefs, thank God, were Jacobites to a man and Catholic, to bring down to teach Edinburgh a lesson and drive the William-ites into the sea. Moreover, James himself would be landing a large Irish-French army on the west coast any day. So – cannon-fire and no surrender. The Duke's replies were inaudi-ble. Dundee clambered down again, to the huzzahs of the dragoons, and rode back into the city.

Graphic accounts of this feat swept the town like a forest-fire, Andrew obtaining various versions of it at a meeting of the dissident Williamites in Penston's tavern that evening. So far there was no cannon-fire however.

Next midday the Convention reassembled in a great hum of excitement, although with a smaller attendance than heretofore owing to fears that the castle guns might well open fire on Parliament Hall as their principal target. Andrew saw that there were three new spectators sitting near himself, all wearing military red coats, and was informed that these were General Mackay, Sir Thomas Livingstone his cavalry com-mander and an English aide called Major Bunting. There was no sign of Dundee when Hamilton opened the proceedings, which some took as ominous.

However they had barely started when Graham made an entry and, in dramatic fashion, flinging wide the doors and stamping in, booted and spurred, with actually a dragoon trumpeter to blow a flourish and so gain approximate quiet and adequate attention, drowning out the outraged Hamilton's voice.

"I come to this unlawful gathering for one purpose and one only – to warn you all!" he announced, into a quivering hush.

"To warn you of wrath to come, in King James's royal name. I am leaving this city forthwith – but the Duke of Gordon is not! His cannon are trained on this hall. *I* do not stay another day, thanks to one honest man, one John Binnie, a master-dyer, who overheard a dastardly plot being hatched to murder myself, the Earl of Balcarres and Sir George Mackenzie, the Lord Advocate, this very night. I remove myself from this company of assassins and traitors! I ride to Stirling where I call a true Convention and Parliament, in King James's name, to meet on 18th April – by which time I hope the King may be there to preside in person – and with a large French-Irish army to add to the Highland host I shall muster forthwith. Then we shall march on this wicked city and it will be the day of reckoning indeed! By then every traitor and rebel will be well advised to have left Scotland. That is all that I have to say to you – save to command all loyal subjects of the King of Scots to leave this hall behind me!"

Signing to the trumpeter to sound again, John Graham marched out.

In the pandemonium which succeeded, every Jacobite in the Convention rose to follow his lead, this time the Marquis of Atholl going also – and some who were not avowed Jacobites but merely men of discretion.

After a while, and some consultation with Dalrymple, Tweeddale and Lothian, the Duke of Hamilton hammered loud and long on his table, to restore order and his authority. He declared stiffly, that this Convention of the Estates of Scotland was still in session, that they were well quit of all Popish and contumacious supporters of the tyrant James Stewart, and that their business must go on. He ordered the officers to lock the doors of the hall and to lay the keys on his table, so that none unauthorised might enter – and clearly, no more were to leave. And he called upon Sir James Dalrymple to speak on a new clause which could be incorporated in the proposed Claim of Right, urging King William to support a federal union of the two kingdoms, which would undoubtedly greatly redound to Scotland's benefit.

The Lord President thereafter did his able best on this theme, emphasising the advantages of increased and mutual commerce with England, equal trading rights in the overseas colonies, the use of English ports, the removal of the risks of war, and much else. Andrew was not convinced – but then he had rather pronounced views on independence, in nations as in men. Dalrymple may have been more successful with others, but he was up against difficult conditions for convincing oratory, the fact being that the commissioners were really in no state to heed and consider theory and long-range policy just then. Their thoughts tended to be elsewhere, notably on the Duke of Gordon's cannon, trained on this building; and what that devil Dundee might be up to now. Indeed, before very long it was Tweeddale himself who interrupted the Lord President, calling on Hamilton to adjourn the session and lead an authoritative party up through the barricades to as near the castle entrance as they could get, there to demand the surrender of his fellow-duke forthwith, with his garrison, under pain of eventual execution, to end this intolerable threat to honest men. The cheers and stamping which greeted this proposal left even Hamilton in no doubt as to the feelings of the assembly; and although he declared that *he* certainly was not going to go shouting surrender-terms to that fat and deplorable Gordon, he conceded that it might be as well to warn him that General Mackay's forces, when they arrived in full, would be well equipped with cannon with which to batter the castle into submission, and the consequences for himself and his people when that happened. A deputation from this Convention could accordingly proceed, to that end. Since the Lord Tweeddale seemed so concerned, he could lead it, with say the Earl of Lothian, the Lord Lyon King of Arms and a trumpeter.

To relieved cheers he added that the session would reconvene three days hence, by which time the situation in the city should be more clear and Mackay's cavalry, it was to be hoped, patrolling the streets. Meeting adjourned.

Thereafter the would-be legislators certainly found the streets thronged with excited crowds – but this held its own reassurance, for if Dundee's dragoons had been on the rampage the populace would not be so much in evidence. Swiftly the news spread. Bloody Clavers was gone, quite gone, pray God for good! He and his troopers had ridden out of the city, shouting that he was going to follow the spirit and example of his great kinsman, Montrose, by the West Port, on their way to Stirling, admittedly promising to return one day in vengeful might. But meantime the town was free of them, at least, and all the prominent Jacobites were scuttling off too. And no cannon had been fired from the castle. It seemed that the Gordon was not of the same stuff as the Graham.

Edinburgh, despite chill April showers, blossomed into holiday mood.

Next day Mackay's cavalry began disembarking at Leith, and Major Bunting was sent, with some three hundred horse, in a sort of token pursuit of Dundee, to try to keep him moving and if possible prevent any sort of muster or assembly at Stirling.

Andrew Fletcher was glad to get out of that volatile and noisy town and to ride eastwards, with Johnnie Belhaven, for Beil, until the Convention reassembled. Although he scarcely admitted it to himself, he was rather inclined to avoid Saltoun these days, Henry's bliss with Margaret being difficult for him to swallow, however much he berated himself.

It was a shrunken Convention which resumed after the interval, all the Jacobite lords and commissioners absent and quite a few of the less politically-conscious non-Jacobites also left the city, having had enough of affairs of state, domestic affairs drawing them home. Indeed the session, although productive of results, was something in the nature of an anti-climax and lacking in drama. When the adjusted Claim of Right was put to the vote there were only five against it and its explicit offer of the crown to William and Mary. If Andrew was perturbed by that new clause incorporated, referring to a federal union of the two kingdoms, he was at least consoled by the decision to include Sir James Montgomery as one of the three representatives to go to London with the Claim. He was to represent the commissioners of the shires, Argyll the lords and Sir John Dalrymple, the younger, for the burghs – for, although a west-country laird's son, oddly enough he sat for the royal burgh of North Berwick in Haddingtonshire.

Apart from this all-important matter, and a hasty decision to go ahead with the raising of militia companies, calling upon all

Protestant males between the ages of sixteen and sixty to be ready for mobilisation, little other business was done. They heard from Tweeddale that the delegation summoning the Duke of Gordon to surrender the castle had been entirely fruitless, but at least had provoked no artillery fire in response. Once Mackay's cannon came up, things would be different. Meanwhile, unfortunately, the news from Ireland was not good, with all the Catholic South and West declaring for James and only the largely Protestant Ulster counties opposing. The dangers for Scotland did not have to be stressed.

Hamilton adjourned the series of sessions until 21st May, by which time they should have William's answer. Assuming acceptance, the King would be asked by the three representatives to name the resumed Convention a full Parliament, so that all necessary steps could be enacted. Meantime let them pray Almighty God that Dundee in Scotland, and James Stewart in Ireland, both came to grief.

So that chapter, at least, was closed.

Andrew Fletcher was too proud to plead, thereafter, with Montgomery, that he should urge William to revoke the forfeiture on himself and Saltoun estate; but he did point out the importance of emphasising that other unredeemed forfeitures by James's regime were not only contrary to justice but seriously hampering William's own cause by souring relations and preventing proper representation in the Estates of Parliament. It was to be hoped that Montgomery would take the hint.

15

The two riders reined up on the birch-clad ridge above the Birns Water, to gaze out over the spreading, rolling countryside which sank before them in ever more gentle waves and folds, from these foothill braes down to the comparative levels of the fertile Vale of Tyne, pasture and old woodland and tilth, as fair and rich a prospect as was to be seen in all Lowland Scotland, all backed by the blue waters of the Firth of Forth and the distant hills of Fife beyond. Yet fair as it all was, and so much of it his own birthright, the man's eyes surveyed it with less than satisfaction and not merely with the hot resentment which went with his temper that this meantime was *not* his, because of unjust laws and royal spite, but with a more constructive and calculating frown, assessing, planning.

The woman watched him rather than the vista.

He pointed, there and there and there, and shook his head. "A waste!" he said.

She raised her lovely brows. "Surely not? Beauty, rather. Is it not one of the finest estates in Lothian. Few that I know can compare. Certainly none that the Carnegies own."

"Beauty, yes, I'll grant you. But neglect, failure to cherish and improve."

"Henry does his best." That was defensive, almost reproachful. "What can he do? He is allowed to spend little or nothing. All has to go to the Douglas . . ."

"No, no – I do not mean that, Margaret. It is not Henry's fault. Indeed, if fault there is, it is my own – for *I* did not develop Saltoun as I could have done when I was lairding it. I did not know, to be sure, did not see it all as I can now. I have learned much on my travels – more than just soldiering and politics and the like."

"And you would change it here?"

"Aye, change much, improve, make it blossom and yield and flourish, as it could, as it should. Look yonder – there, beyond Lempock, and there. Bright green. That is bog, marsh, flooded ground – but good bottom land, gone to waste. These, and others should be drained, ditched and dried out, to grow grain, barley. Those long slopes, the Skimmer Hills and Greenlaw and the rest – they carry cattle, yes, but they are too good for beasts. They could almost all be ploughed, the stones cleared and built into dykes, and grow corn and crops and good hay. Much of the scrub woodland should be cleared, the roots grubbed out and the land turned to use. The braesides up here should be cleared of whin and broom and thorn, to carry the beasts from the lower slopes. This rig cultivation, in long

228

strips, is wasteful, in land and in labour. Large fields are better, walled-in. The ground should be fed, with dung and sea-wrack and marl, as they do in Holland . . ."

"A mercy, Andrew! Who is to do all this? And how? Are you for playing God? Thinking to change the very face of the land!"

"Far from playing God, lass – *worshipping* God! Making two or three or four ears of corn grow where only one grew before – is that not a true worship? Are we not to make the land blossom as the rose? This land of mine – or what *was* mine – could yield fourfold and more."

"To what end? The greater wealth of Andrew Fletcher?"

"That might be. But that is the least of it. You have read of the sin of burying talents in the ground. Here is a talent indeed, going unused. Or not used as it should be. To bring work and prosperity and betterment to all the country and folk around. You must see it, Margaret? In Holland every yard of land is used, worked, more ever being won from the sea, drained, lovingly tended. What we see here would be unthinkable. I lodged in a farmhouse in Holland, near Rotterdam, a miller's farm. I learned much."

"Henry says that Cockburn of Ormiston talks of this. Not of Holland but of land improvement. Henry was interested – but could do nothing meantime."

Henry Fletcher was away on one of his quarterly visits to Douglas Castle in Lanarkshire where he had to go to render account of his stewardship of Saltoun to the Marquis of Douglas, Dumbarton's brother – who was also Hamilton's brother, of course. The moneys he took would be sent on to Dumbarton, in France, a sore and sorry business for the Fletchers. But at least this occasion provided opportunity for Andrew to see Margaret lacking his brother's presence which, however bitter-sweet a privilege, he greatly desired. It was not proving any easier, with time, to accept that he had lost her to Henry. This ride over the property was the first they had had together.

"It is not only land improvement I learned from the Dutch," he told her. "But milling – barley-milling in especial, such as we know not here; pot-barley, as they call it. And weaving of linen – Holland's. And flax-growing, likewise. They have much to teach us."

"And you intend to do all this, put what you have learned into effect, when you get Saltoun back?"

"Aye. Or *if* I get Saltoun back!"

"Surely you must, in time, Andrew? They cannot leave it in the hands of a Jacobite exile! Will Dumbarton not be forfeited, in turn, as a rebel?"

"Who knows? He is Hamilton's brother, after all. And Hamilton is powerful, and now very close to William. And he does not like me! It could be long enough before I am the Laird of Saltoun again . . . !" And smashing down a clenched fist on his knee, he jerked his mare's head round harshly in his anger and frustration. "Come – let us have a race! Yours is the faster beast. To yonder sheep-stell on the hill – a race, to run the grudging devils out of me!" Without awaiting her agreement, he dug in his heels, kicking his mount forward.

Threading the scattered birches and pounding over the slanting grassland beyond, tossing up clods and scattering cattle and sheep, he thundered on downhill, to splash across the Birns Water in a shower of spray and on up the braeside, making for a circular dry-stone shelter for sheep, the best part of a mile ahead, beating the same clenched fist on his horse's flank as they went. Exhilaration took over, an elemental relief which had served him well before this.

At the stell he wheeled round it – and was surprised to see that his companion was still a long way off, just across the burn indeed – which was not like her, for she was an excellent horsewoman and mounted on a fine animal, a gift from her father. He rode back towards her at a canter, wondering, his mare snorting.

"I am sorry," he called, contritely, as they came together. "I should not have done that, dashed off, assumed that you would wish to race also. I have an evil temper – as you know well. It helps, at times, to ride at the fastest. You are not displeased, Margaret?" That was urgent.

"No, no – not that," she assured, smiling. "It was . . . otherwise. I did not wish to ride too fast. Not today."

"Forgive me, lass. I am headstrong, I know. I should have

asked you. But . . . I was hot against fate, just then. As not infrequently I am! Henry now, would not have done that."

"No, Henry would not!" she agreed, with a short, almost nervous laugh. "But then, to be sure, Henry would have known. I am to have a child, you see."

He stared at her, varying emotions expressed in his eyes. "Margaret – you are? You . . . you . . . a child!" He flung himself down from his saddle and ran to reach up to her. "My dear, my dear!" he cried.

Biting her lip she looked down at him, and a hand went out to touch his cheek, briefly. She said nothing.

"My God – I am sorry!" he exclaimed. "Fool that I am! I had no notion of it. You are not . . . ?"

"I am very well, Andrew, I assure you. Nothing amiss. It is just that I am best not to risk . . . upset. Perhaps there is no danger, as yet. I do not know very much about these matters – my first, after all!"

"How long?"

"Five months yet."

"And you have not told me!"

"Should I have done so? I did not think that . . . I wondered whether you would . . ." She left the rest unsaid.

"Whether *I* would approve!" he finished for her. "Sakes, Margaret – what do you think me? A monster?"

"Scarcely that, Andrew," she smiled. "But – you were not pleased at my marriage. I know. You might well not be pleased at the, the fruit of it?"

He shook his head. "I am a selfish man, yes. Much concerned with my own advantage! But, lassie, lassie – in loving you, think you that I will not love this part of you? Because you are not, not for me, am I to begrudge you joy?" He scanned her face keenly. "It *is* your joy? You wanted this child?"

"Yes."

"Then I rejoice. With you. And with Henry. He will be . . . most happy."

"Yes."

"Then why not I, who love you both?"

She reached down again, to grasp his hand. "Andrew, dear," she said.

231

Impulsively he kissed her fingers. Then he stepped back. "Now we must get you home. And heedfully. If we go round by the riverside and through the wood. It is longer but more gentle, easier riding . . ."

"Mercy, Andrew – I am not so fragile a flower as that!" she protested. "Not yet awhile, if ever. We rode here safely enough, did we not? We can ride back as easily as we came – or ride on, if you wish. No need for cosseting me . . ."

Nevertheless they went back to West Saltoun by the roundabout, low-lying route and at a walking-pace – which, of course, had its own compensations on a fine late-May afternoon, with the cuckoos calling from a dozen braesides, the woodpigeons croodling and the first martins darting around them. Oddly, Andrew was more at peace with himself and at ease and in harmony with his companion than he had been these many weeks. Why, he did not ask himself. Margaret responded.

At the dower-house they found visitors, half a dozen strange horses tethered champing, in the yard, armed men drinking ale in the stabling. Andrew was immediately wary, at the sight, ready to bolt, since he was still legally an outlaw and any man could arrest him. But Leezie Duncan came out to announce that these thirsty scoundrels were in the tail of Sir Patrick Home of Polwarth, who was ben the house awaiting the Laird.

It was Home's first visit to Saltoun, and he was obviously uncomfortable; yet as obviously he had come for some specific purpose. Of late he had exhibited something like a guilty attitude towards Andrew, almost as though he blamed himself that his situation should be so much better than that of his friend, his forfeiture remitted, his rights and privileges restored, indeed enhanced. He had lain noticeably low throughout the recent Convention, most evidently at pains not to get on the wrong side of the new regime. He was not, to be sure, one of the Penston's Tavern club.

So there was just a little constraint, at first, in this encounter. But a glass of wine and Margaret's friendly reception presently eased matters and Sir Patrick began to shed his stiffness. He was, in fact, full of news. The trio of representatives were back from London. William had agreed to the Claim of Right

232

provisions, accepted the Scottish crown and indeed, with his wife, had taken the coronation oath in the Scottish form there and then, before the three emissaries, in some haste, evidently. He had hesitated a little at only one item, the swearing to maintain the Presbyterian form of national Church government and to root out all heretics and enemies of that religion, declaring that he would never be a persecutor, like his predecessor – the commissioners as hastily declaring that such was not implied or intended. So now the Convention was to be reconvened as a full Parliament, which would formally proclaim William and Mary as King and Queen of Scots. A new chapter in the nation's story would commence.

Yet, all was not entirely well, it seemed. William was not all amenable. Two of the three representatives had come home dissatisfied, Montgomery especially so. He was an ambitious man and had made no secret of the fact that he hoped for high office, preferably that of Secretary of State. Argyll, too, had expected some major position, preferably Lord High Commissioner to the Parliament. But the new monarch had other ideas – or, since he knew nothing of Scotland personally, listened to other advice. Lord Melville was to be High Commissioner and Secretary of State for Scotland also. Moreover, the highly influential office of Lord Advocate, which Montgomery had sought as second-best, had gone to Sir John Dalrymple, the youngest of the trio, displacing the Jacobite Sir George Mackenzie. All Montgomery had been offered was the decorative but far-from-pivotal post of Lord Justice Clerk – which he promptly refused. So only Dalrymple had come home happy, however important the tidings they bore – and Montgomery, it appeared, had stormed off to his own Ayrshire in high dudgeon.

"And . . . my Saltoun?" Andrew asked, levelly.

"I fear . . . nothing," Home had to report, with some embarrassment. "William, it seems, once he had the crown and swore the oath, was not in a receptive mood. Or was receiving contrary advice."

"From whom? Who has his ear in London, now? Hamilton? Or his chaplain Carstairs, still? Not Gilbert Burnet, for sure."

233

The other shrugged. "Who knows? Save that it must be a friend of Melville and Dalrymple."

"But no friend of mine!"

"Sir Patrick!" Margaret exclaimed. "Does this mean that Andrew is still to be kept out of his inheritance? And by a Jacobite exile! Remain as good as an outlaw? It is wicked! Shameful! After what he has done for William of Orange. What has Lord Melville done, to deserve what *he* has been given? Or this Dalrymple? Whilst Andrew is treated like a leper! Oh, it is beyond all belief! Why? Why?"

Home shrugged helplessly. "Lord Melville is a man of . . . compliance. He will do as he is told. Andrew is . . . otherwise, we all know. Has a mind of his own – and speaks it! Not always to his own best advantage, I fear. I presume that William has been warned that Andrew could be, shall we say, awkward? And so thinks to teach him a lesson."

"Yet I gained the impression that William was a fair and honest man," Andrew averred.

"No doubt. But princes and rulers act otherwise than ordinary men, whatever their qualities. They must needs do so, I suppose."

"I still say it is shameful!" Margaret insisted. "Can nothing be done? By Andrew's friends – not only by his enemies?"

"That is why I am here, Mrs. Fletcher. Andrew has the name of being a rebel, an able and honest man but a rebel against authority. So both the Jacobites and the Williamites look askance at him. Both fear that he could harm them. But, I say that if he was to show that he means no harm to William's regime, now that it is settled lawfully, make *active* cause with it, then attitudes could change – *would* change, I am sure."

"You would have me to turn toady, Patrick? Lickspittle? That I shall never do."

"Nonsense, man – be not so quick! Nor so proud. You are ever too ready to take offence. What I propose would cost your devilish pride nothing! And could greatly help your state. And it would seem apt enough, likewise – for you it was who sought to reduce the standing army and introduce instead local militia companies. Well, your view is now accepted by those whom William trusts. In Scotland, at least. For one thing, there is little money to pay any standing army – James and his henchmen have squandered it all. Mackay's forces are being paid from London – which I think you will not like? So militia, raised by lords and lairds and even burghs, and paid only whilst they are on duty, would save much money, as well as constituting no threat to the population of the country, as does an idle army. But – you know all this – you advocated it all eloquently enough."

Cautiously Andrew nodded.

"And now the matter is urgent, the need great. Dundee has gathered a large clan army in the Highlands, ever growing, with many of the chiefs flocking to his banner. Mackay, chasing after him, prevented him from having his assembly at Stirling. And Mar, in Stirling Castle, wisely saw the way the wind blew and would not surrender to Graham. He went to his own house of Dudhope, at Dundee, to raise men from that city, and Balcarres, his lieutenant, went to raise Fife. Mackay sent cavalry after both, and they captured Balcarres at his own house; but Dundee escaped to the Highlands. Now he has raised James's standard in Lochaber. Keppoch, Glengarry, Locheil, Ardsheil, Glengyle and others of their like have flocked to him. He has marched eastwards from Glen Roy with over two thousand broad-swords and is raising more all the while. He says that James is sending over a force from Ireland, and that they will have Scotland out of William's hands before the summer is out. So – the thing is serious and there is no time to lose. Mackay has some fifteen hundred horse and will have twice that number of foot, when they arrive. That is all. Dundee 'could raise three times as many Hielantmen in a month."

Still Andrew made no comment.

"We therefore have little time to raise the necessary militia," Home went on. "And no money to hire regular troops from elsewhere. So we must act swiftly."

"However swiftly you act, Patrick, you will not *train* your new militia to face Highland broad-swords in a month or so."

"I know it. But if at least they can be mustered, armed and part-trained, they can be used to garrison cities, ports, castles

235

and the like, releasing regular troops for Mackay. It is the best that I can do."

"*You* can do . . . ?"

"Yes. I have been appointed, in William's name, commander of all Militia in Scotland."

"Good Lord!" Andrew stared, perhaps not very graciously. "But you, you . . . ?" He left the rest unsaid.

The other nodded. Home had fairly minimal military experience. "I know what you think. I myself questioned their choice. But we on William's side have few experienced soldiers. At least in Scotland. For long, all the soldiering has been done by Charles's and James's men. So – I come to you for help, Andrew."

His friend shook his head, unhappily. "Patrick, you cannot expect me to do this. To become a soldier again, for William who has spurned me. Sakes, man – I am an outlaw still! A felon, unpardoned . . ."

"Here is the way to change all that. Aid in this and you change your entire position. You were Master of Horse to Monmouth, a colonel against the Turks, one of William's staff. If any man could make this militia project succeed, it is you. And win your way back into William's favour, have all here beholden to you."

"No – I do not turn my coat so readily as that!"

"It is not turning your coat, man. You have always been against James and for William. It is but *proving* your loyalty."

"I could call it otherwise! Such as kissing the hand that struck me! No, I will not go soldiering for William while he sets his face against me."

"Then do it for the nation, for Scotland. You do not want James back, tyrannising over us? *You* would be one of the first to suffer."

"If it comes to that, I will draw my sword, yes. Not before."

"Andrew – could you not consider this?" Margaret asked, all but pleaded. "I do not want you to go fighting, God knows. But could you not go some way with it? Aid in the matter? Somehow you must improve your state . . ."

"Yes, if you will not join me in arms, Andrew, at least help to raise the men, the Haddingtonshire militia. If you were commissioner for the shire, as you were and should be, you would be having to do this. Belhaven, your friend, has agreed to be its colonel."

"He has? But he has no experience as a soldier. Never drawn sword nor fired a shot!"

"No – but you could guide him. Help your country, help your friend – aye and help me also. For this is a heavy task laid on me. Who have little enough experience of war my own self. I have agreed to it, for the need is great. And my own position none too secure, with William. Now that he is King, I would be a fool to stand too much on my dignity."

"As do I?"

"I think that you might, man. And I say it as a friend."

"Do it, Andrew," Margaret urged. "For Henry and myself, also. Remember, we also suffer in all this."

He paced the floor for a turn or two. "Very well. I will aid, in some degree. In the raising and training of this county's militia. But only that. For your sake, and Johnnie's, more than for William's."

"Praise be for that, at least! It will greatly help. The common folk much respect you. Recruiting will gain by it. And training. And . . . it must help your own position. None can treat you as outlaw if you are working with the King's forces."

"The less said about that aspect of it, the better!"

"But *I* say thank God!" Margaret exclaimed. "Somehow you have got to win back to your own place, Andrew. This could be the start of it. And not only for you but for all of us . . ."

* * *

It took a little while for Andrew to adjust to his new situation, in more ways than one. Suddenly he found that he need no longer go furtively, watchful all the time, ready to make himself inconspicuous – and it had become more of a habit and frame-of-mind than he had realised. Large numbers of people had known of his presence in the country, inevitably; but the cautious had kept their distance. Now this all changed and folk were ready to greet him again, and not only in his militia activities. His reputation, exaggerated as he insisted out of all proportion, and which had hitherto marked him off as a most dangerous man, now worked the other way. He was now the sort of man the nation needed, an experienced officer and campaigner, in a cause sadly lacking in such, reputed to be of almost heroic stature. Since clearly he was working for King William, the new monarch's known displeasure could surely no longer apply. So he was safe to greet and accept.

Dramatic events on the national scene much contributed to this general attitude. The reconstituted Convention, now a full Parliament, was scarcely the source of excitement, proceedings being mainly formal and legalistic, however necessary for due constitutional launching of the new reign, all under the uninspired presidency of Lord Melville, as High Commissioner. But as the sittings went on, every other day brought tidings from the north to provide an ominous accompaniment to the proceedings. Dundee all the time was gaining in strength, quartering the Highlands from Lochaber to the Moray Firth, rousing the clans and gathering an ever-growing army, raising James's standard wherever he went and declaring that soon he would turn southwards and demonstrate who really ruled Scotland. General Mackay, although himself a Highlander, had no Highland troops, and, in that wild country, trailed far and ingloriously behind. The news from Ireland was consistently bad, with James's forces almost everywhere in the ascendant and Ulster hard-pressed. There were rumours that matters were looking so black that William himself was to go across to try to bring his father-in-law to account. All this produced a general state of agitation and apprehension in southern Scotland, in which rescuers and strong men were in great demand. Few were to be looked for in the Parliament, it seemed.

But mediocrity was not entirely on one side. In mid-June the Duke of Gordon surrendered Edinburgh Castle, on terms which allowed him and his garrison to march off unimpeded to his northern fastnesses – and the capital celebrated the non-event as though it was a mighty victory.

It was in these conditions that Andrew and Johnnie Belhaven, with Cockburn of Ormiston, went about Haddingtonshire recruiting, enrolling officers, mustering, training, commandeering arms and horses. They had little difficulty in finding men, and even horses, but arms and ammunition were a different story and adequate training scarcely possible. Inevitably the responsibility for this came to rest mainly on Andrew's shoulders, as the only man available with any real idea of what was required. He found it a frustrating business, demanding of a patience he did not possess. Yet at least it kept him fully occupied and feeling necessary, a state he had not been in for long. He made better company at the dower-house of West Saltoun in consequence.

Six weeks or so of this and there were further developments. Sir Patrick Home arrived, to announce that the maximum number of militiamen must proceed northwards at once, however inadequately-trained, to join General Mackay in south Perthshire. When Andrew protested that it was as good as sending lambs to the slaughter, Home declared that he could not help it. He had his orders. Dundee was indeed marching southwards with a very large force of some of the toughest fighting-men in Christendom, MacDonalds, Camerons, Frasers, Macleans, Mackintoshes and the like, to join the Murrays of Atholl and Tullibardine, the Hays, the Drummonds and other Perthshire clans. Somehow they must be halted, and Mackay needed every man, however ill-prepared. It would be a tough baptism for the new militia, but they had no choice.

So two days later Andrew watched Johnnie and his other equally callow officers ride off to war at the head of an enthusiastic but painfully green squadron of the Haddingtonshire Militia, with foreboding and self-recrimination. They ought not to be going – but since they must, *he* ought to have been going with them, he who had persuaded many of them to join, who had taken much responsibility for their training, who at least knew something about warfare. It had been easy to say that he would not draw sword for William; and wise judgment agreed with Home that he would be better employed anyway in training more men. Nevertheless . . .

If Andrew had been less than enthusiastic about his military labours hitherto, now he threw himself into the work with a new determination and vigour, driving himself and his recruits hard. Reinforcements for the squadron would be forthcoming, and the best-trained of any of the new part-time soldiers.

In the event it was all unnecessary. On 29th July, Scotland was shaken by the news that two days previously there had been a great battle in Atholl, at the Pass of Killiecrankie – and, brilliantly handled, the Jacobite forces had won, Mackay outmanoeuvred. But in the hour of his victory, John Graham had been killed, slain by a musket-ball penetrating below his upraised sword-arm. Bonnie Dundee or Bloody Clavers was dead. And the Highland army, shattered by the loss of their renowned leader, and with no obvious successor, Balcarres still being a captive, threw away the fruits of victory in typical inter-clan rivalry, quarrelling over the booty of Mackay's captured baggage-train and then dispersing back to their glens. The beaten Mackay fled back to Stirling, to lick his wounds – then discovered, hardly able to believe his good fortune, that he was left with command of the field. The immediate danger to King William's regime was over.

At Saltoun they heard the news with mixed feelings, relief yes but regret also. John Graham had not been an easy man to associate with or to know well, something of an enigma, admirable and sinister, courageous and ruthless, good and evil – but then were not all men so, in lesser degree? But at least he was a *man*, of a stature rare at any time and notably so in the Scotland of the second half of the seventeenth century.

There was word of Belhaven and the Haddingtonshire squadron. They had come off lightly, scarcely distinguishing themselves but suffering few casualties. It had not been a cavalry battle, fought in the main in a deep and rocky defile where horses were of little use. So they had been kept largely in reserve until Mackay's defeated infantry began their headlong retreat, when they had been useful in covering the retiral. But by then the knowledge of Dundee's death was sapping the Highland fervour, and the abandoned baggage-train a mighty temptation, so that the rout was the less hard to stem.

Andrew Fletcher thanked God for that, at least, even if he was less wildly excited than most of Lowland Scotland appeared to be, with church-bells ringing, flags waving, singing crowds parading and cheers for King William. Surely never had a defeated general come back to such a hero's welcome as did Hugh Mackay of Scourie – symptomatic of the state of dread which had prevailed previously.

Only the more apprehensive – or more thoughtful – eyes now turned towards Ireland.

Part Four

16

Andrew Fletcher surveyed the table in his great hall at Saltoun with some satisfaction mixed with assessment and a little apprehension. As to the brilliance of the company there could be no question, nor of the power and influence represented; but as to the outcome, the success or otherwise of the evening, there was no knowing. Socially it was already a success, to be sure, a notable achievement at least, for the man who had been outlawed, condemned felon and out-of-favour with the monarch, to have assembled here in his own house such a galaxy of the leaders of the nation and the height of fashion. It represented changed days indeed for Saltoun Hall. But Andrew had invited them here for a purpose, and that might well fail. At least in one aspect of it all his satisfaction was certain; his gaze, in its regular scanning of the richly-dressed and bewigged gathering, kept ever returning to the most distant seat, at the other end of the long table, where Margaret sat, acting his hostess. Even that held its bitter-sweet flavour, of course; but the sight of her, so lovely, so graciously assured, so seemingly at home at his table, dispensing his hospitality, could not be other than a delight to that man, even though Henry sat so much closer to her than did he.

He leaned to his right, to pay heed to what his principal guest was saying – John Hay, Earl of Tweeddale, now Chancellor of Scotland no less, chief minister of the realm. At the other side, his left, William Paterson made laborious conversation with Lady Tweeddale, the Dumfriesshire farmer's son with the aunt of the Duchess of Buccleuch and Monmouth. Next to them sat Margaret Belhaven and Lord President Dalrymple, now promoted Viscount Stair, with across the board his son John, now Master of Stair, Secretary of State for Scotland, and Lady Ormiston whose husband, Adam Cockburn was made a Lord of Session, indeed Lord Justice Clerk. And so on down the table, the new rulers of Scotland and their ladies sat at ease, after an excellent repast, sipping their wine, in the mellow glow of innumerable candles. Sir Patrick Home was now Lord Polwarth and a member of the Privy Council, with a pension of £400 sterling a year, as reward for organising and commanding the militia. Even Johnnie Belhaven was a Privy Councillor and Lord Clerk Register – a more or less honorary office but carrying various privileges and perquisites.

Andrew's inner smile at it all tended to be slightly twisted, cynical. So much for choosing the right side at the right moment – no doubt the art and essence of politics. For himself, he was less agile at it, although possibly the most concerned with and interested in the theory and practice of good government of any present. He was, it seemed, still the awkward one, the odd-man-out, the unfortunate who failed to perceive when to tack before the winds of reality. So there were no titles or privy-councillorships for him. Admittedly he was Laird of Saltoun again, forfeiture cancelled at last – but it had taken almost a year after Killiecrankie for this to be conceded, and without any sort of compensation or even message from William in London. But then, to be sure, William was not much in London these days, much more often back in his own Netherlands. After his great Irish victory on the River Boyne in the summer of 1690, with James Stewart losing all and fleeing back to France, William seemed to have recovered his fondness for soldiering and now found campaigning on the Continent against Louis much more to his taste than playing at kingcraft in England. As for Scotland, he appeared to have no least interest; indeed he was reported to have declared that he wished that country a thousand miles away, with the Duke of Hamilton its king, so that he could be rid of them both.

It was February 1692.

Presently a glance and raised eyebrow from Margaret drew a nod from Andrew and she pushed back her chair and got to her feet. All rose thereafter, and amidst much bowing and pretended deprivation, their hostess led the ladies from the hall to their withdrawing-room. The men settled themselves back, refilled their glasses and lounged the more at ease. After a brief pause, Andrew spoke up.

"My lords and friends all – pleasing as is your company for its own sake, and excellent our mutual converse, I believe that we may be privileged tonight to hear of a matter which could be of the greatest interest and profit to us all and to our whole nation, a matter, a project, which I for one will be surprised and much disappointed if this distinguished company fails to consider closely or undervalues. It will be put to us by my friend Mr. William Paterson, of whom you all will know, more especially those who had occasion to sojourn in the Low Countries in exile during the previous reign where, at Amsterdam and Rotterdam and elsewhere, he acted banker for many of us in that time of our great need, taking many a risk and loss on our behalf. My lords of Stair, Polwarth, Melville and Argyll, as well as my much humbler self, were then much beholden to Mr. Paterson. I think that we, and a great many others, will have reason to be still more so, hereafter."

There was an expectant murmur but some wary glances also.

"Before asking Mr. Paterson to speak to you," Andrew went on, "for those who may be less well acquainted with his name and fame, I should perhaps say a few words. Hailing from Skipmyre near to Dumfries, he was reared largely in England, at Bristol, that great trading-port for the Indies. Then he learned the arts of trade and commerce and went voyaging in their pursuit. Nevertheless he was never a mere merchant-adventurer, being a man of faith as well as of enterprise, so that in the West Indies and the Carolinas he brought the Gospel to many, as well as trading with great success. I mention this as indication that our friend's concern is not wholly with the profit of the purse but also with that of the soul! I suggest that this is unusual, to say the least!"

There was some exclamation at that, not all of it enthusiastic, and the wariness increased rather than diminished. Paterson kept his gaunt-featured head lowered, as though embarrassed.

Andrew smiled, however, and patted his shoulder. "Lest some doubters may consider this last less than an added qualification for commercial advancement and profit, let me add that Mr. Paterson has also been labelled buccaneer, on account of his activities in the Indies and the Carib Sea. But I am assured that such charge emanated only from his English

247

rival traders, who resented his success and the trust he established with the colonists and natives of those parts, in which *they* deemed themselves to have a monopoly. We all know too well of the English trade monopolies, to our cost, my friends – and to this Mr. Paterson will, I think, refer. So for those who doubt whether gospel-preaching and trade go hand-in-hand, be reassured by the buccaneering!"

That drew the anticipated laughter and a distinct heightening of interest.

"Thereafter, trading led Mr. Paterson to money-lending and banking," Andrew resumed. "The Dutch are the world's greatest practitioners of this commerce, as we all know, so it was perhaps natural that he should settle himself in Amsterdam, where he proceeded to teach the Hollanders not a little of their own trade, and so was happily placed to aid myself and so many another from Scotland, whom King James's policies had driven into exile and consequent financial difficulties. I may say that King William himself was glad to avail himself of Mr. Paterson's good service in financing his expedition to England."

Andrew paused to sip at his wine, gauging the reaction. Paterson was a poor speaker, less than persuasive. It was important therefore that the company should be suitably informed and interested beforehand, predisposed to receive his proposals with some eagerness however dully presented. At the same time, these lofty ones must not be bored with too lengthy an introduction, any more than scornful of the humble background of the Dumfriesshire farmer's son. He reckoned that it was time for specifics.

"Since William's accession, my friend has not been idle. With the King's support, indeed at the King's request, he has raised for Charles Montagu, the English Chancellor of the Exchequer, a government loan of no less than £500,000 sterling, to help restore the English Treasury which James Stewart left in such bad state. Half a million pounds sterling, my friends!"

The speaker had no call to be dissatisfied with the effect of that on his hearers. Half a million sterling, privately-raised, was almost beyond the comprehension of most present.

"Furthermore, in order to aid the more in the troubled English economy, and at the same time bring profit and well-being to many subscribers, he has conceived the notion of a *national* banking venture, not a private one, although with individuals participating, which he is calling the Bank of England, and in which he has interested some of the highest in that land. It is a great project, which could well change the entire scope of government spending and taxation – and which we here should examine with the greatest of interest. But, my lords and friends, William Paterson, having done all this for England, does not forget that he was born a Scot. And he would seek to do as much for the land of his birth. And that we have need of some such help none here will deny. Never can our land have been in more sorry state of poverty, stagnating trade and empty purses. We have won freedom from persecution at last, freedom to worship as we will, a parliament to protect our laws and rights. But after two reigns of tyranny and turmoil, the rule of favourites from far-away London, and neglect of all the nation's welfare, Scotland is in dire need, commerce at a standstill, the land not being tilled as it should be, our Treasury, like our pockets, empty. I am told that there are over 200,000 beggars and homeless vagrants in our land! Certainly the countryside, as well as the towns, are full of these sad folk. In these circumstances, my friends, I ask you to listen to what Mr. William Paterson has to say."

There was no dissent. All eyed that spare, rather sad-faced individual expectantly.

Paterson made an unimpressive start, clearing his throat, gulping down some water, fumbling with his clothing. "My lords. And gentlemen. Your lordships . . . I am much beholden. To you all. To Mr. Fletcher. For his kindness. For your attention. I am grateful . . ."

"Speak up, man – do not mumble!" Melville, now Earl thereof, was growing a little deaf.

"I beg your pardon, my lord." Paterson almost shouted that, his voice somewhat difficult for his hearers to follow, more West Country English than West Country Scots. "I'll not delay your lordships for long. I, I plan to set up a company. A Company of Scotland for Trading to Africa and the Indies.

That is what I intend. Aye." He nodded, almost apologetically, and returned to his water-glass. He never drank wine or spirits.

His hearers stared at each other.

"Well, man – well?" Tweeddale prompted.

"A company," the other repeated. "To trade, you see. More than that. To plant colonies. Scots colonies, with sole trading rights and monopolies. To rival England's."

There was utter silence now.

Paterson looked round them. "A company," he repeated. "With subscribers. Scotland's company. Scotland's colonies. Where some of these vagrant folk may go. As colonists. To a new life. And to reap riches, for themselves, for the company, for Scotland. Great riches, as I know."

"Where, sir – where?"

"How can this be? All the colonies are already taken up."

"The English, the French, the Dutch, the Spaniards – these have taken all, have they not?"

"We are too late, man – too late."

From all around the table voices were raised. Ineloquent or not, he had their attention now.

"Not too late, my lords. There is still a great opportunity – the greatest, perhaps." Paterson warmed to his theme. "We could be the envy of Christendom. For a few hundred thousands of pounds we could hold the world to ransom!" He blinked at his own extravagant hyperbole; it was not often that that man put his soaring vision into soaring words.

Doubts and exitement, distrust, question, speculation were voiced.

"Where is this great opportunity? Missed by all others?" the Chancellor demanded. "We are not bairns, sir, to be told tales."

"Nor is Mr. Paterson, my lord," Andrew pointed out, strongly. "He *knows* what he says. He has not done what he has done by idle dreaming or child's talk but by achievement, by making two pounds where there was only one, or less, before. The banker cannot afford to deal in bairns' ploys."

"I did more than preach the Gospel amongst the Caribs, my lords, more than trade and exchange. I used my eyes and my wits. Aye, and my legs. Buccaneer I was not – but I sailed with some who might be so-called. Into places where few Christian men had ever penetrated. And in one I discovered a wonder. Aye, and dreamed a dream which I have never forgot. A dream which it is time was fulfilled. Or so Mr. Fletcher says."

"Mr. Fletcher himself is something of a dreamer, I fear!" the Master of Stair observed, thinly. "Much as we all admire him, to be sure."

His father was more tactful towards their host. "Mr. Fletcher's dreams may still serve us well. As to Mr. Paterson's, who knows? But I did not hear him name his projected company of Africa and the Indies? Not of the Carib Sea."

"That, my lord, is but a device." Paterson it was who now did the staring. "A necessary device. To preserve our secret. Your lordships and gentlemen must bear with me when I demand . . . or, forgive me, *request*, your promise of secrecy over what I now would tell you. For if it became known, in London especial, there would be no Scottish company, no Scottish colony, believe me! The territory would be annexed to the *English* crown there and then. Have I your lordships' word?"

Intrigued, men nodded. There was little lounging now round that table.

"I name Africa and the Indies to divert attention. My colony is to be far elsewhere." Paterson leaned forward, to sketch with his finger, dipped in water, on the table. "See you, the Americas, North and South, are joined thus by a great sickle of land, washed on the east by the Carib Sea and on the west by the Pacific Ocean – Central America with the West Indian islands. Spain holds most of this mainland, although there are small Dutch and Portuguese colonies also. But at the very south of this Central America is a narrow isthmus of land, shaped like the letter S. It is little-known or esteemed, for its Carib coast is swampy, flat, with no fair prospects, and there is so much fair land elsewhere for the taking, thousands of miles in every direction. The buccaneers call it Darien and the Carib Indians Panama." The man's dull voice actually quivered with excitement as he pronounced those names, part of this unlikely dreamer's vision.

The excitement notably failed to communicate itself to his hearers.

"Is *this* where you would plant your Scots colony? This small unwanted swamp?" the Secretary of State asked, incredulously.

"Aye, my lord. And for good reason. For I did more than eye that swampy coast. I ventured inland. And found fair country but a few miles beyond the swamps. Fair for cattle, fair for crops and fruits. And a great bay with narrow hidden mouth to lead into it, for anchorage and port. Much excellent land awaiting settlement. Few Indians. But, my lords, more important, I found something else. I found that this isthmus, between the Gulf of Darien and the Pacific shore, is in places a bare thirty miles in width." He paused expectantly, gazing round at them.

Apart from Andrew Fletcher, already in the secret, he perceived scant reaction.

"Do you not see?" he exclaimed, irritation at their ignorance giving him a sort of eloquence at last. "Thirty miles! Between the Atlantic and the Pacific Oceans. No more than from your Forth to Clyde, from Edinburgh to Glasgow – less! Unclaimed by any nation. It is scarcely believable but it is fact. Plant the Scottish flag in Darien, gain a charter from King William as King of Scots, and we hold the key to riches unimaginable!"

Still they did not see it, these men who were amongst the most able in the land.

"You must explain, Will," Andrew said. "We do not all have your understanding of commerce, trade-routes, shipping and the like."

"Aye. Although I would have reckoned it clear enough for any!" The farmer's son's respect for his betters was wearing thin. "Where does the greatest wealth in this world come from? Whence do the nations of Europe draw their prime riches? From the Indies, from the Spice Islands, from China, from Peru and the like. Gold, silver, jewels, jade, silks, spices, oils, perfumes – the riches of the Orient and of the West coast of the Americas. And what have all these in common? They are on the Pacific Ocean – and so must be reached for and brought two-thirds round the world – further because of Africa and

India, which must needs be sailed around. To China is thirteen thousand miles, by sea. To the East Indies, eleven thousand. To Peru, sixteen thousand. Yet to cross the Atlantic Ocean is but four thousand from Bristol, less from Spain. Then but thirty miles across land, and all the Pacific is open to the voyager. The journeying less than halved, the storms of the dread southern seas avoided."

At last they began to perceive. Talk broke out everywhere.

Stair summed it up. "You mean, then, that this company should be concerned not only with colonising but with transporting, porterage, Mr. Paterson? Developing the land but also carrying goods from one ocean to the other across this narrow neck of land?"

"Exactly, my lord. At a price. And not only porterage – although that at first. The Dutch are famed for their canals. I have seen great ships floating twenty miles inland from the sea. This isthmus of Darien is flat, flat as Holland. From the profits of the porterage the company could pay Dutchmen to fashion a canal. And then, and then, my lords, ships could sail through from seas to sea, without having to unload. A toll-gate of the oceans. And *we* would hold the key!"

Something like awe was generated around that table as the scale and scope of this conception dawned on men's minds. None now could fail to recognise the possibilities. All there, even the least concerned with matters outwith Scotland, knew of the vast profits of the English East India Company, of the gold and silver treasures of the Spanish Main largely brought from Peru, of the legendary wealth of Cathay, China and Japan – and also of the almost year-long round voyages, the great losses sustained to shipping as the price of laying hands on all that wealth. The potential profit, in more than halving that cost, in time and shipping and risks run, did not have to be argued.

For a while excited talk prevailed.

But there were some supreme realists present, notably John Dalrymple, Master of Stair and Secretary of State. His strong Ayrshire voice presently predominated.

"Mr. Paterson, your project sounds . . . inviting, none can deny. But certain questions occur to me. Firstly, to build such a canal in such a place would demand a vast deal of money. To pay for it, the profits of the porterage which went before would have to be great. Have we reason to believe that such would be forthcoming? That shippers, the Spanish, the French, the Portuguese, the Dutch – aye, and the English for that matter – would indeed use your porterage? It would save them much voyaging, yes – but would mean transhipping, unloading vessels at one side, then cargoes to be carried across the thirty miles and then loaded on to other ships. Double the amount of shipping required and much labour. More costly, perhaps, than the voyaging?"

"No, sir. See you, the shipping is already there. It needs only to be disposed differently. Instead of a voyage from China or the Spice Islands taking, say, six months each way, it could be done in little more than two. So, much shipping would be saved, not at sea for so long. So it would pay well to have Atlantic ships and Pacific ships, pay the porterage dues and still make handsome profit."

"H'mm. I must take your word for that, sir. But one or two other points. This porterage. Are our Scots colonists to till the land or to become mere porters, carrying others' goods, like slaves? I think that few would choose to go to your Darien to such labour."

"Indians, sir, would provide the labour. And blacks. From the Carib islands. With mule-trains and ox-carts. There is no lack of labour already there. Our settlers would be overseers, farmers, planters, cattle-rearers, traders, with the company merchanting their produce, for their profit and ours."

"It sounds notably fine, sir. But will all this profit, from the portage, the land, even the projected canal, not draw others? Will it be left to us? Would not covetous eyes be bent on all? Spanish, French – even English? Will they continue to pay toll to *us*? Having developed it all, others might well step in and take it all from us, by force of arms. In such distant parts."

"That is why I plan both a settled colony *and* the transportage, sir. The one supporting the other. The settlers in the colony would be there to rally and protect the porterage. And with a royal charter we would have a governor, forts, militia. Do not tell me that Scots would not protect their own!"

"Well said, sir," the Secretary's father commended. "But –

254

does not much of this great project depend on winning that royal charter? Without that, all would be at risk. Have you reason to believe that King William will grant one? Without the advice of his English ministers? Who, if they learned of it, might well persuade him otherwise and themselves move to take over the project! We all know how jealous they are for their monopolies and colonial and trading privileges."

"That danger I have not overlooked, my lord. But I think that you need have no fear. King William requires my services. As does his Chancellor. For further loans, for this Bank of England project and otherwise. I have aided him in the past. I have already mentioned to him the notion of a Scottish colony. And although he showed little interest, neither did he show any opposition. He is interested, I think, in but one matter – soldiering for the Protestant cause. Charters ever have to be paid for in royal dues. If those dues, from a *Scots* colony and company, are specifically to be paid to the King direct, not to the English Treasury, William will sign it, never fear. And the charter will be for the founding of a colony at Darien and the setting up of the trading company. No details as to the trade need be given, certainly not word of the transportage project, which will be but part of our trading activities."

Patrick Home, now Polwarth, spoke up, briefly. "How much?" he asked – which in itself was indication that he, for one, required no further persuasion as to the scheme's worth and practicality.

"For the setting up of the company, the chartering of the necessary shipping to take out the colonists, provisioning, arming, the first year's trade goods and the like, I estimate between £300,000 and £500,000."

There were some gasps at that.

"All to be raised from Scotland, sir?" Tweeddale demanded.

"Certainly, my lord. You would not have the English let in on this, would you? For most certainly they would seek to take over all."

"No, no. But . . . it is a deal of money, Mr. Paterson. And the country is in a poor way. I do not know whether it could be raised . . ."

"I have promised £1,000. Sterling," Andrew put in quietly.

255

"And I likewise, £1,000," Johnnie Belhaven supported.

"I also," Polwarth added.

"So there is one-hundredth spoke for before it is started . . ."

"A fiftieth – since I myself will invest £3,000 of my own," Paterson added. "In shares of one pound. Each to rank for full interest."

"What interest do you anticipate, sir?" Melville asked.

"Who can tell? The first year, none. The second, little. But thereafter I shall be disappointed not to win twenty per cent."

"Lord – twenty per cent. Each year?"

"Why not, my lord? Once the porterage is established, that will be as nothing to the profits earned, I believe. Have you any notion as to the values of the cargoes coming to Europe each year from the East Indies and Spice Islands alone? Or from Peru to Spain? The buccaneers know! They took seven hundred thousand pounds worth of gold and silver from one galleon alone, whilst I was there. A small percentage on the worth of each cargo, for transportage dues, and your investment could be repaid in very short time. And once the canal is built . . ."

After that there was little more debate. Practically every man present subscribed, and although some went no higher than a few hundred pounds, others would have gone well above one thousand. But Paterson said that he would prefer to set that figure as a limit, meanwhile, backed by Andrew. If it was to be a project for the whole Scottish nation, as it should be, opportunity must be offered to all to join in, even the smallest men. It would not do for too much to seem to be taken up by the privileged few.

It was whilst they were busy making lists and writing out notes-of-hand, that a servant brought a mud-spattered courier into the hall and went to speak to Andrew, who nodded and gestured the newcomer to where John Dalrymple, Master of Stair, was sitting.

The courier moved to murmur a few words in the Secretary of State's ear, whereat the latter rose and went with him to a corner of the apartment, where a letter was produced and read. Little or no attention was paid to this by the company, for the

Secretary was of course frequently at the receipt of despatches and official papers. But on this occasion, Dalrymple was evidently much exercised by what was brought, elated even, sufficiently so not to be inclined to keep it to himself.

"Tweeddale," he called, to the Chancellor, "our trap is sprung! And has caught the fox! MacIan is dead, and his brood with him. A notable blow struck for the welfare of the realm."

"MacIan . . . *dead*?" The Chancellor stared. "Dead, you say – and others with him? But – how, man? How? What happened?"

"What happened? Why, they paid the price of rebellion, that is what happened. So perish all the King's enemies, I say."

"There has been a fight? Some battle . . . ?"

"Not that I am informed. This letter is from Glenlyon. He says nothing of any fighting. Merely that he has carried out his instructions. That all is well. MacIan of Glencoe, and sundry of his barbarous tribe of Hieland scum, are dead – and Scotland is the better place for lack of them!"

All were gazing at him now.

"Dead! Slain, then?" Tweeddale's voice quivered a little. He was made of different stuff from Dalrymple. "Was, was this . . . necessary, John?"

"Entirely," the Secretary of State said crisply. "An example had to be made. Or these Hieland Jacobites would be ever at our throats and a danger to the King's Grace. This way we avoid *real* bloodshed. Avoid any more Jacobite risings, battles and many honest men being slain. The other chiefs will thus learn their lesson, I have no doubt. Old Glencoe and his MacDonalds are small price to pay for peace in the North."

Into the silence that followed, Andrew spoke. "Master of Stair – are we hearing aright? Are we to understand that MacIan of Glencoe, that old man, and a number of his MacDonald people, have been slain? Not in battle but in cold blood? By Campbell of Glenlyon – acting on instructions?"

"As to cold blood, I know not, Fletcher. But they have paid the penalty, yes – for rebellion. For having failed to take the due oath of allegiance to King William in the prescribed time. They all had ample warning. So no one is to blame save MacIan himself."

"But – good Lord, man, this is unbelievable! Are you telling us that the Campbells had *orders* to murder the old chief, his family and his clansfolk?"

"I do not like your choice of words, sir! Murder is quite ridiculous. That rebels and traitors pay for their misdeeds at the hands of the King's militia is no murder. But necessary justice. For the benefit of the entire realm."

"Without trial? At the hands of Campbells, hereditary enemies of the MacDonalds. You, a lawyer yourself and son of the chiefest judge of this kingdom, say that?"

"I do, sir. And say, also, that you, Fletcher, should not meddle in matters of which you know nothing and have no least responsibility. Your understanding of the law of the land has in the past proved . . . lacking!"

"I am a free citizen of this realm and again a commissioner to its parliament – however unworthy. I am entitled, indeed in duty bound, to seek to see the law upheld. By whomsoever. On whose orders and instructions were these people slain?"

"On the King's, sir. And on mine, as Secretary of State. On his Grace's personal and written directive."

That silenced even Andrew Fletcher for the moment. All there knew that the simmering Jacobite revolt in the North worried the government; and after the Battles of Killiecrankie and Cromdale, although the clan army had dispersed, its cause was by no means abandoned. In an attempt to pacify the Highlands a proclamation had been issued offering free pardon and indemnity to all chiefs and leading men who would take the oath of allegiance, before their local sheriffs, prior to the last day of 1691. At first few did so; then word arrived from James in France, now broken in resolve and health, that they should all do so and suffer no more on his lost behalf. Most had then made their token submission. But apparently MacIan, chief of the MacDonalds of Glen Coe, had delayed.

Chancellor Tweeddale was clearly unhappy. "I knew nothing of this," he disclaimed. "I, I could not have approved it. I should have been informed. How many? How many died?"

"Glenlyon's message does not say. Only that MacIan and sundry of his tribe are dead."

"May we ask what were Glenlyon's orders?" Andrew said,

"Has he exceeded them? Or is this, this massacre, as *you* instructed, Master of Stair?"

"I am not responsible to such as you, Fletcher, to give account of my actions. Nor indeed, even to you, my lord Chancellor. I remind all that I am the *King's* Secretary of State, not Parliament's. I take my instructions from His Grace – and His Grace's orders were to extirpate that sect of thieves. Those were his actual written words. The King's command has been carried out, it seems. If you have quarrel with it, gentlemen, then your quarrel is with the King's Grace, not with me." And narrow-eyed, the Master looked round the company, threat scarcely veiled.

Andrew Fletcher's temper was ever apt to rise to threats. "And is the King's Grace above the law?" he demanded. "My lord Viscount Stair, as senior lawyer here, can you tell us that?"

The elder Dalrymple was in no hurry to answer. He toyed with his wine-glass. "The monarch is not above the law, no. In *this* realm. But he is, shall we say, the law's ultimate interpreter and guardian. If he so interprets the law, for the best benefit of his subjects as a whole, then to challenge it would be . . . difficult."

"Difficult or no, *I* challenge it! As must all here, if we value our honour. I conceived William of Orange to be an honourable man – even though, like others, he can act mistakenly. But this – this is beyond all bearing. Execution without trial, without legal sanction, of a group of the King's subjects, in time of peace, Scots people – on the orders of a man who has never so much as set foot in Scotland . . . !"

"On the orders of the lawful King of Scots, sirrah!" the Secretary cried. "I advise you to watch your words! Which verge upon treason, sir – treason!"

There was uproar round that table now, men rising, exclaiming, gesticulating. Patrick Polwarth and Johnnie Belhaven sought to calm their friend's guests, but the matter had gone too far for that. John Dalrymple was declaring that he could no longer remain in this disloyal and seditious house; and various others took their prudent cue from him.

So the gathering broke up in disorder, with some agreeing and commiserating with their host, others arguing amongst themselves, some hurrying off to collect their wives.

"I am sorry about this," Polwarth said to his friend. "After so successful an evening, over Paterson's ploy. And your good hospitality. You will have to watch for John Dalrymple, mind, Andrew. He could make a bad enemy."

"I would rather have that one as enemy than as friend!"

"Perhaps. But he could be dangerous. He has William's ear, and the power that goes with it."

"I shall watch him, never fear. Now that we see how he uses his power! But – it is Mr. Paterson, here, whom I am sorry for – since it is too late to be sorry for the MacDonalds! This is an ill ending to the night's business, Will."

"None so ill. This trouble does not affect my project. And I have notes-of-hand here for over £13,000 sterling – which is no bad start for the company. Even Dalrymple's own for £500. *I* am satisfied, my friend."

* * *

Strangely enough, the very developments which so dramatically broke up the Darien scheme dinner-party at Saltoun proved, in course of time, in fact to aid it. As the details of what became known as the Massacre of Glencoe were disclosed, the repercussions reverberated far and wide, not only in Scotland but down in London and indeed over the Channel, where William was, as so often, campaigning against the French 'Grand Monarch' and Louis the Fourteenth's visions of hegemony. And William perceived that he had made an error of judgment.

It transpired that the entire Glencoe episode had been even more reprehensible than it had sounded that night at Saltoun. The old chief, MacIan, had indeed gone in time to register his oath of allegiance, at the new fort at Invergarry, which General Mackay had built to try to overawe the Jacobites of the Lochaber area, and was being called Fort William. He arrived there with a day or two to spare before the year's end; but there proved to be none there who would accept his oath, commandant or magistrate, and he was directed to proceed to the Campbell seat of Inveraray, nearly one hundred miles south-eastwards across the snow-covered mountains, where the sheriff, a Campbell, was domiciled. In grimmest winter weather it took MacIan six days to reach Inveraray. His oath was accepted nevertheless, although thus late, and he returned to his glen and his own people, assuming that all was in order. Just under a month later, the militia colonel, Campbell of Glenlyon, had arrived at Glencoe with a company of one hundred and twenty men, announcing however that he had come in all friendship – despite being a hereditary enemy of the MacDonalds – and requesting permission to lodge and shelter his force amongst the glen's folk during this savage spell of weather, before proceeding on northwards to collect arrears of cess and hearth-money, a new tax the government was imposing. Highland hospitality demanded that, once accepted as guests, they be kindly treated; and in fact the militiamen stayed a fortnight with their hosts, billeted in the cottages and cabins, Glenlyon in MacIan's own house. Early in the morning of 13th February, the grim order was given. Men, women and children were to be slain, without exception, there and then, in their own houses. The Secretary of State's instructions were that the government was not to be troubled with prisoners. The butchery began. MacIan was shot in his bed, and his elderly wife stripped naked and so maltreated that she died the next day. Pickets had been sent to close both ends of the narrow Pass of Glencoe to prevent any escape, for such as might manage to get out of their homes and away. In driving snow some did make good their escape, directly over the icebound mountains, although others died in the attempt. But over thirty had been shot, stabbed or bayoneted to death.

When all this became known, even the normally uncaring and self-concerned were shocked. In general, the Lowlanders looked upon the Highlanders as barbarians, all but savages, partly because they spoke the Gaelic instead of good Scots Doric. But such deceit and treacherous wholesale slaughter appalled. Even in England the thing raised eyebrows, Catholics especially protesting, and everywhere James and the Jacobite cause gained by the revulsion.

So William perceived his mistake, as reports of anger, unrest and blame reached him. In May the English naval victory of La Hogue enabled him to return to London, temporarily, and he consulted with his ministers, 'Cardinal' Carstairs and even sent for Gilbert Burnet. Thereafter he issued a statement announcing that he had been badly served by his Scottish advisers, in especial his Secretary of State, denied any personal involvement and threw the whole responsibility upon John Dalrymple, whom he declared as dismissed from his office.

In Scotland there was much agitation, Andrew Fletcher to the fore. He urged the recall of Parliament. But this required the King's sanction and would obviously not be in William's interest meantime. Nothing was done. He then led the demand for the arrest and trial of the Master of Stair, declaring that dismissal from his position was utterly insufficient retribution. In this he was joined, amongst others, by Sir James Montgomery, who now issued from his sulking retirement in Ayrshire again to take part in affairs – possibly hoping for the vacant Secretaryship of State, out of which Dalrymple had earlier manoeuvred him. But he still found no favour in William's sight, any more than did Andrew, and the King appointed a little-known individual, by the name of James Johnston, to act as Secretary in the interim – it was widely believed merely as a stop-gap to keep the seat warm for Dalrymple who would be reinstated when the fuss had died down. Certainly all attempts to bring the Master to trial, along with Glenlyon and his chief, the Campbell Earl of Breadalbane, came to nothing, the general opinion being that William's own implication must then be made public.

However, unsatisfactory as all this was, the King did find a way of placating Scottish opinion. He smiled kindly upon William Paterson and his Darien project, giving him the charter he required and even encouraging him, and the Scots, in the idea of a new colony. Admittedly this cost William nothing and might well bring him profit; but it did please opinion north of the Border.

So the great subscription campaign was launched – and, since Paterson had to spend much of his time in London, concerned also with the contemporaneous launching of the new Bank of England project, Andrew found himself more or less leading the effort, with assistance from others, notably Johnnie Belhaven. It was remarkable how enthusiasm for the scheme grew and developed, even though at this stage nothing was being said about any possible canal, even the porterage prospects not being emphasised lest envious hostility be aroused outwith Scotland. The enthusiasm was for an overseas colony which Scotland could call her own. If this might seem a strange source of satisfaction for the Scots, it had to be remembered how successful had been the English colonial ventures, since Elizabeth Tudor's time, how enormous the riches which had accrued, what fortune-spinners were the East India and Africa Companies and how jealously the English guarded their trade monopolies, their various Navigation Acts prohibiting commerce with any of their colonies save by English merchants, all goods entering or leaving the colonial ports to be carried only in English ships. Small Scots enclaves had been established for nearly a century in Nova Scotia and the Carolinas; but the actual territories belonged to England and the prohibitions applied there also, the Scots settlers being treated very much as second-class citizens. So the idea of establishing their own crown-colony in the Americas appealed to almost all, as a matter of national pride as well as profit – and it was assumed that the profits would be no less great than those coming from the renowned English, Dutch, Spanish, French and Portuguese dependences.

So Andrew found himself in a strange position, in consequence – popular. From being the furtive fugitive and the awkward man to be seen with, he quite suddenly graduated to being one of the key figures in this great national enterprise, a man to know. His campaign for bringing Dalrymple and Glenlyon to trial, however unsuccessful, also commended him to the populace at large if not to the government and its immediate supporters. But even these were, in the main, now involved as Darien subscribers; so that there was a curious dichotomy with regard to Andrew Fletcher – approval and the reverse. King William's favour towards William Paterson – from whom he was again negotiating a loan for his military adventures – was likewise a factor to be considered in assessing how closely to get involved with Paterson's friend and colleague – even though no direct royal favour was detectable towards Andrew himself.

These circumstances enabled Andrew to score a quite major personal success at the Parliament of 1693, when he was prominent in putting through the assembly a Bill for the Encouragement of Foreign Trade, which gained an overwhelming vote and became an Act. Its details had been drawn up by a new Committee of Trade, a novel development for Scotland in itself, wherein much that Andrew had learned during his foreign travels was brought forward, in addition to Paterson's own proposals. Although the latter was now himself a commissioner to Parliament, representing the burgh of Dumfries, he was unable to attend either committee or assembly with any regularity owing to his problems in the south. The Bank of England design was taking up a lot of his time and though going ahead was meeting with a lot of opposition from established money and usuary interests in London and their spokesmen in both Houses of Parliament. The powerful East India Company had reached the stage of almost automatically opposing all that William Paterson did, fearing competition – and some of the most influential figures in English public life were connected therewith. Inevitably word of the Darien charter and scheme leaked out from Whitehall and Paterson found himself embarrassed, not so much by the enmity but by the clamorous support and demands for shares in his company – this largely by interests excluded from and envious of the East India Company, who saw it as a means of stealing a march on that great monopoly. On Paterson's assertion that it was a Scots-only venture, the applications were merely channelled through the many Scots in London. In the end he had to give way, in some measure, for many of the applicants were the same men with whom he was working over the Bank of England. And, of course, compared with Scotland, London was awash with ready money for investment, and quickly over £300,000 was subscribed, whilst Andrew and his colleagues in the north had reached only half that, splendid a figure as this had seemed to them at this stage. So, much rethinking had to be engaged in, or the entire scheme would slip into English control. It was decided to delay the actual parliamentary procedure of setting up the new company officially meantime, to discourage the London speculators, and to content themselves with this Act for the Encouragement of Foreign Trade, which prepared the way in general for the more detailed company legislation and allowed the organisers to keep their options open.

Andrew for one had not realised that trade and commerce could involve almost as much infighting and strategy as politics and warfare. His skilful sponsorship of the new Act, however, and the lead he was taking against what seemed like one more threat from London, gained him much prestige and recognition as a leading parliamentarian, to help overcome his reputation as a loner and awkward rebel against authority. He still did not lead nor belong to any party but nevertheless he acquired a sort of following, on whose votes he could more or less rely, led by the lords Belhaven, Polwarth, Annandale, Eglinton and Ross and commissioners such as Cockburn of Ormiston, Pringle of Torwoodlee, Swinton of that Ilk, Maxwell of Pollock and Montgomery of Giffen, largely members of the former Club. The last's kinsman, Sir James Montgomery, was less dependable, a disappointed man with a grievance, however able. But as a member of the Committee on Trade he did good work and spoke eloquently on behalf of the Act.

The Scots were a people who appeared to need to be preoccupied, theorists to a man. In the past they had been preoccupied with war, fighting for freedom or just fighting, feuding; with religious reform or at least change; with theological hair-splitting. Now, of a sudden, it was trade, commerce and the better life to be gained thereby. Some saw this as a grievously mundane and earth-bound deterioration, almost shameful in a people who should have their minds above the merely material and sordidly mercantile. Andrew saw it otherwise, he who surely was no materialist. All this, of course, referred to the southern or Lowland Scots. Their Highland compatriots were a different kettle-of-fish. *They* had a simpler outlook, less concern with theories and certainly no preoccupation with commerce. One hundred and thirty years after the Reformation they were still mainly Catholic, thirled to the old ways, patriarchal and clan-conscious. The Stewarts had become a clan, despite Norman origins, and James Stewart was still chief of chiefs whatever his faults and failings. The

Glencoe affair profoundly shook and alarmed the Highlands. *Their* preoccupation was far from schemes of foreign trade and social betterment. The sword commended itself to them, at this juncture, rather than the word, the edict, the vote and the subscription-list. Highlands and Lowlands were on a collision course.

17

It was not often that two gentlemen of Lothian should find occasion to ride over the Highland Line, even the very southern skirts thereof, as now. But circumstances can conspire to even such drastic measures, and in the summer of 1695 circumstances were sufficiently so to impel Andrew Fletcher and Johnnie Belhaven to these lengths. With a suitable escort of half a dozen troopers of the Haddingtonshire militia, drawn from their own two estates – for none would question but that they were venturing into dangerous territory – they trotted up the west bank of the Water of Ruchill in the wide vale of Strathearn, of a late August afternoon, and were in fact surprised to find it all so fair, so fertile-seeming, so far from the barbarous wilderness of crags and mountains and foaming torrents against which they had been warned. Mountains there were but they stood well back, to form a pleasantly blue backcloth to the sylvan strath, the Water of Ruchill was a fine peat-brown river but no fearsome cataract and there was not a crag nor yawning chasm in sight. Strathearn, of course, although just within the Highland Line clan-country, was scarcely truly Highland; and the clan in major possession was that of Campbell, which made a difference.

And it was with the Campbells that the pair were mainly concerned, heading for Aberuchill Castle, seat of Sir Colin Campbell, Lord Aberuchill of Session, Privy Councillor. The fact was that, after so encouraging a start, the Darien scheme was in danger. Not from any failure in the conception or

266

planning, nor yet from any lack of support in Scotland; but wholly on account of opposition in England. William Paterson was paying now for having, against his better judgment, allowed subscriptions to be raised in London. For the East India and Africa Companies had combined to bring overwhelming pressure to bear and had succeeded in getting the English Parliament to declare the entire project unlawful and an infringement of their statutory monopolies. This, to be sure, carried no weight in Scotland, but it meant that it was illegal for any persons domiciled in England to hold shares in the Company; therefore all the £300,000 subscribed there had to be paid back.

This had severely upset all their arrangements and preparations, which had been nearing completion. For revised estimates of initial capital requirements amounted to £600,000, of which Scotland had managed to raise approximately half. Now, with the other half having to be paid back, the crisis situation did not have to be emphasised. Somehow that £300,000 had to be replaced; for the new Company, duly set up by Act of the Scots Parliament only a month or two before, was committed to major expenditure, in especial the building of two new ships suitable for carrying out the settlers and their gear and livestock to Central America, ordered from shipyards in Amsterdam and Hamburg, a third vessel having already been bought from Leith merchants. Paterson, in some desperation, had hurried over to the Continent and managed to raise at short notice something over £100,000 from his Dutch and German associates; but that left £200,000 which had to be produced from Scotland, and quickly. Hence this and other attempts by Andrew and Johnnie – the latter appointed chairman of the new Company of Scotland for Trading with Africa and the Indies, since it was judged politic to have a lord as figurehead, especially as he was now made a member of the Privy Council.

They were thus probing into the Highlands for good reason. Admittedly there was, in the main, precious little money to be found north of the Line, plenty of cattle, broad-swords, pride and flourish but little gold and silver. But such as there might be was undoubtedly largely in the hands of Clan Campbell. It was strange how different from all the other clans were the Campbells, as Celtic in origin as any, yet totally different in outlook, in style of life and especially in acquisitiveness. They were nowise less concerned with pride and status and flourish, but they sought to display and enhance these by the pen and the parchment rather than with the sword, using the law, legal processes, politics and sheer ingenuity – as well as carefully-planned inter-marriage – to gain and hold and expand their influence, lands and riches. Inevitably, although they remained Highland and based, in the main, north of the Line, their eyes were apt to be turned southwards, unlike the other clans. And they multiplied and prospered exceedingly, to the envy and hatred of the rest, who affected to despise them; so that from Argyll, their homeland, they had spread all over the North – and southwards into Ayrshire, for instance, where one of their chieftains had become Earl of Loudoun – so that they had now three earls in the clan, Argyll himself, Breadalbane, who was Campbell of Glenorchy, and Loudoun. Also sundry baronetcies and half a hundred lairdships, many of them very rich and productive.

Hence this journey. Hitherto, although certain Campbells linked to the establishment and government had invested in the Company, by and large the Highland-based lairds had not been involved. Aberuchill himself had shares in a modest way; and at Andrew's suggestion had agreed to call together a selection of his most prosperous fellow-clansmen for approach on the subject. If these could be suitably impressed, a large proportion of the extra capital might well be raised.

That was one aspect of their mission. The other was very different. The authorities in Edinburgh were worried about continuing rumours of Jacobite activity in the North, suggestions of planned rising. It was known that there were constant comings and goings of couriers between the Highlands and James at St. Germain, where he now held court at the expense of Louis of France, who still saw fit to recognise him as King of Scots, and of England too, to William's wrath. It was important for the government to discover how serious a threat this constituted; and this mission to the Campbells seemed an excellent way of attempting a discreet enquiry, with the co-operation of Lord Aberuchill. The Campbells themselves were not likely to be involved in overt seditious activities – they were much too well aware on which side their bread was buttered for that, at least until the other side looked like winning; but undoubtedly they would have their sharp ears very close to the ground and might give useful leads. This was really Belhaven's business rather than Andrew's, as one of the militia commanders and Privy Councillor – although the other was concerned also that James Stewart and his tyrannies should not be restored.

With the mouth of Glen Artney opening southwards before them, out of which this Water of Ruchill issued, they swung off to the west on a road gravelled with marl and grit from the river, something unusual for the Highlands, marks of carriage-wheels thereon. This led through grassy pastureland dotted with birchwoods, where many black cattle grazed, with some tilled land walled off by stone dykes. Andrew in especial was interested, noting that the land-use was superior to much that they had seen since leaving the Lowlands at Dunblane, but perceiving where improvements could be made, in liming, drainage, stone- and scrub-clearance and the like.

Presently the castle of Aberuchill appeared before them, under a green hill, not very large, a fairly typical tall oblong tower of four storeys with angle-turrets and crowstepped gables, whitewashed and spruce within a high-walled court-yard with gatehouse and outbuildings. The yard proved to contain three coaches, horses unhitched. For Highlanders, the Campbells clearly travelled in style.

They were well received, if somewhat cautiously eyed by their fellow-guests, who evidently were on their guard against being sold a horse which might not run. There were half a dozen gentlemen present already and more kept arriving, one creating a major stir, drawing up in a black and yellow coach with what Andrew considered to be a vulgar display of heraldic paintwork reminiscent of the Duke of Lauderdale, now deceased, and six matched black horses with yellow harness, liveried postillions and outriders. This proved to be John Campbell of Glenorchy, first Earl of Breadalbane, second only to Argyll in the Campbell hierarchy, a smooth-faced, bland, cold-smiling man in a full-bottomed wig, in his late fifties, with whom the others were all obviously much impressed. Andrew for one did not much like what he saw, but recognised that if he could convince this man to invest, much of his task might be done, for undoubtedly others would be apt to follow his lead. The fact that Breadalbane had come at all, from Balloch Castle near the foot of Loch Tay, a good forty miles, was encouraging in itself. Whatever else he was, this was a shrewd and able character, ruthless by reputation, a manipulator, and alleged to have urged Dalrymple on to the Glencoe affair, as a means of adding to his territories at the same time as getting rid of his old enemy MacIan – even though already it was Breadalbane's boast that he could ride from the North Sea to the Atlantic on his own land.

The two Lowlanders were surprised to discover that every one of the fourteen other guests was named Campbell; but that, despite this notable demonstration of clan solidarity, not one of them wore Highland dress. The nearest to it was Breadalbane himself, who arrived wrapped in a tartan plaid, despite the August warmth.

Although there were brief references to Darien and current problems, in casual conversation, it was not until dinner was over and the wine was flowing that Aberuchill actually introduced the object of the gathering. He explained that the Lord Belhaven and Stenton, a colleague of his on His Grace's Privy Council, was chairman of the great new company formed to promote Scotland's prosperity and influence; and Mr. Fletcher, whom they would all know by repute, had been largely responsible for advancing the man Paterson's project in Scotland. They had points to put forward which, he was sure, would be of interest to all present, interest and possibly profit. He called upon Lord Belhaven.

Johnnie recognised that when it came to eloquence and persuasiveness he was no match for Andrew. He spoke only briefly, stressed that what was to be discussed was of vital importance, admitted that he was chairman, appointed by Parliament, of the Company of Scotland for Trading with Africa and the Indies, but declared that the real authority in the project after William Paterson himself, was his friend Saltoun, who would explain all, much more ably and fluently than could he.

Andrew, looking round those Campbell faces, well understood that he was dealing with hard-bitten realists who would be unlikely to be swayed by appeals to national sentiment, the good of the many, amelioration of social conditions and the like, any more than by splendid visions of colonial adventure and advancement. Personal advantage and sheer gain, which could be transformed into land-ownership, was what would count here – although there was probably one string on which he might harp to some effect, namely pride, pride in their name and reputation, their clannishness and their embattled situation against the hatred of other clans. Also, of course, there was what could amount to a real weakness in that none of those present would be any stronger, nor dare be, than John, Earl of Breadalbane, their chieftain. So Andrew would direct his attention almost entirely upon that individual, hard case as he undoubtedly was.

He had, to be sure, come prepared and had asked Aberuchill to try at all costs to ensure Breadalbane's presence. He had made a point of discovering quite a lot about John Campbell of Glenorchy, his background and his character. He knew, for instance, that he was not on the best of terms with his own nephew and chief, the young tenth Earl of Argyll, MacCailean Mor, and assumed it stemmed from jealousy. He knew that he was ambitious as to rank, preoccupied with status, as that display of painted heraldry on the coach had proclaimed; so much so that some eight years before, when he was plain Laird of Glenorchy, he had mortgaged his lands and gone to great risks, in order to pay the debts and buy up the estates and assets of the spendthrift Sinclair, Earl of Caithness, on condition that that ancient earldom, granted with special destination to heirs of assign, would revert to himself; whereupon he assumed the title of Earl of Caithness, something which had set Scotland by the ears. Charles the Second had, at first, weakly acquiesced in this, no doubt with suitable sweetener; but on the true Sinclair heir raising legal objection, backed by the law and most of the scandalised nobility of Scotland, the King had had to take back his agreement; but had got over the difficulty by creating the

Campbell Earl of Breadalbane. Andrew knew also that the new Earl was at odds with his own eldest son, the Lord Ormelie, and had obtained special royal permission for his earldom to descend to his *second* son. Furthermore he had learned that the Earl had played a very dubious part in 1691 when, having convinced the government that the Highlands might be pacified largely, and the Jacobite threat contained, by the institution of a sort of irregular militia formed from amongst the clans themselves, to be known as Highland Watches, and the chiefs encouraged to set these up by substantial money payments from Edinburgh. He arranged a so-called hunting-party at Achallader Castle in Rannoch, one of his most remote seats, there to convince the assembled chiefs and to distribute the government largesse, no less than £12,000 sterling, a vast sum by Highland standards. Little of this was thought to have got beyond Breadalbane's own treasure-chest, and the Highland Watch got off to a very limping start. It went against the grain for Andrew Fletcher to seek the co-operation of such a character, but the Darien enterprise had to be salvaged somehow, in the nation's interest.

After explaining the scheme in general therefore and emphasising the transportage and canal possibilities – although making a point of the need for secrecy on this score meantime – he went on to aim certain aspects specifically at Breadalbane. He said that, although William had ceased meantime to smile on the venture, after his English government had declared participation in the company unlawful, nevertheless the King had not sought to withdraw his royal charter. Moreover the monarch was still desperately in need of monies for his military adventures on the Continent, into which he had thrown himself with additional urgency since the death of his Queen the year previously – and for which the English Parliament was loth to finance him. So the royal frowns would most assuredly turn to smiles again if and when profits began to accrue to him, as charter-dues, payable to the King personally. And when William found cause to smile on his prominent subjects, titles and promotions were apt to follow, as they all knew. It was no secret that certain Scots lords who were substantial supporters of the new company looked to their participation as a means of advancement in rank and degree as well as profit. For instance the Marquises of Douglas, Montrose and Atholl hoped to become dukes – even though the last, as they were aware, had been for King James; but his eldest son Lord Murray was of course the new Secretary of State; and another son, Lord Mungo Murray had joined the company's service. The Earl of Tweeddale was already new-promoted Marquis thereof; and those of Melville, Lothian, Roxburgh, Dundonald and Southesk hoped for a like advancement. And so on.

Andrew paused to assess the impact of this thrust. The Marquis of Atholl was known to be Breadalbane's particular foe and bugbear, rival in these central Highlands, almost as great a landowner as himself, whose presence hedged the Campbells in on many fronts. Any promotion for Atholl would sting.

If this line of persuasion was not lost on Breadalbane, his reaction was oblique. "If His Dutch Grace is like to be so favourable towards those who may signally support this venture, Mr. Fletcher – how is it that you yourself do not appear to be a beneficiary of the royal kindness?" he asked shrewdly.

Andrew could not fail to recognise the calibre of that shot. "The King may eventually show me some favour, my lord – who knows? And he has, of course, restored to me my forfeited estates. But I fear that I offended His Grace at one time, spoke my mind over-plainly, on the subject of royal powers. I imagine that he has not forgotten."

"So – this is why you labour so hard in this matter, sir? You seek to win back William's favour?"

Andrew took a quick breath and managed to swallow the hot retort which sprang to his lips. After all, if the Campbell liked to think this, and it made it all more understandable to his acquisitive mind, why argue?

"I seek profit on all accounts, my lord," he answered carefully. "For myself, to be sure, but also for all, for Scotland, for the country as a whole. Profit, wealth, is much needed, you will not deny, in this pass."

"Aye," the Earl nodded, smiling his chilly smile. "Proceed, sir."

"There is undoubted advantage to be gained by investing substantially in the project at this stage, my lords and gentlemen. The company has been set up by Act of Parliament only since last June. So the fullest participation in its direction and governance is not yet complete. My lord of Belhaven, here, is chairman, and Mr. Paterson will chiefly manage all, at first. But there is room for a number of others, as directors and in positions of much influence and responsibility. Obviously those gentleman of ability and standing who subscribe in major amounts will be best-placed to be considered for office, and consequent advancement in further investment and exploitation of the colony's resources and wealth. Which will undoubtedly be very great. Not only for themselves but for their families and associates, for much leadership will be required. For instance, my Lord Justice Clerk Cockburn of Ormiston has become a director, and his son John an officer. As has the Lord Provost of Edinburgh. Sir Robert Cheisley, Commissioner of the Exchequer Sir John Maxwell of Pollock, and others."

If this was blatant, it had its effect. There were murmurs all round the table and calculating glances darting this way and that.

"This of the possible canal?" Breadalbane broke in. "It would be a most costly design. Thirty miles, you say? How is it to be paid for? Out of the moneys you seek?"

"No, my lord. What is being sought now is for the setting up, equipping and funding of the colony itself, shipping, trade-goods, gear and the like. The canal scheme will be a separate issue, to be paid for by profits from the transportage enterprise between the two oceans. There should be no lack of money for that – for the portage will be as good as any gold-mine."

"Proof, sir – proof! I would not put any siller of mine into dreams and calentures!"

"As to proof, gentlemen, sober estimates of the value of cargoes coming to Europe each year from the Pacific and India Oceans amount to over ten millions of pounds sterling. Even a small transportage charge for one quarter of that would provide a notable revenue. And such transportage would save months and dire hazards on every shipment."

That appeared to satisfy most. There were other questions,

similar to those that had been raised at the original meeting at Saltoun. Then Campbell of Barcaldine, sitting next to Breadalbane – he was his chamberlain – and after a whispered exchange spoke up.

"It seems to me, Mr. Fletcher, that this gold-mine of yours, if it does yield the gold, will be bound to attract envious eyes and grasping hands. How will your company protect it? The colonists may well prove insufficient. And who will pay respect to the royal charter when the English themselves decry the enterprise as unlawful?"

Andrew hesitated slightly. This was in fact his own most serious doubt. "It is planned to build a line of forts," he explained. "There will be a governor and a militia force. Do not tell me that we Scots are incapable of defending our own? We have held our kingdom inviolate from attack for seven hundred years. Shall we fail now?"

"But numbers, man? Across the ocean, we could not have the numbers to repel determined assault. By the Spaniards, the French – or the English themselves."

"By the time that the colony has proved its value and profit sufficiently to attract the covetous to take it over, so it will have attracted sufficient Scots to man and defend it, surely? You, here in the Highlands, have fightingmen in plenty, I am told? Too many for some! Would not regiments of these be gainfully employed protecting Darien? I can see the company paying well for a regiment or two of Campbell Fencibles!" That was the best that he could do.

It produced some nodding and agreement. Then Breadalbane resumed the initiative.

"Is not the key to this matter English opposition? Remove that, and there will be little danger or problem. So, I say, we should turn our minds to changing that enmity instead of fighting it. Co-operation instead of the old hostility. The English fear that this will take away some of their prosperity, their monopolies. If we *shared* the venture with them – and not only this venture – all would be changed."

"How can we share, my lord? They *were* allowed to share. Then their government forced all English shares to be handed back. They would not consider it again."

"Not that sort of sharing, sir. Or not only. But greater, much greater. Union!"

There were sharply indrawn breaths from all around. Campbells would question the Earl of Breadalbane on that emotive issue.

"If Scotland and England were united in one polity, then all such hostility would fade," the Earl went on, authoritatively rather than persuasively. "King James the Sixth united the two kingdoms near a century ago. He should have united the states, likewise. One realm. But it could still be done, and should. Then every privilege open to Englishmen would be open to Scotsmen also. The Navigation Acts would no longer close their ports and colonies to Scots shippers. Trade would be freed. We could share in their prosperity – and they in ours. There would be no need to protect Darien from attack – for with English favour, none would dare assail it, Spanish, French or other."

None spoke. Andrew looked around them, and at Belhaven, frowning.

"My lord," he said. "This is a greater issue – much greater. Which we can nowise decide upon here. There are so many aspects of it on which we would have to debate. Moreover, I think that the people of Scotland would never agree to it. To voluntarily yield our freedom and independence, after all the centuries! For the sake of trade?"

"Not our freedom, man – nor yet our independence. I do not say that we should all become Englishmen – God forbid! But a federal union. Each kingdom keeping its own rights, laws and parliaments; but united in one polity. As are the Germanic states and the Empire. It will come, I swear – and better sooner than later. Scotland is too small to stand alone, these days. And your company need fear no interference."

"Save that it would quickly become an *English* company, my lord! And Darien an English colony. That *I* swear!" Andrew realised that he was speaking hotly now, and strove to control himself; also to steer them back to the vital subject, much afraid that he had lost ground. "Parliament has made this a purely Scottish company and venture, my friends. Surely we can show that we are capable of enterprise as well as any

Englishmen, Frenchmen or Spaniards. Does Clan Campbell, famed for its enterprise and acumen, say otherwise?"

That challenge at least produced some reaction. "How much?" Campbell of Lochnell, a rich Lorn laird, demanded. "How much have you raised? And how much still to go?"

"The total required, sir, is put at £600,000, by Mr. Paterson. Much of it for the new ships. We had raised half that, in Scotland, the other half through Scots in England. Now that half has had to be returned. But Mr. Paterson has promised to raise £200,000 from his banking associates in Hamburg and the Low Countries. So we must raise a further £100,000 in Scotland."

There was a pause, men eyeing each other. Aberuchill spoke up.

"There was a limit of £1,000 when I subscribed. Does that still hold, in these changed circumstances, Mr. Fletcher?"

"No, my lord. The limit has been raised to £3,000. And the minimum £100."

"Then I raise my £1,000 to £2,000," their host declared.

Andrew cast him a grateful glance.

"I go to but £1,000," Lochnell said.

"I have but a few stony acres. £500 will do for me," Sir Duncan Campbell of Auchinbreck declared. There were chuckles, he being one of the richest men in the room.

"I always said that you were a faint-heart!" his younger brother exclaimed. "Put *me* down for £1,000!"

There was another pause. All eyes were apt to turn on Breadalbane. The Earl smiled tightly.

"I shall sleep on it, Mr. Fletcher," he announced.

"Excellent, my lord – how wise!" Andrew said quickly. "No doubt others will wish to do the same. Perhaps Auchinbreck may then decide to up his offer by, say, £50?"

Amidst laughter they left it there and the talk reverted to argument about possible union with England, those against much outnumbering those for, despite Breadalbane's advocacy.

Later, in the upper bedchamber they had to share – for the modest-sized castle was full indeed – Johnnie congratulated his friend.

"You managed that passing well, Andrew," he said. "I could never have dealt with them as you did. Nor anyone else that I know. Breadalbane in especial. He is a slippery fish, that one! Think you that you have hooked him? And can land him?"

"Who knows? But I am hopeful. He is shrewd enough and will not fail to perceive the possibilities of Paterson's Tollgate of the Oceans. He will not turn down the possibility of riches lightly. Forby, he was annoyed I think, that so many failed to follow his line on this of union. He sees himself as leader. He may not wish to be superseded, in this of the company, by Aberuchill or Lochnell. Others will also subscribe, I believe. Breadalbane may well be jealous for his leadership."

"I hope so. And if *these* Campbells subscribe strongly, others may well follow. For there are scores more. We would then have cause to rejoice over this night."

"Rejoice? I wonder? Over the subscriptions, perhaps. But tonight leaves a bad taste in my mouth, nevertheless. This talk of union. I do not like it, Johnnie. It much perturbs me. If men of Breadalbane's stature can contemplate it, even advocate it, who knows what may be in store? He even said that it was bound to come. I tell you, here is a threat to our nation to make all others of little account."

"Aye, and I have heard others singing the same song who should know better . . ."

A knock at the door heralded their host. "Ah, you are not yet bedded – that is good," Aberuchill said. "Our, er, friend, is here. He chooses a strange hour to come. But then, he is a strange man! I had not thought to see him until tomorrow's eve – when most of my guests will be gone. Will you come down? I do not wish to bring him through the house . . ."

In the half-dark, they followed the Lord Justice Clerk down the twisting turnpike-stair and out across the courtyard to an outbuilding against the curtain-walling, actually a cow-byre. Therein two men waited – although the newcomers hardly noticed one of them, so extraordinary was the other. This was a massive individual, in Highland costume of great kilt, long calfskin waistcoat or sleeveless jerkin, silken shirt and bonnet sporting a single eagle's feather, broad-sword hanging from a

278

jewelled shoulder-belt, silver buckles and cairngorm-stones gleaming redly in the light of the stable-lantern. The redness was not all the effect of the light, however, for he appeared to be all red, red-haired, red-bearded, clad in red and green tartans. Yet, although striking enough, it was not this which held the attention so much as the man's unusual build and presence. At first sight he did not seem particularly tall; but because of his enormous width of shoulder and great barrel-chest, his height did not greatly impress. What could not fail to register was the quite phenomenal length of the silk-clad arms, which reached down actually to the knees. Yet the total effect was not grotesque nor off-putting but indeed impressive, dramatic almost, eloquent of mighty physical strength and vigour – this last emphasised by intensely blue and alert eyes, vivid even in that light.

"This is MacGregor, of whom I spoke," Aberuchill introduced. "Although he must needs sign himself Campbell! Captain of Glengyle Highland Watch . . . and other things! Rob – here is my Lord Belhaven and Stenton and Mr. Fletcher of Saltoun, seeking a word with you."

"Delighted I am to meet the gentlemen," the enormous young man said courteously – for he could not be more than in his early twenties – his soft, lilting Highland intonation matching but strangely his formidable appearance. "This is Mac-an-Leister, my friend, gentlemen." There was more than a hint of reproof in that, for the Lord Justice Clerk, who had failed to introduce the other man, a tall, thin, dark individual, much less striking of aspect and costume and a few years older.

Surprised not only at this rebuke but at the cultural manner and gentle voice of the speaker, the Lowlanders bowed, distinctly at a loss as to how to deal with these characters, even how to address them.

"Good evening," Johnnie said briefly.

"It is good of you to come to meet us, sir," Andrew said. "And you, sir." He looked at the thin man with some interest now. "Did I hear you named Leister? I have not the Erse tongue, I fear – but I have heard that Leister means fletcher, my own name? Am I right?"

"Indeed you are, sir," the other nodded. "My name, in your

279

tongue, means Son of the Arrow-maker, or Fletcher. I come of the line of Achallader – now alas, Campbell!" And he glanced at Aberuchill, with a half-bow, half-grimace.

"That is extraordinary!" Andrew said. "For there is a tradition in my family that we also come of the Fletchers, or Leisters, of Achallader, some way back. My grandfather was Lord Innerpeffer, of Session. Innerpeffer is not far from here, in Strathearn, I think?"

"To be sure, sir. So we may be kin. Our house is in sad decline!" There was a sardonic twist to the thin man's lips as he said that.

"Shame on you, Mac-an-Leister!" the big man cried, but grinning. "What way is that at all to be speaking to Sassenach gentlemen?"

Aberuchill nodded, a little stiffly. "I will be leaving you to your, h'mm, discussion." And he turned to go.

"Och, he is a Campbell, just!" That came by way of explanation, with a hoot of laughter, and before the Lord Justice Clerk of Scotland was through the open doorway.

Andrew coughed. "How are we to address *you*, sir? Mr. MacGregor? Or Mr. Campbell? Or . . . other?"

"Neither, at all. I am not Mister anything, friend. I am a Highland gentleman, sir, and we do not go in for mistering. I am third son to the former Colonel Donald Ghlas MacGregor of Glengyle, who died for supporting his rightful monarch! *Magni nominis umbra*! You may call me Captain, if you wish. Or, if that sticks in your gullet, I have a few poor acres on the shore of Loch Katrine, so you could name me Portanellan and Inverlochlarig. But, och, most honest men just call me Rob Roy, whatever – and add MacGregor when you are after feeling courageous! Or *In lapsus memoriae*!"

Andrew shot a glance at Belhaven. This was, in theory, his affair; but Johnnie was clearly quite content to leave the handling of this curious Latin-quoting Highlander to himself. He knew, of course – all Scotland knew – that the name of MacGregor had been prescribed by James the Sixth as unlawful to use, in wrath against that clan for their warlike activities against the Macfarlanes, the Colquhouns, the Murrays, the MacNabs and of course the Campbells; and this prescription had been renewed by Parliament as recently as two years ago, 1693, largely at the behest of the Campbells again. So not only was it an offence to call oneself by that name but no such signature was valid in law. Therefore for all legal documents, charters and the like, the MacGregors had to use another name for signing, a source of much heart-burning for a proud folk whose favourite exclamation was 'As Royal's my Race!', referring to their descent, as Clan Alpin, from Kenneth MacAlpin, first King of the United Picts and Scots.

"Captain MacGregor will serve very well, I think," Andrew said. "Forby, it is as captain of a Highland Watch, in the main, that we wish speech with you. That, and the fact that you are, nevertheless, a Jacobite. Or so we understand sir? Or were."

"I fought for King James at Killiecrankie, yes. As did Mac-an-Leister."

"Yet you now lead a militia company of a sort, in the name of King William!"

"Why not, at all, Mr. Fletcher? The King's peace must be kept, whoever is King, must it not?"

Andrew strove to keep his face straight. From all accounts Rob Roy MacGregor's methods of keeping the King's peace were unusual, to say the least, with cattle acquisition reputedly a major part of it and penalties in kind for those who failed to co-operate.

"H'mm. An excellent sentiment, Captain MacGregor. Which confirms Lord Aberuchill's good judgment in suggesting that we should speak with you."

"Och, Colin Campbell has his glimmerings of sense, see you – for a judge!" The big man laughed again, heartily. Evidently he found much amusement in life. "And in what, at all, does he judge I am to serve you, sir?"

"It is in the matter you have already mentioned – the keeping of the King's peace. Here, in the Highlands. The King's government is concerned. It hears rumours. Of couriers from St. Germain, of French gold, of attempts to stir an uprising. How much of this is true is not known . . ."

"I am hoping, Mr. Fletcher, that you are not after coming here for to try to be making a spy out of me?" That

281

intervention was none the less telling, but all menacing, for being so softly, carefully spoken.

"No, no, sir – nothing like that. Our purpose is concerned with *giving* information, more than seeking it. The government naturally wishes to maintain the King's peace north of the Highland Line. Hence the Highland Watches. But it feels that more could and should be done. Not only to counter possible Jacobite movements which is, shall we say, negative, but more positively to show the King's and his ministers' goodwill, to bring the Highlands into closer harmony with the rest of Scotland, to spread the benefits of what has been achieved in better governance, freedom from tyranny, religious bigotry and the like . . ."

"Spread King William's goodwill!" Again the quietly sibilant but tense intervention. "After Glencoe, you talk of that?"

"Glencoe was evil, a disaster, a shame on the government. Also a grievous mistake and error of judgment. But that lesson has been learned. The men responsible brought down . . ."

"But not tried and hanged, by God! Dalrymple is still a free man, I am told. As is my uncle."

"Your uncle . . . ?"

"Glenlyon was my mother's brother – to my sorrow!"

"Save us – I did not know that!" Andrew's thoughts raced. This explained much. Why this young man of such peculiar reputation and of an almost outlawed clan, should have been raised to the position of captaining a Highland Watch; for Campbell of Glenlyon, the man who carried out the Glencoe massacre, was first cousin to Breadalbane himself – so that this Rob Roy was also the Earl's close kin, and Breadalbane it was who had been responsible for setting up the Highland Watches. It explained also why the MacGregor signed himself Campbell. But it likewise meant that he could be the more influential in their present project – something that Aberuchill had not enlarged upon. Moreover, if he felt some guilt by association . . . ?

Belhaven's mind must have been working the same way for he spoke into the pause. "Then you are the more the man we need. To make clear the government's change of heart –

although Glencoe was never the Scots *government's* plan or desire."

"You speak, my lord, as from the government in Edinburgh. Yet you are not in that government, I think? Nor is Mr. Fletcher, by all reports!"

Andrew nodded. "You are correctly informed, Captain. Lord Belhaven is a Privy Councillor but no sort of minister. Whilst *I* am more of a thorn-in-the-flesh to government than its representative! But it was thought best that first approaches and soundings should be made by such as ourselves to such as yourself, quietly. Better that than rushing in, unsure of reception. Governments are thin-skinned in such matters – especially after Glencoe."

"And the said matters, sir? Of which your masters are wary?"

"Scarcely our masters! But the proposals, in general terms, are these. Annual payments – pensions, if you like – to chiefs, chieftains and great lairds, to keep and enforce the King's peace. Proper representation in Parliament – which has never been established in the Highlands. Burgh status, with its trading and other privileges, for suitable communities. More Highland representation on the Privy Council. Indemnity for all Jacobite prisoners. Other benefits and improvements also, but these for a start."

"And the new Darien project to offer much encouragement for Highland settlers in the colony. And to employ troops of Highlanders in its defence," Johnnie put in.

"Well, well, my goodness – all that!" the MacGregor exclaimed, with exaggerated approval. "As Royal's my Race – the government must be loving us all greatly, of a sudden, to woo poor Highlandmen this way! Or else, be much afraid of its ability to be controlling a rising for King James!"

"M'mm. Put it this way, Captain. We are making a new start in Scotland. We have got rid of much that has plagued our nation for long – misgovernment from London, the rule of favourites and their military, religious oppression, Parliament ignored or gagged. There is much more to be done. I myself have worked for this end for near twenty years. But if the Highlands remain outside it all, fertile soil for uprising and foreign intervention, then the rest is ever at risk. Scotland should be one polity, not two. There will always be Highland and Lowland – but they could and should work together for the benefit of the nation as a whole."

"A noble prospect, Mr. Fletcher, whatever. But something sudden, is it not? Myself, I have seen no signs of this new love for the Highlands, this vision of brotherhood – before yourselves, gentlemen! *Auspicium melioris aevi*, perhaps? But sudden. The Highlandman is still treated as dirt, in the streets of Edinburgh. My own father was held in Edinburgh's Tolbooth for five years like a common felon, Highland gentleman as he was. The Highland cattle-drovers are cheated at every tryst by Lowland dealers – as I should know! You, sir, may be strong for this splendid new start – but how many others are? What has changed? Is it sudden love – or fear, just?"

"The new Secretary of State, Lord Murray, is a Highlander, I would remind you. Heir to the Marquis of Atholl," Johnnie mentioned "He supports this enterprise."

"John Murray would support this today and the opposite tomorrow, whatever! I know him, as I know his father – I, who have had to collect mail from them these four years!"

Andrew blinked. "You mean . . . he pays you? To protect his cattle? The Secretary of State himself!"

"When he remembers! I have to be after reminding him, now and again. Like Colin Campbell."

"Aberuchill, you mean? Does he, too . . . ? Surely not? The Lord Justice Clerk!"

"Why not, at all? Their cattle need protecting just like other folk's, Mr. Fletcher, do they not? A kyloe is a kyloe, whosoever owns it. And costs siller. And there are some terrible thieving scoundrels about these days – are there not, Mac-an-Leister?"

That man nodded, grimly.

Again Andrew's wits went birling. If all they heard was true, Rob Roy MacGregor's methods of ensuring that his clients paid their mail, as he called it, for the protection of their flocks and herds, was to raid and drive them off himself if they omitted to do so, using his Highland Watch for the task – blackmail, the process was being called. If even the Secretary of

State and the Lord Justice Clerk were prepared to give into to this, how could normal conditions of honest dealing ever be established north of the Highland Line?

But this was neither the place nor the time to argue that aspect. "That all may be so. But what we have told you represents betterment, a hand outstretched on the government's part, a move in the right direction. Do you not agree, Captain?"

"It could be that, whatever. Or it could mean but more cream on the milk of some and no benefit at all for the rest. As before."

"Before . . . ?"

"To be sure. This is not the first time your masters have tried to buy peace in the Highlands. I am told that £12,000 was sent north for the chiefs, to set up the Watches. But three Watches were raised – and my Glengyle one got only a few hundreds of pounds. We have to be making up our expenses . . . otherwise! Surprised I'd be if more than £2,000 of it all ever got beyond a certain lordly pocket!"

"You think so? I . . . that is unfortunate. And must not occur again. Better arrangements must be made this time."

"Then you will have to be after watching your Campbells, whatever, Mr. Fletcher! What do you want from myself, then?"

"We want you to sound out opinion, quietly. Amongst the chiefs and landed men. You, we understand, are in a good position to do this, as captain of the Watch and as, h'mm, cattle-dealer. Also your father's son. You will remember the main proposals?"

"Och yes, fine. And the money? How much, at all?"

"No actual amounts were given us. But we are assured that they would be substantial."

"Substantial? Just that – substantial. Och yes, well. And it will not be into John of Breadalbane's hands?"

"No, sir. That, I think, I can promise you."

"Aye. And what else can you promise me, Mr. Fletcher?"

"The gratitude of the King's government, shall we say? Which can take many forms."

"Gratitude, Mac-an-Leister – do you hear? Och, King

285

William's gratitude to Clan Alpin and Sheep Robbie! Well, well! For spreading the good word. Och, I think there might be something more you are wanting, no?"

Belhaven cleared his throat. "It would be of advantage, sir, if we knew the state of the Jacobite threat. How strong for James are the chiefs? Is money coming from France – Louis' money? Such information would help this initiative."

"I was thinking it would come to this, in the end, my lord! And I told you, did I not – I would not play the spy?"

"We do not ask you to, Captain MacGregor," Andrew put in hurriedly. "We ask you for no details, no names. Only the general position which, you will agree, we need to know if we are to proceed with this Highland project. And which, surely, we are entitled to ask the captain of one of King William's Watches?"

"Is it King William's Watch, then? And here's me after thinking it was Clan Alpin's Watch! Och well, we're learning things this night. *Hominis est errare*! How say you, Mac-an-Leister – have we any gossip that we can spare for good King William in Holland?"

"He is nearer to King James, his own good-father, there than are we, I'm thinking," the other said. "But och, no harm in a word or two for the gentlemen to be taking back to show that their journey into the wild Highlands was not wasted, just!"

"My own feeling, entirely. A pity to disappoint, whatever. We could tell them that it would not be very difficult to outbid the French louis-d'ors that have come so far – and most of which have stuck to the fingers of the Skye and Island chiefs, whatever! They could be after asking King William's friends there! And we could tell them that there is more bickering amongst the chiefs over who failed who at Cromdale fight, and who might become King James's Earl of this or Marquis of that, than plans for a rising."

"Is that so?" Andrew's glance at Johnnie, although brief, was eloquent. How seriously to take this character was doubtful; but if what he said was reliable, then they had what they had come for. "We take it, then, that there is little danger of any rising meantime – to interfere with this better understanding which is to be promoted, sir?"

286

"Och, you must take what you think best out of what is no more than common gossip just. Which is all that we are after repeating, mind. Myself, now – and Mac-an-Leister, I am sure – would not ever act the informer! But – we would not wish King William's government to be discouraged at all from good works – late as they are! And we would be happy to receive some small token thereof!"

"I see. Then we are much obliged to you, Captain. And to you, Mac-an-Leister. It has been an interesting and valuable meeting."

"Just that, indeed. But it might be, och, inadvisable to speak of our meeting tonight, gentlemen, with the other Campbells here, see you. My lord and cousin of Breadalbane in particular. Not all are so discreet, shall we say, as Colin of Aberuchill. *Verbum sapienti sat est*! Now, if you will excuse us, we have some hours of riding ahead of us . . ."

Back in their upper room the two Lowlanders considered the problems and agilities of dealing with Highlanders; but decided that it probably had been a worthwhile exercise as well as an edification. And in the morning, when Breadalbane weighed in with £1,000 for the Darien project, and some did even better, they set off for the South with fair satisfaction.

The only question at the back of Andrew's mind was – did they in fact speak the same language as these people, even when they were not speaking in the incomprehensible Gaelic? Or in Latin?

18

It would be safe to say that never before had the Port of Leith experienced anything to compare with the scenes of 26th July 1698; not even in 1561 when the cream of Scotland assembled there to greet Mary Queen of Scots on her return from France, nor in 1590 when her son James the Sixth brought back his bride from Denmark. On both these occasions it had been representatives of the ruling hierarchy, together with the provost and magistrates of Edinburgh, with such citizens as felt sufficiently enthusiastic for the two-mile walk down to the port – plus, of course, the good folk of Leith itself. But this fine summer's day all Scotland seemed to have converged on the harbour-area in vast numbers and in high spirits – and for once all Scotland meant just that, Highlanders as well as Lowlanders being quite strongly represented, something unknown hitherto and not altogether approved of by some. However, there had been little or no trouble so far, and a holiday mood prevailed, despite the problems caused by overcrowding in narrow streets, wynds and quaysides.

Andrew Fletcher had difficulty in pushing and working a way for his party, through the excited and cheerful throng, to the dockside from the Tolbooth Wynd where they had to leave the horses, despite the fact that his company included the prime mover and instigator of it all, William Paterson himself. None was more excited than Andrew's eight-year-old nephew and namesake, to whom he clung with one hand whilst he thrust people aside with the other, and Margaret clutched his coat-tails, Henry's arm around her, with Paterson helping Johnnie to steer Margaret Belhaven in their wake. They had been much delayed, unprepared for the huge crowds which had packed the route down Leith Walk all the way from the city.

At least they had no problem as to direction, for the tall masts and rigging of the great ships thrust up high ahead for all to see, their blue-and-white St. Andrew's Cross flags flapping bravely in the breeze. They were moored, five of them, in a line along the principal town quay, known as The Shore, where the Water of Leith river entered the Firth of Forth estuary and provided deep-water berthing, three large three-decked vessels to carry the first twelve hundred settlers and militia and their gear; and two cargo-ships to transport the livestock, stores, provisions, trade-goods and the like. The large craft were suitably named – *Caledonia*, *St. Andrew*, *Unicorn*, and the others *Dolphin* and *Endeavour*; and all represented a mighty investment of capital.

Andrew's pushing, and natural air of authority and bearing,

288

won them through to the quayside at length, itself of course equally crowded, between the tall warehouses and the water. But at least here there was some order in the busy scene, with militiamen keeping lanes open through the throng, shepherding important folk hither and thither. Edinburgh's Lord Provost, himself a major shareholder in the Company, was very much in charge here, bustling about importantly, and at present in some agitation, faced with an unexpected problem – namely the discovery on board each of the ships of innumerable stowaways, some even of gentle blood, who had to be put ashore and dealt with somehow, with everybody far too busy and in no mood to cope with them. Places on the voyage had been over-subscribed five or six times and, with twelve-hundred, the vessels were already overfull.

"Thank God you have arrived!' Patrick Home greeted the newcomers. He was now an earl no less, advanced from being Baron Polwarth to Earl of Marchmont on his appointment as Lord Chancellor of Scotland, a man who made better use of his opportunities than did his friend. "Everybody has been calling for you, Paterson. We were afraid that there must have been some trouble. The shipmasters say that if they are to catch the tide, they must sail within the hour."

"No need for alarm, my lord," Paterson said. "I have only to go aboard, and say goodbye to these my friends. I was here until late last night, putting all matters in order. Everything is ready. We had no notion that there would be so many people."

"Aye, it is extraordinary. I have never seen anything like it. There are folk come from every airt. You have done your work almost too well, Andrew. The land is all but run mad! There are scores, hundreds, still beseeching us to let them sail. As colonists. And not only gangrels, tranters, vagrants, cadgers and the like. Or Hielantmen! But laird's sons, merchanters, men of some substance . . ."

"These stowaways, Mr. Paterson, sir – what are we to do with them?" the Provost interrupted. He had to shout, they all had to shout, for pipers were blowing lustily at the gangways up to every ship and the noise was appalling, with the stowaways yelling, women screeching, militiamen bellowing orders and the vast crowd in full cry.

"We cannot allow any to stay aboard. We are over-loaded already," Paterson declared. "We have many weeks of sailing. Conditions will be bad enough as it is . . ."

"Well, Saltoun – are you satisfied?" The new Lord Stair came up. Old James Dalrymple had died and John, the man who had planned Glencoe, was now the viscount and nowise inhibited from taking fullest part in the affairs of the nation, despite unpopularity. "I will say this for you – you and Belhaven and Marchmont have managed your business to some effect. Quite set the heather on fire, it seems – our Scots heather! Whether whatever they have for heather in this Darien will burn so well, we shall discover! Let us hope that it will prove all that you foretell – or Scotland is going to be a sorry, not to say an angry, land."

"I have every confidence, my lord – or I would not have laboured as I have done," Andrew said stiffly. "William Paterson's dream is about to become a reality. The first part of it. And if we cannot make the second part come true thereafter, we are not the folk I have believed we are. But – I had scarce expected to see *you* here!"

"Why not, man? After all, I am now a shareholder, to the tune of my late father's perhaps rash investment of one thousand pounds. I hope that I shall see some fruits of it!"

Paterson led them up the gangway and aboard the largest ship, *Caledonia*, young Andrew dragging his mother after him eagerly, for a tour of the vessel. Most of the notables followed her, to cheers from the colonists-to-be already crowding the decks. Paterson took them below, to dispense wine in his own cabin to all who could squeeze inside amongst the crates and baggage, and success and a speedy voyage were toasted. But with shipmasters concerned with time and tides, there was pressure to get the formalities over, and the Lord Provost soon had them all hustled up to the high poop-deck at the stern, where he had the city trumpeter blow a flourish. He had to blow loud and long, to overcome the combined efforts of pipers, street-vendors, barking dogs, screaming gulls and the thousands of excited voices. But eventually an approximate hush was achieved, at least nearby.

The Provost then made a speech, rather lengthy. Just what

he said after the first minute or two was unclear, even to those around him, as the chatter began again to drown him out – but undoubtedly it was in congratulatory and well-wishing vein. Then he called upon the Lord Belhaven and Stenton, as chairman of the Company for Trading with Africa and the Indies. Johnnie was as brief as the other had been fulsome – but went equally unheard by most. All he said, in fact, was God-speed to the great venture, thanks for all the wonderful support – and to introduce William Paterson, the begetter of it all.

Paterson did not so much as move forward to the Provost's side, mumbled a few words, raised his hand to wave, and was done. Few there probably knew who he was or what he said.

Then there was a change. The minister of the High Kirk of St. Giles, recently restored to that status after being for a while the cathedral of the unpopular Bishops of Edinburgh, stepped forward and raised both arms high. Quickly the level of noise subsided, tribute to the godly respect for the Kirk amongst the Scots folk at large, the black Geneva gown and white linen bands at throat clearly distinguishing its representative. So he had a better start than the others; but even so he would probably have been heard, for he had a rich and sonorous voice, trained to fill great echoing spaces and to project itself to far corners. Everywhere folk fell silent, save for the far-distant. Eloquently, vehemently, he addressed the Almighty, inform-ing Him of the situation, declaring the essential rightness and worth of their enterprise, the need for it to prosper, the great sacrifice of goods and gear the Lord's faithful Scots people had made to launch it, against the malice of ill-wishers from elsewhere; and beseeching God's most strenuous and compre-hensive blessing upon the entire project and His incessant vigilance on their behalf. Amen. They would now sing to God's praise, in the Psalms of David, number One Hundred.

So, led by the powerful, resonant tenor, the people that on earth do dwell sang to the Lord with cheerful voice, somewhat doubtfully at first and then, as embarrassment gave place to fervour, in growing power and volume until the summer air rang and quivered with the ages-old affirmation and dedica-tion, bringing a kind of wonder to the materialists and moisture to many an eye, if cynical comment from one or two.

Surely seldom had a trading, commercial and colonial endeavour been launched in quite this fashion.

Somebody, after a moment or two of peculiar hush at the psalm's end, started to cheer, and everywhere it was taken up in wild acclaim. On and on the vociferation went, the crowds surged this way and that, some impromptu dancing began, where there was room, on quayside and street, and clearly that was the end of all formalities. Relieved, the shipmen commenced the difficult task of ushering the important visitors off the vessels, and crews were ordered to get busy with ropes and canvas.

The pipers resumed.

Andrew turned to shake Paterson by the hand. "I could wish that I was going with you, Will," he said. "Perhaps, one day. But meantime, there is too much to be done . . ."

"No, no. Your place is here, friend. There are plenty who can direct what has to be done in Darien; few indeed who can win the battle here, keep the folk contented until they can see something of their harvest. The enthusiasm will flag and fail long before the colony is fully established. You will require all your powers and eloquence . . ."

"Good fortune, fair winds and God's blessing, Mr, Paterson," Margaret broke in. "Our thoughts and prayers go with you all."

"I will come too, when I am a little older," young Andrew asserted.

They said farewell to a number of others, in a quite emotional scene, all disagreements, enmities and political rivalries forgotten meantime. There were, in fact, not a few personal friends, and the sons of friends, going on this first expedition. Over three hundred young men of the best families in the land amongst the twelve hundred, an amazing proportion of aristocrats as against sons of the soil, tradesmen, clerks, soldiers and the like, including half a dozen Campbell scions and Atholl's third son, the Lord Mungo Murray, the Secretary of State's brother. Paterson, in fact, was a little perturbed at this profusion of blue blood, for a task which would inevitably entail much hard labour and rough conditions; but his subscribers were not to be gainsaid, and many sent their sons to where their money went.

At last all was ready, the determined lingerers, fond mothers and proud fathers all but pushed down the gangways, the cables loosed and drawn inboard, the first sails hoisted. With a shoal of row-boats to tow her prow from the quayside, infinitely slowly *Caledonia* moved out into what was still the tidal mainstream of the Water of Leith. Canvas began to fill and the great vessel nosed her way, to ecstatic acclaim, towards the harbour-mouth and the Firth of Forth, one by one the other craft following. It was a slow process, of course, and throats were sore from cheering before all five ships were heading seawards. Guns fired a final salute from Leith Fort.

"How does it feel, Dand, to see that argosy sail, at last?" Henry Fletcher asked. "You have worked hard for it, hard and long. For another man's design. At much cost to yourself. Do you feel that it has been worth it?"

"Worth it in material gain and profit, we must wait to see. But that is not what has been my main concern, these many months."

"No? What, then?"

"I have seen this entire enterprise as something far greater than that. Think you that I would have devoted myself, as I have done so fully, to a mere scheme to make money? To develop trade? Even to found a colony? Have you ever known me to be concerned with merchanting and adding pound to pound? No — I have seen this project otherwise, as something like a crusade, Henry! Scotland needed it. Or needed something like it, desperately. Something which would unite and rally the people. We have come through grievous times, oppression, tyranny, civil strife, religious wars, and these have left their mark. The nation was despondent, riven with factions, poverty-stricken, suspicious of all authority. We could well have become a prey not only to anarchy but to English domination at last. There are plentywho talk of union, as you know – the union of the sprat with the mackerel! I used this vision of Paterson's to grow into a different kind of vision of my own. Of a people with a purpose again, something we could unite and struggle for – Presbyterians, Episcopalians and Catholics, town and country, gentry and merchantry and

293

commonality. Lowlands and Highlands. That it had to be money, the lure of siller, profit, troubled me at first. But what matters that if it served the purpose? Whether we approve or no, profit is the way to the best endeavours of many. Sadly, it has little to do with creeds or policies or rank. So, I said let us use the urge for profit to yoke our folk together and lead them on, in this pass." He waved a hand around him. "And you see the results!"

"So that was it, Andrew? I wondered," Margaret said, as they watched the ships diminish with distance. "You never spoke of this. Are you satisfied now? Seeing all this? And raising all that money?"

"So far, yes. All this today must mean something. The nation is stirred, at least."

"All the opposition from England? Did that not make you fear for *your* vision? As well as William Paterson's."

Andrew allowed himself a grim little smile. "To be honest – no, my dear! Indeed, I almost welcomed each blow the English Parliament, the East India Company and the London merchants struck against me. Nothing is more calculated to unite and arouse the Scots than open English interference and hostility, in especial aimed at Scots pockets! It is when they are more subtle and seek to divide us from within, Scot against Scot, that I fear!"

"Are you going to say as much at the parliament on Thursday, Dand? Explain your position?" Henry asked. "This of the English opposition is bound to come up."

"Lord, no! I am considered a sufficiently odd fish as it is! But, come – I think that the crowd is thinning now. We can get through . . ."

* * *

The Scots Parliament of 1698 was scarcely one of the most important; but it had certain distinguishing features. For one thing it was particularly well attended, for many far-away lords and commissioners, who often did not bother to make the journey, had come to see the sailing of the Darien expedition. There was a notable increase in the number of Highland representatives, partly for the same reason but also as a result of the new policy. Again, in the present euphoria, there was less overt acrimony. Also, contributing to this, was the unusual situation whereby King William, involved on the Continent once more and less than ever interested in Scotland, had not bothered to send up a High Commissioner but had merely ordered the Chancellor to act in both capacities. So the new Earl of Marchmont presided and led the discussions, a moderate and amiable man – which was a change at least.

All this affected Andrew Fletcher. Although still outside the government hierarchy, a determined individualist and belonging to no party, he had gained a sort of popularity over his connection with the Darien scheme; his co-operation over the Highland situation was appreciated; and he was known by all to be a friend of the Chancellor. So he in fact was in a position to take a more prominent and influential part in the proceedings than heretofore, and to be heard with respect.

Inevitably the Darien business was foremost on the agenda and in men's minds, and it was of course, very much the concern of Parliament, the Company having been established by official Act; also a great many of the members were financially involved. The main debate was on the scale of English hostility, its manifestations hitherto and what might be looked for in the future. There was much indignation, needless to say, and justly so. The principal offence was the activity of the English Resident in Hamburg, one Sir Paul Rycaut, who had persuaded the authorities there that England looked upon it as an inimical act if Hamburgers supported the Scots enterprise, the Company of Beggars as he called it, and had prevailed upon the Senate to declare the investment unlawful and to order the £100,000 subscribed there to be withdrawn, as in England, on pain of trade sanctions. The Dutch investors whom Paterson had also enrolled, followed suit on the orders of the States-General at the behest of the King of England – who appeared to be serenely unconcerned that he was also King of Scots. So another £200,000 had had to be repaid, that amount extra to be raised in Scotland, over and above the rest, and quickly, or the expedition ships being completed in the Hamburg yards would have been confiscated. That these vast sums had been produced from a nation notoriously poor in money-supply was further tribute to the enthusiasms engendered and the devotion and skill of the fund-raisers.

Discussion of all this, naturally, raised the assembly to a fine pitch of resentment and eloquence – which Marchmont had to try to control and seem to damp down, although it suited Andrew's own purposes very well. His personal interventions were more concerned with the future than the past. He declared that it was unlikely that having gone so far to try to stop the entire project, the English would now sit back and seek to interfere no more. He believed that they must look for further opposition and certainly non-co-operation at the colonial scene. What might be attempted was hard to gauge, but they must be prepared, both the new colonists and themselves at home.

There was much further outcry and demands that King William be left in no doubts as to the wrath of his Scots subjects and their undoubted rights and *his* duty. All this was somewhat basic and incoherent; but presently Marchmont caught the eye of the new Lord Advocate, Sir James Stewart, of ominous name but meticulously correct bearing, who asserted soothingly that their lordships and commissioners were right to be perturbed but that the remedy lay not in wild flourishes and declamations but in the quiet application of due processes of law. He pointed out that, however hostile the English Parliament and the powerful East India Company, they were neither of them above the rule of law, their own law. Therefore legal recourse should be taken by the Scots Parliament. He proposed that a Memorial should be submitted on Scotland's legal rights in the development, emphasising their irrefragable rights in both constitutional and public law to set up their own company and colony, within the provisions of the royal charter already granted. Such Memorial should be sent both to the King and to the English Lord Chancellor. The latter was bound in law to act in the matter and to advise the King accordingly.

Stewart was supported by no less than the new Lord President of Session, Sir Hew Dalrymple of North Berwick, old Stair's second son and brother of the Glencoe instigator. He said that this was the correct and probably most effective action to take. The English were, in theory, strong on the upholding of the law, their legalists influential in the House of Lords. Such an approach would carry far more weight than protests, resolutions and counter-threats.

Andrew, for one, was far from convinced. But he saw no real harm in the proposal – and if it was rejected by the English it would only add to the ire in Scotland and so help to maintain the temper and Darien-enthusiasm of the nation during the difficult and unprofitable months whilst the new colony was being established. So he gave it his moderate blessing.

Then another lawyerly Dalrymple voice spoke up, that of Stair himself. He announced that while he had no quarrel with his respected brother over this matter, nevertheless he urged all to consider whether their cause was best served by all this attitude of confrontation and mutual hostility, which had been the curse of their two realms for so long. Might not an outstretched hand and a smile be more productive than the shaken fist and the angry frown?

This, from the instigator of the Glencoe atrocity, certainly made the assembly sit up.

Warming to his theme, Stair went on to extol the benefits of union, a union of the two parliaments and governments, as there was already a union of the thrones. Surely this was the answer to most of their problems? An end to bickering and enmity, to sanctions against their trade and navigation and enterprises. Co-operation rather than suspicion and hatred. The smaller and less powerful nation could never win against the larger and richer and mightier. Would it not be better, therefore, to recognise the fact and join forces rather than go on fighting as they had done for centuries? It was known that there were far-seeing and influential men in favour of such a development, in London.

This was too much for Andrew. He was on his feet almost before the other had sat down. "My lord Chancellor," he cried. "The noble lord advocates union. What would such union mean? When the small unites with the great, what happens? The greater absorbs and engulfs the lesser. It is ever so, must be. There are near ten times as many English as Scots. Think you that when the ten becomes eleven, the eleventh will *partner* the ten? Or be swallowed up by the ten? Is this what my lord of Stair wants? An end to Scotland, the most ancient nation in Christendom, a kingdom when England was but a medley of warring tribes, from whence Christianity spread to the English, a people with their own Kirk and laws, their freedoms and customs and pride, rightful pride. Is all that, for which our forefathers have fought for untold generations, to be thrown away, for the sake of trading benefits and navigation protection? As all here know, I have worked hard and long for this trading and colonial venture. But I, for one, would rather see all our endeavour sink to the bottom of the ocean than that we lost one least part of our cherished independence and ages-old identity."

He sat down to loud and prolonged cheering.

But Stair was not so easily put down. "Mr. Fletcher roars like a lion – but his roaring hides a timorous heart!" he asserted. "He fears a union. Why? Scotland would still be Scotland. We would not be incorporated in England, only work with her instead of against her. Is not harmony to be preferred to enmity? We should be confederate states. As are those of the Netherlands, the Germans and the Empire electorates. They fare well enough in unity. Why not Scotland and England?"

"I agree with Stair." That was the Earl of Breadalbane, making an unusual appearance at Parliament House, along with other Highlanders. "If the richer will unite with the poorer, is the poorer likely to become poorer still? Will he not rather gain? I say that we have little to lose by union and much to gain."

"I say the same, my lord Chancellor," Campbell of Lochnell said. "I have put £1,000 of my siller into Mr. Fletcher's venture. *He* may be prepared to see it sunk in the ocean – but I am not!"

"There speaks a man of some sense!" James Ogilvie Earl of Findlater, another Northerner commended.

Andrew bit his lip. Had he damaged Scotland's cause by his foray behind the Highland Line? Amidst growing uproar in the hall he caught Marchmont's eye and stood until the latter's gavel restored order.

"My lord Chancellor – I sorrow to learn that I am timorous

298

of heart!" he declared. "Also to learn that these last speakers are so forgetful of the elementary facts of nature, and of mankind, that they believe that the lesser joins the greater it can remain itself and maintain its whole identity. When a bit of a burnie joins a river, which streams on? The burn or the river? When a pike swallows a minnow, in all unity, who chooses the direction to swim? When a man joins a crowd, can his voice be distinguished amongst the shouting? No, my lords and friends, you all know the answers to these questions. Could it be so different for us? I urge you to consider this of union no further. Even if some of your souls appear to be in your pockets! Have you considered English taxation? The English, my friends, have ten taxes for every one of ours. To pay for all their armies and fleets and ambitious projects. Do you wish to pay these taxes also – as we must if we were united with them? Would this suit your pockets?"

He had them there. Into the sudden silence, Johnnie Belhaven spoke.

"I say Saltoun is right. This talk of union is folly."

"Aye, aye!"

"Have done with it!"

Clearly the great majority present were of this mind. The Chancellor beat for silence.

"My lords and commissioners," he said. "May I remind you that there is no motion before the house on this subject? Nor would I entertain anything such, at this stage. We waste our time in this talk. I must bring you back to the business of the day. We shall deal with the progress of the militia companies, including the Highland Watches. My lord of Annandale, will you speak to it . . . ?"

19

They sat in the small library at Saltoun Hall, at a table drawn up before a well-doing fire of aromatic birch-logs, papers spread, young Andrew seeking to help, his small sisters Kate and Meg, on the deerskin hearthrug, playing with the three dogs – a cosy, domestic scene. Margaret, pen in hand, was reading carefully, brows furrowed, ink drying on the quill, immersed in the meaning rather than in the words; whilst her brother-in-law frowned, pursed his lips and scratched out here and added there, pen much more busy.

It was a new task, for both of them, the correcting of printer's proofs. Andrew had long been in the habit of setting down his ideas and theories on paper; but only recently had he decided on collating and rewriting some of his voluminous notes and diaries, to turn them into publishable form. Now here were the first-fruits of his literary endeavours, in the form of sheet-proofs from the printing press, smelling strongly of printing ink, two lengthy essays or treatises, one a *Discourse on the Affairs of Scotland*, the other a *Discourse on Government with Relation to Militias*. He, for one, found the checking and correcting of these pages a trying and distracting business. He had been looking forward to seeing his brain-child in print, and admittedly this was exciting and gratifying. But he had not realised that, in seeming so much more authoritative and convincing than in his own handwriting, it would also produce in him constant urges to change this and improve that, to cut here and amplify there. In fact, his first reaction on reading through the two sets of sheets, after the brief glow of superficial satisfaction, was to rewrite the whole thing. But that would, of course, greatly delay publication, and he had all the new author's essential conviction that this great matter should be put before the privileged public at the earliest. Moreover publication was an expensive business and the printers had warned him that every alteration and especially every addition, once the type was set up, would much add to the cost. So he had brought Henry and Margaret into the issue, to read and give guidance – although whether he would accept any advice was another matter. Henry had been only moderately interested, he not being greatly concerned with national affairs and governmental theories, confining himself almost wholly with factoring the Saltoun estates for his brother, which he did very well. He had seen little to amend or enlarge upon. But

Margaret was different. She was fascinated and flatteringly impressed, most anxious to help. And she had a good brain and could even suggest improvements, in a modest way – even though Andrew scarcely sought such. But there were slight repetitions and elaborations which a fresh eye could see as unnecessary; and one or two of these the author was constrained generously to accept.

So they worked side by side before the fire, that chilly day of early May, he on the Militia discourse, she on the Scottish Affairs one, each frequently interrupting the other, to read out this passage or that for comment; whilst young Andrew sought to put together the corrected and as yet unnumbered sheets in approximate order, with constant demands for guidance and unnecessary questions.

Margaret, impressed as she was by the clarity, penetration and scope of it all, was just a little concerned over the possibility, indeed probability, of giving offence in certain quarters. She agreed that it was almost impossible not to, in dealing with political and governmental matters; but felt that certain personal references might perhaps be toned down and actual names omitted. After all, anybody with any knowledge of the subject would know who was meant and who was pilloried, in almost every case, without having to risk angry repercussions by stating names in print – Lord Stair, for instance. And Lord Melville. Even Sir James Montgomery and the Reverend Carstairs. Andrew declared that this would enfeeble and emasculate all – not to be considered.

They were debating this, the woman tactfully, the man vigorously, when the door opened to reveal Henry, with Johnnie Belhaven and a squat, tough-looking individual with a weather-beaten face, vaguely familiar to Andrew. There was a to-do of greetings and dogs.

"Lord Belhaven has brought you a visitor, Dand," Henry said. "Captain Jamieson of the Company ship *Olive Branch*."

"Ha – I thought that I had seen you before, Captain. So you are back. You will have brought us news? From Darien? Or New Caledonia, as we must now call it. Here is Mrs. Fletcher – Mrs. *Henry* Fletcher."

301

"Grave news, I fear, Andrew," Johnnie said.

"Aye, sir – grave it is," the shipmaster agreed heavily. "Sorry as I am to be bringing it."

"Darien, you mean . . . ? The Company?"

"Aye."

"But I understood that all was going well. After your uneventful voyage out and successful settling in there?"

"Och, aye, that was fair enough, sir. We dodged yon English Admiral Benbow's frigates, that tried to stop us – we had the good fortune of a fog – and the landings and settlement went well enough. Although a wheen o' the gentry – if you will pardon me for saying it, sir – were right sweir to soil their white hands wi' honest toil! But after that . . . och, well, it's a long story."

"Sit down, then – sit down. A glass of wine?"

"I shall see to refreshments, Andrew," Margaret said. "Come, children."

Jamieson's account brought ever grimmer expressions to his hearers' faces. The five Scots ships had reached the Gulf of Darien safely, on November 3rd, in fair order and good morale, despite two or three deaths on the long and cramped voyage, and the efforts of the English warships to intercept. There was no opposition to their landing, indeed they were welcomed by the local Indians, the more so when they offered to *buy* all the land which the Indians would sell, an almost unheard-of proceeding, where Europeans considered any colonial territory inhabited by savages as theirs for the taking. They chose, for the first settlement area, level land at Acta, near the narrowest part of the isthmus, at the head of a sheltered bay with a good anchorage, in the lee of Golden Island. They named it New Caledonia, and the settlement New Edinburgh, and gave thanks to God for their safe arrival; one of their first activities, indeed, the building of a wooden church.

So far so good. Whilst erecting hutments for the new town, warehouses and port facilities, they likewise and promptly built a stronghold, which they named Fort St. Andrew, on high ground behind the settlement area, for protection and as a possible refuge, moving into it the fifty cannon they had brought from home. Also they lost no time in trying out their skills at canal-building, under Dutch guidance, cutting an access across a low peninsula, to improve the approaches to the port in certain winds. Tree-felling and drainage and land-clearance for crop-planting progressed. Much cheap and even eager Indian labour was available, greatly facilitating this initial construction work.

Nevertheless it was partly the plenitude of Indian labour which was behind the first signs of trouble. Although tasks were alloted to all, by Mr. Paterson and his lieutenants, many of the young Scots gentry, with siller in their pockets, saw no reason why they should toil like serfs when they could hire natives personally to do it for them. The other settlers, less well provided, resented this. So there were workers and idlers – and idle young men are always apt to get into mischief. The Indian women in especial attracted and were compliant, and there were protests from their menfolk. Mr. Paterson rebuked the trouble-makers, but he was not strong enough, as a leader, to enforce his will.

Another difficulty was that they found that much of the provisioning brought out from Scotland was unsuitable for life in a hot climate; and until they could grow their own crops there were shortages, some of them serious. So missions were sent out to the English colonies to the north, to purchase the required supplies – and it was discovered that orders had been sent from London to all English governors that there was to be no trade or intercourse of any kind with the new colony, that these Scots were rebels against the King of England and were to be treated as foes, on the allegation that the whole Panama area belonged to Spain, by a declaration of a Spanish governor over a century before, although no recognition of this had been given hitherto, no settlements made, no Spanish presence attempted. So the missions returned empty-handed but with the threat of hostile activities by the English fleet in American waters, in support of King William's present policy of harmony with Spain in his efforts to keep a balance against the power of France.

The Scots did not take the threat of hostilities seriously – until they were attacked by a Spanish expedition from Carta-gena in Colombia, and this with the English fleet cruising in the offing. This attack was beaten off successfully, giving the lairdly element something to do at last. But it was ominous for the future and an indication that the colonists must devote more of their efforts and manpower to defence considerations.

So passed the first four months. Then the situation became very different. Hitherto it had been winter, even though much hotter than any Scots summer. But with the damp heat ever increasing, and shortage of essential supplies weakening both the wills and the bodies of the settlers, fever and sickness set in, and with it disillusion, dissatisfaction and dissention. Mr. Paterson himself fell ill, with consequent weakening of the central authority. It was in the low coastal region that conditions were bad, with miasmas rising and mosquitoes in clouds; but the higher ground inland was cooler and healthy, and thither all who could, and many who should not, tended to remove themselves. With the result that essential works were neglected and the affairs of the colony stagnated. That was the situation when Captain Jamieson sailed for home, for help, supplies, guidance and reinforcements – especially for physicians and physics.

Depressed and anxious at this sorry tale, the three other men cross-questioned the shipmaster. Was new leadership required? Who was responsible for the indiscipline? Surely there were plenty of potential leaders amongst the landed class? William Paterson should not have to act the governor. He was a banker not a leader of men. Was the climate in summer so bad that the colony was indeed not viable, at least on the low ground? They had been assured that the Darien territory was unclaimed by an European power. Was there any truth in this Spanish assertion?

As to the last, Jamieson believed that there was none. Indeed it was the general opinion that the thing was an *English* invention, designed to give them a further excuse for ruining the Scots enterprise. King William was greatly concerned over the Spanish Succession situation and the balance of power in Europe, and so was anxious to please the Spaniards – and this would suit him, as well as the East India Company and their other powerful opponents in England. However the English

304

had not actually taken part in the Spanish assault; so it seemed as though they were unwilling to engage in outright warfare, only to use underhand efforts. But the Scots could not be sure, and more arms, cannon, powder and militiamen were required; for New Caledonia, as well as having to cope with heat, fever, lack of supplies and ineffectual leadership, felt itself to be almost in a state of siege; for if the Spanish, their nearest neighbours, were being encouraged to attack them, would not the French Caribbean colonists, the Portuguese and the Dutch reckon them to be fair game also?

For long the four of them discussed the situation, trying to decide on the best course of action. Andrew felt inclined to go out to Darien himself, but the others pointed out to him that his place was more than ever here at home. Once the word got out in Scotland – as it undoubtedly would, sailors from the ship were bound to talk – there would be great unease and recriminations, as men worried about their investment. No, all Andrew's eloquence and energies would be required here. On the leadership question, they must send out some suitable and strong individuals, used to asserting authority; in especial an experienced military commander. For the rest, Jamieson's requirements regarding supplies, arms, ammunition and medicaments must be met, with all haste, and sent off. Also new colonists and militia recruited. They must all devote their most urgent efforts to this, and have the ship turned round and sailing with the very minimum of delay. Also strong representations must be made by the Scots government, through the Secretary of State and the Chancellor, to William and his London advisers, leaving them in no doubts as to Scotland's reactions. A campaign for possibly separating the crowns again might well be the most effective pressure they could bring, to aid their New Caledonian compatriots, Andrew suggested.

It looked as though authorship and essay-publishing must be forgotten, for the present.

* * *

It made a busy summer and autumn for Andrew Fletcher, the affairs of the Darien Company demanding much of his time and patience and much from his pocket also. Straight away he and his colleagues were confronted with problems, for with speed over supplies and medicines for the colony the first priority, it was decided that the *Olive Branch*, large and slow and anyway requiring repairs, should be held back for a later voyage. A faster, lighter vessel had to be found and chartered, in haste; and in only a week or two Captain Jamieson sailed off in this, with its much-needed freight. They also shipped some personnel. Tried leaders could not be found and persuaded, at such short notice; but a few useful individuals, from amongst those previously disappointed, were enrolled – although the enthusiasm was markedly less than heretofore as rumours of difficulties and disappointments swept the country.

Two more smaller vessels were despatched in August.

By late September, however, the results of much hard work, and some very difficult supplementary financing, enabled a convoy of four more ships to sail, with the arms, munitions and no fewer than thirteen-hundred men, largely military. These included a veteran of the Continental wars, one Colonel Campbell of Finab, of the Earl of Argyll's Lorn Regiment, with one of his former officers, Captain Thomas Drummond, plus three hundred of his own Campbell militia – the Clan Campbell concerned for its investment. It was hoped that this Colonel Campbell would become in effect military governor of the colony, with William Paterson's backing. Also sailing were four ministers of the Kirk, to provide moral leadership, one of the two previous clergymen-colonists having died and the other fallen sick, when Jamieson left. The convoy sailed this time from the west coast, taking all the Campbells aboard at the Isle of Bute, to avoid possible interception by English warships ever lurking in the North Sea.

Andrew and his friends could do little more meantime, although they continued to try to drum up reluctant finance. They had little difficulty in engineering a Scots official protest to King William; but this in due course produced only an entirely negative response, to the effect that ". . . the present juncture of affairs obliges the Kingdom of England to carry fair with that of Spain," and no commitments made anent improved attitudes. But it was hoped that the scarcely veiled threats made by the Scots, and the renewed talk of possibly separating the crowns once more, which Andrew busily promoted, would in fact cause William and the English government to take pause.

And then, with the century turned, William Paterson himself arrived back at Saltoun, in late January 1700, broken almost in health but by no means in spirit. What he had to tell them was scarcely believable – New Caledonia was abandoned. Or had been, when he left it in June, for New York – although presumably the second expedition, of May, was there now. But the original settlers had given up, surrendered to English pressure, under-nourishment, sickness and dissention. It would all have to be done again.

Appalled, Andrew listened and questioned. Paterson had been ill. No, it was not fever. The ignorant and the guilty were saying that it was the place, that Darien was fever-ridden, impossible for white men to inhabit, a death-trap. But it was not so. It was hot in summer, yes – scarcely to be wondered at, so near the Equator. And there were mosquitoes. But that was only at the coastal flats, in the swampy low ground – and even there it was no more inhospitable than a score of thriving colonies in the Americas and Indies. No, it was the lack of food, of proper feeding, of suitable provisions. All were half-starved; and what they *had* to eat was wrong, for the climate. No vegetables, fresh fruit, fresh meat. The stores sent out in some of the ships were beyond belief in folly. One crate, which they expected to contain oatmeal, held fifteen hundred bibles. Another, four hundred periwigs! Whoever packed them was witless. No, it was not fever which struck them down, himself included, but under-nourishment which made them liable to all manner of sicknesses in such climate. They had expected to be able to buy food from neighbouring colonies and islands, until their own crops grew and cattle multiplied. But the Spanish, the French and the Dutch would not sell; and the English, who might, were forbidden to have any dealings with them, by royal command. Even the Indians were forbidden to trade with them. They were shunned like lepers!

"And you had no time to grow your own crops?"

"Time we had, yes – but not the correct seeds. We tilled our

307

soil, some small acreage, and planted yams, Indian corn or maize and Jamaica peas. These came to perfection in only five weeks. The ground is fertile beyond belief. But it was only a little, and not the food which was required. None had tasted fresh meat, only salt, for five months. Men and women died daily."

"You lost . . . many?"

"Three hundred died before we left. Worse, another four hundred, taken sick aboard ship, died before we reached New York."

"Good Lord! Seven hundred dead – out of twelve hundred!"

"Aye. God's hand was heavy upon us. But – we should never have left. I forbade it. But . . ."

"You were in charge, were you not, man?"

"Only as adviser. There was a Council of Seven elected. And these were weak, quarrelsome. Incompetent, well-born bunglers. When I was stricken with sickness I was carried out to the ship, unconscious. For they believed that it was the land which was the killer, the fools! And the ships, crowded with sick, were worse, a hundred times! Many did not wish to leave. But those damned councillors insisted. At forty-eight hours' notice. None were to stay. I was carried with them. We should have stayed, we should have stayed!"

Andrew stared at the man. "It is scarcely to be credited! After all the labour, the high hopes, the money!"

"Aye. All to be done again."

"But – the second expedition? Thirteen hundred men. When they arrived, it would be to find all gone, deserted?"

"To be sure. But the houses, the fort, the cannon and works would still be there. Pray God these were better led. And had the right supplies . . ."

"Yes, yes – we saw to that. Captain Jamieson told us. But – they would face the same conditions. And without *your* guidance. Have we but thrown good money after bad? Not that the money is the worst of it, but men's lives . . ."

"No, no. If we keep them well supplied. Until they can grow their own crops. Send live beasts, cattle, sheep, pigs, poultry . . ."

"The Company has no more money. Already it is in debt."

"Then we must raise more. At once. That is vital."

"Will, my friend – I do not think that you understand. It will be very difficult to raise more. What we did raise was a miracle – a series of miracles! Half the total coin of the country! The land is bled dry of moneys. And now, folk will be despondent, believe all to be wasted. They will not readily find more."

"They must be told. Understand that if they would save their investment they must find more meantime. The project has not yet had a chance . . ."

"They will be hard to convince. You did not commence the transportation?"

"No. How could we? The few mules we could gather had to be eaten for meat. We did dig a small canal, as ensample. It was a notable success. But there was not the time for more."

"You say that you sailed for New York? Why was that?"

"I did not so choose. It was the shipmasters who believed that the orders from London to the governors of colonies, not to deal with us, would only apply to those nearby – Jamaica, the Barbadoes, the Jerseys, the Carolinas. And further north, in New York, Massachusetts and Acadia there were numbers of Scots and we would be better received. It was not so – not in New York, where we had much trouble. And we lost two ships by storm . . ."

The tale of disaster went on.

Andrew was proved all too accurate as to Scotland's reception of the tidings from Darien. Disappointment, disillusion, resentment, anger – these were the usual reactions. The main wrath was against England and King William, of course. There was talk of outright war; the separation of the crowns became a popular slogan; and Jacobite and even republican sentiment flourished. But some of the ire spilled over, inevitably, on to those most prominently connected with the venture – including to be sure Andrew Fletcher, whose comparatively brief spell of popularity came to a sudden end. William Paterson was booed in the streets of Edinburgh. The fact that he had lost more than anybody else in the collapse did not save him. Especially when the news arrived that the second expedition, after a successful voyage and landing, had also abandoned the

309

colony. This completed the Company's disesteem, almost disgrace. It seemed that almost at once, whilst the new settlers were surveying the deserted New Edinburgh they were attacked by a large force of Spaniards in a fleet especially sent out from Seville, an English squadron again standing by and watching. Campbell of Finab, with his trained fighters, defeated a force six times their numbers. But more than a military victory was required to convince this second party that they could succeed where the first had failed and gone. If Paterson himself had been there, it might have been different. Moreover these were more soldiers than settlers. Abandonment again.

Paterson, recovered somewhat in health, was not put down in spirit. Of all things, recognising that Scotland would have none of him meantime, he decided that his vision might still be saved by convincing *English* opinion that there was vast wealth in the transportation and canal scheme. England's finances were scarcely prospering under Godolphin; and the Bank of England was veering this way and that without its founder's direction. And the King was always needing money for his foreign adventures. So south he went, promising that he would try to save the great Scots investment yet; and that the terms he would demand for English participation would produce financial compensation for the Scots loss. None believed him, and his going went unlamented.

Andrew, Belhaven, Tweeddale and their colleagues could not take this route out. They had to stay and suffer, in varying degrees, in disrepute, unpopularity and loss of office as well as in their pockets. Part of Andrew's price was the loss of his Haddingtonshire seat in that year's Parliament, voted down for the first time.

He was not alone in that, to be sure, many others falling in a wave of reaction. The peers, who sat by right of their title, remained, of course, but it was a sadly weakened legislature at a time when Scotland needed strength, with poverty, despair talk of war, the Jacobites rising again especially in the Highlands, and much reform undone.

Strangely, talk of union grew, at least amongst the aristocracy.

The eighteenth century had started badly.

20

On how small a matter may hang the fates of men and even nations. In March of 1702 William the First of the United Kingdom, the Third of England and the Second of Scotland, was thrown from a nervous horse, broke his collar-bone and died a few days later. And, as at a stroke, all was changed, dynastically, politically and, for many, personally. For he died childless. And whatever the Dutch situation, the accepted heir to his thrones of England and Scotland was Anne, his late wife's younger sister, and daughter of James, married to the ineffective Prince George of Denmark. Protestant Anne, therefore, almost automatically mounted both thrones – although admittedly she had the half-brother, whose birth had caused so much heart-burning in 1688, exiled in France. Their father had died the year before.

This situation had two important consequences, other than the inevitable ones relative to any change of monarch. First of all, it meantime took much of the heat out of the Jacobite cause, for of course Anne herself was a Stewart; so the Stewart-supporting Jacobites no longer had much of a case; only the Roman Catholics had anything to fight about. Secondly, however, the problems and controversies were only post-poned, not solved. For Anne was now thirty-seven, unlikely to bear any more children – and the last of her numerous but sickly offspring had died in 1700. Which left the succession once again in major doubt. The nearest Protestant heir was distant indeed, the Princess Sophia, daughter of Elizabeth of Bohemia, Charles the First's beautiful daughter, married to the late Elector of Hanover, her son George being the present Elector. This was a far cry from the ancient Stewart dynasty – but the alternative was Catholic James, now in his fourteenth year and in the care of the King of France. After Anne's last child died, the English Parliament, in typical fashion, had hastily passed an Act of Settlement, settling the crown on this Sophia and her son – the *United Kingdom* crown, not just the English one, with no consultation with Scotland. There had been, of course, vigorous protest by the Scots, notably by Andrew Fletcher, although being no longer in Parliament he had to make it privately and in pamphlet form.

Now, suddenly, much was altered, even if that situation was not. Anne was an Episcopalian, and although not a woman of any strong character or convictions, was under the influence of fervid Episcopalians of the Tory persuasion, and chose her ministers in England accordingly, shunning the more liberal Whigs. Unfortunately she did the same for Scotland, where the Episcopalians were an unpopular minority. So a new ministry, under the Douglas Duke of Queensberry and the Ogilvie Earl of Seafield, formerly Findlater, was appointed – and of all things, Stair created an Earl – much to the people's wrath. And this had the effect of making popular those who publicly opposed the new ministry. Since Andrew was prominent amongst these, he was a beneficiary. The blame for his share in the Darien disaster tended at last to be overlooked and he was able to take a more active part in politics again. With Belhaven, Marchmont, Tweeddale, Annandale and the new Duke of Hamilton – the old autocrat had died some years earlier – something that came to be called the Country or National Party began to form, in which Andrew took a leading part.

This process was expedited by a new development, a policy promoted by the English government for an incorporating union with Scotland. Hitherto many English politicians had mooted it, in a general way, as a means of silencing the troublesome Scots once and for all. Now it became an official objective and Queen Anne backed it, largely over the succession issue. Loud was the outcry, the people angry, the Country Party vociferous, even some Tories uneasy. Andrew's old theme of separating the crowns came much to the fore and he began to be cheered in the streets of Haddington and Edinburgh – a change from Darien boos.

In the election of May 1703 he was returned once more as commissioner for Haddingtonshire, in resounding fashion. None was happier over this than his sister-in-law, for she had found it galling indeed to watch him fretting and frustrated, month after month, having to hold himself in, his energies and abilities unwanted, his eloquence gagged. There were no fewer than four new works ready for the printer, but this was insufficient outlet for his vigorous spirit. He had more and more turned his mind to land improvement; but, although he was Laird of Saltoun again, the estate had been for so long Henry's responsibility and there were inevitable differences of opinion and priority.

Now Andrew could take the lead on the national scene, and that he did, with a will. He managed to gather a group of the most prominent and influential members of the Country Party, the evening prior to the opening of Parliament, at Holyroodhouse of all places, in the quarters of the new Duke of Hamilton, to thrash out with them a strategy. If it might seem extraordinary that such magnates as the Duke, the Marquis of Tweeddale and the Earls of Marchmont, Annandale, Leven and Southesk should acknowledge leadership by a mere East Lothian laird, all recognised that had not Andrew so consistently opposed and worked to reduce the powers of each monarch in turn since Charles the Second, he too undoubtedly would by this time have been amongst the ennobled. Offence towards the fount of honour was not the way to such promotion.

Andrew proposed both a strategy and tactics therefore. He listed no fewer than a dozen headings for which they should press, to be included in an Act of Security – to ensure the continued independence of Scotland, to limit the powers of the crown, to maintain freedom of religion and to improve the government of the realm. On three or four they might possibly be prepared to negotiate or even yield, meantime; but on the main principles they must stand united. The vital issue was that Parliament should be supreme, the will of the people the touchstone.

This went down reasonably well with his hearers. But when he went on to indicate the necessity of restricting the powers of the crown, he was less well received. He emphasised that all monarchs, being human, could do ill, especially those who ruled from a distance. And a woman monarch could be worst of all, since she was liable to be swayed and manipulated by unscrupulous men. Queen Anne was known to be weak. So

313

the Scots Estates must *rule* and Anne *reign*. The crown must not be able to manipulate Parliament, as in the past; by failing to call it, by creating unlimited numbers of lords; by appointing to high office irrespective of parliamentary will; by refusing royal assent to acts passed; by declaring war or peace without consent; and so on. The alternative was to have their own separate monarch once more, here, where they could exert the required control.

Despite the coughs and raised eyebrows, Andrew did get general agreement on the strategy. Tactics were to press hard from the start, to put their requirements forward in the right order, and clause by clause so as to enlist the support, or at least the non-opposition, of the Whigs, the Jacobites, even the Catholics. It should be possible, with care, to get their Act of Security through. The burghs and shires, would, he believed, be preponderantly in favour. It was the lords who would present the difficulty, so many new-appointed peers with eyes firmly fixed on Whitehall.

Sundry new-appointed and promoted peers present pursed noble lips.

Next morning, as they were assembling in the palace forecourt and beyond for the ceremonial Riding of Parliament up through the city, the grooms bringing foward the hundreds of stamping, sidling, whinnying horses, Andrew gripped Johnnie Belhaven's arm.

"I have been asking who is that small, sharp-faced man in the large periwig yonder, talking to Queensberry. I knew that I had seen him before. He is, or was, Colonel John Churchill, now General, indeed Captain-General, and created Duke of Marlborough."

"Sakes – you mean the famous – or notorious – Churchill? Whose wife . . . ?"

"Aye – whose wife Sarah all but controls the Queen! The same. An able soldier indeed but a plotter. And no friend of Scotland."

"But what does he do here?"

"Anne has made him Duke and chief of all her military forces. But before that, Charles created him Lord Churchill of Eyemouth, in the peerage of Scotland, at the urging of the then

James, Duke of York. Eyemouth in the Merse. So he can claim to be a Scots Lord of Parliament, like yourself. And vote!"

"Surely not? An Englishman, with no links with Scotland. Captain-General of England's army. Come to vote in the Scots Parliament?"

"Aye, and there are others, I believe. He will be here to spy, also. To guide and influence Queensberry. It bears out what I said last night."

"This is shameful . . . !"

The Lord Lyon King of Arms' trumpeters blew their summons for the marshalling of the Riding procession, and for a while the crowded forecourt was a scene of utter confusion, men and horses milling everywhere. Gradually Lyon and his colourfully-tabarded heralds achieved some order. First a jingling troop of mounted Grenadiers formed up, to lead. Then the sixty-seven burgh representatives, riding two abreast, soberly-dressed and with the prescribed black horse-trappings, all provosts' and bailies' robes left behind. After them formed up the eighty-five shire commissioners, with rather more flourish, Andrew riding beside young Cockburn of Ormiston. There followed the officers of state and judiciary, in gorgeous official apparel; and then the lords, robed in scarlet, each splendid horse led by liveried footmen two for each baron and up to eight for a duke. The Lord Lyon himself, with his heralds, came next, leading three noblemen who carried the Honours Three, Crown, Sceptre and Sword-of-State, symbols of the royal authority, these riding immediately before the High Commissioner as representing the monarch. Behind Queensberry came his entourage, including today, the Duke of Marlborough. A second troop of cavalry, the Royal Horse Guards, brought up the rear as guard-of-honour, under the new MacCailean Mor, Argyll, promoted to duke. Over five hundred mounted men, apart from the servitors, were involved, and the marshalling a major task, with the resultant procession over half-a-mile long, so that the head of it was most of the way up to Parliament Square before the tail left Holyrood.

Fortunately it was not raining and the Riding less of a trial than it might have been. The streets were thronged with the citizenry, who cheered and jeered and not infrequently threw things at unpopular figures. Children yelled, women skirled, dogs barked and got between horses' legs, and every window of the tall tenement 'lands' on either side of Canongate and High Street held outleaning spectators – who had to be eyed heedfully, and it was not unusual for the contents of chamber-pots and other unpleasantness to be hurled down upon offending legislators, not always with exact aim. If the people could not actually take part in the parliamentary procedures, at least they could make some of their attitudes known beforehand.

This occasion produced no such unseemly incidents, although there were not a few boos for the High Commissioner himself, as representing far-away London authority. All reached Parliament Hall safely, outward dignity exemplified, at least.

* * *

The parliamentary session extended over many days, formalities, opening speeches, manoeuvrings for position by the various magnates, groups and parties, taking up a deal of time. Then there were the disputed elections, of which there were always a number; for with such limited electorates often decisions could be effected by one or two votes. Indeed on this occasion, Andrew's colleague, John Cockburn, had to defend his election, by only one vote, against allegations by Sir George Suttie of Balgone. All this delay irritated Andrew Fletcher, for one, eager to get down to the real meat of the session.

At last battle was joined and Andrew quickly took the floor, and held it. He was indeed at his most eloquent and shrewd, rapier-quick with his thrusts, repartee and asides, reasonable and logical in his arguments, retaining the attention of friend and foe alike. Margaret and Henry had come to listen, unchallenged this time. The woman sat entranced, recognising that this was Andrew at his peak, at long last, dominating, almost orchestrating the proceedings, playing on men's minds and emotions both as on a chosen instrument. She was proud, excited and thankful too.

He led off by expressing his personal loyalty to Anne, their undoubted Queen, and wishing her God's blessing, good guidance – in which they all held a responsibility – and a long life to reign over them. This last was important in more than in Her Grace's personal felicity; for after her, who was to be the next King or Queen of Scots would present problems indeed – which problems it was now their duty to try to solve, for the benefit of her ancient kingdom. Thus, without delay, he threw down the gauntlet. This Parliament had one task above all others – to decide upon the correct succession to the throne, as far as Scotland was concerned, in the interests of the right, good government, the independence of the beloved land and the maintenance of the Protestant faith, whilst securing religious freedom for all.

That evoked widespread cheers, if wary looks from chair and throne.

He went on to point out that the English Parliament, for its own purposes, had already chosen to nominate the Princess Sophia of Bohemia, widow of the late Elector of Hanover, as first heir; but since this lady was aunt to and older than Queen Anne, in effect the English succession was settled upon her son George, the present Elector. That was within their right, for the *English* throne. What was not within their right was to nominate this German prince, nor his mother, for the throne of the United Kingdom, as they had done, without reference to Scotland. It was a joint throne and one partner thereto could not dispose of it without the other. So, in effect, what the English parliamentarians had done was to imply the *separation* of the thrones after the present incumbent's demise. They had chosen their own successor. None could deny that. Would it be this German princeling?

For a while Andrew could not go on, so loud was the noise in the hall. Undoubtedly there were far more agreeing with him than disagreeing. A number of members were on their feet, but it was the Earl of Stair whom the Chancellor noticed and who declared that such talk was little short of treasonable, denying the monarch's own wishes as to her own heir, a limitation of the royal prerogative. He was supported by the Earl of Home, who demanded to know who were the possible alternatives? Dare any man name them?

That put the cat amongst the pigeons. Andrew perceived the dangers to his cause and was not to be drawn. There was, in fact, only a very limited choice, so short of heirs had become the royal Stewart line. Young James in France already calling himself King James the Third and Eighth; the Earl of Dalkeith, son of the Duchess of Buccleuch and the late Monmouth; and the far-out claim of the present Duke of Hamilton to a more remote royal ancestry. None there elected to nominate any of these at this juncture.

Andrew pointed out that it was not the monarch's prerogative which he wished to diminish but that of her English ministers over Scots affairs. He said that they should not seek here to appoint any successor to the Queen but to declare Parliament's right to choose one in due course. That choice to be subject to certain proper limitations for the safeguarding of the realm's weal.

Stair was swift to pounce upon the word limitation. What limitations did Mr. Fletcher dare to impose upon the crown? Andrew could have announced the dozen clauses agreed that evening at Holyrood. Instead, as he had suggested then, he brought forward only one at a time. He put it that the crown should not grant any amnesty or pardon for any transgression against the public good, without the consent of Parliament. When Stair interrupted that a royal pardon could by no means be denied by any subject, even the present speaker, he was shrewdly silenced.

"It is not to be wondered at that his lordship is against this limitation. For had there been such a law, he would have been hanged long ago! For the advice he gave to King James and for the murder of Glencoe! Aye, and for his whole conduct since the Revolution."

That brought scores to their feet whilst the rest shouted, largely acclaim.

Although Seafield fumed, thumped and demanded apology – and got it, if but a smiling one – a vote was immediately pressed for on this first clause of an Act of Security. And won handsomely – Stair's unpopularity saw to that. And it all put the assembly in a mood to consider more, despite the frowns of High Commissioner, Chancellor and ministers.

One by one, then, the clauses were announced, with brief and telling explanatory asides, and passed seriatim – the need for annual parliaments, each appointing its own president; extra shire and burgh commissioners for every peerage created above the present balance; none to vote save Lords of Parliaments of Scots domicile, and commissioners; the crown to have no power to refuse assent to Acts duly passed; none to make war or peace without consent; no standing army, only a national militia; no judge or sheriff to sit in Parliament; and lastly, if the monarch should break any such limitations once accepted, he or she should forfeit the crown and Parliament choose a successor.

All this was not accepted without a fight, many fights. And it took days. But thanks to skilful timing as well as advocacy, and the fairly consistent Country Party vote, some of the most far-reaching, democratic, indeed almost revolutionary improvements in the long story of Scottish government were agreed upon and established as law – once they had received the royal assent, to be sure. The effect was to make the Scots Parliament supreme, to establish the will of the people – or at least their representatives – as superior to the will of the monarch. It was all too much for many; and time and again Queensberry adjourned the sessions in alarm and wrath. But by seeming to concede small points, to retreat here and to compromise there, but never departing from basic principles, Andrew, ably backed by Belhaven, Tweeddale, Annandale, Baillie of Jerviswood and Lockhart of Carnwath, even the Duke of Hamilton on occasion, got his limitations voted through. And when they were summed up in the final Act of Security, the reformers had won by a clear seventy-two votes, utter government defeat, even with the Duke of Marlborough and other English-based peers against.

The assembly went wild with excitement, delight and consternation. Never had there been so great a victory against reaction, such trouncing of the administration, in living memory.

After vainly trying to restore order, Chancellor and High Commissioner announced adjournment and hurried out.

Andrew, Belhaven, Roxburghe and even the Duke of

Hamilton, found themselves hurled upon by the crowd of yelling, laughing legislators and carried shoulder-high round the hall – to great ducal offence.

When at length Andrew struggled free it was to find himself clutched in a different kind of embrace, as Margaret flung herself into his arms.

"Oh, Andrew, Andrew – you did it!" she cried. "You won, you won. You were magnificent! I am so proud of you. At last you have shown them! Dear, dear Andrew!"

He held her tight, there before them all, for a moment – and then all but thrust her back towards the grinning Henry. "Thank you – thank you all!" he panted. "It is good, yes. But . . . there is much to be done yet. This is only the start. There is the royal assent, mark you! And other reforms. There will have to be many more votes and fights. But I think that we shall win through. Aye, I think it now . . ."

Part Five

21

"I knew a very wise man once, who believed that if a man were permitted to make all the ballads, he need not care who should make the laws of a nation," Andrew observed. "Although, myself, I have spent much time seeking to make and improve laws – as have you all – I am prepared to admit that my old friend may have been right. So I accept Sir Christopher's sentiment as to the decay of morals and growths of vice as exemplified by these lewd songs and infamous ballads he deplores. They are but a symbol of a deeper malaise, I am sure."

"Aye, that is the point," Bishop Burnet asserted. "It is the spiritual decadence which produces the corruption of manners and these wretched songs, lampoons and ungodly talk which we hear on every hand, in every street and club and tavern of this city, even in the House itself. So I do not see that your former mentor could be right, Andrew. It is not the songs which produce the sin but the sin which produces the songs! So where the gain in writing the ballads as against improving the laws?"

"And yet what men sing and say and show forth in their daily conduct must affect as well as reflect their inner selves and morals," Andrew held. "So the making of a nation's songs could indeed influence men greatly – and by songs I include so much more, the arts and poetry and literature of the day. Surely it is in the decline of these arts, the graces of your nation, that Sir Christopher bewails and sees as the mirror of your troubles – troubles which we in Scotland by no means escape, although ours take different shape."

"Exactly," Musgrave agreed. "The decline of the graces of the nation – that is apt. England's graces are indeed in sad decline. Who are the folk who today make most noise in this city of London? Gamesters, stock-jobbers, jockeys and wagerers! From London they infest all the places of diversion in England and may be justly called the missionaries of this city . . . !"

"Rubbish!" Sir Edward Seymour interrupted with a snort. "Nonsense, man! These are but the froth on the surface, to be blown away. The brew beneath is sound enough, as good as ever." He took a deep draught of his brimming beaker of ale, to emphasise his point. "England is not in decline. Scotland may be, I well believe – but England is as England was and will be. Sound, I say! And be damned to your gloomy maunderings! When you have as many years and as much experience of affairs under that wig of yours as have I, you will learn to let *them* speak of England rather than your poetic vapourings!" And he belched, deeply, out of long practice.

"And as much beer under your belt – which can also speak quite loud!" Burnet added, but genially, as became their host.

Sir Christopher Musgrave did not make retort. As the comparatively new Member for Carlisle and a courteous man of liberal views, he forbore to challenge the former Speaker of the House of Commons, twice his age. But his colour rose a little and the fingers toying with his wine-glass quivered.

"Your troubles in Scotland, Mr. Fletcher?" he said, turning. "Are they as ill as we hear? Great poverty, even starvation? Certainly in Carlisle we see large numbers of vagrants and folk in sorry state coming over the Border . . ."

"Aye, flooding the country, by God!" Seymour exclaimed. "A scurvy, abject tide! It should be stopped, I say. *There's* a law which should be passed, and without delay, instead of worrying about your damned songs! All beggarly Scots to be sent back whence they came. I've told Godolphin so. It's a scandal!"

"And yet you, sir, I am told, support this policy for a union!" Andrew charged, striving to keep his voice under control. "Surely, if you are so hot against the Scots, you should not seek to join us?"

"Join you, sir? God forbid! All we seek is an end to this everlasting bickering and folly. Your intransigence towards Her Majesty. The threats and petty posturing of your so-called parliament . . . !"

"Ah come, Sir Edward – it is more than that," the Bishop protested. "Better than that. We aim at an altogether better relationship between the two nations, at a healing of old wounds. At a productive partnership instead of age-old hostility. Our purpose is a noble one, unity instead of strife. And to Scotland's great benefit."

Andrew did not fail to note that 'we' and 'our' in his old tutor's assertion. To be sure, Burnet was now one of the spiritual peers of England, a member of the House of Lords. Presumably he was sincere and honest in what he said. But he sounded sadly like an Englishman, not a Scot any more.

The four of them sat in the Bishop's pleasant chamber of his London lodging near Whitehall, overlooking the busy Thames. Andrew was on a visit to London, where he had come mainly to see William Paterson, who was now settled in London again, at Queen's Square, Westminster, in connection with trying to wind up finally the affairs of the ill-fated Darien venture; but also, quietly, to seek information and sound out opinion on matters political connected with Scotland. He was staying with Paterson; but Burnet had suggested that he meet privately these two quite influential Members of Parliament, as representing two very different attitudes in the Commons, Tory and Whig, although perhaps neither was entirely typical.

"And if Scotland does not desire this union?" he asked, reasonably. It was no part of his objective to try to convert these people – hopeless a task as that would be with Seymour at least. It was information that he sought, on a number of aspects of the situation – for Scotland was full of rumours, some of them dire.

"Ah, Scotland will learn the rights of the matter, Andrew," Burnet declared. "At the moment there may be doubts and misgivings. But these can fairly readily be set at rest. Scotland's real interests are not threatened – quite the reverse. And the gain in trade and commerce and prosperity will be very great and much needed."

"Of that I would wish to be assured. But even so, there is more than trade and moneys to be considered here. Are there not matters of the spirit as well as of the pocket and the belly?

Independence, freedom, national pride, the management of our own affairs . . . ?"

"Do not tell me that such things weigh with the starveling Scots, above the full bellies we can give them! Aye, and the full pockets of those who will make the decisions!" Seymour broke in. "Whether our good English money is well spent is another matter. But there will be no lack of takers, I assure you, Fletcher – already there are!"

Andrew bit back retorts – for this was part of what he had come to try to find out, allegations of massive bribery from London. "Surely you are not right in that, sir?" he said carefully.

"You think not? Then little you know of your own folk, sirrah. Your lords have their hands stretched for gold, even if only behind their backs! To vote accordingly. These dogs, I swear, will not bite the hand that feeds them!"

"One or two, perhaps. Some are for the union anyway. Stair and Loudoun and their friends. But not many, not of those who will decide the issue. These would not sell their country for gold."

"Men will sell their mothers for gold! More especially Scotchmen! Oh, it can be dressed up, for the nice – pensions, offices of profit, green ribbons of the Thistle, even seats in our English House of Lords, I've heard. You, Bishop, will know about that?"

"One hears idle talk," Burnet said, frowning.

"Is £20,000 idle talk? I have it on the best authority that the Queen sanctioned Godolphin to send that sum to Scotland, to pay these hucksters not to obstruct the union."

"Sent to whom, sir?" Andrew demanded, voice quivering.

"Why to your ministers, to be sure. Who else? That Seafield, your Chancellor, is but a blank sheet of paper on which to write the terms of this union! But at a price – oh yes, at a price!"

"The government is different now. From what it was. Perhaps you have forgot? Since the ministry was outvoted at the last Parliament, new men have been brought in – Tweed-dale, Roxburghe, Marchmont, Mar, Lothian. Seafield is still Chancellor, yes – but the colour of the ministry is changed. These are friends of my own . . ."

"You think so, man? You are an innocent then, I say. I wager that you will find your precious friends will all be voting with their pockets when it comes to the day – your Roxburghes and Marchmonts and the rest."

"Damn you, sir" Andrew burst out. "I'll thank you to spare my friends your calumnies in my presence! I will not sit here . . ."

"Andrew! Andrew – a mercy!" Burnet exclaimed. "In my house we'll have none of this! Seymour – spare us your spleen, I beg of you. This is no way to behave, and serves nothing . . ."

Sir Christopher Musgrave sought to aid his host. "Mr. Fletcher – what ails you so much against this union? It can only be for the good of your country and people. The poorer allying with the richer can only gain."

"Poor in what, sir? In money and numbers, perhaps. But not in spirit, in skills and enterprise, even in land and its products."

"Even so, will a union destroy these? Will it not rather give them added value? Surely it must widen your opportunities, increase your trade and therefore your wealth. And so offer a better life for your folk?"

"At the price of our independence, our ancient freedom to decide our own fate? Tell me, Sir Christopher – is this why England has become so anxious for union? To widen Scotland's opportunities and increase her trade and prosperity? England scarce took that line over our Darien venture! Is it not that you see it to *England's* advantage? England has been trying to swallow up Scotland for seven centuries. She could not do it by force of arms – so now she seeks to do it by trade and money. Do not let us pretend that it is all care for Scotland's benefit."

"Oh, England will gain also, to be sure. That is the excellence of it. Like a true marriage, it will benefit both. An end to war and strife, suspicion and envy."

"This marriage will not be made in heaven, I think – but in the back-rooms of this Westminster! And why? Why now, of a sudden? I will tell you – although you all know. Because of fear. You English fear the separation of the crowns, when Anne dies. You fear that Scotland, with her own King again could ally with France, your enemy, as she has done in the past – the Auld Alliance. You fear that she could challenge you overseas, in colonies and trading enterprises – as at Darien, which you destroyed, in fear. With the King in London's help! You fear for your monopolies and foreign trade, fear us as rivals. It is the Succession which has brought your fever for union. It is since the Scots Parliament passed its Act of Security, which Queen Anne has refused to ratify. Deny it if you can?"

"We do not have to deny it, man," Seymour declared. "Certainly it was that foolish and treacherous Act which finally forced this policy upon us. Opened the eyes of all England to the dangers, the threat of secession."

"Secession, sir? How can an independent nation secede? Secede from what? We share a crown, by accident of royal birth – that is all. Because your Elizabeth Tudor did not marry and beget an heir. So our Scots King James mounted her throne. How then could Scotland secede by choosing a different monarch when Anne has no heir?"

"This is a profitless discussion, Andrew," Burnet said. "I had hoped that we could arrive at some common ground, some useful compromise which we might put to our colleagues. Not this opening of old wounds . . ."

"There *is* common ground," Musgrave insisted. "Surely Mr. Fletcher will not deny this – the Jacobite and Catholic threat? We hear all too much of this, these days – and Scotland is the weak link in our Protestant chain of defence. We know that King Louis will put the young James Stewart, whom he calls the Chevalier de St. George, on both his father's thrones, if he can, and restore the rule of Rome in these islands thereafter. He will start with Scotland, where the Catholic Highlands are, we are told, solid for James. This is why we must have a Protestant succession assured – and there is none save the prince in Hanover."

"Again I take issue with you, Sir Christopher. I hope that I am as stout a Protestant as you, however unworthy. But, first, I do not agree that there is no other Protestant of the Scots blood-royal, save George of Hanover. And second, that the Highlands are solidly Catholic or for James. Although a Hanoverian on Scotland's throne might make them so!"

"Damn it, man – do you expect us to believe that?" Seymour

328

broke in. "When it is common knowledge that your Highlands are a hot-bed of Jacobite intrigue. And being armed from France. Our every informant tells us so. Why think you your Atholl was made duke and given his £1,000, if not to try to buy him away from that seditious crew?"

"Atholl . . . ? £1,000 . . . ? You cannot mean me to believe that . . . ?"

"Indeed I do. His share of the £20,000 I spoke of. And there are others – Breadalbane, they say. *I* say it is a waste of good money. But there is no doubting the Highland Catholic threat. This man Lovat is busy, always. Like a weaver's shuttle between France and London and the North. And there is said to be another, one MacGregor – Robert MacGregor that some call Campbell for some reason. Atholl's agent. Or Breadalbane's – God knows which! But going round amongst the clans, distributing French louis d'ors to buy arms."

"You sound very knowledgeable about our Highland affairs, Sir Edward. How is that, I wonder?"

"Oh, we are not complete fools, here in London, sir. We have our sources of information. As I say, Scots – or most of them – can be bought! So we keep our ears to the ground."

"H'rr'mm," Burnet looked uncomfortable. "I think we are treading dangerous ground again – not the common ground I spoke of. What *is* common, Andrew, is that what is best for our two nations in the long term should be decided upon, and our differences resolved. To that end we must all work."

"But you, my lord Bishop . . ." and it was not often that Andrew called his old tutor that ". . . are, it seems, now firm for union?"

"Yes, Andrew, I think that I am. I hope with God's guidance."

"Is this the same God you taught me to worship as a lad, at Saltoun, I wonder . . . ?"

That broke up the little gathering effectively.

Later, in William Paterson's house in Queen's Square, Andrew put it to this other friend – who also now seemed convinced that union was the only answer, with commercial rather than heavenly guidance, presumably – that with his financial links with London government, he could discover what truth might be in these bribery allegations, and who was getting what. For surely, even if he believed in union, he would not wish it to be built on corrupt foundations? Paterson was doubtful about that, not unnaturally, but defended the £20,000 grant to the Joint Secretaries of State, now Mar and Roxburghe, for Scots aid and compensation. After all, Scotland had lost grievously by English action, over Darien; and £20,000 was a mere drop in the bucket. He himself was working on a vastly more ambitious project, to aid his native country, seeking to gain Treasury agreement to a payment of the equivalent of the Scots losses in that venture, their *financial* losses that is. He was negotiating for as much as half a million pounds sterling – although he might have to accept a little less – which sum would surely greatly help to put Scots trade and commerce back on its feet?

"How is it, my friend, that these hard-headed English politicians and money-men are prepared to listen to you singing that sort of song? When they so scurvily sank your Darien venture?"

"It is because they have found that they have need of me – that is why! The English Treasury has been desperately mismanaged. My Bank of England likewise. Men who know nothing of finance have been in charge too long. And William's foreign wars have bled the Treasury white. Godolphin and Marlborough called me in, and I have put them on the right road again. I have advised and started a Sinking Fund for the conversion of the National Debt – which is now £18 million, no less! The Bank is deeply involved. So meantime they cannot do without me. And I can aid Scotland."

"But only if Scotland agrees to this union!"

"Yes – I fear that is necessary. The Equivalent, as I am calling it, could be paid only if Scotland and England were united. The Treasury could nowise pay half a million pounds to a foreign country. You must see that? I have been given the task of compiling the financial terms for a Treaty of Union – and I promise you, we shall win back our Darien losses, or I resign."

"But – good God, man, is this not just more and greater bribery? I came to you hot against £20,000 for buying a few

Scots lords. Now you talk of twenty-five times that to buy the entire Scots nation! Its independence."

"Nonsense, my good friend! The union is necessary, and will come, without *any* payment. Of that I have become assured. This money, the Equivalent, is something in addition which I can achieve, to help compensate for hurt done by the failure of my venture. It is no bribe, but a just recompense."

"Aye." That was heavily said. "And meantime what of the *Annandale*?" The *Annandale* business was largely what had brought Andrew down to London at this juncture. It was the last of the Scots ships still in the company's hands; and putting into the Thames with a cargo of goods for sale, had been promptly seized by the English authorities and ship and cargo held, as having infringed the East India Company's trading privileges – much to the fury of the Scots.

"I am doing my best, Andrew. But it will take time. It has to go before the Court of the Exchequer, and that is a slow process. But I have no doubts that all will be well in the end. Godolphin, Marlborough and company will see to that. They will not risk the union for the sake of one ship."

Frustrated, helplessly Andrew shook his head, staring at Paterson. "How happy will be the Scots to hear me tell them that!" he exclaimed.

"Tell them about the Equivalent, my friend . . ."

In his perplexed and anxious mood, as he rode northwards two days later, going over it all in his mind, Andrew decided that he could at least try to contrive some benefit out of his depressing London visit. Clearly the Scots people must be warned of what was being perpetrated against them, even by well-wishers. Somehow. He had to do what he could. Parliament was not sitting meantime and he could only speak to the few. But he could still write and print. His treatises and pamphlets had been very successful and even influential. He could write a warning and have it widely distributed. Indeed, he could use that discussion he had had, in Burnet's house, for the purpose. Use the views and attitudes of these English Members of Parliament to drive home his message. In the form of their discussion and arguments, it would be the more readable and telling. The two attitudes of the English exemplified by Whig and Tory – both demanding this union. He did not wish to pillory his old mentor, Burnet, however valuable to use as the dangerous pro-union Scot. Besides, he had contributed little to the discussion. Better to invent another to take his place – a prominent Scot who was known to be pro-union. But not one already unpopular, like Stair or Seafield. Say George Mackenzie, Viscount Tarbat, recently promoted to be Earl of Cromartie. *He* would serve – typical of the sort of Scot who was steadily rising in the world by looking to London for preferment. That was it – Seymour. Musgrave and Cromartie urging union from their different viewpoints and himself indicating the dangers and fallacies. A pamphlet of this conversation, improved and added to where necessary. That should help to bring the menace of it all before folk in Scotland – at least the sort who would read pamphlets . . .

He compiled it all in his head as he rode.

* * *

But when Andrew arrived home, although his pamphlet project remained very much with him, it was pushed rather into the background by the implications of the situation he found awaiting him. Whilst he had been away there had been resounding developments. An English ship called the *Worcester*, two hundred tons and twenty guns, had put into the Forth on account of the weather and anchored off Leith. From the talk of her crew in Leith taverns, the notion spread abroad that this vessel was responsible for the fate of another of the Darien Company's ships, the *Speedy Return*, which had disappeared with all hands some time before in strange circumstances. According to the stories circulating, this *Worcester*, licensed privateer, had attacked the *Speedy Return* off the Malabar coast on a voyage to India, slain the crew and thrown the bodies overboard, stolen the cargo and sold the ship to slavers. In the present situation, with the *Annandale* held arrested in the Thames, the effect on Scots public opinion could be imagined, with clamour for justice to be done increasing.

But there were some who had not waited for the ponderous processes of the law. One, Roderick Mackenzie, the new secretary of the Darien Company no less, decided that the company's interests demanded immediate action. He had gathered about a score of volunteers, gone down to Leith by night, rowed out to the *Worcester* in three small boats and clambered aboard. There they had taken possession of the vessel, with its master and crew, many of whom had been helpless with drink, thirty-six all told. Not content with this, they had sailed the ship across the Forth estuary to Burntisland in Fife, where presumably they felt more secure, and from there demanded forfeiture to the Company of ship and cargo, and trial of Captain Green and crew.

The administration was much embarrassed, foreseeing dire trouble with London, and would have recovered the *Worcester* and promptly depatched her from Scottish waters; but the jubilation of the populace and the swelling demand for reprisals and even hangings, deterred them. They passed the problem to the Privy Council, weakly, who ordered the ancient High Court of Admiralty, an almost forgotten body, to look into the matter. This, with commendable celerity, met, decided that the Company had a case and remitted Captain Green and his mates and crew for trial forthwith, before the Privy Council.

This was the situation when Andrew returned to Scotland; so that whilst the Court of Exchequer in London was dilatorily examining the case of the Scots *Annandale*, a committee of the Privy Council in Edinburgh was sitting much more expeditiously on the case of the English *Worcester*. Ministers in both capitals were much upset, and threats and commands volleyed back and forth. In Edinburgh streets mobs paraded, windows were smashed and the death of Green and his men demanded.

Andrew was intrigued to find that two of his own Privy Councillor friends were on the hastily-empannelled committee of judges – Johnnie Belhaven and Cockburn of Ormiston, both of course prominent Darien supporters and therefore perhaps scarcely u-nbiassed. At any rate, it did not take them long to hear the evidence, almost entirely depositions of the *Worcester*'s crew who had turned Queen's Evidence, and which produced a dire list of piracies, mrders and sinkings – although whether the *Speedy Return* was actually one of the victims remained in doubt owing to conflicting accounts. However, there was ample evidence to convict of multiple murders, and the Privy Councillors had no difficulty in appeasing angry public opinion by hanging Green and his two mates whilst letting the rest of the crew go.

Queensberry, Seafield and the other ministers were in a state of alarm. This sort of thing could play havoc with Scots-English relations and might even sink the union talks.

Andrew, from what he had learned in the South, thought otherwise. But he discerned something important from the incident – however much he doubted the legal niceties of it all. That was that the people were tougher, stronger, than their so-called leaders; that the common folk could be lions – or wolves, perhaps – where their betters were mice; and that it would therefore be profitable to bend his attentions more upon the commonality than upon the nobility and gentry, in what was clearly going to be a fight to save Scotland's independence.

Pamphlets were all very well, but they would scarcely be read by the folk in the streets. He must think of something to mobilise the mob.

22

So, deliberately, Andrew Fletcher changed tactics and began to try to address himself more to the people. He did not cease in his efforts to warn and convince his own kind and class. He published his pamphlets, including the one entitled *An Account of a Conversation concerning a Right Regulation of Government for the Common Good of Mankind*, which had a distinct success. All sought to bring home the dangers, for the lesser partner, of any political union, but especially of an incorporating union such as the English seemed to be contemplating. But he also engaged himself in a campaign of public speech-making and tavern oratory – which he did not enjoy but which enabled his views to reach many of the ordinary folk and made him much talked about and well-known amongst the populace at large, particularly of course, in the East of Scotland. Also, arising out of these meetings, he went on, after much heart-burning and frustration, to found and nurture two popularly-based organisations, not so much of members of the Estates but of the people at large. One he named the Scottish Home Rule Party and the other, to try to bring in the younger people who were going to be needed in the struggle hereafter, the Young Scotland Party. He admittedly found these last efforts difficult and heavy going; it was a new conception for Scotland, this of political participation and party-membership for other than the ruling classes, and folk were reluctant to join, however vociferous in their attitudes and their broad convictions. And, unfortunately, amongst those who were prepared to take active part, were apt to be all too many undesirables, extremists, agitators, irresponsibles and trouble-makers, to give all a bad name. Andrew found it all an uphill and less-than-rewarding, indeed often a distasteful task; but persevered the more as he perceived the pressure from the South on the Scottish leadership ever building up.

And then, in the spring of 1705, erupted a development which, although vehemently emphasising the need for Andrew's efforts, at the same time cut them short. The English Parliament passed an extraordinary Act, Queen Anne herself present at its final stages, which, by its very title, threw down the gauntlet – An Act for the Effectual Security of the Kingdom of England from the Apparent Dangers that may arise from Several Acts passed by the Parliament of Scotland. Which title was reduced in common usage to The Alien Act. The terms of this Act were sufficiently explicit.

A union of the Parliaments was demanded. Commissioners to treat for such union were to be appointed – and on the nomination of the Queen, in both countries. And unless, by the following Christmas, the Scots Parliament had agreed to settle the succession to the throne in the same way as it had already been settled by England, namely upon the Electress Sophia of Hanover or her son George, then a state of hostility would exist between the two realms. In consequence, all natives of Scotland in England, Ireland or any of the colonies, would be treated as aliens, including those presently serving in the armed forces; all Scottish goods and commerce, such as coals, linen, cattle and the like, would be excluded from entering England, and no English goods or arms to enter Scotland; the towns of Berwick, Carlisle and Newcastle would be fortified and garrisoned and regular regiments sent to line the Border, with the northern militia mustered and put on a war-footing.

It made a rough wooing towards a marriage of convenience.

Scotland was thrown into an uproar, needless to say, and the Queen's ministers into panic. A Convention of the Estates was called for as soon as possible, forty days' notice being obligatory.

Meanwhile the nation seethed, crowds demonstrated in the streets, meetings were held behind closed doors and members of the administration were pelted with filth and stones if they allowed themselves to be seen in public. Andrew devoted most of his time to lobbying fellow-members of the Estates, in the interests of votes, leaving the populace meantime, as fairly reliable in their reactions, more so than their legislators.

Talking to these, he began to hear of a new grouping within the Country Party, and amongst its most prominent members. At first he dismissed this as mere political gossip. But as the stories persisted he commenced to take it seriously, especially when he heard that the group had even been given a name, and a strange one – the Squadrone Volante. When it was alleged that amongst those forming this group were none other than his former colleagues, almost his pupils, Roxburghe, Rothes, Montrose and Selkirk, even Tweeddale and Marchmont being suggested as adhering, he became intrigued, even a little anxious. For if all these were colloguing in some new association, yet he himself had not been approached, it must be for some purpose of which it was felt he would not approve. And it began to occur to him that these lords might well have been avoiding him recently.

So he sought out Marchmont who, as an old friend, he felt owed him an explanation. And from him he learned that there was good reason for excluding himself from the Squadrone

Volante's ranks – for they had come to the conclusion that union with England was inevitable and decided that, since it would be pointless to oppose it fruitlessly, it was better to make the best of it, which they had agreed meant fighting for a federal instead of an incorporating union such as the English appeared to want. A federal parliament dealing with matters of mutual concern, the crown, foreign policy, the armed forces, the colonies and the like with national legislatures still handling domestic matters, laws, trade and commerce and so on, would leave Scotland reasonably free and independent in her own affairs and still to a large extent mistress of her destiny, whilst allowing the benefits of the English connection, they believed. But they had feared that Andrew would not see it that way, dead set against union as he was. So . . .

Grimly Andrew agreed that they were right in that respect, at least.

He was much upset and perturbed. His first inclination was see it all as little less than treachery. Further consideration, however, convinced him that all these friends of his could not be traitors; they must believe sincerely in what they had decided, since it was against all their former professions. Nevertheless he could not find it in him to absolve them thus of weakness, even of moral cowardice, even though they might call their change of front realism. For they were wrong, wrong – of that he had no least doubt. Was it arrogance, then, on *his* part, to be so sure? Or merely stubbornness? No – for he could do nothing else. To *know* the right and resile from it – that was something he could not do. Moreover, their attitude was fated to failure, he was certain, selling the pass before the battle was joined. The English would see it only as the first step toward surrender. They were strong, whatever else, and would understand only strength used against them. A weak meeting of them halfway would gain nothing.

Andrew failed to convince any of his former colleagues to change back. He knew, as probably did they, that things would never be quite the same between them again. Only Johnnie Belhaven, of his intimates, remained staunch.

His apprehensions increased a few evenings later when, at Saltoun, Margaret rather doubtfully intimated that a Mr.

337

Campbell had come to see him, and thereafter ushered in the curiously-built and so impressive young man who, despite nondescript Lowland dress, could be none other than Rob Roy MacGregor. Surprised, naturally, he greeted him warily.

The other gave no impression of wariness, all courteous bonhomie and smiles, expressing pleasure at the honour of meeting Mr. Fletcher again and his admiration for the fine house of Saltoun Hall and its wide and fertile lands.

It took a little while, in all this spate of Highland flourish and Latin tags, to reach the object of the visit. When at length it began to emerge, Andrew could scarcely believe his ears. It seemed that the MacGregor had come to try to convert him to Jacobitism, or at least to involve him in co-operation with that cause.

The strange thing was how reasonable the visitor made his representations sound, how persuasive towards such an improbable alignment – and how well-informed he was. When he could get a word in, it was this that Andrew commented upon first.

"You are very knowledgeable about our Lowland affairs, Mr. MacGregor – I beg your pardon, *Captain* MacGregor. I would scarcely have expected it."

"Och, we are no so ignorant, north of the Line, Mr. Fletcher, see you. I have my sources of information, whatever. In the cattle trade."

"Then the cattle trade must be an interesting one, in the Highlands, sir! Hereabout at markets, we do not seem to discuss much more than the price of beef, the cost of hay and the honesty of dealers. Matters of state and politics hardly come into it."

"Perhaps you're after going to the wrong markets, Mr. Fletcher! Or buy and sell beasts for the wrong folk. I, now, sell cattle for such as my lords Duke of Atholl, Marquis of Montrose, Earl of Breadalbane and even the Duke of Gordon. Indeed it is on Duke Atholl's business that I am here, just."

"Ah. But the Duke is in London, I think?"

"But his Duchess is not, sir. She is in his house in Edinburgh."

"And this concerns me, Captain?"

338

"It could, Mr. Fletcher. Och, I think it could, yes. You see, there is a plot to bring down the Duke – and more than the Duke. It is to split the cause against this union and to damage the Jacobites as well. Och, a right clever conspiracy, as you might say. *Fas est ab hostibus doceri!*"

Andrew searched the other's ruddy features. "Go on," he said.

"Yes, then. This is why I think that you and your friends should be after fighting on the same side as the Jacobites in this warfare – since we both would damn this of union. When it comes to the bit in your Parliament you are going to be needing every vote you can raise."

"Perhaps, sir. But it is a big jump to suggest that I come to terms with the Jacobites. I am a Protestant and will not contemplate Romish rule again."

"My goodness, Mr. Fletcher – am I not after being as good a Protestant as you are, whatever? This talk of the Stewart's bringing back the Roman Church to power is but a device of our enemies. My lord Breadalbane is no Catholic. Nor is the Earl of Mar. Nor, for that matter, is the Duke . . ."

"Aye – Atholl. Where does he come into this? You spoke of a plot?"

"Plot, yes. You will have heard tell of MacShimi? The Lord Lovat, chief of the Frasers of the North, him who ran off with first his cousin, then his aunt? Aye, well – he is now close to Queen Mary of Modena, James Stewart's mother, in St. Germain. To the sorrow of all honest men, my God! He is a snake, that one! He has just been here, to Scotland. He was after calling a meeting of chiefs and great ones in the cause, at Drummond Castle. He brought letters from the Queen. Och, I'll not be troubling you with what was in the letters or what the meeting was about, see you – since you are not concerned with Jacobite affairs, Mr. Fletcher. But this I can tell you – there were three letters. One to the Duke of Gordon, one to the Duke of Hamilton and the third to the Duke of Atholl . . ."

"Hamilton? But Hamilton is no Jacobite. Why Hamilton? As for Atholl, he *might* be a secret Jacobite sympathiser. His father, the late Marquis, was ever of that persuasion. Although the Duke, as Lord Murray, was William's Secretary of State and is now Anne's minister. After all, she made him a duke."

"Just that, yes. As to the Duke of Hamilton, *his* letter was but to urge him to be fighting the union and not to push his far-out claim to the succession. MacShimi – Lovat – was after reading it out to the meeting. But the Duke of Atholl's letter, now, was different. Och yes, different. It was after seeking his help in the struggle, telling him of plans and dates and offering him a command in the Jacobite forces. Right . . . explicit."

"Lord – Atholl! The Queen's Lord Privy Seal! This could be as good as a keg of gunpowder! Atholl as close as that to St. Germain . . . ?"

"Och, no – that is just it, Mr. Fletcher. It is a plot, I tell you. I have known my lord Duke for long. I sell his cattle for him and do other small things. And he has no dealings with St. Germain. He is no real Jacobite – although a wheen of his clan are. No – this was Lovat's work. The other letters were addressed in the same hand as wrote them. This was not. This was addressed to Atholl in a different hand – I jalouse Lovat's own."

"You mean . . . ?"

"Aye – it was an open letter from Queen Mary. To be given where it would do the cause most good. But Lovat hates Atholl – clan trouble. Atholl's aunt married the previous Lord Lovat and the title was to descend to her offspring, half-Murrays. But this Simon Fraser claimed it as heir male. Took it by force when the old Lord died. The Murrays have tried to unseat him. He abducted the women. So he is outlaw and exile – as once you were, Mr. Fletcher! And he hates Atholl."

"But – I cannot believe that he, Lovat, could endanger his whole cause for the sake of a private spite. If he is indeed close to Mary of Modena, her envoy . . . ?"

"You think not, at all? Then hear this. Before coming to Drummond Castle, Lovat went secretly to see the Duke of Queensberry and showed him that letter."

"Queensberry! Not Queensberry, the High Commissioner? Save us – Queen Anne's chiefest man in Scotland! You have your dukes wrong, surely . . . ?"

"I have not, then. Queensberry it was."

"How do you know this, man? I warrant Lovat did not tell you!"

"You will have been hearing of a man named Defoe, sir? Daniel Defoe. No? Och well, he is an Englishman just, who does be doing business in Scotland. He . . . comes and goes. I see him from time to time. At cattle-trysts. He has his friends in high places, it seems – and plenty of siller . . . !"

"In other words, an English spy!"

"Och well, that is not a word I would be using myself. But he has useful information whiles, see you. And sometimes seeks information from the likes of myself."

"I see."

"Likely you do not see at all, Mr. Fletcher! We'll not be looking into that, just now. But he is close to the Duke of Queensberry, whatever."

"But – what is the point of all this? Why should Queensberry receive the exiled Lord Lovat, a known Jacobite and outlaw?"

"I asked that, my own self. But if Lovat was *more* than just a Jacobite, see you – what then? If he was working for the English government as well, would it not all make sense? How think you he can move so freely about Scotland and England too? I am told he dined openly in London."

"You mean he works for both sides? For Mary and James and for Anne also? A traitor! If this is so, why should this Englishman – Defoe, did you call him? – tell you so? Against his own masters."

"They tell me that there are two sides in England, too, not loving each other. Whigs and Tories. This Defoe plays his own game, for one or other."

"Even so, I fail to see the reason for this of Queensberry. If true."

"Why, to bring down Atholl. To split the Protestant Jacobites from the Catholics – Atholl is Protestant and could act as bridge. And to break up those who work against the union. Atholl is against union, as is Hamilton. And they are not to be bribed, these two dukes. They tried to bribe Atholl, with £1,000 – but it did not serve."

"So you hear tell of bribery also?"

341

"Who does not? So I come to you, Mr. Fletcher. On behalf of . . . others. To urge you to be acting with the Jacobites, over this of union. Atholl will be disgraced – for I am told that Queensberry sent a copy of the letter to Queen Anne. He will have to leave the ministry. Many here will name him a Jacobite schemer, and hate and fear the Jacobites the more. To Scotland's loss. If *you* do not make that mistake, and seek to keep the vote against the union united, much of the harm will be undone, whatever. Men respect yourself, Mr. Fletcher. *Honos habet onus!*"

"Not if I seem to be turning Jacobite, sir."

"Och, you can say that you but make common cause, just. You, who are against military rule, they tell me."

"Eh . . . ? What do you mean, Captain MacGregor?"

"You have fought against standing armies, have you not? Support only militias, like my own Highland Watch? Well, then – there is danger again."

"Why do you say that? How could that be? There is only the Royal Horse Guards as regular troops in Scotland now – the High Commissioner's guard."

"It is *English* troops which will be the danger, whatever. I hear that the Earl of Stair, a curse on him, has written to Queen Anne, and the man Marlborough, advising that they send an English army into Scotland to suspend parliamentary government and impose military rule. Because of the danger of what they are after calling secession, of a Jacobite rising, and of this union being voted out by the Estates."

"Good God! Stair, again! Is this true, man?"

"Those who sent me believe it so."

"But – this is almost beyond belief! I would be interested to know just who these *are* who sent you, Captain?"

"Och, just some gentlemen who have Scotland's welfare at heart, sir."

"Your friends, the Campbells? Not your cousin Breadalbane, I'll be bound!"

But the MacGregor was not to be drawn on this subject, however informative on others. When, presently, he departed as courteously amiable as when he came, he left the Laird of Saltoun a very thoughtful man indeed.

* * *

When the Estates met, on 28th June, 1705, the excitement in
Edinburgh seemed to throb in the streets as it did in Parliament
Hall. Known supporters of union were booed and spat upon
on their way to the assembly, opponents cheered. There was
no doubt as to the feelings of the populace, at any rate –
although known Jacobites and Catholics were also jeered. The
divide-and-rule philosophy always worked well in Scotland.

In the hall itself tension was at a high pitch. Talk of bribery
and coercion, the English Alien Act, threats from London, the
fall of Atholl – who did not appear – and Jacobite alarms,
reverberated. Lords and commissioners eyed each other with
more suspicion than anyone could remember previously.

There were ample other matters to exclaim over. For one
thing, there was a new High Commissioner sent up in place of
Queensberry – the young Duke of Argyll, the new MacCailean
Mor, a professional soldier and lieutenant of Marlborough's in
the Continental wars, no doubt sent by the Queen on that
favourite's advice. It was extraordinary for so young a man,
not yet twenty-five years, to be appointed to represent the
crown; and men saw it as an indication that the sessions were to
be ruled military-style. Seafield was still Chancellor, Queensberry being given the Privy Seal and Cromartie Lord Justice
General, whilst Loudoun was Secretary of State. In other
words, a solidly pro-union administration, with Atholl out.
That Stair was not in it was the only surprise – but no doubt he
remained a power behind all.

Argyll's speech from the throne was the briefest in living
memory, delivered in staccato style like orders in the field. He
was a red-haired, high-coloured young man with hot pale-
blue eyes, very different from the last three chiefs of Clan
Campbell who had all had a dark and foxy look. He announced
baldly that the business before them was to deal with the
succession to the crown again, since the Queen was dissatisfied
with the previously-passed Act of Security; to consider terms
for a Treaty of Union; and to find ways to aid the poverty-
stricken state of the nation – although the said union would
much assist in that. The Chancellor to proceed.

343

Queensberry and Loudoun had not yet arrived from London, and Seafield was fairly evidently reluctant to start on the major controversies without these union stalwarts. So he elected to take the poverty issue first, to Argyll's frowns, and announced consideration of two schemes for improving the financial state of the nation, by printing paper money, in the wake of the Darien disaster – one by Law of Lauriston, a Scot presently making his name in the councils of France, the other by an English banker named Chamberlain. Recognising the Chancellor's anxiety to delay the union and succession themes, and the High Commissioner's impatience, Andrew at once jumped up to try to dispose of this time-wasting device. He declared that Law's scheme was no more than a contribution to enslave the nation, and that Chamberlain's was not worth considering. To get rid of the entire subject he proposed that the two financiers should be asked to appear before the Estates at some future date, to put their projects in person; meantime to pass on to more pressing and important matters. Although clearly this pleased the vast majority present, and even Argyll nodded, oddly enough it was not Seafield but Roxburghe who protested. He hotly announced that Mr. Law's scheme deserved better treatment than this, and that it was unmannerly to bring him before them all to defend it. He for one had better manners, and moved debate.

Surprised, Andrew considered. Why was Roxburghe seeking delay – he who was no financial expert? Was he also in favour of awaiting the arrival of Queensberry and Loudoun – which would indicate a pro-union stance indeed? And was he likely to be backed by the rest of his Squadrone Volante? If so, their votes and prestige could get this thing through, and the session get off to an exceedingly ominous start. Swiftly he made up his mind, and chose dramatics. Deliberately he adopted a truculent attitude. Did the previous speaker accuse him of unmannerly conduct, he demanded – judiciously allowing his reputation for hot temper free rein for once?

The haughty Roxburghe had his own temper – and, as far as Andrew was concerned, probably a bad conscience. If the cap fitted, Mr. Fletcher could wear it, he returned.

There was uproar in the hall. This was as good as a challenge-of-honour. Andrew quite intentionally took it that way. He challenged the Earl of Roxburghe to a duel forthwith.

Wild scenes for and against erupted, the tension in the entire assembly thus abruptly if deliberately released. No amount of gavel-banging quietened it all. Furious, redder-faced than ever, Argyll rose from the throne, ordered an adjournment of the House, commanded the two disputants to be confined, and stalked out.

Andrew had at least spoked that wheel. And if knew the populace outside he would have crowds responding in huge enthusiasm to the dramatic situation. It might be a strange method of aiding the democratic processes, but it could be effective against the forces they were up against.

Although in theory under arrest, he found no difficulty in gaining the open High Street, in a knot of vociferous well-wishers who communicated the news to the crowd. Perceiving that Lord Charles Kerr, second son of the Marquis of Lothian and a far-out kinsman of Roxburghe, was one of these, he sent him off to deliver to the Earl his challenge to meet him that evening at six on Leith Links, to settle this affair-of-honour like gentlemen. He scarcely expected Roxburghe to appear – but that would only assist the effect on public opinion, if as he believed, the Earl could be nailed as a pro-union convert.

It did not quite work out that way, for Roxburghe duly turned up, with young Baillie of Jerviswood as his second – who tried hard to induce both principals to call it all off. He explained to Andrew that the Earl had a weakness in his right leg, which would put him at a disadvantage in sword-play – whereupon Andrew produced a pair of matching pistols, for Roxburghe to take his choice. It was at this stage that a troop of the High Commissioner's Horse Guards appeared upon the scene, to arrest both contestants, who managed to fire their pistols in the air and shake hands before being escorted back to their lodgings in Edinburgh.

It was all distinctly childish and artificial, but none the less effective in that it aroused passions, helped to unify anti-union opinion, upset the plans of the administration and made the Squadrone Volante suspect – however unfairly. Andrew was cheered whenever he appeared in the streets.

So when the session was resumed two days later there was a different atmosphere, tension still present but attitudes hardened, the authorities less confident. The Duke of Hamilton, who probably resented having so often to play second fiddle to a mere laird like Fletcher, led off by rising quickly when the Chancellor intimated that they would discuss the matter of the succession first and then the terms for a Treaty of Union. He asserted that this was unnecessary. They had in the previous Parliament already decided on this matter and passed the Act of Security. There was no point in doing so once more. He moved that they get on with and dispose of this talk of union, straight away. Besides, the one would encompass the other. He had no lack of seconders. Stair moved the reverse and got in some biting remarks anent irresponsibles, trouble-makers, rabble-rousers even republicans, staring pointedly at Andrew. But when Marchmont added his voice to Hamilton's motion, indicating that the Squadrone would vote that way, the thing was settled. It was passed by a large majority that they should deal with the union forthwith.

So at last the decks were cleared. Queensberry was still missing but Loudoun had arrived. Seafield led off. He declared that union was sensible and inevitable, indeed necessary, in these islands, for four good and sufficient reasons – the security of the Protestant religion, England being staunchly of that faith with little Catholic Jacobite sympathies; the great and vital advantages of free trade; the securing of their essential freedoms, as proudly held by all Englishmen; and the absence of any other means of settled and permanent peace between the two nations. He urged the assembly to pass an Act for appointing commissioners to treat for union.

Andrew held back to allow Hamilton to lead the rejection; but that man sat still, talking low-voiced with his neighbour on the ducal benches – none other than Atholl, who had just arrived, creating a major stir. All eyes on him, Andrew launched out on what he recognised might well be the most important speech of his career, to date. Vehement but eloquent, he based his opposition on the hated English Alien Act which so insulted the Scots. How could they, he demanded, as free and honourable men, contemplate union with a nation

346

whose Parliament had passed, so recently, so imperious and hostile a measure, which not only affronted and threatened their ancient kingdom but gave them an ultimatum to favour an incorporating union by Christmastide or be considered to be in a state of war? English guns and swords were to be the persuaders of this unnatural and shameful union – which indeed would be no marriage of equals but an abduction and rape! Carlisle, Newcastle, even their own Berwick-on-Tweed were to be garrisoned against them and an English army moved up to the Border. Well, in the past, they had had English armies attempting to cross their Borders – and they had sent them back whence they had come bloody-nosed! They would do so again . . .

For a while he could not continue, for the deafening cheering and stamping. Argyll was glaring and the ministers sitting looking uneasy.

When he could resume, Andrew struck still harder. If any thought that this of armed intervention was a mere threat and no more, let them take note that he had heard it from, so far as he could tell, a reliable source that certain Scots of the government persuasion – one of whom was sitting there on the lords' benches – had written urging Queen Anne and her London ministers to send up an English army *into* Scotland, not just to the Border, to suspend the rule of Parliament and impose English military rule in its place. If this was not the case, let the said lord stand up and deny it!

Pandemonium broke out. Neither Stair nor any other rose from their seats.

In these circumstances, Andrew concluded, there was no need for any detailed and reasoned debate of the principle of union or terms therefore. He moved that Parliament promptly rejected the Chancellor's proposals, at least until such time as the English might put such forward in a more neighbourly and friendly manner.

He sat down to resounding applause – and hasty conferring amongst ministers and their close associates.

The Duke of Hamilton rose to second.

A new voice was raised on the government side, David Boyle, first Earl of Glasgow, a clever lawyer and said to be

347

Queensberry's adviser, recently promoted to the peerage. He said, silkily, that before they voted, it would be advisable to hear what Mr. Fletcher would substitute for union. On a previous occasion he had put forward twelve limitations on the crown to be embodied in the unfortunate Act of Security which so offended Her Grace. If there was to be no union, what then? The House was entitled to know what limitations the opposition still required.

Recognising a delaying tactic, Andrew pointed out that his limitations referred to the succession to the crown, on the Queen's death, not to the union of the Parliaments. Hamilton agreed and said there was no need to discuss that now.

But Glasgow, supported by ministers, insisted; and the Chancellor ruled that the House was entitled to hear and decide whether or no these limitations or objections were relevant to the union vote, as the Earl claimed.

So, effectively baulked and seething with anger, Andrew had to spend the rest of that day going over and defending his twelve limitations on the crown, detail by detail, whilst the House grew bored and all the fine fervour dissipated. By a process of niggling question and amalgamation, the dozen clauses were eventually reduced to four, and even these were watered down. The holding of annual parliaments was reduced to tri-annual; officers of state were to be appointed by the Estates, not the crown; Scotland was to have its own ambassadors to foreign powers; and holders of treasury-paid offices should not be eligible for Parliament.

After four hours of this, many members had disappeared and the House was in a state of torpor in July heat. Stair rose to declare that since these four clauses appeared to be agreed, they should be incorporated as a safeguard in the proposed Act appointing commissioners to treat for union. He so moved, and Glasgow seconded.

Hotly Andrew leapt to his feet. Never, he cried. This could imply that he was in favour of union. None must be so tricked.

Johnnie Belhaven sought to save the situation by suggesting that these basic requirements should be incorporated in another Act, for Regulating the Constitution, not naming union. Rothes seconded.

To avoid a vote, the ministers agreed to ask Queen Anne to repeal the hated English Alien Act – although Andrew for one was scornful as to their chances of success.

Hamilton then proposed a clause to the proposed Act appointing commissioners to treat for union, which would preserve the fundamental laws, liberties and offices of the Scottish realm – which would prevent any incorporating union. Andrew declared that this was an admission of the principle of union and urged withdrawal. Hamilton angrily insisted, and in some confusion a vote was taken – and lost by two votes, some abstaining and not a few members now absent.

The government, feeling more confident at this, straightway got the vital issue put to the House, that commissioners to treat for union be agreed and appointed forthwith. Andrew proposed the direct negative. Hamilton, nettled, jumped up to propose an amendment – not to Andrew's negative but to the government's original measure. Shocked, the anti-union members heard the Duke suggest that the said commissioners to treat should not be appointed by the ministry nor yet by this Parliament but by the Queen herself.

Appalled, Andrew began to protest, to demand whether the lord Duke realised what he was saying, when Seafield ruled him out-of-order. Gleefully the Chancellor declared that the government would accept Duke Hamilton's amendment in place of their original motion. The matter was now clear-cut and simple – the commissioners to treat for a union of the two Parliaments to be appointed by Queen Anne; or the direct negative. The House would vote.

Sick at heart, Andrew saw the Squadrone Volante, all twenty-four members, vote with Hamilton and the government. The motion was carried.

Like a stricken man, Andrew Fletcher left Parliament Hall. Few of his former colleagues dared to meet his eye, much less to speak with him. That a full dozen of the Duke of Hamilton's own personal supporters stormed out with him, declaring that there was no purpose in staying longer in this Parliament when their Duke had deserted and basely betrayed them, was of scant comfort.

349

23

Dire as was the blow, the battle was not yet irrevocably lost. Commissioners to treat for a union would be appointed; but that did not necessarily mean that a union would eventuate. Admittedly it implied that Scotland's legislature accepted that there could be a case for union; and the fact that the Queen in London was to appoint the commissioners – which in effect meant that her English advisers would appoint them – would mean that they would be all prejudiced in favour from the start. But there were other forces to be reckoned with. There were the people of Scotland, firm against union, if they could be roused. There was the Kirk, almost solidly against. And there were, to be sure, the Jacobites, to whom anything of the sort would spell the end of their hopes. And, of course, the terms of the treaty negotiated by the said commissioners would still have to be passed by the Estates of the Realm – although, after the late performance, Andrew did not place much confidence in that.

So he went to work. He would fight this thing with every weapon that came to his hand. His own kind had largely failed the nation – he would not spare these. He would try to rouse the people. He would forge his Home Rule movement and Young Scotland Party into the weapons which were required, to arouse and warn, even to threaten if need be. He would seek to rally all the forces inimical to union for one combined effort, however mutually suspicious and hostile they were.

So Andrew Fletcher entered upon the busiest year of his life. He started by issuing a public demand for new elections to Parliament. It was three years since the last ones, and those had been held on the issue of the succession to the throne. To decide on this great new issue of union, the electorate must have the opportunity to express its will. He had little hope of this being accepted by the administration, since almost certainly a large anti-union majority would be returned. But the attempt had to be made, and was worth making, since rejection would all help to stir up public feeling and resentment. So he stumped the country and burghs, holding meetings, amidst popular acclaim and enthusiasm and much recruitment for his Home Rule and Young Scotland movements.

It was at one of these meetings, in the burgh of Dumbarton on the Clyde, that he found that he had a most unlikely ally. He and Johnnie Belhaven had many well-wishers and co-operators, of course, amongst the country gentry and town provosts and magistrates; but to find one amongst the Queen's ministers was a surprise indeed. Especially as this was a man whom Andrew had never liked, looked upon as a mere place-seeker and time-server – Sir James Stewart, the Lord Advocate, no less. An elderly man now and somewhat prosy and bumbling in manner, he came forward alone as the gathering was dispersing, dressed in nondescript fashion and with his cocked hat pulled down well over his wig.

"I congratulate you, Saltoun, on your public spirit as on your eloquence," he said. "The seed is well sown – although I fear the harvest will be but meagre."

"You, Sir James! Am I dreaming? I scarcely would have looked to see the Queen's Advocate here tonight!"

"Why not, sir – why not? I can love my country as well as any other, can I not? I agree with you that there ought to be new elections over this matter of union. Only a specially elected parliament would be competent to ratify or otherwise whatever decisions are come to by the union commissioners. And so I have advised the Queen and her Grace's ministers. But I fear that they are unlikely to take my advice in this."

"Then our fears coincide, Sir James. I too have no expectation of elections being called. The result would be too painful for your friends and colleagues in the ministry! I but seek 'to muster public opinion."

"Quite, sir – quite. And I wish you well in it. But I cannot think that it will much affect the issue. There will be no elections."

"Then the people will be the more wrathful."

"Perhaps. But their wrath will not turn into votes. And votes decide."

351

"Their wrath could *affect* votes, if strongly enough expressed!"

"Aye, there's the rub, Saltoun – how to express Scotland's wrath? There are many besides yourself considering that problem, just now. With differing answers."

"Then I am glad to hear it, sir. For I sometimes feel that the Lord Belhaven and myself are the only two who care. Or at least, who can be relied upon to do anything. After Hamilton's and the Squadrone's defection."

"Not so, Saltoun – not so. There are others, many others, who are concerned. And seek their own solutions. The pity that they cannot work together rather than thus separately."

Andrew stared. "Do I hear aright, Sir James? Do I hear the Lord Advocate, one of the Queen's most important ministers, advocating united opposition to the Queen's ministers' policy?"

"In this of union I believe that they are mistaken."

"Then, sir, would your course not best be to resign from the ministry?"

"I think not. I believe that I can continue to serve Scotland better as Advocate than as a private subject, sir. By the nature of my office, I hear much, learn much. Which could be . . . invaluable."

"I see. And you come to me with some of that information?"

"You are the acknowledged leader of the forces against union in Parliament, Saltoun."

"I would have said that the Duke of Hamilton was that – until he betrayed all."

"Be not too hard on Hamilton, sir. He is a strange man and of uncertain temper. But I believe that he is honest against union . . ."

"Then why did he sell the pass? Propose that commissioners to treat should be appointed by the Queen – which means her *English* ministers?"

"It was a mistake, I agree. But he thought that though he could not prevail upon the ministers here or in London, he could perhaps prevail upon the Queen. Personally. He had Argyll's promise to have him appointed one of the treaty commissioners, if he did this, moved that motion. And he hoped that he would then get the Queen to appoint others, who would work for a *federal* union, not an incorporating one. Some of your so-called Squadrone . . ."

"Lord! Is the man witless? So innocent as to believe that! Queen Anne will not move a finger without Marlborough's and his wife's guidance. And Marlborough and Godolphin are set on an incorporating union. Hamilton must know that . . ."

"He thought otherwise. Although he has since learned that he was mistaken. For he is *not* included amongst the commissioners. And nor is the Duke of Argyll himself – who has refused to serve because his promise made to Hamilton was not honoured."

"Ha! So MacCailean Mor chooses his own kind of honour! But – the commissioners are chosen, then?"

"Yes. Thirty-one of each nation. The list reached me three days ago."

"And all the Scots safe men, I'll be bound?"

"All but one – and he is a friend of your own. George Lockhart of Carnwath."

"But he is against union, almost a Jacobite!"

"Aye, but his mother is sister to the English Lord Wharton, one of the chiefest commissioners on the other side. Why he got Lockhart chosen is unclear, but there will be a reason behind it, never fear."

"Yet I trust Lockhart. Whatever the reason, he will not sell his country. And who are the others?"

"Few surprises, sir – save that all three Dalrymples are in; Stair and his two brothers, Sir Hew, the Lord President of Session and Sir David, Queen's Solicitor. For the rest, what you would expect – Queensberry, Seafield, Loudoun, Mar, Marchmont, Morton, Sutherland. And most of the officers of state."

"But not yourself, Sir James?"

"Not myself. I have not hidden my views on union. Argyll does not sit – but he has seen to it that his brother Archie does, created Earl of Islay at the same time!"

"So – all lords except Lockhart?"

"No. There is Grant of Grant, Seafield's kinsman. And Sir Patrick Johnston, who was Lord Provost of Edinburgh. Aird, the Glasgow man also. I fear the result is not in doubt."

"It never was, once Hamilton shifted his stance. It will be an incorporating union, whatever Marchmont and the Squadrone hope about a federal one. When do they start treating – if that is the word?"

"In April. In London, of course."

"Naturally! Then we must try to ensure that Scotland's voice is heard, loud enough to reach London! Since it will not be uttered by those commissioners. You spoke, Sir James, of others working to this end? And of the need to work together. May I hear who and what?"

"That is what I came to tell you, Saltoun – only, *my* name must not be brought into it, you understand? Or I could not remain Lord Advocate. And that is important. First of all, Atholl. He is in disgrace anyway, over that Lovat business. He aims to take over Stirling, with his Murray clansmen, and so hold open the passage of Forth so that a Highland army could come down at short notice. Pray God it does not come to that, to fighting – but the threat may be useful."

"That could bring the Jacobites down on us."

The other shrugged non-committally – and Andrew began to wonder whether this James Stewart was, in fact, totally out of sympathy with that other James Stewart in St. Germain.

"Then the General Assembly of the Kirk is preparing a statement to be read from all pulpits, against union."

"That I know of. Indeed I had some small hand in the matter."

"Arrangements are being made for most of the towns and burghs to draw up protests against union, to be presented to Parliament when it meets. But you will know well of this, since you were advocating it here in Dumbarton tonight, as you have done elsewhere. But you may not know how widespread is this move, all over the country."

"I helped draft the Haddington and Dunbar protests. But it is good to hear that it spreads. It should mean that the burgh commissioners to the Estates vote accordingly."

"That is less certain. There is talk of substantial payments being made to the sitting burgh members. Or some of them."

"Ha – the bribery weapon again! I heard that the lords were being bribed, from London. I suppose that it was too much to expect that others should be overlooked."

"Then there is the matter of the Cameronians. This I am concerned about, for it could be dangerous. My main reason for coming to you, Saltoun. You know how violent can be the passions of these extreme Covenanting sectaries of the South-West. The folk Claverhouse fought. They are much enraged largely because they believe that Scotland will hereafter be ruled by Episcopalians from London. And they still have hidden arms in large quantities. They threaten to march, when it comes to the vote. March on Edinburgh. That might not be so ill, if it was under control. But there is a wild man you may have heard of, who has put himself at their head – Cunninghame of Aiket. He was one of your Darien adventurers. And he is now preaching what almost amounts to a holy war. Not only against union and Episcopalians but against Catholics. And, as you know, much of the Highland force which Atholl could bring down would be Catholic."

"Ah – I see. This could be dangerous indeed. I know of this Cunninghame. A firebrand."

"There could be civil war. Which could play into the unionist's hands. Excuse for the English army to march over the Border. To restore order. Stair has already urged that – and Stair's will be the loudest voice amongst the commissioners. So – can *you* seek to keep this Cunninghame within bounds, Saltoun? He may heed you. I could have him apprehended – but that might well only provoke uprising."

"I do not know that I could do much – but I will try. I am seeking to arrange a descent upon Edinburgh, my own self. Of a different sort of electors. Of the men who would be electing the new shire commissioners to the Estates – if there *was* an election. Lairds, lesser barons, country gentlemen. Hundreds of them, from all over. If these can show their teeth, then present representatives may think twice. I am in touch with a number in the South-West and Galloway. I will write to them about Cunninghame and the Cameronians."

"That is good. These are the men we need in this pass. I am glad to hear of your enterprise, sir. If I can help, I shall. We must keep in touch. But secretly, Saltoun – secretly. Or my usefulness is gone . . ."

The winter, so busy for Andrew, gave way to a belated spring, and Scotland as it were held its breath, as the commissioners to treat of union sat in London, amidst great secrecy. Travellers reported no comparable tension in England nor even public interest, although in London one or two mercantile groups linked to the East India Company demonstrated against union, fearing loss of trading monopolies to the beggarly Scots.

Although the treaty sittings went on from 11th April 1706 until late July, all the principal decisions were made within the first nine days, only the working out of details, mainly financial, taking up the time. These details, indeed even the general terms of the proposed treaty in twenty-five Articles, were not published, all to be kept secret until they could be laid before the two Parliaments for approval or otherwise. Nevertheless, with as many as sixty-two commissioners, much leaked out inevitably, to reach Scotland and set the nation by the ears, the worst fears surpassed.

Andrew, through his new links with the Lord Advocate – who was of course officially informed – did not have to rely on rumours and hearsay. Whatever the details might subsequently reveal, the main Articles were, from the Scots aspect, appalling. All was to be as England desired. It would be an incorporating union, under one authority sitting in London, to be named the Parliament of the United Kingdom, but in all major respects it would be the English Parliament continuing. On this the Scots would be allowed only forty-five elected members to the Commons and a mere sixteen peers to the House of Lords – although the Scots peers who sat on this treaty commission were to be sweetened to agree by each being granted an *English* peerage, so that they might take seats. The Scots had asked for sixty-six M.P.s, which would be one-sixth of the membership of the Commons, comparable to the population ratio of the two countries – whereas they got only one-thirteenth in the two Houses. Much was made of Scotland retaining its own laws and judicature; but it would lose its Privy Council and would have to pay taxes and customs-dues at the same level as England. It would become responsible for a share of the English National Debt, which now amounted to £18 million sterling, equalling three years' revenue, thanks largely to King William's Continental wars; since Scotland had only £160,000 of public debt, to enable her to pay her annual contribution, that £160,000 would be remitted the first year by being added to the Equivalent which William Paterson had worked for and which was to be looked upon as compensation for the Darien losses. This Equivalent was to total £398,085 – 10 shillings, calculated none knew how. Instead of the boasted addition to Scotland's wealth, of which so much had been made, they were thus to shoulder an enormous loss, in funding the English National Debt. Trade was to be free, in principle – but the English trade monopolies were to remain, and the Scottish coinage was to be assimilated in that of England. A land tax was to be instituted, and the Hanoverian succession was settled. The only small crumb of comfort in it all was that the loathed Alien Act was to be withdrawn as no longer applicable.

When the gist of all this became known in Scotland there was the predictable fury. The nation seethed, with rioting in the streets of cities and towns, arson on the estates of pro-union lords, the commissioners burnt in effigy. Stair, who as expected had taken the lead in the so-called negotiations, was hated above all, and being named the Curse of Scotland. Discreetly the said commissioners either remained in England meantime or came home secretly and lay very low.

The Scots Parliament was called for 3rd October, to debate the treaty provisions, but no elections were to be held. Meanwhile, Andrew and others like-minded sought to orchestrate the tempest of anger and protest into something which could be controlled and harnessed as a powerful force to influence even a corrupt, bribed and non-representative assembly – no easy task.

He had most success, not unnaturally, with his country gentry, the shires electorate, getting promises from over five hundred of them to rally in Edinburgh, with their retainers, to express their opinions in no uncertain fashion. At meetings with leading churchmen, he stressed the point that while the English Episcopal bishops had twenty-two seats as Lords

Spiritual in the House of Lords – more than the total of Scots peers permitted – Church of Scotland ministers had no representation, putting their Presbyterian system in obvious danger. So, in addition to the pulpit condemnations, the General Assembly agreed to present a vehement overture to Parliament against the terms of the proposed treaty. This, of course, was not enough for the Cameronians and their sympathisers in South-West Scotland, who were already digging out their hidden arms, drilling and parading. These, to the number of some eight thousand, actually took over the town of Dumfries, the 'capital' of that region, burnt a mock-up of the treaty at the burgh cross, and prepared to march north. Efforts to tone down the wilder excesses of the man Cunninghame of Aiket were partly successful; but the situation was complicated by the appearance on the scene of a rival leader called Ker of Kersland, about whom nobody seemed to know much but who appeared to be sowing dissention. Ker, spelt with one 'r' was the family name of the Earl of Roxburghe – the Marquis of Lothian's branch of the clan used two; and there were doubts as to whether this new man was in fact an *agent provocateur* sent down by the Squadrone to disrupt any concerted action. Andrew, for one, did not know whether to welcome this intervention or otherwise. In the north, Atholl was said to be mobilising his Murrays and the other clans, largely Jacobite inevitably; and though Andrew had little influence there, he did keep in touch through Rob Roy MacGregor who, because of his cattle-dealing activities, came and went in the Lowlands more or less at will. The town and burgh protests were being organised into a most impressive series of proclamations, score upon score of them, all bearing signatures running into thousands, and all to be presented by innumerable delegations to Parliament. It was significant that of all these, only one was in favour of union, from the burgh of Ayr, where Stair had much influence – and even there a counter-manifesto, with many more signatures, was drawn up to accompany it. And so on.

All this was reasonably heartening for Andrew, Belhaven and their colleagues. But gradually a curious doubt began to form at the back of Andrew's mind. It was the MacGregor, on one of his clandestine visits to Saltoun, who was instrumental in bringing that doubt from the back to the front of his host's mind, only a few days before Parliament was due to sit.

"My lord Duke does not like this of Hamilton, whatever," he said. "He does not. It is not the right place, at all."

"Place . . . ? You do not refer to *Duke* Hamilton, then?"

"Och, well – that too, yes. But it is this of the *town* of Hamilton that does be troubling my own duke. The South-landers from Dumfries and Galloway, these Covenanters – they are after having the Duke of Atholl and his Highlandmen to be joining them there, at Hamilton, to march on Edinburgh. And my duke is not much liking the notion, see you. Stirling it was to be, just – to be holding Stirling and the Forth crossing."

"Save us – Hamilton! I knew nothing of this. The two forces to join at Hamilton? I do not wonder that Atholl does not like it. This could provoke outright war. Excuse for the English army on the Border to march."

"Yes, then. Holding Stirling is one thing. To march south into Lanarkshire and join these wild men at Hamilton is another, whatever."

It interested Andrew to hear this Highland fightingman, cateran and cattle-lifter refer to the Cameronians as wild men. "But why choose Hamilton?" he wondered. "The Duke's own town and palace. They would hardly march there without the Duke's agreement."

"That is what my duke says. Forby, he has heard tell, as have I, that Duke Hamilton is for making a national address to the Queen, declaring that almost all Scotland is averse to this union and that, according to our laws, it is as good as high treason to consider an entire union. And that if the Queen's Scots ministers insist on bringing to Parliament, he himself will lead all against out of the House, whatever. Which Duke Atholl says is a foolishness."

"I say so also. I knew of the address – indeed I suggested it to, well to another. But not this of walking out. The ministers would just pass the treaty without us. Folly, indeed!" It clicked in Andrew's mind, then, that more than one of his shires gentry had proposed that Hamilton was the man to head up *their* united demonstration to Parliament; and that leading churchmen had named the Duke also, to present their overture. Was there just too much of Duke James in all this? It was understandable, of course. He was the premier peer of Scotland, allied to the royal house, and had been strong against union. But after that let-down at the last Parliament, Andrew was not disposed to trust him – not so much as to dishonesty but in his judgment and consistency.

"We shall have to watch Hamilton," he said. "And I think that Atholl is wise to wait at Stirling. Or his men, at least – for we shall need him here."

* * *

The 3rd of October dawned cold and grey, with a thin drizzle of rain off the North Sea, to put a frown on even Edinburgh's fair face. But the weather no wise daunted the crowds and the streets were thronged from an early hour – indeed many had been out all night, for the city was bursting at the seams, accommodation all but unprocurable, with thousands flocked in, deputations, petitioners, demonstrators and the retainers of all the lords and gentry. The taverns were doing a roaring trade. And the capital was as full of rumours as it was of excited folk – the Jacobites were coming, the Cameronians were marching, the English had invaded across Tweed, Glasgow town was on fire and its Provost hanged, there had been a battle at Stirling, the country was sold for English gold, and so on.

In this heady climate, so at odds with the weather, the members of the Estates had to make their way up to Parliament Hall, no easy matter anyway through the packed, narrow streets and wynds. Unfortunately there was no way in general of identifying the pro-union from the anti-union commissioners, or even who was a commissioner and who was not. To be on the safe side, the crowds more or less assumed that every well-dressed man whom they did not recognise was one of the hated unionists – or else perhaps a Jacobite in disguise. So even the most rugged opponents of union had to run the gauntlet, were mobbed and hooted and spat upon. Those who had discreetly surrounded themselves with bodyguards of retainers were, in fact, particularly picked upon, as obviously guilt-stricken, no doubt, and paid for, and had to make their way up the High Street in one long battle. Those lordly ones who could rise to coaches, thinking that they were safe therein, were quickly disillusioned, many of the vehicles' windows smashed, outriders unhorsed and some of the noble occupants dragged out and assaulted. Andrew himself, thanks to his campaign of public appearances, escaped all this, being quickly recognised and applauded. Even so, progress was difficult.

When he and Belhaven eventually reached Parliament Hall, breathless and dishevelled, it was to find the place besieged, indeed doors locked to keep the crowds at bay – and keeping out the commissioners likewise, to be sure. Although they tried the rear entrances, by narrow wynds up from the Cowgate, these too were impassible. It was not until, with much clatter and trumpet-blasts, the Lord High Commissioner's great coach arrived from Holyrood with an escort of two troops of Horse Guards, swords drawn and swiping flat-bladed, that the waiting and alarmed legislators were able to enter their building – and even this arrival, ironically enough, had apparently only been possible by Queensberry's coach and escort keeping close behind the Duke of Hamilton who, coming from his suite in the same palace, was carried up Canongate and High Street shoulder-high by relays of stalwart citizens, to cheers and acclaim, the darling of the populace, a strange thing by any standards, with Hamilton himself as mystified and embarrassed as any.

Once within and the doors locked again, it was evident that no business-like procedure was likely to be possible for some time. For one thing, quite a large proportion of the members had not been able to get there, including many of the ministerial team. And everyone was in a state of excitement, agitation and resentment. The first day of any new session was apt to be much taken up with ceremonial anyway, and this no one was in any mood for. Eventually it was decided that, since the crowds outside were growing ever more vociferous and the door-banging worse, probably the best thing to do, to try to appease the populace, was to announce that the innumerable deputations out there amongst the clamouring throng should be allowed in to present their petitions, overtures and protests, the Horse Guards to seek to keep the unauthorised out.

So, after much noisy delay and false starts, this was put in process, beginning with the General Assembly of the Kirk's overture. No lengthy speeches were permitted and even the reading out of the petitions was curtailed. Soon nobody was listening. It seemed that the Kirk, and indeed some of the burghs, expected the Duke of Hamilton to present their protests for them – and were disappointed, for that nobleman curtly refused and went to hide himself in an anteroom. Just how it had come about that Hamilton had become, as it were, the focus of the nation's hopes and fears, was hard to understand; but clearly it was so, and he proved to be something of a broken reed.

This petition presenting went on and on, Andrew's public campaigning proving all too successful. The lengthy process did help to diffuse the tense situation outside but that was about all it did, for inside little attention was being paid to all the announcements and eloquence save by the parliamentary clerks and a few activists like Andrew himself. Indeed when, during one deputation's egress and another's ingress, somebody plaintively demanded what they were to do with all these petitions piling up, the Duke of Argyll suggested that they make kites of them.

So much for the voice of the people.

Andrew had deliberately planned his country-electorate demonstration for the second day, recognising that the first would be fairly fully occupied with formal business. But he had scarcely foreseen that nothing at all would get done on the opening day, other than the receiving of these petitions. But that was the situation. After hours of deputation-visits, controlled with difficulty, the crowds outside grew bored and began to disperse. And recognising a relative quiet, and the opportunity presented to make a reasonably safe departure, Seafield and Queensberry announced adjournment till the morrow, and all were glad enough to call it a day.

But, of course, the excitement and its causes were not removed nor exhausted, only transferred to the houses, taverns and streets of the city, for commissioners and populace alike, and by no means lessened by being damped down throughout the day by inaction. Edinburgh passed a wild night. Indeed, since only a small proportion of the crowds had been able to besiege Parliament Hall, the rest appeared to have gone on the rampage elsewhere. The houses of known pro-union figures, including that of the hitherto popular ex-Lord Provost Johnston, had been broken into and sacked. Windows were smashed, effigies hanged and burned and marchers through the town chanted "No union!"

But there was word of more serious upheavals than these. The town was buzzing with stories that the Cameronians were on the way north in their thousands, in arms. Some put them already at Hamilton town only thirty-seven miles away, where they were said to be only awaiting the Duke thereof to put himself at their head and to descend upon the capital, to show the unionists what Scottish independence meant. There were tales of large numbers of Highlanders congregated at Stirling, with dire prophesies as to what they were liable to do; but since the Duke of Atholl had been in Parliament Hall that day, behaving normally, Andrew for one discounted any dramatics from that quarter.

Next day the streets were as crowded and noisy as ever. Some of the High Commissioner Queensberry's personal following had been set upon overnight and maltreated. Argyll, Mar, Loudoun and even Montrose, of the Squadrone, complained of being attacked and insulted at their lodgings. The Earl of Erroll, High Constable of the Realm, had been brought in to keep order, at least around Parliament Hall, but declared that he could not trust the militiamen allotted to him. In this spirit the great debate began.

Andrew scored an early victory by demanding, and winning, the House's support that the Articles of the union treaty be debated one by one, each to be voted upon separately. This should at least prevent any pushing through of the measure by a catch-vote. The ministry, evidently recognising that it might be touch-and-go, decided to give in on small details in the hope of getting the main provisions swallowed. They accepted part of the Kirk's overture, that the Coronation Oath should bind the monarch to maintain the Presbyterian form of Church government. They agreed to recommend the reduction of the Salt Tax, for Scotland – a sore point in a country which manufactured salt in large quantities and one of whose greatest exports was salted-fish. They conceded that the English Malt Tax imposition should be delayed. And cunningly they let it be known that numerous vacancies in profitable office, especially of judges of the Court of Session and of sheriffs, would not be filled until Parliament concluded – and that Queensberry had been given a blank commission to fill them. Also that there was an extra £15,500 sterling available from London for 'arrears of pension'.

By these means the first Article put to the vote was passed by a majority of thirty-two, most of the Squadrone members voting with the government. Had they voted otherwise, the union would have been lost.

Grimly Andrew recognised that now it was time to apply outside pressure.

He discovered, however, that a serious hitch had developed. The five hundred or so county electors, who had come to Edinburgh, during these two days had decided that, in view of the reception accorded to all the other petitioners the previous day, it would be better not to present their protest to Parliament as such but directly to the High Commissioner, from whom they hoped to get agreement to see them, as representing the Queen. Andrew saw some point in this. But in order to obtain Queensberry's attention they had decided that only an approach on the highest level was likely to be successful, by someone that duke could scarcely refuse. So they had elected to ask the Duke of Hamilton, premier peer, to act their spokesman. And Hamilton had agreed – and then later sent word that his agreement depended upon the electoral group's acceptance of the succession to the crown of the Electress Sophia and her son George. This bombshell, so utterly unexpected from one who himself had been named as a possible royal successor, had quite shattered the country gentry, of whom many were Jacobite sympathisers and almost all against the Hanoverian succession. There had been an angry and unruly meeting, whilst the Estates had been sitting, and the five hundred had split up into factions, Jacobite, Catholic, Episcopalian, Presbyterian, yeas and noes. Quite a large proportion had thereupon marched out and gone home.

Appalled, Andrew sought to gather what he could of those remaining in the city for a petition-presenting on the morrow. In the process, that evening, he discovered that this was not Hamilton's only contribution to the day. He had apparently sent off urgent messengers to Hamilton town countermanding the Cameronians assembly there and ordering all connected therewith to return home – allegedly because he had heard that their marching was to be used as an excuse by the English army at Berwick to invade.

That night the mood in Edinburgh was noticeably changed. There was an element of despair evident now in the city, even though there was a wilder note in the demonstrations and disorders. Hamilton was no longer cheered in the streets. Windows in his wing of the palace were smashed.

Next day Queensberry, no doubt well informed, refused to accept Andrew's request to receive his gentry. Only a modest deputation was permitted to make one more brief presentation of protest-note before Parliament itself – a grievously disappointing expression of all their hopes.

Depressed, Andrew and Belhaven sought desperately for some remedy to counter the creeping, thickening miasma of defeat.

Delay at least they could achieve. In the days following, they and their friends took up most of the Estates' debating time by èloquence and tactical devices. Johnnie especially distinguished himself by speaking literally for hours, with of course interruptions, on an expanding theme that saw their ancient Mother Caledonia, like Caesar, sitting amongst them all and beholding ruefully how she was betrayed, covering herself with her royal garment before breaking out at last with '*Et tu, mi fili*!' This drew tears from some and laughter from others; but Andrew saw that this theatrical representation could be used with effect on many and could be applied daily to almost all the clauses debated; master of parliamentary tactics as he was, he saw to it that it was so.

So they managed to postpone the voting.

The delay they used to endeavour to muster and revitalise the demoralised county-electorate gentry who, properly handled, might still be a potent force. But Andrew found it hard going, the aura of failure, corruption and treachery widespread and spreading. He also found that the Duke of Hamilton had been busy again. He had informed some of his supporters amongst the gentry – and there were not a few Hamiltons therein – that union was now inevitable and that they must concentrate on trying to make it a federal and not an incorporating one. He believed that they could achieve this by trading their agreement to the Hanoverian succession. It was the only way, he was convinced. If they would back him in this, he would carry the anti-union vote in the House, and the Squadrone too, sufficiently to give them a majority.

Andrew was more than doubtful, more especially in that the Duke had not approached *him* on the matter, indeed seemed to be carefully avoiding him these days. He was prepared to admit that the anti-union cause was in great danger; but to accept any kind of union went sorely against the grain – and he was by no means convinced that England would agree to any federal union, even with the Hanoverian succession granted. He urged the gentry not to commit themselves to Hamilton's plan, asserting that they had not yet reached so desperate a remedy.

Oddly enough new ammunition for his fight reached him that same night, when an anonymous caller handed in a letter to his town lodging. It contained a list of payments made to Scots lords and commissioners from moneys sent by the English Treasury. There was no signature nor indication from whom the list had come – but Andrew could imagine no source other than the Lord Advocate's office. Some of the names and figures thereon raised his eyebrows high indeed.

So next day, distasteful as he found his task, he threw gentlemanly scruples to the wind and went into all-out attack. After Johnnie Belhaven had exhausted himself, and the House, and yet two more clauses were passed by the usual majorities, Andrew rose to challenge the clause which accepted that the Scots representation in the United Kingdom Parliament should be only forty-five elected members and sixteen peers. Did they all recognise what this meant, he demanded? In the Commons, the Scots voice could always be outvoted by thirteen to one. And in the Lords by twice that – even the

English bishops alone could outvote Scotland. Moreover the treaty terms, limiting the Scots peers to sixteen, put no limits on how many peers of England the crown could create. So it was all a travesty of fair dealing as it was of representation.

He paused, and jabbed an accusing finger in various specific directions. Does the House know, he asked, at what price this shameful surrender of their country's rights has been purchased? The worth of Scotland's honour, to some of her accepted leaders? He would give them one or two examples – although the list was long. And he would start with his old friend and comrade-in-arms, the former Sir Patrick Home, now Earl of Marchmont. Marchmont's price was £1,104.15.7 sterling, paid through the Earl of Glasgow from the English Treasury!

A roar of mixed astonishment, outrage, protest and fury shook the hall, the Chancellor's gavel scarcely to be heard. As it continued, Marchmont rose, set-faced, stared at Andrew and then, without even bowing to the throne, hurried from the chamber.

When the noise abated sufficiently for the Chancellor to be heard, Seafield declared that this was utterly disgraceful and not to be tolerated. The commissioner for Haddingtonshire must apologise to the noble Earl and to the House and make no more such outrageous statements.

"I do not apologise, my lord Chancellor. Nor can you muzzle me! This is a matter of public moneys of which this House has the right to hear. None can deny that, even if the payments were intended to be secret! Some other friends of mine – or at least they *were* my friends – have done almost as well. My lord Marquis of Tweeddale, for instance, has charged £1,000 for his vote – although he used to be against union. My lord of Roxburghe only got £500 – but he is younger, of course . . . !"

Again the eruption of clamour and outcry.

Tweeddale was on his feet. "I protest, my lord Chancellor – I protest! Such sums as I have received were only arrears of pension. For the time that I held office in Her Grace's ministry . . ."

"Mine also," Roxburghe cried.

367

"Call it what you will, my lords. Since when did serving your country, Scotland, merit *English* pensions? Tell me that! Besides, there are others, many others, on my list, who served on no ministry, could claim no pension. My lord Marquis of Montrose, another member of the so-called Squadrone, and bearer of a proud name. How would the noble James Graham, the Great Marquis, have viewed his great-grandson's acceptance of £300 for his vote, I wonder? Plus the Garter, of course! Or my neighbour Lord Justice Clerk Cockburn of Ormiston's £200? Or my lord Earl of Balcarres there, whom some call Jacobite, his £500 . . . ?"

"Silence, sir – silence!" Seafield shouted, hammering. "This is not to be borne. Sit down – or leave the hall."

"When I have finished, my lord. Do not fear – I shall not fail to reveal your own moderation and modesty! *You* only are down for £490 – a mere pittance for all that you have done for England! Barely covering your expenses of travel to and from London! Or is that paid for separately? But, to be sure, there is the £100 paid in the name of your new peerage as Earl of Findlater. These modest sums are eclipsed by others, of course, which some may consider extraordinarily little to accept for a man's honour. For instance, my lord Elibank's £50 and my lord Banff's only £11 2 shillings. One wonders how this was computed – his lordship's or the Treasury's estimate?"

Andrew had a strong voice, but even so he had difficulty in making it heard.

"But lest you take it that all these merchants of votes are noble lords, my friends, let me disillusion you. The Provost of Ayr, the only burgh to send in an address supporting the union, got £100 for it – no doubt my lord of Stair arranged that! And the Provost of Wigtown £25 – insufficient presumably, for no support came from Wigtown! Sir William Sharp got £300 and Stuart of Castle-Stuart also £300. But I must not weary you . . ."

"By God, you shall not!" the Chancellor exclaimed. He turned. "Your Grace, I beseech you to adjourn this shameful session!"

"His Grace no doubt will oblige!" Andrew hurried on before Queensberry could speak. "But surely not before we learn that *he* has not been wholly neglected either, by a grateful English Treasury. Since he receives the suitable sum of no less than £12,325. 10 shillings for equippage and expenses! And, of course, we heard the other day that there is still another £20,000 to disburse. So that those voters as yet unbought need not lose hope . . . !"

"Session adjourned!" the High Commissioner got in, and stamped from the chamber.

The House broke up in chaos for the week-end, without voting.

* * *

That vote, thereafter, would be vital, all perceived. How much effect Andrew's disclosures would have, apart from losing him many friends, none could tell. For now he had shot his bolt. His country gentry, however, decided that they too should strike whilst the iron was hot. They would present themselves at Parliament Hall with their amended resolution for the Duke of Hamilton to announce – no incorporating union but a federal one, in exchange for acceptance of the Electress and her son on Anne's demise. Andrew remained aloof.

The session resumed in a nervous and subdued state, the gentry assembled and were ready to process to Parliament Square when a messenger arrived from Holyrood. The demonstration must be cancelled. The Duke of Hamilton had toothache and would not be able to attend.

In dire confusion and irresolution, not knowing whether to take this as a postponement or one more resilement, the county electors dithered, argued and did nothing. And in a sullen and far-from-full House the vote on the representation clause was taken, the government winning by 113 to 83.

It was not yet quite the end – but there could be no doubt now how the final vote would go. Andrew had lost his battle.

The obsequies for the old independent Scotland seemed to take an interminable time, everybody very busy about particulars and face-saving details now that the major decisions were taken. Sick at heart, Andrew put in only token appearances now. But when, at last, the day was set for the final and total acceptance of the Treaty of Union, now being accorded capital

369

letters, he was in his seat and prepared, as it were, to sink with his ship.

It was a strange and melancholy occasion, even for those in favour of union – or most of them. Not the Earl of Stair, however, who was at his most bitingly eloquent and vehement, declaring the obvious benefits of the union, emphasising the wisdom of those who supported it and the short-sighted folly, if not worse, of those against, who clearly saw themselves as large frogs in a small pond and dreaded the challenge of larger waters and wider shores. At this stage the Duke of Hamilton walked out, followed by some of his supporters – and so avoided having to face the distress and reproach of being on the losing side in the final vote. Not so Andrew Fletcher, who rose to pour withering scorn on Stair and his like, to reiterate that man's long history of wounding his native land, to which he now added gloating over this concluding assassination. Stung, Stair gave his enemy the lie direct, which Andrew as swiftly took up, hotly offering to substantiate his words elsewhere with sword or pistol. The Chancellor's gavel halted this exchange, apologies being demanded of both and duly if stiffly given.

This, however, was the only excitement of a dreary and pedestrian debate, all relevant issues having been gone over *ad nauseam* previously, and the end a foregone conclusion. Or not quite, for when at length Seafield put the ultimate question, the Act of Union was passed with a majority of only nineteen votes instead of the anticipated thirty-odd, not a few faint-hearts clearly abstaining from the terminal dagger-stroke.

But the result was the same. Scotland had voted away a thousand years of independence – the final betrayal of the land of Bruce and Wallace and Montrose, or taken the great step forward into the eighteenth-century enlightenment, which-ever way one liked to consider it.

There remained only one last flourish, the signing of the Treaty by the union commissioners. It was accepted that this should not be done in Parliament Hall where all members would have a right to be present and trouble would undoubt-edly ensue. The problem was, where? Edinburgh seethed with angry mobs looking for victims of their ire and disgust, and any public place would be besieged. Secretly Queensberry and Seafield prospected private houses and lodgings but without exception the word got round and the commissioners, like furtive fugitives now, and even in fear of their lives, had to flee by back-doors and alleys. Eventually they thought that they would be safe in an ornamental summer-house in the garden of Moray House, in the Canongate; but barely had they started the business when the mob found them again and they had to disperse. When the Treaty was eventually signed it was in a cellar below a mean shop in 177 High Street, opposite the Tron Kirk – a fitting venue, as Andrew commented when he heard next morning. Seafield's comment, as he signed, was reported to be "There's an end to an auld sang!" and was made as much in relief as in cynicism.

The news of the signing was overshadowed next day by the astonishing information that the Earl of Stair had died, at almost the same time, in a fit of apoplexy. There were not lacking those who declared that it was God's judgment – and hoped for as much for others. Some even suggested that he would have been better, after all, to make an end with Andrew Fletcher's sword or bullet in his heart.

24

Andrew sat in a lofty small chamber in one of the topmost towers of Stirling Castle, an eagle's-nest of a place, with one of the most wide and splendid views in all Scotland – to compensate for the fact that he was a captive, confined within these narrow walls of the royal fortress, a prisoner for the first time since Bilbao in Spain. And, of all things, a Jacobite prisoner, laughable as this might seem to many. It did not make Andrew laugh.

He had been there for some weeks. Admittedly he was well-treated, as comfortable as somewhat spartan quarters would permit, with a fire in his room, his papers and books around

him, and well-fed, even wined, – his gaoler, Colonel James
Erskine, being also his friend, brother of John, Earl of Mar, the
Secretary of State, who was Hereditary Keeper of the castle.
Nevertheless, Andrew fretted for his freedom, never a man to
accept shackles of any kind patiently – especially when they
were imposed on such pathetically ridiculous pretext.

His arrest and incarceration as a Jacobite was only a device,
of course. There had been an abortive Jacobite rising within a
year of the union being signed, when James Stewart, the young
Chevalier de St. George, and his advisers, sought to take
advantage of the anger and unrest in Scotland over that debacle.
It had all been grievously mismanaged and postponed whilst
James had measles. When that rather depressed and dilatory
twenty-year-old at length arrived off the Forth with an
inadequate French force, the thing had gone off at half-cock
and failed on all fronts, the Pretender as he was being called,
being promptly carried back to France by quarrelling and
apprehensive French admirals. And thereafter there had been
a great rounding-up of Jacobites, known or suspected –
although, to be sure, not the ones who mattered, safe behind
their clans in the impenetrable Highlands. But as well as these,
the opportunity was seized to apprehend many others whom
the administration did not like, however far-fetched their links
with Jacobitism. These included Johnnie Belhaven, the Duke
of Gordon, the Marquis of Huntly and eighteen other mainly
Catholic peers, although the Duke of Hamilton was also
included after a fashion, being requested to present himself
before the Privy Council in London. The rest were less civilly
treated and sent south as prisoners. Andrew's charges were
that he had had secret meetings with the notorious rebel and
felon Robert Roy Campbell, calling himself MacGregor, and
had worked in concert with the Duke of Atholl – according to
one Daniel Defoe, government agent, whose name was vaguely
familiar. Since the said Atholl was too powerful to arrest and
Rob Roy was safely behind the Highland Line also, Andrew
was taken instead – and was not in a position to call these others
to witness to his innocence.

Not that the authorities either in Edinburgh or London had
the least belief in his Jacobitism, to be sure. But they had a good

reason for wanting him behind bars meantime. For this was election-time for the new United Kingdom Parliament – and Andrew had notified his intention of standing for the now single seat of Haddingtonshire. At first, after the union had passed both Parliaments, Queensberry and Seafield had merely picked their own sixteen docile peers – Hamilton agreeing to be one, oddly – and the thirty shire members with fifteen from the burghs, all assured unionists, and that had been that. But elections could not be postponed indefinitely and well aware of the temper and attitude of the nation, the government had little doubt as to how any elections would go. So another campaign of buying votes had to be initiated, although they were apt to find it much cheaper just to imprison the opposition candidates. So the failed Jacobite rising came as a godsend and Andrew Fletcher one of the most obvious victims.

In a way he considered himself to be fortunate. For whilst most of the alleged Jacobites had been sent under guard down to London for trial and probable banishment to the plantations, he had only been brought here to Stirling. Just why, he was uncertain, although Erskine suggested that his former friends in high places would prefer not to have him brought to trial, certainly not in London, when he might make uncomfortable revelations. If this was so, then he was not likely to be tried at all and might well just be quietly released once the elections were over.

He had whiled away the time with writing and reading and long gazings out over that magnificent vista, where Highlands and Lowlands met, the very hinge of Scotland, and thinking, thinking. His thoughts, naturally, on the whole had been less than happy; but he had come to certain conclusions. Today he was in better cheer. For he was to have visitors – the first allowed him. It was to be Henry and Margaret.

It was early afternoon before James Erskine personally showed them in – a moving occasion, with Margaret throwing herself bodily into Andrew's arms, to the grins of Henry and the embarrassment of their eldest son, Andrew's godson and namesake, now in his late teens and training to be a lawyer.

In her late forties, Margaret had become a comely, capable

matron, still attractive, satisfyingly-made and a stronger character than was her husband. She did not often gabble but she gabbled now in a breathless flood of greeting, love, concern, question and exclamation. Andrew was not unaffected either. She felt so very good within his arms. He had missed her more than he could say, or even admitted to himself.

It took some time before they were able to settle to coherent converse – and when they did it was not to Andrew's joy. Henry it was who broke the news.

"Johnnie is dead, Dand," he said thickly. "Belhaven. He died. In London."

Wordless, his brother stared.

"Andrew – oh, Andrew, it is dreadful news to bring you," Margaret said, pressing his arm. "They say that it was an inflamation of the brain. He was arraigned before the Privy Council – the *English* Privy Council! He was no Jacobite, as all knew well. He refused to recognise their authority over him, a Scots peer. They could prove nothing, of course, and eventually he was released on bail. But took this stroke. It had been . . . too much for him."

"Johnnie!" Andrew got out. "Johnnie . . . !"

Henry hurried on, as though to cover this emotional abyss. "The others are still being questioned – Gordon, Huntly and the rest. But not Hamilton. He is released and in great favour with the Queen. They say that he is to get an English dukedom. Which much annoys Seafield, who expected as much for himself but has not been given it. Even a Scots one, as Roxburghe has been promoted. But Queensberry is now Duke of Dover and granted a pension of £3,000 a year. Did you hear of his reception?"

"No." That was flat.

"He went south with forty-six coaches in train, no less. And hundreds of horse. Like a royal progress! The Queen met him, with all her court. It was a hero's welcome!" It was Henry's turn to gabble. "He joined in the service of thanksgiving at St. Paul's Cathedral. It was as though the millenium had dawned! Cannon fired from the Tower of London and bells rang by the hour! One of their ministers announced that they had catched the Scots and would hold them fast! The Archbishop of

Canterbury preached a mighty sermon on the blessings of unity . . ."

"But not the Archbishop of York," Margaret broke in. "He said, in the House of Lords, that the union was little better than a disaster. For England! He said 'God forbid that I should assent to union with a people who are not as much as initiated in Christianity!' Those were the words, were they not, Henry? And added that the Scots were even averse to good English ceremonies and vestments!"

"The Kirk agrees, at least as to the disaster," her husband commented.

"The Assembly has decreed a day of fasting for the nation . . ."

"Johnnie . . . dead!" Andrew said.

There was silence for a little.

The young Andrew tried. "All are now saying that you were right, Uncle Dand. None have a good word for the union. Have you heard – Mr. Paterson's Equivalent money, so long delayed, is now paid – but only one-quarter in coin. The rest but in paper – English Treasury bills which no one trusts. How much the Darien shareholders will get, none know. The Honours of Scotland, the crown and sceptre and sword, have been bundled up in a chest and stowed in the cellar of Edinburgh Castle! Like, some old worn-out lumber. And English press-gangs are already out seizing Scots seamen."

"Sir David Dalrymple, Stair's younger brother, is the new Lord Advocate," Henry added, "With Sir Hew, Lord President of Session, the Dalrymples have done mighty well."

"Have you heard the result of the election?" the youth went on eagerly. "*Your* election? Or at least, Haddington-shire . . . ?"

"I think, Andy, that your uncle is scarcely in a mood for all this," his mother intervened. "Later will serve."

"I may as well hear it now, lass."

"The man Morrison of Prestongrange, the salt-merchant, is in – half-wit as he is! Do you know, he believes that the Apocalypse of St. John was written at Prestonpans! Now he represents your old seat, Uncle. In London, of course."

"In London, yes!"

"So, Andrew, we hope and believe that they may release you soon," Margaret declared. "Now that, that . . ."

"Now that I can do them no more harm?"

She swallowed. "Oh, my dear!" she said.

"Not that they needed to worry," he went on, levelly. "For I have decided to give it all up – politics. To retire from public affairs. I have thought well and long on this – I have had much time to think, in this place. It is enough. Nothing will change the union now, or Scotland's destiny. The course is set. I am in my fifty-fourth year. It is time that *I* set a new course, for such years as may remain to me. I have squandered sufficient, in chasing dreams."

They eyed him with varying expressions.

"I have achieved little or nothing for all my labours, in nearly thirty years. Whereas you, Henry, have achieved much. It is said that the greatest achievement for a man is to make two ears of corn grow where only one grew before. *You* have done this. Now, so shall I, God helping me. I shall devote the rest of my days to that – to try to make the land burgeon better. You shall still manage Saltoun for me, Henry, as you have done so well for so long. But I shall seek to improve the land and what it produces. This at least I can still do, for Scotland. For this land desperately needs improvement. For the people's sake, not just for wealth. It could yield five times, ten times, what it does today. In better crops, better seed, better tillage and husbandry, better drainage, better beasts and stock. I have thousands of acres for which I am responsible – not you, Henry, *me*, God forgive me! I shall make up for the wasted years. And one day, who knows, men may say – 'Andrew Fletcher? Was not he the man who put an extra ear on every stalk of corn?' Would not that be an epitaph to work and hope for? Instead of, of . . ."

Margaret swallowed a lump in her throat. "Andrew – oh, Andrew, that is good, good! My dear, I could weep for joy to hear you say it! For long Henry and I have said this. At last you will gain what you have never had – true fulfilment. Live at peace with yourself, and others. Stay in your own place, tend your own people and your own lands, fight no more battles – save against the seasons and the soil . . . !"

"Wait you, wait you!" he interrupted her, and his eyes had regained something of their accustomed lustre. "I am not going to turn old man, sitting in Saltoun Hall and mumbling of crops and the weather and the price of oats! Heaven forbid! I am going to travel and look and learn. I am going back to Holland, if they will let me – to learn more. There is much that the Dutch can teach us. I mind a mill that Peter van Heel had, at Bergschenhoel, near to Rotterdam, where I lodged for a while. For husking the barley. The most cunning device – machinery of iron. We have nothing of the sort in all these islands. I shall go back there and learn the secret. And there was another mill, I saw elsewhere, a fanner for winnowing grain. I told you of them . . ."

"And the weaving machines, Andrew – the linen looms you also spoke of. For making hollands," Margaret intervened, eyes shining. "I greatly wish to learn how to make holland linen. We could do great things with that . . ."

"No doubt. If I have time and opportunity. That would require a trained weaver to understand it. Then there is the making of tiles, for field-drains. Pipes. And pantiles for roofing. We have the clay. The Dutch have the knowledge . . ."

"Andrew – I could come with you! I have always wished to travel, to see other lands. Henry – we could go also? To Holland."

"Not all at the same time, my dear. Not myself, with Andrew. Or who would look after Saltoun? You, perhaps. But not Andrew and myself both."

"Very well, then. I shall go. With Andrew. Andrew – you will take me to Holland with you? And I will take a weaver, to discover this of the looms, whilst you visit the mills. Would not that be splendid? Then we shall make Saltoun flourish indeed – and all Scotland gain!"

"And what would our good neighbours say, Margaret lass? What would Scotland say? Andrew Fletcher traipsing off abroad with his brother's wife!"

"Nonsense! At our years! I am not some skittish quean – the mother of seven! Besides, we could travel separately and meet there. That is what we shall do."

"I do not know . . ."

"She will do it, Dand – if she sets her heart on it. Nothing surer," Henry said, smiling. "Perhaps you are safer here in Stirling Castle! But . . . can you bear to give up your politics? After a lifetime?"

"I think that I can. I was never a true politician, Henry. I was not cast in the right mould for it. Politicians, I find, must flock together. I have always played a lone hand. And they must compromise and hedge and bargain. They are merchants, in fact – whereas I would rather be a grower, a producer. So I shall turn back to the land, which I should perhaps never have left, and leave the chaffering to those who find it to their taste. And there are plenty so-minded, I have learned – and in the highest places."

"And all that you have learned and fought for, these long years? Is it all to be forgotten, wasted, lost?"

"I have still my pen, lad. I shall write. Whilst coaxing that extra ear to sprout from the corn-stalk. Who knows, my pen may prove a sharper weapon than ever my sword has done, or my tongue . . . !"

"Bravo, Andrew Fletcher!" Margaret exclaimed.

Historical Note

Fletcher never did return to politics. He became one of Scotland's foremost land-improvers, along with his neighbour and friend John Cockburn of Ormiston. He did go to Holland in 1710, taking James Meikle, mill-wright, with him, and in due course brought back the secret of pot-barley milling, to establish a mill at West Saltoun, there to this day, and which for forty years was the only one of its kind in the British Isles. Margaret went also and returned with the designs for weaving fine holland linen, for which she set up a manufactory, likewise at West Saltoun, and which became almost as famous and even more profitable. Andrew continued to travel, and was in Leyden the year before his death in Paris in 1716. Margaret far outlived both Andrew and her husband, who died in 1733, living to a ripe old age and seeing both the Jacobite rising of 1715 and the beginnings of that of 1745. Young Andrew in due course became the noted judge, Lord Milton, of Session.

Each year Andrew Fletcher's memory is celebrated at a ceremony at Saltoun kirk, where his body lies – which is more than can be said of any of the other actors in this story.

Nigel Tranter
Aberlady, April 1980

NIGEL TRANTER

MᴀᴄBETH THE KING

Across a huge and colourful canvas, ranging from the wilds of Scotland to Norway, Denmark and Rome, here is the story of the real MacBeth.

Set aside Shakespeare's portrait of a savage, murderous, ambitious King. Read instead of his struggle to make and save a united Scotland. Of his devotion to his great love, the young Queen Gruoch. Of the humane laws they fought for, the great battle they were forced to fight. And the price they paid.

A Royal Mail service in association with the Book Marketing Council & The Booksellers Association.
Post-A-Book is a Post Office trademark.

NIGEL TRANTER

THE WALLACE

William Wallace – a man of violent passions and un-
quenchable spirit, the natural leader of a proud race.

Scotland at the end of the thirteenth century was a
blood-torn country under the harsh domination of a
tyrant usurper, the hated Plantagenet, Edward Long-
shanks. During the appalling violence of those unsettled
days one man rose as leader of the Scots. That man
was William Wallace. Motivated first by revenge for his
father's slaughter, Wallace then vowed to cleanse his
country of the English and set the rightful king, Robert
the Bruce, upon the Scottish throne. Though Wallace
was a heroic figure, he was but a man – and his chosen
path led him through grievous danger and personal
tragedy before the final outcome . . .

CORONET BOOKS

NIGEL TRANTER

THE YOUNG MONTROSE

James Graham – the brilliant young Marquis of Montrose.

One man alone could not change the course of history. But James Graham was determined to try. A gallant soldier, talented leader and compelling personality, his fame has echoed down the centuries. For the young Marquis of Montrose was to give his utmost in the service of his beloved monarch.

The first of two magnificent novels about THE MARQUIS OF MONTROSE.

CORONET BOOKS

NIGEL TRANTER

TAPESTRY OF THE BOAR

During the reign of Malcolm the Fourth, King of the Scots, Hugh de Swinton and his fellow mosstroopers helped keep the rampaging Galloway rebels at bay. But it was for his expertise in the killing of wild boars, as protector of the Swintons' sheep flocks, that young Hugh was brought to Malcolm's attention.

But Malcolm was a pious man much concerned with the well-being of his people. And he handpicked Hugh de Swinton to mastermind a very special project close to his heart: to establish Scotland's first real hospital for the sick and poor, at Soutra in Lauderdale.

In this gripping 12th century tale of action, chivalry and romance Nigel Tranter's rich imagination and fascinating research once again combine to bring the history of Scotland to vivid life.

CORONET BOOKS

MORE NIGEL TRANTER TITLES AVAILABLE FROM
HODDER AND STOUGHTON PAPERBACKS

All these books are available at your local bookshop or newsagent or can be ordered direct from the publisher. Just tick the titles you want and fill in the form below.

Prices and availability subject to change without notice.

HODDER AND STOUGHTON PAPERBACKS, P O Box 11, Falmouth, Cornwall.

Please send cheque or postal order for the value of the book, and add the following for postage and packing:

UK including BFPO – £1.00 for one book, plus 50p for the second book, and 30p for each additional book ordered up to a £3.00 maximum.

OVERSEAS INCLUDING EIRE – £2.00 for the first book, plus £1.00 for the second book, and 50p for each additional book ordered.
OR Please debit this amount from my Access/Visa Card (delete as appropriate).

CARD NUMBER ☐☐☐☐☐☐☐☐☐☐☐☐☐☐☐☐☐☐

AMOUNT £ ....

EXPIRY DATE ....

SIGNED ....

NAME ....

ADDRESS ....

....